INTOTHE**HEAT**

Taking her shotgun, Dee got out of the truck. She kept the spotlight trained on the vehicle, which was about two hundred yards down the road. She could hear its engine running. The driver hadn't stopped because of a breakdown or a lack of gasoline.

He wanted to come out and play.

She inched out into the scrub, watching for the wink of a gun muzzle. It was all the warning she'd have.

She had just stepped down into a shallow depression when a force—huge, swift, hammering—struck her chest like a fist. She watched her arms float outward and the shotgun tumble away. Heat followed, and the night turned a painful orange . . .

Other Avon Books by
Kirk Mitchell

BLOWN AWAY
HIGH DESERT MALICE

DEEP VALLEY MALICE

KIRK MITCHELL

AVON BOOKS NEW YORK

DEEP VALLEY MALICE is an original publication of Avon Books. This work has never before appeared in book form. This work is a novel. Any similarity to actual persons or events is purely coincidental.

AVON BOOKS
A division of
The Hearst Corporation
1350 Avenue of the Americas
New York, New York 10019

Copyright © 1996 by Kirk Mitchell
Published by arrangement with the author
Library of Congress Catalog Card Number: 95-95058
ISBN: 0-380-77662-6

First Avon Books Printing: March 1996

AVON TRADEMARK REG. U.S. PAT. OFF. AND IN OTHER COUNTRIES, MARCA REGISTRADA, HECHO EN U.S.A.

Printed in the U.S.A.

RA 10 9 8 7 6 5 4 3 2 1

ACKNOWLEDGMENTS

With thanks to Lieutenant Dennis Bacoch, Inyo County Sheriff's Office; Chief Warrant Officer Michael A. Cordoza, U.S.N. (Ret.); the Basque Studies Program, University of Nevada; the Fresno Office of the Bureau of Alcohol, Tobacco and Firearms; and the U.S. Bureau of Land Management.

CHAPTER**ONE**

The Ford Bronco started heating up on Towne Pass, just west of Death Valley. The sky was bone-white, as if the July sun had burned all the blue out of it, and the asphalt pavement looked sticky enough to snare birds by their talons.

Dee Laguerre turned off onto the highway shoulder and killed the engine. After hesitating a moment, she stepped out into the heat. It almost took her breath away. No breeze. And the deep silence made her ears ring. Turning, she scanned the crest of the Panamint Range on which she stood. Rubbly slopes plunged down to alkali wastes and wool-colored sand dunes, shimmering far below through waves of torrid air.

Finally, she opened the hood, using her handkerchief on the latch. The fan belt was frayed.

"Merde."

She got back into the Bronco. Checking the rearview mirror, she glanced briefly at herself. Her eyes were almost the same shade as her bobbed brown hair. A face more European than American, somehow.

Then she started down the long grade, checking the temperature gauge every few seconds. Only a hairsbreadth separated the needle from the red zone.

"Come on," she begged the capricious gods of things mechanical. She'd been up since four that morning.

Fifteen minutes later, she reached the solitary gas station at Panamint Springs, a tiny oasis of tamarisk trees surrounded by endless creosote bush scrub. While the attendant rummaged through the stockroom, she stretched her legs. The perspiration-soaked back of her uniform shirt was dry by the time she'd crossed the gravel lot to the thermometer tacked to the trunk of one of the lacy desert trees—111 degrees Fahrenheit. Nothing remarkable for the last weekend of July along California's easttern edge. Almost sweater weather.

The shadow of the Coso Range was creeping toward her. It was on the verge of falling mercifully over the station when the sun slanted down into a canyon and molten light filled the Panamint Valley again. Dee gave it her back. To the south lay the navy's bombing range, the scrub pocked with craters.

The lank, slow-moving attendant strolled out to report that he had belts for every Japanese car made since Mitsubishi stopped turning out bombers—but nothing that would fit her U.S. government four-wheel-drive. "It's Friday evenin', so I can't get one from Lone Pine till Monday mornin'."

"Merde."

"Pardon?"

"Shit," she explained.

The man smiled. "You wanna tow over into Owens Valley?"

"No thanks." Not yet. Getting towed in off a desert patrol was like hoisting the white flag. It still might come to that, but she wanted it to be the last resort.

She drove on, her visor pulled low against the sun, and climbed slowly up into the almost moon-barren Coso Range. The belt began squealing. Sighing, she rolled down both side windows to make up for the loss of air-conditioning. She couldn't bring herself to run the heater, even though that would help cool the engine. An hour of that and she'd look like a mummy.

She took her left hand off the steering wheel and opened it to the hot stream of wind. The burst of coolness died in the split second it took her palm to dry, but the sensation had been nice. She was testing for a drop in temperature. Each successive parched basin west of Death Valley was usually five or so degrees cooler than the one east of it. It didn't feel that way this evening. The heat seemed to be wrapped around the entire world.

The Bronco crowned the last summit, and the Owens Valley came into view. Darkening tints of gray and brown. It was a deep, flat-bottomed trough curving northward between two towering mountain ranges. The deepest valley in the country.

"Bon," Dee said.

She was nearly back to civilization. Relative civilization, marked by a wider selection of fan belts.

Ahead, the lights of Lone Pine were twinkling through the gathering dusk. Looming behind the small town was the Sierra Nevada. The pale gray granite was fading to black, although the snowfields would go on shining pinkly until the nightfall was complete. *Heaven to be up there right now*, she thought. No more than fifty degrees at this hour. Maybe even a trace of fresh snow had fallen this afternoon: thunderheads had hovered over the crest until the cooling of the day dissolved them. *Heaven to run soft, new snow over my face.*

Yawning, Dee tried to massage a kink out of her back. Her Sam Browne belt creaked and her revolver hammer dug softly into her side as she arched her spine.

Off to the south sprawled Owens Lake, dry now for more than half a century. The snow-fed river that had once flowed into it had been diverted into the Los Angeles Aqueduct in the teens, and the lake, crisscrossed in the last century by steamboats, shriveled into a vast, dusty playa. A garden of salt crystals. Above its old western shoreline, Dee could see an unbroken line of headlights heading north along U.S. Highway 395: vacationers from Southern California coming to fish and frolic in the same waters they used to wash their cars and fill their swimming pools.

She suddenly let up on the accelerator.

Something strange had caught her eye. Two dark wisps of smoke had just materialized above the lake bed and were curling in on themselves like little tornadoes. She was reaching for her binoculars when the roar broke over her.

She crouched, involuntarily, and swore.

The pair of F-18s streaked over the road. The jets flew so low they rocked the Bronco and made Dee's shotgun rattle in its rack. They banked off toward the Inyo Mountains, on the east side of the valley, their afterburners glowing redly, and quickly vanished into the nightfall.

Dee sat up, gripped the wheel with both hands, and exhaled. "Bastards."

The navy pilots from the nearby base at China Lake loved nothing better than buzzing hapless drivers on their terrain-hugging approaches to the target areas in the Panamint Valley she'd just left. Legend had it that Tyrus Foley, the 350-pound sheriff of Waucoba County, had been buzzed once too often. He'd pried himself out of his Dodge sedan and blazed away at the offending aircraft with his automatic pistol.

Dee stopped at the intersection with Highway 395, waited for an opening to appear in the line of motor homes, vans, and boat-towing cars. An invading horde of pleasure seekers bent on mechanized fun. She checked her wristwatch. Nine-thirty. And another forty-five minutes until she reached home near Big Pine. Something long and cool to drink, then bed. She dug a tube of Chap Stick out of her pocket, ran it over her lips.

Finally, a break in the traffic appeared.

Lone Pine, like all the widely scattered towns of the Owens Valley, was small and compact. It had once spilled out into farms, orchards, and ranches, a checkerboard of lush greens ten miles wide and eighty miles long. But then, in the first decade of this century, the Los Angeles Department of Water and Power had grabbed all the water rights, strangling one of the most prosperous agricultural economies in California, leaving Lone Pine and its sister towns of Independence, Big Pine, and Bishop islands in the sagebrush.

Dee turned into the Chevron station and parked just outside the service bay.

A teenage boy came scuffling through the mini-mart door in a pair of oversized Acme boots. He nudged his Stetson slightly higher on his brow. "Evenin', Ranger Laguerre."

"Darryl." She got out, stretched her back again. "Fan belt's shot. I'll need a new one."

"You bet." The boy went for his tools. "Go far today?"

"Saline Valley."

"Hot?"

"Yeah," she said, "but August is coming on. We've turned the corner."

"What corner?"

"June and July are always the hottest months."

"I thought August was."

"Nope." Hands in the back pockets of her trousers, she went out to the sidewalk and gazed up the short main street. A dazzle of neon signs beckoned the secretly despised Angelenos to stop long enough for gas, a greasy meal, bait, beer. Two of these interlopers—elderly, both in Bermuda shorts—were ambling arm-in-arm toward Dee. They kept peering off toward the saw-toothed crest of the Sierra, which was now silhouetted against a blush of alpenglow.

The husband eyed Dee's tan-over-brown uniform, her revolver. "Which one's Whitney, Deputy?" he asked. "The tallest one there?"

"No, sir."

"I thought Mount Whitney's supposed to be the highest mountain in the lower forty-eight."

"Right. But you're pointing at Lone Pine Peak. It appears to be higher from this angle." She pointed. "Mount Whitney is there, off to the right."

The wife gave Dee a skeptical frown. "How can that be?"

"How can what be?"

"How can it look shorter when it's taller?"

"Mirrors," Dee said with a brittle smile.

The couple stared at her a moment longer, then walked on.

"And I'm not a goddamned deputy," she added under her breath, returning to the Bronco. The triangular emblems on the doors were for the Bureau of Land Management, U.S. Department of the Interior. She was the only federal law enforcement officer on a beat of high range and desert mountains the size of Connecticut. Ten hours of patrolling that beat, much of it without air-conditioning, had left her feeling too withered to politely field questions from the flatlanders.

Darryl was adjusting the new belt. "You see any nudies out there at Saline?" he asked.

"Too many," Dee said, yawning again. Natural hot springs in Saline Valley fed soaking pools that drew every potbellied free spirit or wide-eyed sexual misfit within five hundred miles.

A sharp boom to the north turned Dee's head. "Sonic," Darryl said knowingly. "Goddamn navy broke our bay window at home hotdoggin' over town like that."

"Don't cuss."

"You cuss."

"Yeah, but I've got a gun and a badge."

Darryl chuckled, then let down the hood.

She was handing him her government credit card when an old GMC pickup with a bad muffler thundered up to the self-service aisle. Dee noticed the Winchester carbine in the window rack first, then the sullen-faced driver. Kyle Foley. The sheriff's seventeen-year-old son. He got out and squared his black Stetson on his head with studied ease before uncapping his gas tank. Inserting the nozzle, he smirked around a cud of tobacco at Dee.

"Hello, Kyle," she said.

He stared off, shifted the wad to the other cheek.

"I said *hello*, Kyle," she said, stepping up to the truck. As she did so, she noticed the quart of malt liquor on the front seat. "Enjoying a beer tonight?"

He smirked again, which made her angry enough to reach through the open window and take the bottle.

"Hey, Laguerre, what're you—?"

She shattered it with her nightstick over the trash can.

His face darkened, and for an instant she thought that he was going to come at her. But he didn't. Instead, he hooked the nozzle back on the pump and laughed under his breath. "You just fucked up royal, lady. You got no jurisdiction in town here. Federal officer can't go enforcin' California laws."

"That's right, Kyle," she said evenly. "You want to tell your daddy I fucked up—or should I?"

Kyle spat onto the cement, then grinned as he handed Darryl a ten-dollar bill. "This Basque bitch got herself run off by the ranchers over in Nevada."

"Watch your mouth, Kyle. And nobody ran me off."

"Not what I heard."

"I don't care what you've heard. And I don't care what you think of me or my ancestry. I do expect a little courtesy, the same courtesy I show your father and any other law enforcement officer."

"The badge don't make you a real cop."

"Congress might differ with you. . . . " She started back for the Bronco: Sheriff's Dispatch was asking for any unit in the vicinity of Lone Pine to respond. "And Kyle—if you ever flip me off in public again, like you did last week when I drove past the high school, I'm going to take that middle finger and show you exactly how far federal jurisdiction goes."

"This ain't the end of it, Laguerre."

"I'm sure it isn't," she said, getting in behind the wheel and grabbing the microphone. "BLM-One, at the Chevron in Lone Pine."

The dispatcher asked her to investigate a report that had come over CB channel 9. Water on the highway north of town. Dee acknowledged and backed up. She gave a parting wave to the two boys, but neither responded. Darryl, friendly toward her when alone, was now under Kyle's influence once again.

Cowboy snots.

Dee quickly put Lone Pine in her rearview mirror.

The full moon had risen and was reflecting off the fault scarp that ran along the west side of the highway. The land east of this sandy billow had dropped twenty feet in less than a minute one night in 1872, when an earthquake as strong as the 1906 San Francisco tremor rocked the Owens Valley, leveling the then-adobe village of Lone Pine. She passed the cemetery that held the dead from that night. It stood atop the scarp, the graves marked by rusted wrought-iron fences.

She looked forward again, then said, *"Merde."* She reached for her mike. "Control, advise CHP—traffic's backed up for a half mile below the Alabama Spillway." Here, at the northern end of the Alabama Hills, was a sluice gate that would let Los Angeles DWP return the current to its old channel, the Owens River. In eighty years, DWP had never done so.

"BLM-One," the dispatcher asked, "can you see where the water's coming from?"

"Negative, stand by." Dee flicked on her emergency lights and used the shoulder to bypass the jammed cars. Horns were braying for her to do something.

"Do what already?" she muttered.

She didn't see the flood until her front tires were almost in it. Hurriedly, she turned on her spotlight. A foot of swift, tawny-colored water was flowing over the pavement where the highway dipped slightly. It had already gouged a six-foot-deep ravine into the slope below the roadbed and was rapidly eating away at the asphalt, creating a horseshoe-shaped crater that was growing by the second. Two cars had been knocked sideways by the powerful current, and the occupants—drenched to their waists—ran up to Dee's Bronco, shouting for her to save their cars before they were washed away.

"Hang on," Dee said. "And stand back, will you? This could be a flash flood. It might rise even more." She didn't think that was the case, but it worked: the people headed for higher ground. Realizing that the aqueduct ran just above the highway, she was about to advise Dispatch to roll a DWP maintenance crew on a possible canal breach when she saw a silver Porsche coming southbound along the shoulder just as she had driven north. She switched to her public address speaker: "Don't try to cross."

But the Porsche kept coming.

"Don't cross!"

The driver, squinting against Dee's spotlight, pretended not to understand by cupping a hand behind his ear. His female passenger was laughing at his antics.

"Do not—!"

The current hit the low-centered sports car like a wrecking ball, spinning it around three times before dumping it headlights-first into the crater. The brown water curled over the roof, and through its roar Dee heard the woman screaming.

"Control," Dee radioed, fumbling for her flashlight with her free hand, "roll Lone Pine fire, ambulance, and a tow!" Getting out of the Bronco, she could see the Porsche's tail lamps slowly rising. The water, heavy with sand and silt, was upending the car.

She ran to the lower embankment, slid down on the heels of her boots to the edge of the ever-growing crater—only to be knocked off her feet by a gout of water as the Porsche crashed over onto its roof. She picked herself up, looked briefly for her flashlight, but then gave up and waded into the crater. The ooze was four feet deep. It made a sizzling sound as it poured over the vehicle's chassis. She groped blindly for a door handle. The headlights were still on, but the water was as opaque as creamed coffee.

The couple was hollering, pounding on the floorboards.

"I'm here!" Dee hollered. "Try to open a door!"

The man answered something, but she couldn't make out what.

At last, she found the door handle on the passenger side. She pressed the button and yanked. No good. She braced her feet against the front fender and pulled with all her strength, but the crumpled roof had jammed the door.

She was wading around the rear of the car to try the other door when two flashlight beams slanted down and found her. She blinked up into them. "CHP?"

"Yeah . . . Jesus." The nearest highway patrolman tossed his handgun up to his partner, then jumped in beside Dee. "Driver still inside?"

"With a passenger."

Together, they strained to open the door, but it refused to budge. The overturned Porsche was now buried in silt. The patrolman tried to scoop some of it away from the driver's side window, but more just flowed into the hole. He kicked at the submerged glass, which made the couple inside pound on the floorboards all the harder.

"Wait," Dee said, "they're letting us know they've still got an airspace inside there." And she realized that the front end might have buckled when the car plummeted into the crater, pinning one or both of them under the dash.

The patrolman wiped his wet and gritty face on his short sleeve. "What the hell is this? Flash flood?"

"Aqueduct, I think."

"Crap." The patrolman whistled for his partner's attention. "Pry bar—and Jaws of Life when the fire department gets here.'' Then he turned to Dee again. "How 'bout you seeing if there's any way to shut this water off?''

"Okay.'' The wall around the crater was getting higher as earth slabbed off into the water, so Dee waded down the flow several yards, losing her footing twice before crawling out onto dry land. She took only a moment to catch her breath before jogging back up to the Bronco. There she got her radio handset and spare flashlight.

"Control,'' she transmitted on the run, tearing her trousers on barbed wire as she ducked through a three-strand fence, "tell DWP to shut down the aqueduct . . . Alabama Spillway or above . . .''

"Stand by,'' the dispatcher said.

"Just acknowledge, dammit,'' Dee moaned without keying the button. Her uniform squishing, she trotted over a sandy pasture to the base of the fault scarp. She'd slogged halfway up it when the dispatcher's voice halted her.

"Go,'' Dee answered breathlessly.

"Sergeant advises he wants confirmation of aqueduct damage before we phone DWP.''

"Tell him—either it's damaged or the drought is over.''

"Repeat that?''

"Hang on a minute. I'm almost to the canal.'' She continued up the steep face of the scarp and broke onto the moonlit benchland beyond.

CHAPTER**TWO**

Tyrus Foley had taken over half a booth inside the bar of the Veterans of Foreign Wars Post at Independence, the county seat. He'd never served in the military. Heart murmur. But he counted himself a veteran of one of the bitterest domestic conflicts in American history, the Owens Valley Water War. He'd been only a kid during its last gasp, but he could recall his father's slow slide down into the bottle, the empty, luminous stare that followed the news that DWP had bought out the "upditch" farm, cutting off the Foleys' water—and, finally, the old man dangling from a rafter in the springhouse of their apple ranch. His body still swaying a little.

Foley took a gulp of Jim Beam and Seven-Up to blot out that picture.

In the last few years, his ass had grown too broad for the stools at the bar. Like sitting on a flagpole. He'd fought his weight for a while, even bought a NordicTrack. But eventually he admitted to himself that it was no use. Besides, rural folk liked flesh on their sheriff. Made him seem more formidable, manly.

A voice was echoing through the open double doors to the meeting hall. A deep, white-sounding voice. But the speaker, Ben Whittaker, the head of DWP operations in the Owens Valley, was black. He was trying to soft-soap what everybody present, including Whittaker himself, knew to be a threat. In short, the city was welshing on its agreement with the county over the amount of groundwater it would pump, and if valley people protested there'd be consequences.

Foley had learned long ago that the Los Angeles Aqueduct was insatiable, and each time its guzzling thirst grew the treaty with the natives was broken and a new, less favorable one was offered. It surprised Foley that anybody north of Los Angeles County could be surprised when it happened again.

"Lookit, people . . ." Whittaker was saying, "we've just had a decade-long drought. I hate to tell you the lengths the city's gone to exploring new water sources so it wouldn't have to increase groundwater pumping here in the valley. . . ." The DWP man chuckled. "Damn, we just paid millions for a feasibility study on piping water all the way from Alaska. You know how this was going to be done? Along the bottom of the ocean, for godsake. Down the length of the continental shelf, using wave action to power the pumps. Can you imagine the cost and headaches of a project like that? Hell, there's a chasm off the Monterey coast as deep as Grand Canyon. But what does this tell you about the city's plight?"

A droll voice answered, "Grab the Vaseline and bend over."

"Oh, come on, friends. . . ." Whittaker laughed along with the others.

Foley leaned forward slightly so he could see the DWP man through the open doors. He wondered if black people blushed under all that pigment. Whittaker, like Foley, was a few years past sixty. He was wearing a VFW garrison cap with "Korea" emblazoned on it, and above his left eye was a star-shaped wound from a shell fragment—but he had no friends here this evening.

Somebody had stood. One of the few ranchers left in the county. Those who'd remained leased their pasture from the city, which owned all the irrigation systems and virtually all the land in the valley. What wasn't locked up by the city was managed by the BLM. Overmanaged by the BLM. "Whittaker, tell me it ain't true . . ."

"If I can."

"Tell me that if we don't go along with this new agreement, our grazin' leases won't be yanked."

Momentarily silence, then Whittaker answered, "In all honesty, I don't know if I can promise that. . . . " A groan went up from the small audience, then hoots followed by loud foot stamping on the old wooden floor. "Listen to me, please. That issue's separate and distinct from groundwater pumping. . . . " Now shouted profanity. "Listen—Karl Schoenfeld and his Wetlands Preservation Society went to court to make the city take a hard look at the quality of its rangeland in riparian areas. The verdict—not ours, I remind you—was that the valley's overgrazed."

"Bullshit," another voice said. "Quit irrigatin' the pasture you lease to us and you flatlanders got more water to ship down the aqueduct. That's the plan, Whittaker—you goddamn lyin' son of a bitch."

"Easy there," Foley growled from the booth. He was here to keep the peace.

The hall quieted down.

Foley took another gulp of bourbon and Seven, then slipped a small electronic chess gameboard from the inner pocket of his white seersucker jacket. Water debates bored him. Some of his earliest memories were of nights like these, leaning his head against his daddy's shoulder, half listening to the interminable Ping-Pong match between outraged valley folk and condescending DWP officials. These parleys were meaningless. It all came down to an unbeatable weight differential. Waucoba County had seventeen thousand people and one water lawyer. The city of Los Angeles had over fourteen million people in its metropolitan area and a hundred water lawyers.

"Then here's another issue for you, Ben," a sporting goods store owner from Bishop said. "Is there any possibility the city will close its lands to public recreation?"

"None," Whittaker said.

"You know what no huntin' and fishin' on the valley floor would do to us merchants."

"Yes, I do." The way the DWP man said this was vaguely ominous. "And we might agree here on something—had the city never come to the valley it wouldn't be the pristine draw it is for recreationists. There'd be fifty thousand vacation shacks and a No Trespassing sign every fifty feet—"

"Oh, Christ, now I've heard it all. . . . " A Paiute tribal councilman came to his feet, grinning. "Not only do I gotta tread lightly 'round DWP for fear they'll break the agreement with the reservation water districts, now I gotta thank 'em for restorin' the valley to its aboriginal state. . . ."

Laughing, Foley punched a button and a black pawn advanced on the little screen. He loved chess. Years ago, he'd even won a tournament up at the Hilton in Reno, astonished everybody and tromped a high-toned Russian who tried to eye-fuck all his opponents. But competition meant nothing to Foley. Playing against himself was fine. He just liked keeping his mind busy. A BLM archaeologist had once told him that the ancient Indian petroglyphs in the hills north of Bishop probably had no meaning. They were just doodles chipped into rock by the brightest members of the tribe who couldn't tolerate boredom. And being a fourth-term sheriff was as boring as hell—most of the time.

"Sheriff?" Hank, the bartender, was holding up the phone for him. "Dispatch."

Foley frowned and got ponderously up, making sure his jacket was covering his .44 magnum. He'd once packed only a .38 special, but as he put on more and more weight the smaller revolver began to look like a toy in his hammy fist. Reaching for the receiver, his first thought was that it had something to do with his son. His worry for Kyle was chronic, like a low-grade fever. He was losing his son to something. Eventual manhood, he hoped, although he feared the boy's recklessness until that day. He and his wife had had their only child too late in their own lives, maybe.

Sally, the night watch dispatcher, said, "Sheriff, you're not gonna believe this . . ."

"Try me." He hadn't been surprised in years.

"Somebody went and bombed the aqueduct."

Foley came close to smiling. *"Where?"*

"Just below the Alabama Spillway. A mess all over the highway."

He considered this for a moment, then asked, "You sure it was a bomb?"

"Confirmed by BLM just a minute ago, sir."

He let out a long breath. "Get hold of ATF in Bakersfield. Turns my stomach to look at Ol' Scarface, but we'll

need his technical support on this." Then he hung up and
plodded across the bar to the meeting hall doors.

"People, the agreements with all the local water districts
were already up for renegotiation when—" Whittaker interrupted himself when he saw Foley filling the door frame.
"Yes, Tyrus?"

"You wanna tag along, Ben?"

"Tag along?"

"Yeah, somebody just made that feasibility study on
Alaska water look good again."

Dee clipped her radio handset back onto her belt, then
climbed the lower embankment of the canal, studying the
V-shaped breach. She grabbed a twisted length of reinforc-
ing bar to help pull herself up. The explosion had left an
acrid smell in the air and peppered the flats below with
chunks of concrete. Pieces of the aqueduct's lining. Water
continued to gush out, thousands of gallons a minute foam-
ing under the moon, digging an ever-deeper channel on its
rush to the highway below. There, a fire department utility
truck had just pulled up behind her Bronco.

Inwardly, she kept seeing the dumbstruck faces of the
couple as their Porsche spun in circles. She prayed that the
car hadn't filled with water and silt.

She reached the narrow dirt road topping the embankment and started running.

The gatehouse lay two hundred yards upstream. Its windows were lit, and the stark light spilled down the length
of the canal, showing her that it was running at full capacity. Her boots were filled with sand and gravel, but she
didn't stop to empty them.

She crossed a catwalk to the gatehouse. The door was
wide open. Inside, a man in coveralls was straining to turn
a threaded iron rod with a pair of locking pliers. "Shit
awmighty," he gasped, then gave up, dropped the pliers to
the floor, and ran his hand over his sweaty crew cut.

"You've got to shut the flow off," she said. "People're
trapped—"

"I know, dammit. Been monitorin' my scanner." The
DWP worker pointed in exasperation at the end of the rod.
"Some son of a bitch stole the handwheel again. I can't

turn the fuckin' screw to raise the sluice gate.''

"What d'you need?"

"A big pipe wrench."

"Can I go for it?"

"Naw," he said. "Got one down the hill at my house, but you'll never find it." He started to leave, but she took hold of his arm.

"What about the intake?" she asked. The river flowed into the system ten or so miles north near a bluff called Charley's Butte.

The man brushed away her hand. "That's buggered too. Got a phone system on it. All we gotta do is call a number to close the gate down—but we been phonin' for ten minutes and it ain't respondin'.''

He went out at a half run. Dee heard his truck engine being fired up a moment later.

She leaned over a railing and peered down at the iron plate that could have been raised had the handwheel not been removed. That would have diverted the current down a concrete sluice to the old bed of the Owens River. Bombed canal. Sabotaged sluice gate. No way to shut off the intake except by going out to Charley's Butte and cranking it shut by hand.

Somebody had done it up right this time.

The cramped interior of the gatehouse was stifling. Dee opened a window for some draft. Moths were pinging off the bare bulb in the ceiling fixture. "Control," she transmitted on her handset, "be advised—the Alabama Spillway can't be opened for the next several minutes. Advise CHP and fire units down on the highway.''

"Copy." The dispatcher relayed the information.

Dee unlaced a boot and shook it out. Then the other. She tied them up again and stared out across the moonlit valley. The water glinted like quicksilver as it snaked through the brush toward Owens Dry Lake, eight miles to the south.

"Dammit." She picked up the locking pliers from where the DWP man had dropped them. She clamped them onto the rod and twisted until her knuckles whitened, but it felt like trying to turn the Washington Monument. She drew her baton and tried to think of some way to connect it to the handles of the pliers for leverage. But it was no good.

At last, she heard the DWP man's truck speed up to the gatehouse and brake. Three seconds later, he burst inside, hefting an enormous pipe wrench over his shoulder. "This'll do 'er," he said, thumbing the adjustment screw.

But at that moment, one of the CHP officers radioed the sheriff's office: "Uh, Control," he said, badly out of breath, "roll coroner. . . . Somebody say this was a bombing?"

"That's affirmative. BLM Laguerre."

"Then you've got a double homicide on your hands."

Sid Abramowitz hurried across the darkened tarmac to the waiting Cessna, his field kit in one hand and travel bag in the other. The charter pilot called out over the murmuring engine, "Mr. Abramowitz?"

"Yeah, that's me." Sid braced for what would now inevitably follow.

Leaning closer to take Sid's luggage, the young pilot suddenly froze. It lasted no more than a second, just long enough for the man's shock to wear off. "Let me stow that for you, sir."

"Thanks." Sid climbed inside the cabin, latched the door. From now on, if the pattern held—and it always did with disappointing predictability—the pilot would look at Sid's face only on the sly. Grim little peeks.

The pilot took his seat, kept his gaze trained forward.

"Nice night for it," Sid said, strapping himself in.

"Yeah, sure is. Great moon." The pilot immediately began taxiing.

Sid slumped back, wondering for the thousandth time if it was really that repulsive. The answer awaited him in the reflection of the green instrument lights.

He glanced up.

Yes, he realized for the millionth time in ten years, it honestly was. Shiny scars like melted wax washing over his face, a patchwork of graft mottles where he might still have some hair at age forty-six. Crisped ears. No eyebrows, of course, and virtually no eyelids. But his hands still revolted him worse than his face. He could see them without a mirror.

The pilot cleared for takeoff with the Meadows Field tower, then asked casually, " 'Nam?''

"Right," Sid lied. "Napalm."

"Nasty shit."

"Yeah, nasty shit." Everybody wanted to believe that it'd been the war. The truth was more complicated, and a good shrink had finally convinced Sid that only a trusted few deserved the truth.

The Cessna lifted off, and the pilot quickly banked toward the northeast. "What d'you do for the government, Mr. Abramowitz—if I can ask?"

"Sure, and call me Sid. . . . " He twisted around in the seat, looked futilely for his condominium in Bakersfield's crisscrossing lights. Strange, he realized. He'd never done that before when leaving town. His one-bedroom condo had never really felt like home. "I'm an arson-explosives investigator for Alcohol, Tobacco and Firearms." The Treasury Department's catchall agency.

"Headed to Lone Pine on a case now?"

"Right." Sid peered upward through the window: the full moon was directly overhead. "Looks like somebody bombed the Los Angeles Aqueduct."

"Bad?"

"I'll have to see."

They flew up the Kern River and over Lake Isabella to avoid the 14,000-foot-high crest of the Sierra. Sid could see it off to left, the snow tucked in the craggy folds of the range a brilliant white. The range made the Los Angeles Aqueduct possible: a granite scoop reaching up into the Pacific storm track, storing the heavy snowfall and then slowly releasing it in meltwater over the cool mountain summer.

"Were you doing this kind of work over in 'Nam?" the pilot asked after a silence of some minutes.

"Sorta. Explosive Ordnance Disposal." That much was the truth. He'd left the navy a warrant officer after twelve years, gotten a degree in criminology at Fresno State, then joined ATF. He'd lost his face and nearly his hands a few months later.

They'd crossed the southern end of Sierra, and the pilot

banked for the lower approach to the Owens Valley. Range after range unfolded to the east.

Sid gazed below.

A silver thread undulated along the desert foothills, rising over ridges and dipping into canyons. It looked tiny from this height, but it was actually a ten-foot-diameter pipe, a series of inverted siphons. Therein was the secret to the Los Angeles Aqueduct. Some turn-of-the-century visionary had taken a trick from the ancient Romans in realizing that water would flow over an intermediate height as long as the pipeline intake was higher than its outlet. The city's system was largely gravity-driven, one of the cheapest water projects in the world to operate.

Last year, the head of DWP, worried about sabotage in the light of increasing tensions with the people of the Owens Valley over groundwater pumping, had invited Sid to familiarize himself with its tunnels, canals, siphons, and wells. More than sixty miles of tunnel had been bored through solid rock. The blasting of even a few hundred feet of underground conduit could close the system for months, if not years.

Sid had come away from that orientation convinced that the Los Angeles Aqueduct was one of the most vulnerable major utilities in the country. Almost impossible to guard. Due to the population dislocation caused by its construction, most of its more than 330 miles ran through empty range and scrubland before emptying into Van Norman Reservoir in the San Fernando Valley.

Sid glanced in that direction.

He could see the lights of the Lancaster-Palmdale mini-urban area, Los Angeles's encroaching frontier. Tens of thousands of Angelenos were spilling out into the desert in search of affordable housing. More faucets. More lawns. More swimming pools.

Sid yawned to pop his ears.

The pilot sat straighter as they began dropping down over Owens Dry Lake. The salty surface glistened like sugar. "Any idea when I pick you up, Sid?"

"Never. Sometimes I'm done in a couple hours. Sometimes it goes on for months."

"Not much of a home life that way."

"No," Sid said.

The Cessna was met at the airstrip south of Lone Pine by a white-and-brown BLM Bronco. Sid took his luggage from the pilot and went over to it. A young female ranger got out from behind the wheel. A thin brunette. Pretty, he believed.

"Dominica Laguerre," she said, offering a firm hand. "Everybody calls me Dee."

"Nice to meet you, Dee. Sid Abramowitz."

"I'll lower the rear window so you can stash your gear."

As the window whined down, he tensed. He could feel her eyes on him. He slowly turned. She smiled at him—without suddenly breaking off their glance. He wondered if she could see his face well enough. Yes, he quickly decided, there was more than enough moonlight. For the first time, he realized that she looked tired. A hard beat, Waucoba County. A few years before, he'd flown out to disarm a device found in the then-ranger's mobile home. A warning from the locals to back off.

"Long day?" he asked, going around to the passenger door.

"Patrol since zero-dark-thirty, and then a double homicide at the end of it."

Sid stopped short, his hand halfway to the door handle. "The detective who called me from the sheriff's office said nothing about homicide."

"Could be he didn't know at the time," Dee said.

They both got in. The interior of the Bronco smelled of dust and sweat.

Accelerating toward the highway, she went on. "Man and a woman. The flooding buried their Porsche in silt. Rear window was cracked ... doors pinned." A faint hoarseness came into her voice. "They drowned before the fire department could get them out."

Sid leaned the back of his neck against the headrest. This changed none of the parameters of his job. Knowing this, he'd do nothing different in how he assisted the sheriff. But a faint sadness had come over him, dampening some of the mental pleasure he often took from investigating.

"Do you want to check into a motel or see the crime scene first?"

"Scene first, please." He checked the luminous dial of his wristwatch. Almost midnight. "When'd this go down?"

"Nine-forty-five, approximately."

Terrific, Sid thought. The locals had had two and a half hours to drag their snakeskin shit-kickers all over his scene.

CHAPTER **THREE**

Dee led Sid Abramowitz down the road that ran along the top of the canal embankment. Sweat was trickling down her back. While waiting for the ATF agent's plane at the Lone Pine airstrip, she'd ducked behind the small hangar and changed out of her soaking uniform into a jumpsuit and fresh underwear she kept in the Bronco. The nylon suit was too warm for the night, but it felt better than being wet.

"Just a sec." Sid halted and shined his flashlight down into the now-dry canal.

She could see him thinking, trying not to miss anything. His face had given her a start, but she'd quickly caught the hypersensitivity in his eyes and managed to hide her shock.

"You say the sluice gate was sabotaged?" Sid asked, moving on again.

"Handwheel was missing."

"How'd DWP get the current shut down?"

"They sent a crew out to the main intake—"

"Charley's Bluff?"

"Butte. But before that, the worker at the spillway here got a pipe wrench on the screw rod. That diverted the flow away from the break."

"At the intake . . ." Sid paused, a little out of breath—the 4,000-foot altitude.

"Uh-huh?"

"Don't they have a phone-activated gate?"

"Right," Dee said. "Our blaster might've jimmied that too."

"Might've?"

Dee said, "Continental Telephone's looking into a possible computer failure on their part."

"So sabotage—other than the blast—is only suspected at this point."

"I'd say."

The sheriff's Dodge was blocking the road at a point halfway to the breach. The interior dome light was on, and Dee could see Foley sitting behind the wheel, head slumped. Sleeping? His side of the chassis was tilting six inches lower than the other, and Sid remarked under his breath, "He's put on a pound or two more since I last saw him."

"He's probably added two zip codes since then." Dee cleared her throat as she neared the car. "Sheriff," she said, making Foley glance up drowsily from some kind of electronic gameboard, "this is Special Agent Sid Abramowitz."

Sid offered his disfigured right hand, but Foley pretended not to see it. He studied his gameboard again and said, "We've met. Just tell me what you need, Abramowitz, and you got it—car, driver, whatever."

"Thanks, Sheriff."

Nothing was said for a moment, then Sid shrugged. "Might as well get to work."

"Might as well," Foley echoed.

Dee asked, "Anything I can do, Sid?"

"Not for the moment, thanks." The agent continued on alone to the gap in the lower embankment, where he opened his case on the ground and started pocketing this and that from it. His glass vials and chrome-plated tools sparkled in the moonlight.

Dee had no choice but to stand near Foley's sedan, waiting for something to do. No one from the sheriff's department had questioned her. It was their case, and the federal government was merely assisting. She began mentally composing her report. What would she say about how the driver of the Porsche had ignored her order to stop? It was the kind of thing a defense attorney would use to get a dismissal of the murder charge against the blaster.

She yawned. Up since four that morning. It was hard to stand without feeling unsteady. She leaned against the rear fender of Foley's Dodge and yawned again. Coyotes yipped from the Alabama Hills, then broke into squalls. In another few minutes, the moon would set behind the Sierra.

Ben Whittaker, in a hard hat, could be seen down in the gulch below the breach. He was talking in low tones to some of his city workers. After a moment, he climbed the embankment to Sid, stutter-stepping in his muddy street shoes. Reaching the road, he introduced himself, shook hands, chatted briefly, then came over to Dee. "Ms. Laguerre," he said in that courtly bass voice of his.

"Ben." She rather like the DWP's point man in the valley. Snubbed at every turn, villified, he kept an unflappable good humor. It would probably cost him a massive coronary one of these days.

"I think," Whittaker said, raising his voice slightly for what was obviously the sheriff's sake, "we should all put our heads together at the first opportunity. A powwow. You know, to pool our assets."

"Consider 'em pooled, Ben." Foley heaved himself out of the Dodge. His side of the chassis sprang up, and Dee could almost hear the springs and shocks sigh in relief. "I just told the ATF boy he could have anything he needs." His smallish eyes clicked toward Dee. "Somebody ever gonna tell me what happened to his face . . . or is that a federal secret?"

"I didn't ask," Dee said, "and he didn't explain."

Whittaker said, "I was speaking in general terms, Tyrus—"

"You usually do," Foley interrupted.

"I suppose it goes with the job," Whittaker said. "And the people I have to deal with." The DWP man held the sheriff's gaze for a few seconds. "Until we nab this guy, we've got miles and miles of aqueduct to patrol. That's all I'm saying."

Foley scratched his heavy jowls. "Well, startin' tomorrow night," he finally said, "Laguerre here can cover the system where it crosses the gov'mint lands below Haiwee Reservoir. My boys will take everythin' from the dam north to the county line."

"That's a lot of territory for Dee to work alone."

"She's got a knack of bein' Sally-on-the-spot." Then

Foley added with a shrewd smile, "Like tonight."

"I was responding to a call put out by your department, Sheriff."

"Yes, Laguerre, I'm sure you were."

She wondered if Foley's son, Kyle, had told him about the latest confrontation at the Chevron station. She didn't think so—and would wait until the sheriff brought it up first. It'd probably do no good to remind him once again that she was sick of Kyle's baiting her. Foley no doubt encouraged it. His way of getting back at what he considered an army of federal bureaucrats occupying his county.

"All right," Dee said, too tired to trade barbs. "If somebody can give Sid a lift to a motel when he needs it, I'm going to turn in."

"Done gladly," Foley said. "Sleep well, young lady." The soul of congeniality now that he'd gotten his jabs in at DWP and the federal government.

"Good night, Ms. Laguerre," Whittaker said. "Thanks for your help on this."

"Anytime, Ben." Dee started back up the canal road, her feet dragging. Below, on the highway, the flattened Porsche had been righted and was being hooked up for a tow to the evidence impound yard. She knew that she'd see the faces of the dead couple as soon as she dropped off to sleep.

At dawn, Sid Abramowitz had a deputy sheriff drop him off at the Frontier Motel, just south of Lone Pine. The motif was western films, and he was given the Tom Mix Room. There, he dozed for three hours, showered, then dressed from head to toe in what Howard Rowe, his friend who ramrodded the Bakersfield FBI office, called his Truman Capote ensemble: wide-brimmed hat, sunglasses, scarf, long-sleeved shirt, and cotton gloves. Exposure to strong sunlight brought back that sensation of burning, his flesh drizzling as he watched helplessly, the dry autumn breeze off the Santa Ynez Mountains fanning the flames into a sickening roar. The feeling had to be psychological, for the scar tissue covering his face and hands was virtually nerve-dead.

A sheriff's office detective picked him up at ten, as promised.

"Ray Jelks," he introduced himself, gunning the engine to a sand-pitted department Jeep. As expected, he evaded gazes as soon as he'd shaken hands with Sid. A hollow-cheeked man with a style of mustache that had gone out of fashion during the Nuremberg trials. "Sheriff Foley says I'm yours as long as you need."

"Thanks, Ray. Could use a hand with one thing . . ."

"Name it." Speeding north along the highway, Jelks slipped a pack of Marlboro Lights from the top of his boot sock. The cellophane was beaded with sweat. He lit up. "Like I said, I'm yours."

Sid cracked his window. He hated the smell of anything burning. Even tobacco. "The road that runs along the canal—it's gated and locked near the spillway . . . right?"

"Always. DWP won't even share a key with us."

Sid fell silent. A considerable amount of explosive had been hauled to the scene—several hundred pounds, judging by the size of the crater. How had the blaster done that without leaving any physical evidence, vehicle tire impressions especially? Other than on the canal road, which had been driven over by law enforcement and DWP personnel, Sid had found nothing below the seat of the blast that told him the aqueduct had been approached by vehicle. Maybe the blaster had a DWP key and had somehow slipped past the spillway attendant's residence to use the embankment road. Sid made a mental note: Don't overlook the possibility of a disgruntled employee—the equivalent of the butler when it came to bomb investigations. Maybe even the spillway man. "I'm wondering about those bouldery hills right above the canal . . ." he mused out loud.

"Alabama Hills," Jelks chimed in. "Used for more movies than you can shake a stick at. Everything from *Gunga Din* to *How the West Was Won*."

"Some Alabaman christen them after his home state?"

"No. Named for the Confederate raider that sunk half the federal navy, C.S.S. *Alabama*." Then Jelks added with a raspy, nicotine laugh, "You're in redneck country, mister."

Sid didn't have to be told that. "Any chance somebody with a good four-wheel-drive could make his way through the hills to the blast site?"

Jelks had to think about that. "Maybe. But I kinda doubt it. You'd have a squeeze of it even on a motorbike."

"But you're not positive . . . are you?"

The detective finally gave him a grudging no.

"You mind eliminating that possibility for me, Ray?"

"You sure it's necessary?"

"Yes."

Five minutes later, Jelks dropped Sid off on the highway below the spillway, giving him a radio handset so they could stay in touch. The detective then continued on around the north end of the Alabama Hills to seek a way through from their western side. Sid, toting a small gear bag, clambered over a barbed-wire fence and hiked up along the gulley left by last night's rampaging waters.

A shadow flitted across the ground before him. A hawk riding an updraft.

Sid had to stop. Staring up into the dazzling sun had left him with vertigo. He shut his eyes to get his vision back, then glanced around.

Suddenly, he dropped to his knees in the hot sand. Taking a pair of tweezers and a vial from the bag, he picked up a jagged metal fragment half the size of a postage stamp. He'd found two others last night. All had a bluish iridescence. From the searing heat of the blast—the dim, orangish flash seen by some of the witnesses on the highway, muted because the explosion had been in water. What were they? His gut instinct told him bomb casing shrapnel. Yet, they might also be chips off the rebar used to reinforce the concrete walls of the canal.

An air-curdling sound made him twist around: a navy F-18 was streaking just above the line of dead trees that marked the old bed of the Owens River. Sid winced. The sudden movement had made the supposedly long-healed incisions on his chest and upper thighs ache, the places where skin had been lifted for grafts to his face and hands.

He rose and moved on.

The fragments made him suspect that the explosive device had come wrapped in a single package. Heavy. Most likely, it had not been carted to the scene piecemeal, so many bricks of plastique or sticks of dynamite at a time. That is why he'd sent Jelks in search of a route by which the blaster could have approached the canal by truck, unnoticed.

Sid huffed up the embankment, a lizard scampering in front of him. It had a squirming cricket in its jaws.

He paused on the road and shook his head at the scene.

In daylight, the breach looked even more like a combat bombing than it had last night. A definite cone squarely in the middle of the canal, wide at the top, narrow at the bottom. Shattered concrete and tangled rebar. A ring of earth lay heaped on the bank wherever the water hadn't washed it away. A classic bomb crater, probably from a five-hundred-pounder or better. He'd seen a thousand of them in Vietnam.

A muffled voice came from inside Sid's bag. Jelks's voice. He took out the handset. "ATF Abramowitz, go ahead."

"Listen," the detective transmitted, sounding breathless and exasperated, "there's just no way through from this side of the hills. Spent the last ten minutes high-centered on a big rock. I'm backin' out. A mountain goat couldn't make it."

"Fine, Ray, thanks. Pick me up—I'm about done for now. I'll come back later to do some sifting."

"Copy."

While putting the handset back inside the bag, Sid noticed something between his shoes on the roadway. A shred of nylonlike material. It was blaze-orange in color, scorched around the edges. Standing straight again, he gazed up the empty canal. A hundred yards away, a steel cable had been strung from side to side. Several straps dangled off it into what was ordinarily the current. They too were orange. Handgrabs, Sid figured, in case someone fell in and was swept along.

Growing thunder turned Sid's head.

An A-6 came screaming up the valley floor, the undersides of the Intruder's wings bulging with ordnance. Five-hundred-pounders. Sid glanced from the aircraft to the crater, then his eyes widened and he chuckled incredulously.

"No way," he said to himself.

*   *   *

A rhythmic grinding sound gradually brought Dee out of a deep sleep. She tried to open an eye to investigate, but the painful daylight wouldn't let her. The sound went on, stone against stone. Grist . . . grist . . . grist . . . She could feel a warm breeze, hear it rattling what were probably aspen or cottonwood leaves. Grist . . . grist . . .

"Quit it," she muttered.

But it went on.

Dee groaned, then rose on her elbows and finally forced her eyelids apart. They felt like Velcro. "Jesus."

Everything was a blur, but she saw enough of her surroundings to remember coming in late last night and finding her unair-conditioned bungalow too hot for sleep. She'd dragged her mattress outside and thrown it atop the flat-topped granite boulder in the yard. Indian women had used it for generations to grind foodstuffs, wearing four mortars the size of small mixing bowls into its surface. Tillie Aguirre, her landlord's wide-faced Paiute wife, was pulverizing the last of the previous fall's pinyon nut crop with a *mano*, or hand-stone.

Dee shut her eyes again. "Told you, Tillie—the rock dust in your pinyon mush is wearing down your teeth. Louie's too. Use your Cuisinart." The staff at the county sanitorium had given her one after her twenty-fifth year there as a nurse's aide.

"Don't like it."

"Why not?"

"Zip-zip and the grindin's all done. Makes me wanna take up smokin' again. I got nothin' to keep my hands busy while I think. Besides, Louie told me to come out and wake you up."

"What time's it?"

"Almost noon," Tillie said. "And he's pissed off."

"Why?"

"Let him tell you."

Dee sat up, rubbed her eyes. It really didn't matter that Tillie had awakened her. The sun was close to inching completely around the cottonwood tree that had been shading her all morning. Yawning, she looked out across the yard at the shanties and huts scattered among the locust and cottonwood trees. The Big Pine Indian Colony. Home sweet home. It wasn't part of the nearby Paiute reservation, and legally its dozen residents were squatters on city of Los Angeles land. But they and their forebears had been squatters on this spot since Khufu had thrown up his pyramid, so DWP, fearing bad publicity, had refrained from bulldozing the rickety structures—as it'd done with a vengeance to the old farmhouses on its property elsewhere in the valley. The fewer people on the land, the less competition for the water.

A wooden screen door could be heard slamming shut, and Louie Aguirre came charging around the corner of his and Tillie's small house waving a folded newspaper in his fist. He was a short man, powerfully built. He would go barechested now until the snow flew. "Dominica, *goddammita*," he said, "write me a letter."

She yawned so widely her jaws clicked. "Who to?"

"President of the United States."

"Why?" she asked. He tossed the newspaper into her lap. From the homeland. In Basque, of course. "Louie, you know I can't read this."

"*Bullshita.*"

"No *bullshita*. Papa and Mama had a hard enough time getting me to speak a little Basque, let alone read it." She, like most of the second generation, had resorted to pig Basque: mimicking the grammar by adding the article to the end of nouns. A highway became *highwaya*, a pickup truck *pickupa*, a picnic *pikinikje*. Just enough to convince the old folks that not all was lost. Louie, after more than forty years in America, was just beginning to put English articles in their proper order.

A fly landed on the balding crown of his head. Rather than shoo it, he smashed it flat. Tillie giggled. He snatched the paper back from Dee and strode toward his front door. "I will get my fuckin' glasses. Dominica, *goddammita*—you wait."

Dee sighed. Transferred to California last winter by the BLM, she'd rented the Aguirres' tiny two-room, "guest house" at the urging of Louie's distant cousin, who'd been Dee's landlord in Nevada. Gabrielle, like Louie, was stridently Basque and couldn't imagine Dee living among nonlandsmen, particularly in cattle country. Actually, despite what Kyle Foley had heard, she'd ended her tour in Nevada on fairly good terms with the local cattlemen.

A tenderness played around Tillie's mouth as she watched Louie's return. He still apparently amused her.

Louie's bifocals were propped low on his nose. He scratched the mat of gray hair between his pectoral muscles, then began reading a news article out loud. In rapid-fire Basque. She asked for a translation, but he told her to shut up and went on in the strange tongue that confused most Americans because it sounded neither French nor Spanish, the languages of the two nations that had gobbled up the Basque homeland in the Pyrenees. For a reason that escaped her, most Bascos swore in either Spanish or French.

Gradually, she got the gist of the article. The Madrid government was getting ready to execute two members of Euzkadi Ta Askatasuna, the Basque Homeland and Liberty Party, better known as ETA. They were accused of having blown up a police station, which the Spaniards might have forgiven and chalked up to congenital Basque surliness had not the national director of the paramilitary police been inside the place at the time eating lunch.

At last, Louie lowered the newspaper. "So, you see— you write me a letter, Dominica, *goddammita*."

"Louie, my middle name is not *goddammita*."

"Letter to the president, so he stops this *bullshita*, okay?"

"Not okay."

Louie scowled. "Why?"

"The president's my boss. I just don't drop him a line advising him on international issues."

"But I will sign it, for chrissake."

Sighing, Dee glanced under her sheet. Good. She'd taken the time to put on her pajama bottoms last night. "Write him yourself, Louie. In your own hand. Politicians like that personal touch. And keep it polite."

His eyes darkened, but he finally asked, "You check my English?"

"All right, I'll do that much."

A white pickup truck with Los Angeles City seals on the doors pulled up to a cedar-shingled hut across the stony creek that burbled through the middle of the colony. The broad-shouldered Paiute waited for the dust to settle before getting out. Then, slowly turning, he stared from behind mirrored sunglasses at the threesome on the rock. Finally, he offered a shy wave. Dwight Rainwater, Tillie's younger brother. "You hear, Dee?"

"Hear what?"

"Navy bombed the aqueduct."

"What?"

Dwight never repeated himself. Without another word, he went inside his hut for lunch.

"What he say?" Louie asked.

"Got me," Dee said. "All I know is that somebody put a big hole in the canal below the Alabama Spillway last night."

Louie thrust out his lower lip in surprise, then said, *"La puta madre."* Your mother's a whore. A Basqueism usually reserved for good news.

This made Dee pointedly add, "Louie, two people drowned inside their Porsche because of it."

His forehead wrinkled. "They drive their car into canal?"

"No, the canal water found them."

"Local?"

"Flatlanders," Dee said.

"TV actors," Dwight said out his screenless kitchen window between bites on a hastily made sandwich. "Stars on one of them soap operas. Whittaker's secretary says now they're gonna have to kill 'em off in the show too. They'll write it that way. Have a funeral and everythin'."

Dee slid off the rock to the ground and stretched. The warm, silky dust felt good between her bare toes. "What's this about the navy, Dwight?"

He stared back at her a moment. "They dropped a bomb on the aqueduct."

Louie was as confused as Dee. "Why the navy gonna pick a fight with L.A.?"

Dwight shoved the last quarter of the sandwich into his mouth, chewed, gulped, and hiked his shoulders. "Don't know." He lowered his head to drink from the tap. "It's just what I heard."

Louie turned to Dee. "What kind explosive?" His interest seemed professional. He was a contract construction blaster, his jobs taking him away from the valley about six months out of the year. He'd applied for work with DWP, but so far his application had gone unanswered. "Military? Maybe civilian, huh?"

"The ATF agent from Bakersfield was still working on—"

Dee's phone could be heard chiming through the open door of her bungalow. She hurried for it, grabbing the receiver just before her answering machine kicked in. "Laguerre."

"Morning. Sid Abramowitz. Did I wake you?"

She paused, recalling the poor man's face. It wouldn't seem real until she saw it for a second time. "Close, but no cigar. What's up?"

"Sheriff has asked a favor of us. Feds on Feds, I suppose he figures."

"Pardon?"

"Foley wants us to go down to China Lake Naval Air Station and ask a few questions."

"Is he serious?" Dee said.

"Pardon?"

"What about the handwheel? The telephone activator at the intake? Did navy SEALS take them out first?"

Sid softly chuckled. "That sabotage is more up in the air than ever. Seems every kid in this valley wants a handwheel from the spillway for his bedroom wall. Trophy. Some sort of rite of passage. And the worker isn't sure how long it's been missing this time. Maybe weeks. He never opens the gate. And the phone company now thinks the problem was with their equipment at the intake."

Outside her window, Louie was popping the hood to his old Jeep pickup. He checked the radiator, frowned. "All right," she said to Sid, "let's go to China Lake."

CHAPTER**FOUR**

Dee stopped off at the post office in Big Pine, grabbed several days of mail and a *Los Angeles Times* from the vending machine outside. The wind had risen out of the southeast in the two hours since noon, and she had to get back inside the Bronco to go through the newspaper without having it ripped from her hands. Both ranges flanking the valley, the Sierra and the White Mountains, looked fuzzy and yellowish through tons of airborne dust.

She found what she'd expected on the first page of the Metro Section: "Sherman Oaks Couple Dies in Owens Valley Aqueduct Blast." Powell Gideon, twenty-nine, and Sheila Kane, twenty-six, who'd been returning from a holiday in the mountain resort of Mammoth Lakes. Actors, as Dwight Rainwater had said, in the popular NBC soap opera "Century City." They'd been engaged to be married in the fall.

Dee gently bit the inside of her cheek, remembering their faces, then tossed the paper into the backseat.

She ripped open her bank statement. *"Merde."* Buying a swamp cooler for her bungalow—which Louie, ever the frugal Basco, refused to do—would have to wait another month. She distrusted credit. Forking over interest to small-town banks and merchants had kept her sheepherder father broke most of his life. His dreams—simple, Old World dreams of land and a few grapevines—had always lain beyond the horizon of his debts.

She started south, and Big Pine was soon a dark clump of trees in her rearview mirror.

An earth-lined feeder canal wound lazily, grassily

through a few hundred acres of alfalfa and then a timber lot of locust trees. The valley turned riotously green wherever water touched it, but sagebrush dominated everywhere else. The only signs she saw of pre-aqueduct farms were the old windbreaks, the dead trees bleached silver by the sun, and the foundations of houses razed by DWP.

The Owens Valley Water War.

She'd known of it before being transferred here, but had assumed that it was a closed book. After all, the last revolt of the exhausted farmers and ranchers had fizzled out in the courts more than half a century ago. But then she'd overheard a local mother in the rest room at Denny's in Bishop admonishing her toddler, "Flush the toilet, honey. . . . L.A. needs the water." And there were the bumper stickers: "L.A. Sucks—Stop the Groundwater Pumping."

Thirty minutes later, she slowed for Independence, the county seat. A fine old courthouse, a few gas stations, and then in a blink the sage scrub again, trembling in the wind.

Los Angeles owned the Eastern Sierra's surface water lock, stock, and barrel. Nobody even bothered to contest that anymore. It was groundwater pumping, the tapping of the valley's aquifer and lowering of the water table with its effect on vegetation and wildlife, that had the locals up in arms. They figured Los Angeles was stealing their underground water to keep city government solvent. Water was a product. The more DWP could send down the line, the more it could sell to its customers. The more cops it could hire. That was the issue at present. L.A. had already tried and failed to bolster its law enforcement by increasing airport-use fees paid by the airlines.

Glancing to the side, Dee saw that DWP crews were already busy repairing the breach in the canal. Dwight Rainwater had told her that they were using a special concrete that wouldn't take long to cure. The system would be back in full operation by midweek.

Dee turned in at the Frontier Motel. Sid Abramowitz was waiting out front, clasping a floppy-brimmed hat to his head to keep it from flying out into the brush. It took her an instant to realize that the ATF agent was smiling, not sneering.

"Hello, hello," he said, getting inside the Bronco.

"Lovely weather."

"I'll take it over cold."

Dee got back on the highway. "Where you from originally?"

"Oahu."

"Really?"

"Yeah, Dad was a pipefitter at Pearl Harbor. Transferred from Brooklyn Navy Yard. My mom was a local *hapa* girl, working at the base commissary."

"Hapa?"

"Hapa haole. Half white. Portuguese and Chinese."

Ahead, Dee could see curtains of white alkali dust rising off Owens Lake, sifting down again over the highway. She turned on her headlights. Without even a sheen of water to cover its powdery bed, the dry lake now threatened thousands of high desert residents with silicosis, fibrosis of the lungs. Coal miners' disease. "So we're off to arrest the U.S. Navy?" she asked.

"Not quite. I spent twelve years with them. We might have a tough enough time getting somebody to talk to us, although I phoned ahead to N.C.I.S."

Naval Criminal Investigative Service, Dee realized. "How long you been with ATF?"

"Ten years."

Special agents had to have a bachelor's degree. That put Sid in his mid-forties. She'd gotten no idea how old he was from his appearance, not without a face and hands to judge by. "The whole valley is saying the navy bombed the aqueduct."

His eyes clicked toward her. "I've only told you and the sheriff about this."

"Well, I heard it from a neighbor, a DWP worker, just before you called. So that leaves Foley."

"I told him in confidence," Sid said. "I thought that'd be understood. One cop to another."

"We're not cops to him. We're Feds." Dee tapped her brakes twice as she eased into the foglike dust. She also made sure the air conditioner fan was on recirculation. "And ol' Ty thinks even less of China Lake flyboys than he does of us. Nobody in the valley exactly sees them as Top Gun heroes."

"Flyovers get bitched a lot?"

"Everytime a crack's found in a window." She hesitated, then said, "Two F-Eighteens buzzed me last night about fifteen minutes before the explosion. This was ten or so miles south of where the canal was hit."

"Were they carrying ordnance?"

"I couldn't tell you."

"You see the flash?"

"No, I was at a service station in Lone Pine at the time." Dee squinted into the scudding dust, kept checking her rearview mirror. "Heard the boom, though."

"Was it sharp or rumbly?"

"Uh . . . more sharp than rumbly."

Sid said nothing for a minute, then sighed. "Well, I'm sorry Foley shot his mouth off. I'm not even convinced it was military stuff."

"Can you rule it out?"

"Nope," he admitted. "But I can't begin to identify the type till our bomb truck gets over here from Walnut Creek. Another ten hours, at least. That's why I wanted a lid on this. Navy's more apt to admit to an accidental drop if the brass isn't forced to circle the wagons first." Sid sighed again. "Well, whatever—it's done now. I've learned my lesson with Foley. Let's just hope we get down there before the media does." The Bronco shuddered over a stretch of highway roughened up by heavy trucks, and the shotgun's slide handle began rattling. Sid stilled it, then rested his purplish hand around the barrel until Dee glanced at it. He quickly withdrew it. "You from around here, Dee?"

"No. Born and raised on the Nevada range about a hundred miles northeast of here. The resource area there was my last assignment."

"Why'd you leave? I mean, it being home and all."

She took a moment. "I suppose things got too close. I'd known everybody since kindergarten. The good guys and the violators. It's a hard place, Pinyon County. Nothing ever gets forgotten, let alone forgiven."

"What d'you mean?"

"Feuds. I inherited one the minute I was born. My clan raised sheep. The other side ran cattle. Men on both sides wound up dead. I got tired of carting that baggage to every call I went on."

"Sure," Sid said as if he understood.

Dee and Sid waited almost an hour at the China Lake security office for the on-call agent from N.C.I.S. to show up. He eventually phoned and had the guard give Dee a map marked with the route to the Air Operations control center. "Can't miss it, ma'am," the base cop said. "On the lower floor of the tower. Ask for Commander Torres. He's expecting you."

"How long has he been expecting us?" Dee asked. "About an hour now?"

"Pardon, ma'am?"

"Never mind."

Once they were outside, Sid warned, "Patience, Dee— okay?" His shriveled lips curled into another grotesque smile. "This isn't the United States of America anymore. This is the navy."

Dee drove at the twenty-five-mile-an-hour limit, homing in on the flight tower. Its big windows looked like sheets of copper as they reflected the late afternoon sun. The Bronco overtook a group of young sailors hurrying on foot toward the base recreation hall. She slowed a little for them.

"What're you staring at?" Sid asked.

Caught red-handed, Dee grinned. "Tight asses in whites."

Sid chuckled. "I see I'm gonna have to keep an eye on you, Laguerre."

"Please do. Things tend to happen when I'm around."

"Truly?"

She nodded, then smiled. "That's another reason I'm not in Nevada anymore."

Commander Torres let them wait another twenty minutes in his outer office, then swung open his door, a stiff-backed Hispanic in crisp khakis. "Ms. Laguerre, Mr. Abramo- witz—forgive the delay. Please come in."

Dee took her time following Sid inside, then dallied a bit longer studying the photographs of aircraft on the walls.

"Laguerre . . . ?" Smiling, Torres then asked her in Spanish how the drive had been.

"All right," she answered in English. "Hate to disappoint you, Commander—but my Basque ancestors would spin in their graves if they caught me speaking Spanish."

Torres blushed slightly. "Sorry, I assumed—"

"An easy mistake to make," Dee interrupted, enjoying his obvious discomfort.

"Won't you please sit down?" When all had done so, Torres folded his hands on his desk blotter and asked, "Now, how may I help you?"

Dee looked to Sid, who cleared his throat and began filling the commander in. Torres, to his credit, had no trouble staring Abramowitz square in the eye. Maybe in his line of work he was used to burn victims. Sid, on the other hand, grew increasingly uneasy as he talked. Dee finally figured out that it was the situation. He was a sailor again, bringing bad news to a high-ranking officer. This was confirmed when Torres butted in and asked with a genial smile, "Excuse me, Abramowitz—are you former navy?"

"Yes—warrant officer, EOD."

"I thought so. How nice." Nice had nothing to do with it. Torres was reminding Sid of the pecking order here. "Then you certainly realize that it's not a quick thing to determine the flights that may have used the restricted airspace over Owens Valley last night."

"Why not?"

Torres's eyes snapped toward Dee. "I'm sorry?"

"I don't understand what's so complicated about it."

"Aircraft using the Panamint bombing range come from air stations all over the West. Lemoore in the Central Valley. Miramar and North Island in the San Diego area. Fallon up in Nevada."

Dee said, "But don't they check in with you people?"

Torres sat back, his swivel chair creaking, and his face went still.

"Maybe this will help you, Commander—yesterday at dusk, two low-flying F-Eighteens nearly blew my Bronco off Highway One-thirty-six."

"How do you know they were Hornets, Ms. Laguerre?"

"I didn't watch the Gulf War on CNN for nothing."

Torres smirked. "Touché. But I'm sure they were flying higher than you think."

"I'm sure I could've thrown my nightstick and put a dent in one of them."

"Whatever." The commander came briskly to his feet. "Well, I certainly have my work cut out for me. I'll have to find out which flights were carrying ordnance and get back to you sometime after the weekend. If you'll leave your card out front."

Sid had risen as well, but Dee remained seated. "Commander, do you know Sheriff Foley very well?"

Torres's eyes hardened. "We've met."

"Isn't pretty, is it?"

A flicker of a smile. "No, not very."

"Special Agent Abramowitz and I are down here at Foley's request. It's his investigation. His homicides trump our case for destruction of property used for interstate commerce. But he's asked for us, as minions of the federal government, to ask you, fellow minions of the same government, if there's even a remote possibility a navy jet dropped a bomb on the Los Angeles Aqueduct. If Sid and I go back and tell him the Air Operations officer at China Lake will get back to us on it one of these days—know what he'll do? Tonight, he'll get on the horn to every paper and TV station he can think of and roast you and the navy for covering up the truth."

Torres stared off into a corner of the office for a few seconds, then at Dee again. "What're you asking for, Laguerre?"

"Pilots. I want to talk to any pilots who flew over the southern end of the Owens Valley yesterday evening."

A longer pause, and then Torres sat again, reached for his telephone and began dialing. "There's a snack room at the end of the passageway. If you don't mind."

Out in the corridor, Sid said with a half-serious, half-amused tone, "You're dangerous, Laguerre. *That's* why you got shipped out to California."

She winked. "No, Sid, I'm just a little naive. I honestly don't know how important that starched son of a bitch is, so we may as well use it . . . okay?"

Shaking his head, he dug out some pocket change. He bought them each a cup of coffee from a machine, but set hers on the table rather than directly hand it to her.

"Thanks." Dee took a sip. Awful coffee. "Don't deny it, Sid."

"Deny what?"

"You're almost sure it was a military bomb. Otherwise, you would've cut me off in there."

Abramowitz didn't answer.

A half hour later, they were summoned to a conference room by Torres's petty officer secretary. The commander sat at the head of a long mahogany table, flanked by two young officers who looked as if they'd fished their uniforms out of laundry hampers for the occasion. One was red-eyed, and Dee could smell beer on him. It was Saturday afternoon, she reminded herself, and they'd no doubt been summoned from their quarters. They and Torres rose as she entered, as did a fourth man, a paunchy civilian who was sitting at the opposite end of the table.

"Ranger Laguerre, Special Agent Abramowitz . . ." Torres then introduced the two aviators, Lieutenants Neidrick and Huber. Dee ignored their terse nods and jotted down the names in her pocket notebook. The civilian was Special Agent Christy of N.C.I.S.

"These two officers were over the valley with ordnance last evening," Torres said. "Fire away, Ms. Laguerre."

Dee smiled. "Either of you accidentally lose a bomb over the Owens Valley at approximately twenty-one-forty-five hours?"

The pilots grinned at each other, then Neidrick, the one who'd obviously been drinking, chuckled as if she were out of her mind. Torres silenced him with a look.

"Lieutenant Neidrick," Dee said, "are you trying to tell me that it'd be highly unusual to accidentally drop a bomb?"

"Yes, ma'am."

Ma'amed by everyone. She was beginning to feel like somebody's grandmother. "Educate me, Lieutenant."

Neidrick shifted in his chair, sucked in a noisy breath. "My aircraft, Huber's here—they're all equipped with an ordnance master arm switch. It's kept on safe right till we approach the target. Then we radio back to the tower for permission to arm."

"Was that the case last night?"

"Yes, ma'am."

Dee turned slightly. "Lieutenant Huber?"

"Yes, ma'am. On safe the whole trip up. And we dropped all our ordnance on target over in Panamint Valley. Both aircraft. I saw Neidrick's go, and he saw mine."

"Do these master arm switches ever fail?" Dee asked.

Silence.

Christy stirred and jotted something in a small notepad as Torres said, "These men aren't qualified to answer that."

"Why not?" Dee said.

"They're not aircraft maintenance personnel."

"Oh, Jesus."

"Pardon?" Torres asked.

"I said, 'Oh, Jesus.' It's an expression of amazement or incredulity." Dee faced the two pilots again. "What kind of ordnance were you carrying?"

"Mark Eighty-twos," Neidrick said.

"Forgive me for asking . . ."

Huber clarified, "Five-hundred-pound bombs, ma'am. Both aircraft."

Dee pocketed her pen. "All right, gentlemen, you've convinced me of one thing. You'd no more lose a bomb than you'd buzz a brown-and-white BLM Bronco." She stood while the two pilots gazed vacantly at the tabletop. "Thank you, Commander Torres. That's all for now . . . unless Mr. Abramowitz has something more?"

Sid just shook his head.

Reaching the Bronco, the two of them sat quietly a moment, thinking. The southeasterly, still strong, was slightly rocking the vehicle. A tumbleweed bounced down the length of the parking lot, then was pinned to a chain-link fence. "Well, that didn't prove much," Dee finally said, starting the engine.

"You did all right. Now it's up to Torres to lean on them."

"Think he will?"

"Yeah. He'll defend them from us, an outsider, then tear them new assholes as soon as we're gone. The navy way."

"Good," she said. "You hungry?"

"Oh, not really."

It then occurred to her that he didn't want to sit inside a crowded restaurant. "Nothing fancy," she went on. "I'm on a budget. Saving up to buy an evaporative cooler for my place. Should have enough by Christmas. What d'you say we go drive-through, burgers maybe?"

"Well . . . okay, sure. Maybe I am getting an appetite."

Heading for the exit, Dee saw Neidrick and Huber strolling together for their cars, laughing, assholes very much intact. They couldn't hear the Bronco's approach because of the wind.

"Watch this," she said to Sid, turning the key to off and coasting. When just a few yards behind the pilots, she pumped the gas pedal twice, restarted the engine, and gunned it. The deafening backfire made Neidrick and Huber scramble for their lives. Neidrick went down on a knee, ripping his khakis.

Dee cracked her window and said, beaming, "Paybacks are bummers, boys."

Then she drove on.

CHAPTER **FIVE**

Dee pulled out of the Frosty Cone drive-through and turned west, toward the Sierra. It was fawn-colored this far south, the pryamidlike peaks and V-shaped canyons untouched by the glaciers that, just to the north, had peeled the soil down to the underlying granite. The sun was gone, but a long twilight would last at least another hour.

Suddenly, she slowed.

"What's wrong?" Sid asked, balancing a cardboard box of cheeseburgers, fries, and Cokes on his lap.

"I'm sorry," Dee said. "It's the 'Me Too Hour,' and I didn't give you the chance to phone."

" 'Me Too Hour'?"

"Yeah, everytime I work with an agent, this is when he calls home. Always signs off to mama with 'Me too, honey.' "

"No mama." Sid took a sip of cola. "How about you? Got a pappa?"

Dee accelerated again. "Ex-pappa."

"I'm sorry," Sid said after a moment.

"Don't be. I left him." Through the blowing dust, she could barely make out a line of inverted siphons zigzagging up and down like a roller coaster along the base of the mountains. Huge steel pipes used to cross the canyons between the aqueduct tunnels.

She realized that she'd left an opening when Sid asked, "What happened? If you don't mind . . ." She shrugged that she didn't. "Your old man couldn't share you with BLM?"

44

"No, that wasn't it. I called it quits with Tyler before I got my federal appointment. Although, he depises the bureau."

"Why?"

"Ever heard of Tyler Ravenshaw?"

Sid shook his head.

"He's the Melvin Belli of environmental attorneys," she went on. "Heads the Wilderness Conservancy Alliance."

"So that was it—political differences?"

"Not really . . ." She paused, wondering how to put it.

"What d'you want first here, Dee?"

"Fries, while they're hot." Accepting them, she chewed as she turned north onto Highway 395, then said, "Warm and charming egocentrics. They shine when they need you. If you need them, all the lights go out and nobody's home. I guess I got sick of that."

"I'm sorry," Sid repeated. Then he lowered his head slightly and looked out the windows. "Well, if anything happens this evening, we can't blame the navy."

"Why's that?"

His scarred hand gestured at all the dust swirling and eddying through the atmosphere. "Flights will be cancelled due to this crud."

"Listen," she said, "if it's okay with you, I'll take you back as far as Olancha. That's the little burg we passed near Owens Dry Lake. The resident deputy can shuttle you from there to Lone Pine."

"What're you gonna do?"

"Patrol. Foley wants me to cover the system from Haiwee Reservoir down here to Indian Wells Valley."

Sid said, "No sense in you having to backtrack." He offered her a cheeseburger. "If you don't mind the company."

"Not at all. Seldom get any. Would you unwrap that for me?"

He hesitated, but then did so.

"Thanks," she said, making sure to casually touch his right hand in the process. To make him feel that it wasn't the inhuman claw he kept hiding with the left one in the folds of his ATF windbreaker. Munching hungrily, she put on her left blinker and turned up a wide dirt road toward the mountains. Ahead lay some of the Eastern Sierra's few foothills; most of this slope was a scarp soaring almost straight up from the desert floor.

"How long you been with BLM?" Sid asked, gazing out across the alluvial flats. The long, spindly branches of the creosote bushes were whipping against the ground.

"Two and a half years, counting Glynnco." The federal law enforcement academy in Georgia. Sweltering Dixie. After living most of her life in high desert, the tidewater humidity had nearly killed her.

"You've found a home?" Sid asked.

"I think so."

"Ambitions?"

"Get through this summer in one piece."

He toasted her with his Coke. "Hear, hear."

The road climbed to the mouth of Nine-Mile Canyon. There, beneath a section of siphon raised on concrete piers, a white DWP truck was parked. The driver was sitting inside out of the wind, uncapping a thermos. Elvis sideburns and a cracker grin. He touched two fingers to an eyebrow in greeting.

Dee felt better seeing him out here: Ben Whittaker knew that there were limits to what she could patrol. The DWP man and Dee rolled down their windows.

She shut off her engine. "How's it going?"

"Still and clear," the man said with the same infectious grin. "Still blowin' dust clear up my ass."

Dee smiled. "Out here on your lonesome?"

"Oh, no, we—" The DWP man had to shield his eyes from a blast of flying grit. "We got a truck in damn near every canyon 'tween here and Haiwee."

"See anything so far?"

"Just a van with two kids goin' up the canyon to make out. I got the license, like they told us."

"Good." Dee studied the ten-foot-diameter pipeline. A warning had been stenciled on it in red letters every hundred yards: "Stand Clear—Under Extreme High Pressure!" She'd been told that a stream from even a small leak in the bottom stretch of a siphon could cut flesh.

Sid leaned forward to look past her at the DWP man. "There an automatic shutoff on this section?"

The worker visibly paled before recovering himself. "Yeah. Sensors every so far to check if the flow's been interrupted."

Dee restarted her engine, shifted into reverse, and said, "Well, take care. I'll try to swing by again before I go off shift."

The DWP man nodded somberly, his eyes still on Sid's face.

Dee started down the slope. "Question, Sid."

"Okay." He'd shrunk into his windbreaker.

"Where would you hit the line—if you were the blaster? Saying it's a blaster and not Neidrick or Huber out reliving Desert Storm."

"Wherever I could leave as little physical evidence as possible."

"The damage below the Alabama Spillway—how much explosive are we talking about?"

"Too much for a man to pack in one trip," Sid said. "And an experienced blaster wouldn't want to do that. Track up the scene making several trips back and forth."

She continued northward on the highway. Headlights were coming on in the nightfall. She flicked on her own, then radioed the sheriff's office, asking if there was any traffic for her.

"*Nada*, BLM-One," the dispatcher answered.

"Naturally," Dee muttered, her thumb off the mike button.

"Must be pretty tough," Sid said. "Out here alone. At loggerheads with local law enforcement most of the time."

"I've never known anything but. It was the same over in Nevada." Dee let up on the gas pedal. The highway was four-laned here, and she looked across the median strip at a GMC pickup speeding south. "And it's about to get a lot tougher."

"Why's that?"

Dee jinked the wheel to the left, bounced across the strip, and fell in behind the pickup at a distance. "Sheriff Foley's son. He's a long way from home, even for Saturday evening."

"Any reason to suspect him?"

She eased off several more car lengths, just to make sure

Kyle wouldn't realize that he was being tailed. "He was in Lone Pine last night when things got noisy. The Foleys live in Independence."

"Fifteen miles north?"

"Right." She smiled at Sid, who was finishing off his now-cold fries. "Just a hunch."

"Go with it."

"And it's happened before up here," she added. "Daddy badmouthing DWP for raping the valley, then acting surprised as hell when junior blows up a city well with a homemade device."

Kyle's tail lamps swerved off into a combination store, bar, and gas station that stood alone like a frontier outpost in the scrub. Its flying horse sign was blinking on and off, a reminder of the days before British Petroleum had eclipsed Mobil. Desert people clung to old symbols. All change was resisted.

Kyle parked close to the store entrance.

Dee switched off her lights and crept in behind a tractor-trailer, putting it between the Bronco and the boy. "Mind the radio for me a minute?"

"Done," Sid said.

She got out and hurried to the space between the truck cab and the trailer. Through it, she watched Kyle saunter around a Jeep pickup equipped with a boom and cable pulley, then approach a darkly bearded man. He was sitting on the porch railing just outside the bar door, nursing a long-necked bottle of Coors under the buggy glare of the neon lights.

"Mister—?" Something in the man's face or eyes made the boy pause.

"What?"

"Mind buyin' a sixer for me?"

The man clasped the back of his muscular neck and rubbed. He'd cut away the sleeves of his light woolen shirt, revealing his massive biceps. His body, even at rest, gave an impression of coiled strength. "Too much death on the highways lately."

So he read the newspaper.

But this only mystified Kyle, who grinned stubbornly

and tried again. "I'll give you a couple bucks for your trouble."

"Nobody gives you shit for your trouble. Ever."

"Five bucks."

"Get outta here."

"Well, fuck you too, you goddamn son of a bitch."

The man gave no reaction, his glassy eyes simply followed Kyle back to his pickup, where the boy got in and slammed his door. He chittered his tires getting back on the highway, then soon made the turn for Ridgecrest.

Dee saw no point in following him to the next store.

The man stared off toward the south.

"Anything unusual?" Sid asked as Dee got inside the Bronco again.

"At least nothing out of character." She continued north once again. "Kyle might just be ranging farther afield so Daddy doesn't hear about his carousing."

"He a little terror?"

"Holy terror. Sometimes I think cops oughta be sterilized at academy graduation."

Sid chuckled.

Several miles later, she pulled off onto a flat expanse where a lumber mill had once stood. The ground was black with old pine bark, which still gave off a resiny smell. Taking her bipoded spotting scope from the Bronco's cargo area, she set it up on the hood and glassed the faint line of the aqueduct all the way to where it curved southwest and out of sight. She was searching for headlights on any of the dirt roads that crossed under the pipeline.

Nothing.

The wind was starting to die down, and the full moon, magnified and turned orange by the dust, had risen over the Coso Range.

"Here," she said, standing aside for Sid, "have a look."

He stooped to peer through the eyepiece. "You always want to be a cop, Dee?"

"As a kid, you mean?"

"Yeah."

"Never occurred to me." She pivoted for a glance northward toward the volcanic bluff that marked the southern end of Owens Valley. The tracery of roads above the highway showed no lights. "Where I grew up, out nowhere," she went on, "law enforcement was the career of choice for the functionally illiterate. Diplomas for the high school graduates, badges for the dropouts."

"Then what'd you want to be?"

"Something that'd get me out-of-doors, at least part of the time. I got a master's in resource management."

"No kidding." He stood up and stretched—gingerly, as if parts of his body gave him pain. "Why aren't you doing something related to that?"

"I am. Don't you know? I'm Mother Nature with a Smith and Wesson revolver."

"Is that really how you see your job?"

"No," she admitted, tracing the now-luminous siphons with her naked eye. "I'm a tightrope walker. The environmentalists are on one side of me and the land users—the miners, the livestock operators, the recreationists—are on the other. Both are shouting for me to fall."

"Then what's the satisfaction in it?"

"Not falling."

Her gaze was on Nine-Mile Canyon when something dark and curdling mushroomed up from the peak just north of it. She half believed she'd seen a dim flash just before. "Sid—"

"I saw it," he said, grabbing the telescope.

He gripped the dashboard with both hands as Dee barreled up the unpaved road toward Nine-Mile Canyon. The DWP dispatcher was trying for the third time to raise the city truck there. Sid transmitted for Dee so she could keep a tight hold on the steering wheel. "DWP, this is BLM-ATF, we're just about to the scene."

"Any sign of running water?"

"None so far . . ." Sid paused as Dee shone her spotlight across the hood and into a shallow ravine on his side. Gushing down it was a wave of silty water about two feet high.

Dee jerked the wheel to avoid a jackrabbit bolting out of the ravine. "It shouldn't flood the highway. There's a culvert bridge over this drainage."

"Man," he exclaimed, "that was a shitpot full of explosive."

"Why wasn't there much flash?"

"I'm not sure." Sid started to hold his wristwatch up to the dash lights, but Dee told him that the blast had been at nine-forty-six. Almost the same time as last night's. "The sensors should've kicked in," he said, watching the reflection of the moon run over the surface of the floodwater. "I don't get it."

"Our blaster," Dee said. "Just like he spiked the intake and sluice gates last night. That was no coincidence." She spotlighted the flow again. It was subsiding, having dwindled to a small, muddy creek at this point. "Here we go— DWP's on the ball tonight. They've got the taps turned off." She shifted the beam directly ahead to the mouth of the canyon. "What . . . ?"

"Jesus Christ," Sid said.

It looked as if a wrecked freight train had come to rest on the road, tanker cars strewn atop one another, and a soft white mist sifting over the entire jumble. Dee realized that the tanker cars were actually sections of siphon pipe. Under one of them, she could see the squashed tailgate of a DWP truck. "Oh, God."

"Let me go up and check it out, Dee," Sid volunteered.

"We'll go together."

She'd just braked when hands flew through her open side window out of the darkness and glommed onto her uniform shirt. Her right hand was closing around her revolver grip when a hysterical male voice cried, "Tell'em I'm all right!"

It was the DWP worker with the Elvis sideburns. He was soaked and muddied to the waist—but uninjured as far as she could tell. "Okay . . . let go of me."

"I'm all fuckin' right!"

"Let go, dammit," she said. He finally unhanded her, leaving two twisted knots on her shirtfront. "You hurt anywhere?"

"Hell no!"

Sid radioed the city dispatcher to let them know their man was alive and well, then stepped out of the Bronco. "How'd you get away from your truck in time?"

"A piss, honey!" the DWP man said, giving her a hug.

"A goddamn piss! I went out into the brush to take a leak just as she blew. Boom!"

"Any flash?" Sid asked.

"Just a smidgen. Next thing, the water knocked all the piers out from under half this whole siphon. You shoulda heard the sound that made—like the Golden Gate Bridge comin' down 'round my ears!"

Dee asked, "Did the sensors stop the flow right away?"

"No—the system kept pumpin' for at least five minutes."

She turned to Sid. "You want to go up there?"

"Sooner the better."

She took two flashlights from the Bronco, tossing one to the agent, and they set off up the slope toward the seat of the explosion. It was all she could do not to break into a trot and leave Sid behind. They passed through a strand of mist clinging to the hillside. "What's this from?" she asked, slowing her pace.

"Cool water hitting warm sand, I guess." Sid already sounded winded.

Her beam danced before her in a patch of black sage. The foliage was dripping wet. "Should we be looking for footprints?"

"Usually," he said. "But I just don't know." A quick, gasping breath. "I don't wanna meet the guy who could pack that much shit up this mountain."

They hiked past a pipe section that had been squashed almost completely flat. The ground, decomposed granite, was littered with metal buttons—rivets that had popped loose as the siphon broke apart.

"Stop, please," Sid said. "Lousy lifestyle. Age."

"Altitude."

"You're too kind. But keep it up."

They halted and gazed out across Indian Wells Valley at the linear runway lights on the base, the clustered lights of Ridgecrest. Sid was breathing as if he'd just run a marathon. "Let's go."

"You sure?"

He jogged a few strides, but then slowed again. "No."

Ten minutes later, they reached the crest—and a thirty-foot-wide crater filled with water. The surviving section of siphon was ringed by jagged flaps of steel, all pointing outward. Sid shuffled around, examining the crater, the ruptured pipeline, the churned soil. Finally, he switched off his light and said, "It blew like a trick cigar."

"What d'you mean?"

"Exploded from the inside out." He sat on his heels, doffed his hat, and gently wiped his scarred pate with his sleeve. "And again, a lot of punch."

Dee turned, peered down the plunging slope to the Bronco below. It looked the size of an ant. "Question."

"Shoot."

"Like you said, how'd somebody cart that much explosive all the way up here, plus find a way to stuff it inside the pipe? *Especially* today, with half of DWP staked out along the system?"

Sid faced northward, his eyes on the siphon that rose steeply out of the neighboring canyon. "I've got my own questions, Dee. Like how the devil could the current push a heavy device up that long grade there? It couldn't. Never in a million years." He shook his head. "I just know." Then he said with a feeble laugh, "This bastard scares me."

CHAPTER**SIX**

Sheriff Foley snorted to himself.

DWP couldn't have made its threat clearer than by picking the Mount Whitney Fish Hatchery for the site of the two o'clock meeting on Sunday afternoon with all area law enforcement: *Go along with whatever the city has in mind or the tourists, the few to still come north, will be picking mummified trout out of the dry creek beds.*

Seeing that there were no folding chairs behind the podium for local dignitaries, he snorted again. *Get ready for ten lashes.* DWP had even invited the Los Angeles media to witness the punishment. Each time he turned around, a hard-faced young woman was thrusting a microphone up to his mouth, a videocam staring at him like a cyclops.

Nothing about the media had been mentioned early this morning when that soft Irish accent had come over Foley's telephone. "Tyrus, what d'you say we all have ourselves a gathering this afternoon?"

"Who's *all ourselves*?"

"Everyone concerned with protecting the aqueduct. What d'you say?"

"Monday mornin'."

"Too late . . ."

The number-two man at DWP, Garrett Driscoll, had what might be called an engaging personality. Too engaging to be trusted by anybody from the Owens Valley. No matter how widely he smiled, his pale blue eyes remained as hard as flints. Hard eyes from a hard early upbringing. A Belfast orphan adopted in his teens by a wealthy Catholic family in Bel Air, the sylvan, manicured side of Los Angeles. Degrees in both law and hydrology. Foley kept a mental intelligence file on all of DWP's top brass, and Driscoll had always seemed the one to really watch. He'd come from nowhere and was going places, a volatile mix in a bright, ambitious man with boundless energy.

Dabbing his neck with his handkerchief, Foley strolled over to the pond just outside the hatchery building. A bubble gum dispenser glinted in the sunlight. It was filled with fish food. He grunted breathily, then dug out a quarter and bought a handful. As soon as the pellets broke the surface, lunker trout darted up from the greenish depths and writhed over each other in a frenzy, boiling the waters.

A deep voice asked from behind, "How big you figure they can get in a pond like this, Tyrus?" It was Whittaker, looking as if he'd gotten no sleep.

"No limit to it, Ben," Foley said. "The big ones always get bigger as long as they got no scruples 'bout eatin' the littler ones." Foley tossed out more pellets. "Leastways, you coulda pitched the chairs under some shade for the public floggin' . . . or did you want to see the natives sweat in the presence of the Great White Father?"

"Come on now, Tyrus." Whittaker chuckled wearily. "Give me a break."

"Too much water over the dam for that, Ben."

Whittaker started to shake his head, but then stopped. "Truth is—microphone cord wouldn't reach all the way to the oaks over there."

"Sure."

"Get you something to drink, Tyrus? We've got cold water and coffee."

Foley shook his head, and Whittaker moved on. The sheriff brushed the fish food dust off his palms and sank into a chair at one end of the last row. A kind of protest. Dee Laguerre sat forward of him by three rows, her broad-brimmed campaign hat tilting forward as she read the first section of the *L.A. Times*. His eyes were still good, remarkably good for sixty-three years of desert sun, and he read the headlines:

LOS ANGELES AQUEDUCT BOMBED FOR
SECOND TIME
Ruptured Siphon Spells Severe Rationing

Several cars could be heard pulling into the parking lot at once. The arrival of Driscoll's cortege from the Independence airstrip, just down the hill from the hatchery.

Yawning, Foley took his electronic chessboard from his seersucker jacket pocket, contemplated it before pressing the ON button. Kyle had given it to him for Christmas. He often thought to tell the boy that it had been a fine gift and had spared him countless hours of boredom over the past several months. But each time he tried, the dark cloud that hovered over them descended before he could get the words out. And if he tried again this evening, last night would get in the way—Kyle hadn't returned home till dawn.

Foley frowned.

Driscoll could be heard schmoozing his way toward the podium. The sheriff ignored the man's hello and went on thoughtfully punching buttons, feeding pawns into the jaws of mightier powers.

Dee lowered the newspaper as a beguiling Irish accent said over the microphone, "Ladies and gentlemen, thank you for—" The public address system squealed, and the dark-haired man in his early thirties grinned boyishly. Somehow, his grin made Dee and most everyone else automatically smile. "Well, if that gave you a shiver, we'll call it air-conditioning and give thanks to God Almighty for small pleasures. . . . " He paused, a slight breeze ruffling his expensive-looking razor haircut. "For those of you who don't know, I'm Garrett Driscoll, assistant chief of the Los Angeles Department of Water and Power. I want to thank Ben Whittaker here for organizing this gathering, and each of you for braving the heat to hear me out when you might be enjoying the sabbath at home. . . . "

Dee heard someone grunt once, bearishly. She didn't have to turn around to know that it was Sheriff Foley. She'd been treated to the same noise numerous times over the telephone late last night as she reported Sid Abramowitz's preliminary findings to him.

"First off," Driscoll went on, "I want it known that the chief and I blame no one except the perpetrator or perpetrators for the developments of the past forty-eight hours. By that I mean no blame should be put on local and federal law enforcement here in the valley. I'm convinced that every effort was made to deter last night's blast. Nor will the department tolerate any careless insinuations that the environmental community is somehow responsible." Driscoll looked squarely at Karl Schoenfeld, president of the valley-based Wetlands Preservation Society, who gave a distant nod. Putty-faced, he looked like a middle-aged prizefighter—except for his waist-length, reddish blond ponytail. "But regardless of blame, the aqueduct system has been gravely damaged."

"How gravely?" an overeager reporter asked.

"*If* no further attacks are made, we'll need perhaps a month to replace one quarter mile of siphon in Nine-Mile Canyon. During that period, Van Norman Reservoir, the terminus of the system in the San Fernando Valley, will be drawn down to critical levels. This comes as we approach early autumn, when consumption historically peaks. What I now tell you is unavoidable, no matter how quickly we work—five hundred thousand of our customers will be on rationing at a level not seen before in California."

A reported asked, "Like what? Enough to flush the toilet?"

"Yes," Driscoll said flatly, "once a day."

"You're kidding."

The DWP executive just stared quietly back at him.

"What about city wells in Southern California, Mr. Driscoll?" a woman reporter asked. "Can't they meet some of the demand?"

"They were inadequate at the turn of the century. That's what prompted the building of the aqueduct." Driscoll flared his eyes a little. "Yes, indeed, people—we have a lovely crisis on our hands. I don't want to think what additional sabotage will do to this situation. But I'm paid to do just that. So here's what we must do—all blame aside, the present security structure can't be held to prevent more bombings. Vast patrol distances are involved, personnel are few. Therefore, meeting in emergency session this morning, the city council saw no recourse but to adopt the DWP's recommendation that members of the Los Angeles Police Department's Metro Division be dispatched here to guard city property—''

"Whoa," Foley said.

The sheriff had stood. His lower jaw dangled slightly as his tongue tried to catch up with his shock and anger. He'd been ambushed, and Dee found herself enjoying the moment. Foley was finally tasting the dish he usually served.

"Whoa?" Driscoll echoed, smiling.

"You're not bringin' your SWAT teams to my county. And I don't care if everybody in the San Fernando Valley is down at the beach this fall lappin' up salt water. . . . '' The reporters—to a person—smirked and scribbled down that one. "So you can forget that idea right now, Driscoll. Keep your goons home."

"We're not prepared to do that, Sheriff. Not with another chunk of the aqueduct going up in smoke each night. And they're not goons, Sheriff. Metro is the best—''

"Damn you!" Foley exploded. "It always gets down to this, don't it!"

One of the county supervisors tugged on Foley's sleeve, gave him a cautionary wink.

The sheriff stared at the man briefly, then nodded and took a moment to control himself by wiping his streaming face with his handkerchief. "You didn't invoke the state mutual aid pact in this matter, Driscoll. Hell, Los Angeles County ain't even in the same aid region as us, so how can you jump over San Berdoo and Kern counties' outfits to offer us help we never asked for?"

"Sheriff," Driscoll said evenly, "I understand the sensitivity of Owens Valley people toward this sort of thing . . . '' He then ran his eyes over the reporters as he explained. "During the height of the water troubles seventy-five years ago or so, Los Angeles sent private detectives up here to investigate bombings and such. They often behaved reprehensibly toward the local community, and that's the main reason we've called upon our most disciplined police unit to guard our facilities. . . . '' Dee sat up. It was the first time she'd ever heard a DWP official come close to apologizing for the excesses of its infamous "water dicks," whose favorite mode of persuasion was to break bones with baseball bats. "We have no intention," Driscoll went on, "of interfering with the ongoing investigation by Sheriff Foley's department and the federal officers assisting—"

"You couldn't if you wanted to," Foley interrupted. "Unless your goons come here on mutual aid, they've got nothin' in the way of peace officer powers. Citizen's arrest—that's all the authority they got, and if they stretch it, hello my jail."

For a few seconds, Dee thought that Driscoll had been caught off-guard by this argument, but then he slowly smiled and said, "Why, we wouldn't presume otherwise, Sheriff."

"Oh, you wouldn't now," Foley said bitterly.

"Our people will simply detain any suspect until your deputies can arrive." Finally, Driscoll broke off gazes with the sheriff and asked for questions.

While he fielded them, Dee realized that he'd wanted this public confrontation with Foley, who'd started back for his Dodge, hands fisted. But why had Driscoll preferred not to hold this shouting match behind closed doors? Had he known from the outset that there'd be no cooperation from the sheriff? Did it better serve his purposes to draw the battle lines sooner than later?

There were only a half dozen questions—due to the scorching sun, she figured. Driscoll made his escape with Whittaker inside the hatchery building. Dee had a drink of cold water, then set off for her Bronco.

She'd just gotten the air-conditioning going when Ben came trotting up. "Dee, you have a minute to talk to Mr. Driscoll? He'd sure appreciate it."

She had only a few hours before going back out on patrol. She'd hoped to check in on Sid Abramowitz, who was working with the ATF technician who'd driven a bomb investigation truck over the Sierra from Walnut Creek in the Bay Area. And then she wanted to grab a nap in the shade of Tillie's rock. But she found herself shutting off the engine and saying, "Okay."

Driscoll was standing just inside the cavernous building, patiently listening to Karl Schoenfeld, who was giving him the devil. "Break the pact on groundwater pumping, Garrett,'' the WPS president said, gesturing with a smoldering cigarette, ''and you got a full-scale war on your hands. That's no threat. I'm just stating facts.''

''I appreciate the warning, Karl.''

''Think of the impacts, man. That's where the courts will nail you. You're not an idiot, Garrett, you're an experienced hydrologist, for godsake.'' Schoenfeld—with his Marine Corps tattoo and rock climber's musculature—was something of an original among eco-eccentrics. He'd managed to form alliances with sportsmen, raise funds, and buy wetlands for set-aside all over the West. ''But I wanna thank you,'' he went on to Driscoll, ''you know, for establishin' the tone about this bomb shit. I got no use for DWP and its goddamn aqueduct. But I'm gonna whip your asses in court, not with dynamite.''

Driscoll clasped his hand. ''I have the feeling this could be the start of a beautiful friendship.'' Then he acknowledged Dee for the first time. ''Ah, Ranger Laguerre—thank you for sparing me a minute.''

''Howdy, Dee,'' Schoenfeld said.

''Karl.''

Quickly taking her arm, Driscoll led her past the enormous trout egg incubator. ''You're an angel of deliverance,'' he said when they'd left Schoenfeld out of earshot. ''Hell isn't a place of fire and brimstone. It's where the well intentioned are at liberty to harp at you for all eternity.''

Dee smiled.

''That's the kindest look I've seen all day,'' Driscoll said. Then he halted and peered down into one of the waterfilled trays swarming with fingerling rainbows. ''I want to commend you for your reports. Without them, I'd have no idea what happened up here over the past two nights.''

''How'd you get them so fast?'' she asked with a little frown.

''Of course—sorry. I should've said right off that I've been in communication with your district office in Bakersfield.'' Surveying the incubator, the hundreds of trays, he suddenly grinned. ''Ah, the genius of man. It's been forgotten in all the rightful talk of nature being supreme. But look at this—man sees the process of nature in a gravelly stretch of creek and replicates it a thousandfold for his own benefit.'' Then he quietly added, ''That's not a very politically correct sentiment, is it?''

''I'm too tired to run it past my correctness meter.''

''Of course you are.'' He actually blushed. ''How rude of me, blathering on like this. To the point—''

''I rather like the sound of your blather,'' she said, surprising herself. But she did. It was musical. ''Where from in Ireland?''

''County Antrim.'' Then Driscoll swiftly changed the subject. ''And you're Basque.''

''How'd you know that?''

''Your supervisor told me . . . in warning, I think.''

''Oh?''

''Just joking—he had nothing but admiration for you.''

''What's Basque mean to you?'' she asked.

Driscoll took a moment. ''A distrust of the status quo. We Irish and you Basquos have that much in common, don't we?'' He smiled. A mobile face with ever-changing expressions. Except for the eyes. They remained sharply inquisitive no matter what. ''I'm going to ask for a favor, Ms. Laguerre. I don't believe it's anything out of line, but I'll trust you to tell me if it is. . . . '' They strolled on again, and he carefully inspected the living contents of each tray they passed. ''Some time elapses between the completion of your reports and when I can get them. The sheriff's office has yet to provide DWP with anything. I'd appreciate your phoning me collect whenever you see fit. I'm talking only about information that will ultimately appear in your reports. And give me a fair crack of the whip if you think we're coming on too strong up here. Do I make you uncomfortable asking this?''

''No, but I'll have to ask my supervisor. It's not the way we ordinarily work.''

''Understood.'' Driscoll stopped, took a business card from his wallet, and jotted a number on its back side. ''If it's okay with Bakersfield, call me at either office or home. And at any hour. I've got to tie myself to the mattress, my sleep's so light. Sometimes I wish I had a switch on the side of my head. To shut it all down for a few hours.''

Dee accepted the card. ''Very well, Mr. Driscoll.''

"Did I forget to ask you to please call me Garrett?"

"Garrett. And I'm Dee."

He looked at her intently for a second, then smiled again. "Thank you, Dee."

"Good afternoon."

She looked back at him from the entrance. He was strolling among the trays, arms behind him. He stooped once to examine the plumbing system, rose with an approving nod, and moved on.

Sid Abramowitz sat in an aluminum chair under the awning of the bomb truck, nursing a Coke that had gone lukewarm. The crest of the Sierra was visible over the roofline of the county jail. It must have driven the pioneers nuts on a summer day like this. Creeping along the sun-baked floor of the valley with their oxen and wagons, seeing snow through the heat shimmers, just out of reach above a towering wall of granite. After two and a half days, the heat was getting to Sid. The worst thing about scar tissue was that it had no pores. Unable to sweat, his head was sweltering, even when he could withdraw to his air-conditioned motel room.

"Sid?" a voice called from inside the truck. Jim Curlie, the technician. Former navy EOD, like Sid.

"Uh-huh?"

Curlie thrust his head out the back door. He shaved his head and waxed his mustache into long rat tails that drooped nearly to his chin. An irrepressible good humor that rubbed Sid the wrong way when he got tired. Like now. "You sure you really need me to fire up the Crock-Pot one more time?" The primitive explosive analyzer Curlie had jury-rigged in his spare time. The trucks weren't ordinarily equipped for field testing, as all evidence was supposed to be transported to the forensic lab in Walnut Creek. A seven-hundred-mile round-trip from Independence.

"Yeah, Curlie. . . . I do." With national media now pouring into the Owens Valley to cover the new water war, Sid wanted at least a preliminary idea about the identity of the residue melded to the tiny steel fragments he'd found at both blast scenes.

Curlie sighed, then sang something from Gilbert and Sullivan as he got busy again. Maybe that was his problem: he was a comic opera figure trapped in a world that was smaller than life. Bits of scorched shrapnel. Traces of substances in such trivial amounts they could be viewed only through an electron microscope.

Sid realized that he'd dozed off only when he heard tires crunching over the graveled lot. A BLM Bronco. He stood and tried not to look too pleased that Dee Laguerre was dropping by. She got out, waved. Eyes safely hidden behind his sunglasses, Sid watched her approach, the slight sway of her thin hips. "Well, how'd it go?"

"Los Angeles is sending in the Marines," she said.

"We're offering sodas now, beer in another half hour at five." Sid pointed at a Stryrofoam ice chest, and she helped herself to a Dr Pepper. "Marines, you say?"

"Well, almost—Metro Division of LAPD."

"Really?"

"Yeah, Foley had a shit fit, but DWP held firm."

He broke another chair out of the cargo compartment and unfolded it for her. "They won't have peace officer status unless the sheriff gives it to them."

"The city knows that." She sat, took a sip, and closed her eyes for a moment. "Metro's here simply to guard the system."

Sid chuckled knowingly. "Right. I can see the cream of LAPD asking a county mountie what to do. Let's just make sure we don't get caught in the crossfire."

"You're beat, Sid."

"How can you tell?" he asked before he could think.

"Your shoulders are round. Normally you hold 'em square. Like a navy officer."

"I'm fine," he said. "I'll get a little sack time before tonight."

Then he realized that her look had turned worried. "Sid?"

"Uh-huh?"

"How does an amateur like me try to disarm a device?"

"Don't, Dee. Just don't."

"But if there's no choice."

Sid exhaled. "If you absolutely must, pull out the electrical blasting cap. If it blows, you lose some fingers, maybe your sight. If the explosive goes, you lose everything.''

She nodded. ''Have you come up with the type our blaster's using?''

Curlie stuck his shining head outside the open door again and said, ''Second unofficial return just in—it's probably HBX.''

''What's that?'' she asked, grinning at the technician.

''Bonded high explosive. I'm Curlie.''

''Obviously. I'm Dee.'' She turned to Sid. ''I've heard of tracers being put in explosives, you know—so the manufacturer can be identified.''

''Goes farther than that. You can trace some stuff back to the specific lot number. But not HBX, Dee. It's almost exclusively used by the military, which doesn't see the need to brand its ordnance.''

''Why not?''

Curlie volunteered, ''They figure they got plenty of bodies to guard their magazines.'' Then he ducked back inside the truck.

''Do they?'' Dee asked.

Sid thought about that a moment. ''I'll get on the horn to the N.C.I.S. It could be HBX. FBI too. See if any bombs are missing.''

''Are you convinced they were bombs . . . even though the last one went off inside the pipeline?''

''Reasonably. I'd like to find the strong backs . . .'' Sid noted her confusion. ''Kinda like the spine of a bomb. Supports the lugs that connect to the aircraft. It sometimes survives the blast intact.''

''But not always?''

Sid shook his head. ''When's Metro set to arrive?''

''Don't know. State secret, I think.''

''They're swimming up the aqueduct in scuba gear,'' Curlie said from inside. ''Won't even know they're here till they start poppin' outta toilets.''

Sid rolled his eyes. ''See what I've been putting up with all day?'' Dee smiled. ''What time you going out on patrol tonight?''

''Sevenish.''

''Happy to tag along, if you can stand the company.''

Waiting for her answer, he felt his pulse quicken slightly.

"I'd love the company, Sid, but I think you'd better get some rest as soon as you can. If the pattern holds, you'll be called out again late tonight."

"You're probably right." He raised his scarf over his mouth, trying to hide his disappointed grin. "My old ass is dragging."

Dee rose and started for her Bronco. "Thanks for the soda."

"Anytime."

As she drove off, Curlie hung out the rear door on his arm and said, "I'm in *love*."

"Shut up," Sid said.

CHAPTER**SEVEN**

Dee drove down the rutted dirt road toward the copse of trees that hid the Big Pine Indian Colony. *Make yourselves inconspicuous*, the Paiute of this country had always said by how they tucked away their camps, *or somebody will come for what's yours.* The white settlers of the Owens Valley hadn't seen the wisdom in that: they'd boasted of their bright streams, their orchards, fields, and pastures. They'd won more prizes for agriculture than any other region in the state. They hadn't tried to keep their Eden in the desert a secret.

Smoke was sifting through the trees as Dee crossed the creek. She could smell roasting meat. A community barbecue was under way, spontaneous no doubt, all welcome, come as you are. These people couldn't imagine limiting any activity to the nuclear family. It'd be antisocial. Louie Aguirre was tending the flames in a fifty-gallon metal drum he'd converted into a barbecue. His eyes were red, and his head rocked slightly as he watched Dee park.

"*Merde,*" she said to herself, turning off the engine.

Her landlord was stewed, which happened regularly when time dragged between construction blasting jobs for him. He'd talked all spring of work on a dam site in Utah, but then the U.S. Forest Service had kiboshed the project on the basis of the Environmental Impact Statement. And DWP, with no expansion of the aqueduct system under way, hadn't hired blasters in years.

Getting out, Dee turned to a half dozen kids who were using her fifteen-year-old yellow Fiat for a jungle gym.

"Off," she ordered, and they grudgingly slid to the ground. She hated her personal car as much as anyone could hate something inanimate. Broken down much of any given year, it nickeled and dimed her to death. Yet, buying a new one was out of the question, and good used cars were impossible to find short of a blood relative dying.

"Dominica, *goddammita*," Louie boomed, "I wrote it!"

"What?"

"Letter to the president."

"Oh . . . good, Louie."

Tillie, looking worried, crept up to Dee and whispered, "But then he got pissed off and ripped it up. He don't remember that, I guess."

"Artistic temperament." Dee inspected the hodgepodge of meats on the grill: venison, trout, Basque sausage, even some dove breasts. There was never any furtive accounting of who had brought what. You gave as long as there was need, holding back nothing. An old woman stood at a corner of the drum, browning tortillas. Her crinkled face looked like a dried apple.

Louie shook his turning fork at Dee. "You don't go shootin' no Bascos for free."

"No," she said, licking her fingers before swiping a bacon-wrapped dove breast from the flames, "you should charge admission."

"What?"

"Nothing."

"You laugh at me, Dominica, *goddammita*?"

"No, Louie—I'm too tired to laugh at you this evening." She shuffled on toward her bungalow.

"Auntie Dee . . ." a teenage girl hailed her. It wasn't so much a term of respect, as among blacks, but more a habit born of tightly knit clan life. Any older woman a Paiute girl knew was usually her aunt. ". . . you catch the bomber man yet?"

"Not yet."

"Good."

"What's that supposed to mean?"

"We're goin' out later to watch the bombs go off."

"Terrific." Dee unsnapped the leather keepers that held

up her Sam Browne belt as she went through her unlocked front door.

The message light on her answering machine was blinking. "No evil," she half prayed.

The first voice was her supervisor's, calling from Bakersfield at ten this morning, he said. She'd already talked to him since. The second male voice was far younger. It was also tentative. An obvious attempt was being made to muffle and disguise it. "Ranger Laguerre," the boy said, "you keep an eye on Kyle Foley tonight 'fore he does somethin' stupid." Then a clumsy, hurried disconnection.

Dee stared vacantly through her window a few seconds, then ejected the tape for safekeeping and replaced it with another. She felt justified in having a listed number, even though she got an occasional crank call, including boozy threats not to patrol this or that part of the resource area. She tossed her Sam Browne gear on her bed, ran a handcuff through the trigger guard of her revolver, should one of the kids come snooping inside, then went out again to the barbecue.

Louie continued where he'd left off. "There be plenny hell to pay if them fuckin' *erdaldunak* shoot our boys— you see, Dominica, *goddammita.*" One of those Basque words that defied precise translation, an *erdaldunak* was a Spanish immigrant to the Basque homeland. Or a Spanish speaker in general. But "a piece of dog shit" came closer to the sentiment.

Dee regarded Louie more carefully. "What kind of hell?"

"You name it."

"No, *you* name it, Louie."

He cocked his head to the side, smiled somewhat mischievously, then went back to turning meat without another word.

The old Paiute woman gave Dee a tortilla, which she then filled with a strip of sizzling venison and some homemade salsa. She ate hungrily, trying to remember if she'd had anything resembling a meal since yesterday evening's burgers with Sid. No appetite until now. Nerves, she supposed.

Dwight Rainwater came home in his DWP truck, ducked

inside his place for a nonalcoholic beer, then ambled over to the barbecue. He was smirking, something he—or any Paiute—rarely did. "Hey, Lou—you hear?"

The barbecue fell silent.

"Hear what?"

"LAPD's sendin' up cops."

"Who says?"

"Everybody," Dwight said. "Ask Dee."

She nodded, still chewing.

"When?" Louie asked.

"They get here first thing in the mornin'."

Dee asked, "How d'you know, Dwight?"

He snatched a venison strip, clenched it between his front teeth until it was cool enough to eat. "I'm gonna be their scout."

Louie scoffed. "Their *what!*"

As always, Dwight refused to repeat himself.

He turned, as did everyone else, at the sound of an old Chevy Impala pulling dustily into the colony, its throaty eight-cylinder engine knocking badly. The inside of the sedan was already crowded with raven-haired teenagers, but three more ran to join them for a cruise of the valley.

"No booze," Dee warned.

"That's right," Tillie added. A decade before, she and Louie had lost their sixteen-year-old daughter, Ginny, to the automobile and alcohol. The smashed death car was rusting in the dump up behind the colony, the hood missing and milkweed growing up through the engine compartment.

Louie was studying Dwight. "No L.A. cops. You lie."

Rainwater's eyes darkened, but his fingers remained loose around his Sharp's bottle. The moment passed.

"You get enough to eat, Dee?" Louie asked. Conciliatory all of a sudden. Nothing like an unemployed drunk to turn life into a roller coaster ride.

"Yeah—thanks, Louie."

He reached for his beer. "What they know 'bout this guy's hand?" The blaster's technique, he meant.

"Not much," Dee said. "The investigators usually hold back some detail just to make sure they've got the right moron. You know, in case he confesses."

"He blasted the siphon from the inside," Dwight blurted.

Dee muttered, "Oh, Christ."

"Aqueduct been shut down?" Louie drained the foam from his bottle, then belched.

Dwight said, "Nope. On-line all summer."

"Why do you ask that, Louie?" Dee said.

"How the fuck else you get a bomb down *pipelina*?"

Dwight polished off the last of the venison. "Float it."

"*Bullshita*—turds float, not no five-hun'red-pound bombs." Louie jabbed a dove breast and devoured it off the fork.

Dee frowned. "What makes you think it was a five-hundred-pounder, Louie?"

"I go down there yesterday. To Alabama Spillway. I know what a bomb does and don't."

After a few minutes, Dee went back inside her bungalow and stripped. She wanted a long soak in her claw-footed tub, but then remembered the time. She could taste her own salt when she held her face up into the spray of the plastic hose and nozzle she used to give herself showers. It'd be a long night, particularly going into it with no afternoon nap. She closed her eyes and saw Garrett Driscoll smiling at her. Strange that he'd said nothing of the homicides in his remarks to the press. She lowered her chin onto her breastbone and let the hot needles of water drum against the back of her neck.

"Dee?" Tillie's voice came through the open bathroom door.

"Yeah, Till?"

"You drop me off at work?"

"Sure."

Dee decided that night patrol wasn't worth a fresh uniform. She doused herself with deodorant and, wincing, put on the same shirt and trousers.

Outside, Tillie was waiting in her own uniform, white. She murmured something to Louie, who nodded obstinately, drunkenly, and said, "In a while, in a while . . ."

Dee fired up the Bronco and radioed the sheriff's department, asking if there was any traffic for her. None. Tillie got in and took something wrapped in cellophane from her beaded handbag, two frozen cakes made from pinyon nut mush. A kind of Paiute ice cream. Great for teething babies. Dee was getting partial to it, even though there was enough fat in a dozen mush cakes to justify exploratory heart surgery. "Thanks."

Pulling away from the colony and out onto the rolling sage flats, Dee hesitated, then glanced over at Tillie. "Has Louie always talked a lot about the old country? You know, political things. Like those ETA boys bombing that police station?"

Tillie stared placidly out her open window, nibbling on her cake. "No. Just recent."

"How much?"

"It's all he talks about."

"Why do you think that?"

Tillie didn't answer for a few moments. "Maybe he finally knows he's gettin' old."

"I don't understand," Dee nudged again.

"Old folks try to set things right 'fore they go. 'Specially them that're goin' with no kids livin' after. Don't have to be so careful."

"Set what things right?"

"Whatever they saw young, I guess. See it all the time at the sanitorium. We got one, he's near a hun'red, we figure. He's always tryin' to set everybody right about the water war back then. On account he was there and saw everythin' with his own eyes." Tillie concluded with a shrug. For her, it'd been a speech.

But Dee couldn't quite let up. "Friday, when I went out to Saline on patrol—did Louie go anywhere during the day?"

"Just Bishop."

"How long was he gone?"

"Oh, an hour. Maybe a little more."

"Why'd he go?"

"Auto parts store. He was workin' on your car all day. Saturday too." Tillie glanced sharply at her, and Dee felt ashamed for having asked.

"Sorry," she said.

Tillie just smiled.

*　　*　　*

Seven miles south of Big Pine, a spur of low brown hills rose from the middle of the valley floor. Poverty Hills, named by a frontier merchant whose store in the vicinity had gone bust. An unpaved road wound up to the highest promontory, ending at a wildlife overlook for tule elk, transplanted in the 1930s from their native range in the San Joaquin Valley and now flourishing on city of Los Angeles land. One thing had to be admitted, Dee realized as she sped up the road to the overlook. By choking off agriculture, DWP had inadvertently restored most of the valley to prime wildlife habitat. The Owens drainage looked much as it had when Samuel Bishop drove the first herd of cattle up it in 1859.

She reached the top—and braked in surprise.

A large tailgate party in full swing. Forty or fifty locals turned from their smoking hibachis and greeted her with mock good cheer. "It's the gov'mint," one wag cried, "nobody have any fun from now on!" Their license plate holders told her that they'd come from as far away as Bishop to set up their spotting scopes, grilling hot dogs and hamburgers while waiting for the sun to set and the blaster to provide the evening's entertainment.

An old-timer waved her to a stop with a faded Stetson. "Makin' any progress, BLM?" More people came over, plowing their boots through the dust. Kids began pressing their faces against Dee's windows.

"Progress?" she asked.

"Yeah, we wanna know who this fella is before November."

"Why?"

"We're gonna write in his name for Congress."

When he and the others had finished cackling, Dee said, "Whoever he is, he killed two innocent people."

"They wasn't people," a fat woman with dirty blond hair said between pulls on a cigarette. "They was Hollywood actors."

Dee smiled sweetly, then said as she drove on, "I'm so glad I got assigned to a Christian community."

Nobody had an answer to that.

She got back on the highway and continued south.

Both the sheriff's office and CHP were out in force: she

counted four cruisers between Poverty Hills and Independence. A DWP truck with a two-man crew was posted at each major turnoff onto city lands, even though the locals knew labyrinthine ways around these checkpoints. At the southern outskirts of Independence, a middle-aged couple in square dancing duds stood on the highway shoulder, stretching a bedsheet banner between them:

HONK IF YOU LOVE THE BOMBER

And drivers in both directions laid on their horns, long wails that echoed through the deepening twilight, out into the parched fields that had gone back to sage and rabbitbrush.

Dee tried to put aside her disgust. To understand. These were the descendants of the farmers and ranchers who'd stuck it out despite bankruptcy and endless legal wrangling with the city. They might be wealthy had their families been able to hold on to their farms, some of the most prosperous in the state. They felt as much an oppressed minority as any Basque in the homeland did. Los Angeles was Madrid to them.

But two people had been murdered. Didn't that color their thinking at all?

Sighing, she pulled into the Lone Pine Chevron station and stopped at the pumps. As hoped, young Darryl was on duty. He averted his eyes until she got out and called his name.

"Ranger Laguerre," he said as quietly as he could and still be heard.

"Fill 'er up please."

"Yes'm."

She unlocked the gas cap for him, then made sure the other attendant was inside the mini-mart. "How're you doing tonight, Darryl?"

"Okay, I guess."

She lowered her voice. "I grew up in a small town like this. Smaller than this. I know what it's like . . ." Like being stuck on a cramped ship far from land, yet being ostracized meant stepping off into black waters a mile deep.

"I knew the first names of the parents of every kid who went to my high school."

The boy's gaze remained riveted on the nozzle. "Why you tellin' me all this?"

"Because I want you to know I'm not taking it lightly."

"Take what?" The nozzle snicked, but his hand held tight to the trigger, and gasoline slopped down the Bronco's side.

"Darryl," she said while he wiped up the spill with a fistfull of blue paper towels, "I can't keep an eye on Kyle Foley unless I know exactly where and when tonight."

He finally looked at her. "I don't know what you're talkin' about."

Dee just handed him the government credit card.

He slunk off to the mini-mart door, paused a moment with his hand on the push-bar, then went inside. Dee noticed Darryl's father at the cash register. He looked carefully at the boy, then felt his pimply forehead and asked something. Darryl mumbled a reply, then came back out to Dee with the credit card plate.

His eyes were watering as he glanced up the street and said, hushed. "I can't. And you know why. You just told me why."

Dee vacillated, then allowed, "What if it stays between us?" Not using a named informant might weaken the case if an arrest were made tonight, but she saw no other choice now.

"Lord Awmighty," he whispered, almost crying, mucus bubbling from a nostril. "Charley's Butte. The intake. I'm not sure when, exactly. After dark, he said."

It was already dark. Dee had to force herself not to rush things. "Is he armed?"

"I don't know. He usually totes that ol' Winchester in the truck."

Dee wanted to touch the side of his agonized face, but didn't. "Thanks, Darryl. We'll talk more about this later, all right?"

"No, I'm never talkin' to you again."

"You don't mean that."

He shrugged.

She signed the charge slip, then got into the Bronco and started north.

The intake was about thirty miles distant, not far from the wildlife overlook she'd swept through earlier. Yet, she'd known from the moment she'd played back Darryl's message that phoning him would have gained nothing. He would've denied everything. Still, she disliked turning an informant. It always felt manipulative.

She passed a long line of traffic, then took her color-coded map of the valley from the glove compartment and snapped it open. Green for Forest Service land. Salmon for withdrawn BLM land. Yellow for Los Angeles property. She steadied her flashlight beam on the area surrounding the intake. It was a patchwork of salmon and yellow. Good, she decided, flicking off the light and speeding around a Greyhound bus at eighty miles an hour. There was BLM land in the area that she could justifiably patrol. She wanted to account for her presence near Charley's Butte for a reason that didn't involve Darryl. No one would question her good fortune in staking out the intake as long as the federal government had holdings nearby.

She unclipped the microphone from the radio stack, but then almost immediately put it back.

The sheriff's office might not help the situation. Kyle was Foley's son, after all, and a bit of foot dragging on the part of the deputies could ruin the prosecution even before it got off the ground.

Sid Abramowitz?

No, she quickly decided. The agent was in no shape to go running through a mile of scrub and lava beds to the butte that overlooked the small dam. And driving directly to the intake on the gravel road east of the river was out of the question. The boy would see her coming, even if she drove without her lights. Chrome glinted for miles across the scrub, and the moon, slightly less than full, had already crested Waucoba Mountain.

"What's the rush?" a voice asked over the radio.

Dee glanced back. A CHP black-and-white had just gone by in the other direction.

"Sorry," she transmitted. "So many violators, so little time."

The highway patrolman acknowledged with two clicks of his mike button, and she slowed down until his taillights rounded a curve.

A few miles north of Independence, an isolated hill came into view. It rose steeply above the ribbon of trees hugging the river. Charley's Butte. Named after a black cowboy who, here in the 1860s, during a running skirmish with the Paiutes, gave his horse up to his boss's wife. He was never seen again, but years later his revolver was found, all the cartridges fired. Charley Tyler had been an ex-slave, his boss pro-slavery. One of the countless, half-forgotten ironies scattered over the desert.

Dee parked on BLM land, behind a screen of dead poplars above Taboose Creek.

Grabbing her flashlight and radio handset, she got out and made sure the Bronco couldn't be seen from the highway. A soft breeze was rattling the wizened branches of the poplars, a sound like bamboo wind chimes. She clipped the radio onto her belt and hiked down to the shallow stream that passed by the conduit under the roadway. The cool water felt good against her lower legs. Her nylon hiking boots would soon dry out.

She'd give Kyle no more than ten minutes to show up once she reached the intake. After that, it had to be assumed that he'd come and gone, and she'd contact Sid Abramowitz and Jim Curlie to sweep the site for explosive devices.

Emerging from the conduit, she jogged up the bank of the creek into an expanse of tall sage, much of it higher than her head. Gnarled trunks, clawlike branch tips. The butte, a half mile distant, was barely visible through the dense growth. She slowed as it became even thicker, the twig claws making whisking sounds against her trousers.

Intent.

She had to gamble with time and let Kyle go far enough to prove what he had in mind. Could she catch him with a device in his possession? Maybe not. It might be too late for that.

Something winged overhead, loudly. An owl. Her running through the sage was spooking small creatures, and the owl's keen ears had picked up the rustling of their escapes.

She halted a moment to do her own listening.

Kyle, she was sure, would approach the intake from the east side of the river. But she didn't want to blunder into him. She needed to be ready for him.

Hearing nothing, she broke into a trot again.

The sandy ground became littered with ragged chunks of lava, volcanic bombs hurled miles by an eruption thousands of years ago. She turned an ankle on one of them, but kept moving.

The butte rose up before her, flat-topped, limned by moonlight. She made up her mind to go around it—to keep from being silhouetted against the western horizon, which was still pinkish. The river made itself known to her, the lush smell of the plants it sustained. She slipped through a marsh, dry-bottomed in this season but still carpeted with tules, and halted in some willows within a few yards of the river. Downstream lay the intake dam, a big curlicue of foam slowly spinning in the pond behind it.

She could hear the thirsty, gushing sound of the intake.

And then a human cough across the river.

She dropped to her knees, her right hand finding the grips of her revolver. Bulrushes on the far bank were blocking her view.

Footfalls scuffled across hard ground. The road surface over there, she imagined. Then a vehicle door slammed shut, and an engine was started. Dee sifted through the willows and made her way halfway up the butte, then squatted again. It was a DWP truck, and the driver started north along the graded road at no more than ten miles an hour, probing the rushes and trees with his spotlight. She flattened herself against the rocky slope. The beam swept a footbridge upstream of her, then winked off.

She sat up.

The DWP man, making his rounds, no doubt would have looked over the intake facilities for devices. It was only an assumption, but she relaxed a little.

The footbridge. Kyle would have to cross it to get to the intake. The Owens was deep for its size, with sharply cut earthen banks that readily crumbled, drowning a couple of hapless fishermen each season.

She began to rise to approach the span when a pixel of

light flashed in the corner of her eye, then went out. It had
appeared—unless it had been just some trick of her own
vision—across the river in a lava flow that had gushed long
ago from a vent halfway up the slope. A seldom-used road
switchbacked up there, dead-ending at an open-pit mine.
Volcanic cinders, used on local winter roads instead of salt.

The pinprick of light came on again, making her hold
her breath. This time, it seemed slightly farther down the
slope. It winked out again.

Somebody was making sparing use of a flashlight, just
as she'd been trained to do.

Kyle Foley had learned a thing or two from his father.

Dee waited, hoping that the boy wasn't packing the carbine. She couldn't imagine shooting him, yet knew it could
happen.

Suddenly, a figure appeared out of the lava and glided
into the low scrub on the river terrace across from her. It
was unearthly, a pointed head, massive neck, and shoulders
supported by spindly legs. And before she could make
sense of it, another materialized slightly off to one side,
advancing with the same loose-kneed, gliding gait. A third
converged on the others from upstream.

She could hear only her own pulse in her ears.

Finally, one of them turned broadside.

''*Merde*,'' she exhaled. Elk. Kyle was unknowingly driving some Tule elk before him. They were now craning their
thick necks for a look back toward the boy. The light was
even closer now. Finally, they bolted, splashing into the
river and swimming across to the near bank. They clattered
across the face of the butte and vanished behind her.

Dee ran to the foot of the bridge and hid crouching under
the deck. She grabbed a truss overhead as a slab of bank
broke off under her feet and toppled lazily into the river.

Had Kyle heard?

No, she decided. He was still coming on. She could hear
him breathing. He was winded. His boots began pounding
the bridge deck, heavily, ploddingly. She drew her revolver.
No other way. He had to see the seriousness of this. The
boots stepped off onto the bank, and Dee swung out from
under the span. She clasped her flashlight and handgun to-

gether as she switched on the beam and took aim. "Freeze, Kyle—right now!"

Her circle of light focused on a fat neck. The head slowly turned, confronting her with a wide, sweaty face.

"Tyrus," she gasped.

The sheriff blinked back at her, astonished. He'd come out with his weapon as well but, seeing that Dee had the drop on him, held the automatic pistol down at his side. "Laguerre . . . ?"

"What're you doing here?"

Foley said nothing before abruptly holstering his gun and tilting his wristwatch toward her light. Then he reeled and hurried on, passing downstream along the bank as quickly as his thick legs would carry him.

"Foley!" She followed, not quite ready to put away her Smith & Wesson.

"This BLM land, Laguerre?" he tossed over his shoulder.

"Some of it." Now that he'd holstered, he carried nothing in his hands. No device she could see.

"I mean this very property beneath us."

"No," she admitted.

The sheriff grunted. "That fool kid in Lone Pine call you too?"

It was her turn not to answer.

"Well," Foley went on, "he didn't have the guts to tell me he sang to the Feds too."

Foley meant Darryl, of course. Something had happened after she'd left the gas station. A collapse of nerve, maybe. She could see Darryl confessing all to his father, who'd no doubt told him to call the sheriff and try to repair the damage he'd done.

Foley crossed a catwalk to the locked control panel for the intake. There, still wheezing for breath, he ran his hands atop the steel housing. He suddenly growled with a kind of angry satisfaction and brought down an object, which Dee illuminated for him.

"Turn that goddamn thing off," he snapped.

She did so only because she'd heard of bombs that could be triggered by light. An antihandling mechanism to thwart disarming.

From her brief glimpse, she realized that it was a large pipe bomb. Taped to it was a windup alarm clock, which was still ticking until Foley recklessly tore it off, leaving a thin wire to dangle in the air. Then he glanced at Dee and gave a humorless chuckle. She'd instinctively cringed. "Surprisin' what you gotta learn as rural cop," he said. "A real generalist. That's what you become. City cop can afford to specialize. But not us, eh?"

Dee stood straight again. "What the hell's going on, Foley?"

His jowls were glistening with sweat. He blotted his face on the crook of his jacket sleeve. " 'Member Halloween as a kid, Laguerre?" He peered up at the moon. "How the crazy mood of it all got you doin' things you'd never do any other night of the year?"

She finally put away her revolver, but then took her handset off her belt.

"Well," he went on after a moment, "I just busted up a little prank. That's all it was, a goddamn Halloween prank."

"Set down the device, Foley. I don't want it touched till Abramowitz has a look."

The sheriff chuckled again. "It's a dummy, Laguerre. Just somethin' to scare the city boys." But he was holding the pipe as if it had some weight to it. The weight of several pounds of black powder. "I've talked to Kyle, and he's come to his senses. He knows now that Halloween is over, and it's time to face the music."

"Put it down," she repeated.

She could feel his eyes on her, but he remained silent.

She pressed the mike button and, identifying herself, tried to raise Foley's dispatcher. Both Abramowitz and Curlie had checked off for the night, so she needed someone to phone their motel.

"Unit tryin' to call Control," the dispatcher said, her voice high and her words forced, "you're unreadable. Try again from another location."

Dee didn't bother. Instead, she attempted the DWP dispatcher. Yet, that channel was blocked by a steady hiss.

"Careless of me," Foley said, pocketing the clock and hefting the bomb onto his shoulder. "I was chattin' with

Ben Whittaker earlier on that frequency and musta left my mike keyed when I tossed it on the front seat.''

"Leave the device, Foley.''

He let out a long, whiskey-scented breath. "Tell me the authority by which you can take it, and I shall spring to oblige you, Ranger Laguerre.''

"You know the federal statute.''

"For possession of a device? I only know the state one. Your laws are a mystery to me. Besides, this ain't gov'mint property we're standin' on, and you ain't from ATF or the FBI. Seems to me BLM's out of its league when it comes to bombs and such. Why don't you make yourself useful and go check on somebody's grazin' permit, Laguerre?''

She ached to stuff her muzzle in Foley's face and just grab the pipe bomb—but knew better. Few careers survived a pissing contest between federal and local jurisdiction. Her only sensible recourse might be a serpentine legal path that ran through the U.S. Attorney's office in Fresno, if he even wanted to get involved. That'd take time. Time Foley would put to good use.

"Unless you mean to shoot me,'' he said, starting back for the bridge, "ol' Sid can have a gander at this thing in the mornin'. Send him 'round, say, ten o'clock. I'll have a fresh pot waitin'.''

CHAPTER**EIGHT**

Tillie Aguirre held a finger across her lips even though a kind of reveille was echoing down the corridor of the county sanitorium at Big Pine. Bronchial coughing. Faint, scratchy voices asking questions Dee couldn't quite make out. Bedsprings clacking as frail bodies were rolled over for diaper changings. Tillie led Dee past open doors, stuffy rooms with green walls. She kept an eye out for the floor nurse. Visitors weren't allowed for another three hours, but Dee had persuaded Tillie to let her have a few minutes with the oldest patient in the place.

Perspective.

Over a sleepless night on the grinding rock, listening to the breeze in the cottonwood leaves, Dee had decided that she needed a little perspective before the present overwhelmed her. The investigation was by no means hers, yet each way she turned she seemed to wind up back in the middle of it. She needed to find a beginning somewhere. Fast.

A few minutes after midnight, she'd had a call from her supervisor in Bakersfield. He'd just heard from the congressman of the district that included Waucoba County, who'd just heard from a livid Tyrus Foley. The sheriff was accusing her of having provoked a "situation" and obstructing his investigation of the bombings. No elaboration on how precisely she was doing this, of course. The congressman fully intended to see the national director of BLM in the morning to make sure that Ranger Laguerre was immediately transferred. At that point, Dee had stopped her supervisor cold by saying that she wanted a morning meeting too—with the U.S. Attorney's office. Then she told him what had happened at the intake. Her supervisor had listened, cussed, listened again, and then signed off with a less than adamant "Well, okay . . . we'll stand pat for now. As long as you have a grip on this thing, Dee."

She didn't, not really. She had no idea how Kyle Foley's crude bomb fit into a pattern of sophisticated blastings that still had Sid Abramowitz puzzled.

Tillie thrust her head inside a room, then motioned that it was all right to enter. "Name's Ephraim Bickle," she whispered, then shut the door behind Dee.

For a moment, she thought that she was in the presence of a cadaver. The cheeks were shrunken, the mouth agape, and there was no sign of breath. But then, taking a few steps deeper into the small room, she saw that his slitted gaze was tracking her.

She eased into the only chair. It was at bedside.

Up close, the texture of the skin on his face was like apricots that had begun to spoil. His milky blue eyes seemed to slide out of focus, and he started quietly wheezing. She looked away, out the window. The valley was showing its dawn colorations: tans and golds and russets. These would soon be replaced by the dull gray-greens of sagebrush.

She glanced back at the old man. This wasn't going to be easy, and she was in the mood for easy. "Ephraim . . ."

He sucked in a sharp, noisy breath, then croaked, "You a Witness?"

She shook her head in confusion.

"If you're a Jehovah's Witness, get out—and take your goddamn comic books with you."

Dee tried not to smile. "No, Ephraim. My name's Dee Laguerre. And I want to hear about the old days."

He weakly dismissed the notion with a wave of his purple-veined hand.

"I'm serious."

He rubbed his hand over his bare, liver-spotted scalp, then said, "Started over there in the Tigris Valley. . . ."

She mentally ran through a list of basins in the region with Middle Eastern names. Dozens of them, but Tigris didn't ring a bell. "There was a garden in it. Tenants came along, a man and then a woman. But they bitched it up, got tossed out. That old enough for you?"

Dee finally smiled.

"Well?" Bickle demanded.

"I want to hear about the water war."

"Oh," he said, sounding disappointed, "you've come for the short view." He fumbled for something—his oxygen tube, she realized too late to help him clamp it to his nostrils. "Who recommended me?"

"Tillie Aguirre."

"You her kin?"

Dee shook her head. "I rent from her."

"Did she tell you I'm a convicted felon? An embezzler?"

"No," Dee said.

"Or that I spent five years in San Quentin for robbin' the people of this valley blind?" He glanced dimly back at her, then said, "Go away."

"Pardon?"

"Go away and don't come back till you know somethin' about me."

Dee rose, tight-lipped. What made her angrier than anything was being caught off-guard. Tillie had unintentionally prepared her for a rambling, half-coherent old man, not an ill-tempered ex-con.

"Wait." He stopped her at the door. "What kind of uniform's that?"

"Federal."

"Reclamation Service?"

"Bureau of Land Management. Another agency within the Department of the Interior."

"You squarin' with me?"

"Yes."

Bickle nodded. "Well then, if you got nothin' to do with Reclamation, I'll tell this much . . ." Then he simply said, "Chicanery."

After a few seconds, she asked, "What?"

"I'm tellin' you how it always starts—with a big dose of chicanery."

"I don't understand."

"Course you don't. You're the next generation to be hoodwinked." Bickle paused. "U.S. Reclamation sent an agent here to Eden. He was gonna help us double the amount of land under cultivation. Big irrigation project. He oversaw all the survey work, years of work at taxpayers' expense—and then you know what he did?"

Dee just waited.

"The son of a bitch handed the files over to Los Angeles. Reclamation got Teddy Roosevelt to abandon our project in favor of the city's. Washington had sent a viper to dwell among us. That agent was workin' for the United States gov'mint *and* Los Angeles." He grinned, bitterly, almost toothlessly. "So that's how it was in the beginnin'. Secret plans. Chicanery."

Dee held his gaze a moment longer, then went out.

Foley sat at his kitchen table, playing halfheartedly with the electronic chessboard. Every few minutes, he spiked his coffee with a splash of Jim Beam whiskey. The sun had risen over the courthouse roof and was warming the old Victorian he rented from the city of Los Angeles, making its boards expand, groan, and warble. His wife and Kyle were still asleep. Or pretending to be asleep.

Through the open door to the dining room Foley could see last night's busted chair propped against a corner. Frowning, he took a black rook with a white bishop.

A car could be heard coming slowly down the street.

Getting up, he took his pistol off the top of the refrigerator and went to the window over the sink.

He relaxed after a quick glance.

It was only the woman who delivered the newspaper. He would let the *Times* lie on the gravel drive until the sun began to yellow it. Mustn't seem too anxious. His deputies had both the Big Pine Indian Colony and the Lone Pine motel where the ATF men were staying under surveillance. There'd been no sign of unusual activity from the Feds all night.

He thought about making breakfast, but then decided against it. He was hungry, but didn't feel like dealing with one more mess. His wife had zonked herself out on Valium before retiring last evening. She'd seen it all: Kyle's blank-faced denial, and then Foley's blow to the cheek that had sent the boy reeling into the chair, busting it. Kyle admitted everything after that—yet, with a defiant tone as if he'd been betrayed by everyone, not just Darryl.

Another car was coming.

Foley went to the window again. "Good."

The Chrysler sedan drove to the back side of the house, and Foley went through the service porch to meet the driver, an old man with slicked-back silver hair. The ground felt hard under his bare feet.

"It's done, Ty," the man said, popping the trunk and taking out a burlap sack pulled tight by something heavy at its bottom. "Four hours, just like you asked."

"Thanks, Buck."

"That a bomb of some kind?"

Foley accepted the sack. "Yes, it is. Outta my evidence room. We're gonna make a display of disarmed ones. You know, for public awareness, given what's goin' on. But first I had to make sure there's nothin' toxic left on any of 'em."

"Oh," Buck said, obviously waiting to be invited inside.

But Foley had things to do. "Owe you one, Buck. How 'bout I buy you a drink soon as everythin' settles down?"

"Wouldn't say no."

"Thanks again. Bye." Quietly shutting the screen door behind himself, Foley went through the service porch and back into the kitchen, where he laid the sack on the table. Immediately, he donned his wife's rubber gloves and grabbed the tea towel off the refrigerator door handle. He took the pipe bomb from the sack and wiped it down. Once Buck's latent fingerprints were obliterated, he carried the bomb and a small cardboard box he swept up off the sinkboard into Kyle's room.

The boy startled awake, reared his head from the pillow, and cast a sullen eye back on Foley. The plum-colored bruise on his cheek made Foley's heart sink. But he'd seen no other away yesterday evening, not with the seconds ticking away.

"Put it back together," Foley ordered. "Just like you did in the first place. Alarm clock and all." The boy averted his face and stared off obstinately. Suddenly, Foley's anger was hot and running again. "Do it!"

Kyle's hair was down over his eyes. He brushed it back with his hand and glanced at the bomb. "Where's the blastin' cap? That ain't no real cap."

"Right. When you talk to Ray Jelks this morning . . . and you *will* talk to Ray . . . that piece of radio antenna's what you had plugged in there from the beginnin'."

"That's a lie," Kyle said with an acidy satisfaction.

Foley smacked him. Not as hard as last night, but hard. It was done before he could think.

Kyle explored his jaw with the palm of his right hand, his eyes filling.

"Why?" Foley asked, his voice low and shaky.

"It's what you wanted, ain't it!" the boy cried.

"You outta your mind? What kinda talk's that?"

"You been askin' me to do it all my life!"

He stared in silence at his son. He had nothing to say to that. He was hearing his own voice railing against the city in a thousand different ways.

Kyle sat up, crying, and started reassembling the bomb.

Returning to the kitchen, Foley stripped off the gloves and hurled them into a corner. He dialed one of hundreds of numbers he'd memorized. Like names and faces, once committed to memory they were indelibly his. His gaze absently drifted over his pistol marksmanship trophies on the shelf along the upper wall. All were a dusty, lusterless pyrite color. Fool's gold. He was the most deadly shot in the Eastern Sierra, yet his own son had no fear of him.

"Modoc County Sheriff's Office," a female voice answered.

"Yeah, honey—Sheriff Tyrus Foley of Waucoba County for the boss man."

"One moment please."

Modoc County. About as far as you could get from the Owens Valley without crossing the line into another state. He'd gone hunting there years ago. It'd been a disappointing trip with no big bucks taken, but now Foley recalled it as a wonderful time. Kyle must've been no older than four or five, safely at home, innocent. Small kids, small problems. Big kids . . .

"Tyrus, you ol' son of a bitch. What can I do for you?"

After some obligatory joshing, Foley got down to the

reason for his call. Did Modoc County have an open bed in its juvenile detention facility?

"Well," the Modoc sheriff said tentatively, "I believe we do. . . ."

At this point, Foley admitted that he was having son problems.

"So bad you gotta ship him off, Ty?"

"Yeah, that bad. Can the wife and I consider your facility if things can be arranged?"

"Of course."

Foley thanked him, then dialed the chief probation officer of his own county. "Listen, Nadine," he said as soon as the woman came on the line, "Kyle's completely out of hand. . . ."

Yawning, Dee saw that the city-chartered Learjet had almost reached the same altitude as Mount Whitney. Behind, Bishop was recognizable only as a green stain of trees on the dun-colored valley floor. She faced forward again in her seat, finished yawning.

"Getting any sleep lately?" Ben Whittaker asked.

"Not much," Dee said.

"That's two of us." The DWP head of valley operations was crouching before a compact refrigerator. "These are the only choices, my friends—Scotch sours, Manhattans, vodka gimlets. All canned. Ah, and here's a lonely Budweiser. Dee?"

"Scotch sour, please."

"Sid?"

"The beer," he said quietly, "if you don't want it."

"Nope." Smiling, Whittaker passed out the cans, then eased down into his seat and belted up again. "There," he sighed contentedly as he gazed down on the aqueduct, from this height its feeder streams and canals as indistinct as the traceries on the surface of Mars.

Eyes closed, Sid nestled the beer in his scarred hands. He was still miffed that Dee hadn't called him out last evening, but she was too tired to defend herself.

At eleven this morning, her supervisor had finally phoned back, awakening her out of a light sleep. An emergency meeting with an investigator from the state attorney general's office and a team of L.A. officials was scheduled for three o'clock at DWP headquarters. The California A.G. and not the U.S. Attorney from Fresno, who'd decided to defer to his state counterpart for the time being. Dee and Sid were to attend, transportation to be provided by the city. "What about patrol tonight?" she'd asked. Her supervisor said that two rangers from other resource areas were being detached to the Owens Valley until her return. Something of a compliment, he'd added. Two men to take her place.

She took a sip from the can, then looked across the narrow aisle at Whittaker. He was still smiling. "Feel that good to get away, Ben?"

"I guess it does. Don't know why it should. Out of the frying pan and into the fire."

"How's that?"

Whittaker seemed to hesitate, but then went ahead and said, dropping his voice, "There's a pall hanging over the nuthouse on Hopeless Street. . . . "

Hope Street actually, she realized: DWP headquarters. "Oh?"

"It's finally dawned on everybody—no more easy water waiting out in the boondocks." He raised in his seat slightly and glanced down at the threadlike conduit south of Haiwee Reservoir. "Hell, given the political climate and environmental laws today, a project like the L.A. Aqueduct would be an impossibility."

"What about limiting growth?" Dee asked.

"I'd love to see it. But how? Government can't even get a handle on illegal immigration, let alone discourage your native-born Americans from coming west. And if you promote business and industry, which every city in the country proudly does, you're encouraging water consumption. DWP's being asked the impossible—keep up with demand without impacting the environment."

The Scotch sour gave Dee a quick shiver. "Then what's the solution, Ben?"

"Don't have one," Whittaker admitted. "Maybe that means I'm ready for retirement. Oh, I had a couple ideas when I left engineering school a hundred years ago."

"What happened?" Dee asked.

He smiled wistfully. "Either they had no merit or I didn't

know how to get them across. I'll just leave the can of worms to the next generation.''

"Garrett Driscoll?"

Whittaker shrugged but said nothing.

"Is he the next generalissimo at DWP, Ben?"

Sid cleared his throat. "I think he's politely telling you to put a lid on it, Dee."

"No, no," Ben said. "I honestly don't know. Time was I could've told you who in the department would wind up where and when. It was predictable, as long as a man kept out of the spotlight, made no mistakes that could be pinned to him."

"What changed?" Dee said.

"Hmm." Whittaker paused. "We're almost back to the pioneer mind-set at DWP once more. It's a risk taker's game again, just as it was in the teens with Mulholland."

Sid stirred. "Who?"

"William Mulholland. Chief engineer on the aqueduct project. A natural risk taker, just like Driscoll. Often they win all the marbles. Just as often they crash and burn. Mulholland managed to do both in his lifetime."

"How?" Dee asked.

"His genius brought Owens Valley water to Los Angeles. The most massive undertaking of its kind in history. Then, fifteen years later, the Saint Francis Dam he'd built collapsed. The foundation rock turned out to be water-soluble. The flood killed more than four hundred people." Whittaker glanced below out the window, then sighed. "We're out of the valley." He toasted his escape with his canned Manhattan. "May LAPD Metro Division give us all a quiet night."

CHAPTER**NINE**

Garrett Driscoll asked Sid Abramowitz to kick off the briefing. That's how he put it—"briefing." Dee felt a little uneasy as the ATF agent took Kyle Foley's device from an aluminum case and gently laid it on the glass-topped table before him. Hadn't Driscoll invited the sheriff to a briefing at the Mount Whitney Fish Hatchery and then turned it into a bushwhacking? Yet, Driscoll smiled at Sid, which was better than the others present did. Addison, the lawyerish-looking investigator from the California Attorney General's Office, stared at his yellow pad, tapping it with the butt of his pen. Cragen, an arson-bomb detective from LAPD with gin blossoms on his bulbous nose, gazed out the window at the San Gabriel Mountains. They'd been washed to near invisibility by the late afternoon smog.

Ben Whittaker was absent, closeted with the head man for the rest of the afternoon, according to Driscoll.

Sid was uncomfortable at being the center of attention—Dee could tell by his rigid posture. "I assume," he began with a slight quaver in his voice, "you've all got copies of the various reports on the first two blasts."

"Assume away," Driscoll said pleasantly.

"We owe the confiscation of this latest device"—instead of pointing with a scarred finger, Sid just nodded at it—"to Ranger Laguerre here. . . . " He then repeated what she'd told him about Darryl's tip-off. Since the boy had phoned the sheriff as well, she'd decided to admit his existence but keep him anonymous. She'd keep her word to Darryl, even if Foley fingered him.

Addison interrupted Sid and turned to Dee. "Can we name your informant if the need arises, Ms. Laguerre?"

She took a breath. "No."

"Why not?" the A.G.'s investigator asked, still smiling.

"I promised this person I wouldn't do that."

Cragen snorted. "You what?"

At that moment, the door swung open and a tall, white-haired man entered. His mild eyes were smiling behind gold-rimmed glasses. "Sorry I'm tardy," he said with a Southwestern twang, "but a goddamn truck jackknifed on the Grapevine." A freeway grade at the southern end of the Central Valley.

"Mr. Howard Rowe, everyone," Driscoll introduced him. "Special agent in charge of the FBI's Bakersfield office."

"Hell, that office runs me." Rowe shook hands all around, then winked at Sid. "Pard."

"You're getting senile, Howard," Sid muttered. "You used the jackknifed truck bit last time."

Chuckling, the FBI man sat, and Driscoll brought him up to speed, ending with Dee's refusal to name Darryl. "Sergeant Cragen was expressing his concern about this, Howard, when you came in."

"A whole lotta concern," the LAPD detective said.

Dee tried to go on. "I don't work in Los Angeles—"

"Obviously," Cragen interrupted.

"Easy, son," Rowe said low, "let the lady talk."

"I live and work in a fishbowl," Dee said, struggling now to keep her temper. "If I stab an informant in the back, *everybody* will know about it and I can forget about future cooperation."

The LAPD bomb man sat back and folded his hands behind his head. "What happens if that snitch is the only way we've got to nail this blaster?"

Sid came to her rescue. "I'll get into that issue down the line. . . . " From there, he described her arrival yesterday evening at the aqueduct intake, her brief stakeout and then confrontation with Foley over possession of the pipe bomb. "The sheriff claimed it's what we call a 'tease.' A dummy improvised explosive device, an IED. Want to add something here, Dee?"

"Two things struck me," she said. "First, the urgency the sheriff showed. He checked his wristwatch on his way to the intake. He wasted no time ripping the alarm clock from the pipe."

Addison stopped scribing and frowned. "Anything more pointed to characterize this sense of urgency?"

"Well, it meant nothing to Foley I had my revolver trained on him. He made straightway for the control panel and the bomb." Dee paused. "Secondly, the device appeared to have heft as he held it."

"Heft?" Addison echoed.

"Yes, weight. Like it was filled with several pounds of black powder."

Everyone faced Sid again, who shook his head. "Nothing but air inside the IED when Foley turned it over to me this morning."

"You test for nitrates?" Cragen asked him.

"Yes."

"And . . . ?"

"Solvent. Common gun solvent, we believe. I'd guess the pipe was run through a hot bath."

Driscoll said, "You'll have to illuminate the ignorant, Sid."

"A cleaning apparatus for soaking firearms in solvent. Most gun shops have one in the back room."

Rowe asked, "That a blastin' cap I see protrudin' from the hole in the pipe?"

"Meant to look like one, Howard," Sid said. "But it isn't. A section of car radio antenna."

"Latent prints on any of this?" Addison asked hopefully.

"Yes, where not smudged because of the solvent. Foley's, of course and"—Sid slid a fingerprint exemplar card and photostats of the latents lifted off the device across the table to him—"Kyle Earl Foley's, the sheriff's juvenile son."

Driscoll turned to Cragen and asked, "How is it that every recalcitrant in America has Earl for a middle name? Why, it's like putting the mark of the beast on a poor child."

The detective just glared at him.

"Fast work, Mr. Abramowitz," Addison noted.

Sid's shrunken lips thinned even more over his teeth. A wry grin, Dee realized. "I had help."

"From whom?"

"The sheriff." Sid held up a buff-colored page of paper. "Along with the IED and fingerprint card, Foley gave me this. A booking sheet. Kyle was arrested and arraigned this morning on a state charge of placing a facsimile bomb. It's a flip-flop statute—can be tried as either a felony or a misdemeanor. The sheriff then, after meeting with me, personally transported his son to Modoc Youth Camp in Northern California, for detention pending hearing and disposition in Waucoba Superior Court."

Addison tossed down his pen. "Damn."

Coffee arrived on a tray carried by a female secretary. Driscoll immediately sprang up and said, "Thank you, Betty. I'll take it from here." And he did. Pouring, he said to Addison, "My specialty isn't criminal law, but it'd seem to me that a more serious charge is in order."

"Yeah," Cragen butted in, "a definite felony, not some chickenshit misdemeanor like planting a false bomb. Intent to intimidate by explosives, for starters."

"Cream or sugar, Dee?" Driscoll asked.

"Black's fine."

"Me too. Thanks." Addison accepted his cup and went on, "Foley has removed his son from easy accessibility. The kid's no doubt been well coached by now, with a local attorney standing by in Modoc to sit in on any questioning."

"Let's turn to Foley himself. . . . " Driscoll handed Sid a cup. "Hasn't he tampered with evidence?"

"You bet your ass," Cragen said.

"It's the one thing I won't gamble with," Driscoll said, smiling. "Otherwise, when I'm old I'll have nothing to sit on except my laurels. Black?"

"No, cream and sugar. Lots."

"See what a poor judge of character I am, Sergeant Cragen? I thought all cops preferred a manly cup. Howard?"

"Pass."

Driscoll sat again. He took a thoughtful sip before asking, "Don't we have Dee's statements to establish that the bomb was indeed primed and ready to go?"

"I'm afraid that's all we have," Addison said. "Foley will account for his urgency in some other way." He turned to Dee. "And you never actually held the device, so you can't compare its weight last night to what it is today . . . right?"

"Right."

"Doesn't matter," Sid flatly declared. For once, he looked everyone in the eye, a slow sweep around the table that ended on Driscoll. "This was a copycat. The first two bombings were world-class. I still can't tell you how they were done, exactly—and I'm not going to jump to conclusions. This thing last night was kid's stuff. Even had the bomb gone off, damage to the facility would've been minimal."

Driscoll said, "I think you're right. We shouldn't focus on a herring when we've got a whale to catch. Is there any reason to suspect the sheriff himself?"

Silence.

"Does Foley have explosive expertise in his background?"

Dee finally said, "He said something about a rural cop having to be a generalist. Knowing something about everything. He was referring to disarming the device."

"The graveyards are filled with generalists," Cragen said, "and the way he took down that IED—it works once, if you're lucky."

"That's right," Sid reluctantly admitted to Dee. "Had there been even the simplest antihandling mechanism on it, you and Foley would both be dead." He looked back at Driscoll. "The sheriff has to be considered a rank amateur."

"Still," Cragen said, "I wouldn't have called it an evening till I had that pipe bomb."

"Oh?" Rowe asked. "And you woulda been willin' to shoot Tyrus Foley to get it?"

"In a minute."

"Couple years ago, I investigated the high sheriff of Waucoba County on a civil rights bitch," the FBI man continued. "Foley came out clean, but the Indian gunman he plugged didn't. Two pistol shots to the forehead at fifty feet. Coulda covered the holes with an Eisenhower dollar."

He grinned. "You better take far less'n a minute if you want ol' Ty Foley's pelt."

"All I'm saying—you gotta be creative in this business," Cragen mumbled.

"I wouldn't know," Rowe said, his eyes now hard behind his glasses. "I'm just a poor ol' California Okie from Weed Patch."

Dee smiled. Then she caught Driscoll staring at her.

He quickly glanced away and said, "I have no doubt Ranger Laguerre acted quite properly. The city's more than satisfied with the efforts of the federal government so far." He came to his feet. "Well, we all have some work to do, don't we? Mr. Addison, where do you take it from here?"

"Waucoba County. I'll interview Sheriff Foley as soon as he returns from Modoc."

"Fine," Driscoll said, although it was evident that he'd gathered from the A.G. investigator's tone nothing would come of the episode. "Dee, may I have a word with you in my office?"

She turned to Sid, who said, "Go ahead. I've got to call the GSA motor pool, get something with four-wheel drive to take back up to the valley."

"You won't be flying back up this evening with Ben Whittaker, Sid?" Driscoll asked.

"No."

"And I'll return with Sid in the morning," Dee said. She'd been cleared to spend the night in Los Angeles. And, with two rangers filling in for her, she wanted to take advantage of the respite from nightly bombings. She hadn't slept decently since it'd all started Friday.

"Grand," Driscoll said. He indicated the wall phone at the end of the conference room. "Help yourself, Sid. One of my assistants will drop you off at the Government Services yard whenever you like." Then, smiling, he led Dee out into the hallway. It was lined with Ansel Adams photographs of the Owens Valley and the Eastern Sierra. He checked over his shoulder, then said, "Sorry about Sergeant Cragen. His presence was forced on me by the mayor's office. Still, I managed to nettle him some."

"How's that?"

"Why, the good sergeant's middle name is Earl. I have his file, don't you know."

She laughed, then said, "Thanks for sticking up for Sid and me."

"That's not the end of it, by any means. This way, please." They passed through his outer office, past Betty, who handed him a thick sheaf of messages. "Lovely," he said, rolling his eyes. Closing the door behind Dee and himself, he invited her to sit behind his desk. "Read the letter there, if you will—and excuse me just a minute." Before she could ease into his large swivel chair, Driscoll had ducked through a side door. She had a quick glimpse of a meeting in full swing, men in western attire more suited for Nevada than Los Angeles. "Here's that rascal," one of them drawled at Driscoll's entry. Then the self-closing door sighed shut.

Dee suddenly realized that she'd met one of the men in the meeting. The head of the Nevada State water board.

She scanned the letter on the blotter before her.

It was from the mayor of Los Angeles to the director of the Bureau of Land Management in Washington, D.C., commending Ranger Dominica Laguerre for "professional conduct and personal integrity in the face of unwarranted political attacks on her person and the public trust she represents . . ." More of the same. After last night, the most sleepless and gut-wrenching yet, the words went down like honey. Driscoll had no doubt instigated this.

Beneath this letter was another, this one from Garrett to the director of ATF, thanking him for providing DWP with media-ready biographical information about Special Agent Sid Abramowitz. The packet was attached. Dee's heart sank as she saw the photograph. "Oh, Sid," she said softly, "you were gorgeous." Thick, curly black hair. An impish nose and a killing smile.

Finally, she turned the photo over and went through the short bio ATF had prepared on him. Bronze Star, Vietnam. Went in ahead of the Marines to clear Viet Cong booby traps under fire, paved the way for the rescue of a South Vietnamese unit that'd been cut off. Fresno State, criminology. Injured in ATF service, although how wasn't stated.

Dee looked over the desktop. Tottering piles of Environmental Impact Statements. She riffled through them, glancing at covers. Every last project was for an aborted water-diversion project in either Oregon, Nevada, or California. Schemes that had been kiboshed for unacceptable environmental consequences or political backlash.

The side door swung open, and Driscoll stepped back inside, face expectant.

"Thank you, Garrett," Dee simply said.

"I hope it eases your mind."

"It does. And thanks for getting ready to defend Sid. He may need it as much as I do before this is over."

Driscoll nodded distantly. "He's good, isn't he? Really good?"

"I'm no explosives expert, but I work with enough specialists to get a sense of how capable they are."

"And?"

"Sid will get this blaster. Sooner than later, I believe."

"Grand," Driscoll said, briskly clapping his hands together. "Ah . . . are you at liberty to . . . ?" Then he blushed. "I mean, would you care to go to dinner? Even with the drive, I'll have you back to your motel under Sid's watchful eye by midnight."

"Drive?"

"Yes, I've got the immigrant's weakness for Palm Springs. I'd like Las Vegas fine too, if I didn't find that manner of gambling a bit too tame. What do you say?"

"All right," she said, smiling. "But it has to be Dutch. Federal regulations."

"Dutch even if I'm Irish?"

"Don't confuse the issue."

"It's how I make my living. Don't you listen to those people up in Owens Valley?"

On the way out, she glanced at an oil portrait of a prim-looking man with humorless eyes. "Who—?"

"William Mulholland," Driscoll said, switching off the light that had been burning over the painting, "who with God's help brought forth water from the rock."

Shade.

It was more than a dark place on the ground. Wherever

it fell, a kind of home could be made, the things of life spread out. In the old days, the people had lived out-of-doors from spring to autumn, satisfied with a spot of shade and a windbreak woven out of tules. Dwight Rainwater felt perfectly at home sprawling in the warm sand under a half-dead poplar tree. It had once shaded a farmhouse, but the city had bought the water rights, then the land, and finally bulldozed the house to make sure that nobody would ever live in this place again. But, somehow, the city had forgotten the Paiute. They could live anywhere some shade could be found.

"Mount up!" an electronically amplified voice shouted through the late afternoon stillness. It came from the P.A. speaker on one of two SWAT trucks parked nearby, their generators purring. They looked like bakery vans. For some reason, the SWAT cops had found the shade too hot and had shut themselves up inside their air-conditioned trucks. Dwight didn't care for air-conditioning. It felt unnatural, put the seasons out of kilter. He had only to think of a vaporous winter chill hanging over the valley, that raw gray sky, and even the most torrid summer day felt good to him again.

"You hear me, Chief?" the voice barked. "We're moving out!"

Dwight sat up, tilted his head, and jiggled his ear canal with a finger. Sand. Then, grunting, he came to his feet and plodded over to the lead truck. The engine was already idling, but the driver laid on the horn.

The rear door swung open for Dwight, and an outpouring of cold air gave him a shiver. *Unnatural.*

"Our bird's got something spotted," the Metro lieutenant said, so impatient he grabbed Dwight by the shoulder to hurry him inside. A prematurely gray-headed man with a neatly trimmed mustache the color of bobcat dander.

Dwight glowered at him until he let go, then moved forward.

The benches were filled with drowsy cops, so he found a place on the floor. They all had sunburned ears and necks. Their dull black helmets were too hot for this country, and they'd brought no other hats. His eyes slid shut as the van lurched and vibrated down the seldom-graded road, heading

southward. The lieutenant had made up his mind to use no
paved roads. Greater chance of surprising the blaster, he
figured. Dwight hadn't argued, even though the vans raised
a dust plume that could be seen for twenty miles.

"Still in sight," a voice crackled over the radio, "not
responding to my circling. A Jeep pickup. Nobody visible
in or around it."

This morning, Dwight had been surprised to learn that
LAPD had sneaked one of its fixed-wing aircraft up to the
Lone Pine airstrip during the night. He half hoped the thing
would crash. The pilot had had them chasing phantom
blasters all over the valley since breakfast. Long sweeps on
foot through the hot sage and grass—only to scare the day-
lights out of a fisherman working a feeder stream or a kid
floating down the canal in an old inner tube. They went
forward with a chilling determination Dwight hadn't even
seen among his fellow grunts in Vietnam. This lasted until
the midday heat took its toll on the two five-man SWAT
teams DWP had given him to guide. A deep lassitude began
to infect them, and by three o'clock their lieutenant had to
invoke memories of past glories and promise them cold
beer to keep their whining down.

A hard lurch of the chassis made Dwight bite the tip of
his tongue hard enough to taste blood. "You might wanna
slow down, maybe?" he suggested to the driver. It wasn't
the Paiute way to boss others around. "This road gets
worse. You'll break an axle."

Five minutes later, the driver broke the front axle, and
the disabled van sideslipped into a ditch.

Everybody piled out, and an argument erupted under the
broiling sun over what to do. Dwight stayed out of it. He'd
already said too much—and been proved right, which
strained his sense of etiquette.

"What d'you think, Chief?" the lieutenant asked, fig-
uring maybe that he was being democratic. He didn't understand that Indian-style democracy, clan consensus, was
never achieved by posturing and opinionating. It depended
on subtle gestures, approving or disapproving silences. Ex-
pressive silences.

"I'm not a chief," Dwight said after one such long silence.

"Just a figure of speech," the lieutenant said, chuckling, clapping him on the arm.

"Okay, Your Eminence."

"Your Eminence." The lieutenant chuckled again, this time without the clap on the arm. "Will our van be all right if we leave it here?"

Slowly turning, Dwight gazed northward up the khaki streak of road along the base of the Sierra. The dusk shadow had just crept over it. Pivoting again, he looked southeast at a lone thunderhead stacking up against the distant Panamint Mountains. The evening drop in temperature would shrivel it before there'd be rain over Death Valley.

"No idea," he eventually said.

Driscoll suggested a ride up the Palm Springs Aerial Tram while they were waiting for their eight-thirty reservation at Le Vallavris in town. They could get a cocktail at the bar up at Mountain Station, enjoy the coolness of the 8,500-foot altitude. Dee agreed, but asked if her jacket, blouse, and skirt were semiformal enough for the perhaps best French restaurant in Southern California. "My dear," he answered, gently touching her around the waist while shepherding her inside the tram car, "you could get married in that ensemble."

She had been—but didn't say so. A civil ceremony in San Francisco. At the time, Tyler had been at war with the Roman Catholic Church over zero population growth.

The Palm Springs tourist season had peaked in April, and they had the car to themselves. It'd been over 120 degrees on the low desert today. Both side windows had been let down. Dee crossed to the outer one, impatient for motion, for the stir of a breeze and the cool air waiting above. The car rocked with a giddy sway, and they were off, climbing. Driscoll was clearly fascinated by the interplay of the towers, pulleys, and cables. Dee smiled at him, then peered down into the slowly plunging bottom of Chino Canyon. Rocky. Spiky tufts of yucca, the huge yellow blooms just starting to brown.

"The genius of it all," he said admiringly.

"Yeah, every plant and animal with its place in the mosaic."

He lowered his eyes on hers. "I meant the works of man, like this tramway."

"Oh."

"Not terribly fashionable to be so taken with them, is it?"

She shrugged. She was in no mood for an argument. Even a polite one.

"I'm a dreadful misfit, Dee," he said, smiling.

"A rather persuasive misfit."

"And why's that?"

"I couldn't help seeing the company you were keeping in that little conference room off your office. . . . " The car passed into shadow, and she momentarily luxuriated in it. "The water bosses from a half dozen western states. DWP's competition, right?"

Driscoll nodded. A bit evasively, she thought.

"Something afoot?" she pressed. "Some big agreement in the works?"

"Oh, not really. Not yet. But I do hold the trump card against those cagey lads."

She noted his use of "I" and not "the DWP." "What?"

"I tell them—share your water with Southern California, sustain its economy, or look out. All those tanned Philistines will flood your way, looking for work and cheap housing. Oregon and Washington State are already scared to death of this growing migration. They'd give us the Columbia River if they could, just to keep Californians at home."

The car glided up past a steep rock face. Stunted pines stood perched along narrow ledges, their exposed, snakelike taproots twisting down into fissures. "But maybe that's the way things have to be, Garrett—California's population dispersing, going back to the states from which most of them came."

"Really?"

"Yes, all because it's impossible to concentrate enough resources in one region to support that many people. The same thing's happened countless times through history, huge urban areas collapsing, people scattering, moving on."

He turned for a look eastward. Palm Springs' golf courses could be seen meandering out into the parched desolation of the Colorado Desert. "Resource management at Nevada, wasn't it?"

She nodded, secretly pleased that he'd cared to find out.

"And I agree with you in principle," Driscoll went on. "Entirely. The pot is brimming with people. Overflowing. But on a practical level, I'm not at liberty to argue with the demographics of the situation. I've been given a task to do. It's mine to accept or decline, so I blame no one for the heat I take and the sixteen-hour days. Speaking of the heat . . ." He held a hand outside the car to test the air. "Lovely. Glad we came up, aren't you?"

"Yes." She could smell the pines. "But what if it can't be done?"

"Pardon?"

"What if the status quo, let alone growth, can't be sustained? What if it's impossible? You know the resistance to massive projects better than anyone."

As the car slowed for Mountain Station, he said, "I'm sure you've heard of the Gordian Knot . . ."

It took her a moment. "Oh, the man who could unravel it would rule all of Asia."

"Right." The car swayed, and when she tottered slightly he gripped her around the waist for a moment. His touch was gentle, shy. "Along came Alexander the Great. He looked at this impossible knot that had confounded so many. Then he drew his sword and cut it in two."

"Not very sportsmanlike."

"No, winners are rarely good sportsmen." Then he must have caught her look, for he dropped his eyes and added, "That sounded crass, didn't it? I'm sorry, Dee. Long day, and at this hour the mind turns crass and surly. I need a drink to find my better angels. How about you?"

Something occurred to Dwight Rainwater as he clambered up a sandy hillside behind the lieutenant. He felt the same toward these cops as his great-grandfather probably had toward the U.S. Cavalry. He found them alternately exuberant and morose. They harbored some nameless resentment that mystified him. They had good jobs with the city. Medical, dental, a pension plan. They looked well fed. Yet, they piled out of the van—after a crowded, jostling ride from where the other truck had broken down—as if they meant to kill every living thing they stumbled upon. One of them kept mumbling, "My gun is a tool that turns worthless humanity into valuable fertilizer. . . . My gun is a tool . . ."

The first team trotted ahead to secure the perimeter around the Jeep and the nearest section of siphon, while the second unit duckwalked through the scrub to the pickup. The men all wore their helmets now, despite the heat. These, their dark uniforms, and body armor made them look like the imperial storm troopers in *Star Wars*. He'd seen the movie at the Bishop Drive-in before it'd been torn down. Each time Darth Vader appeared on the screen, the Paiute would chant from their vehicles, "Custer . . . Custer . . ."

"Vehicle's clear," the sergeant of the second team radioed the lieutenant, who smartly responded with two clicks on his handset key.

"We got the bastard now," the lieutenant whispered gleefully as he and Dwight crested the hill and squatted in some bitterbrush.

"Got who?" Dwight asked.

The lieutenant held up a fisted hand for him to be quiet.

The Jeep pickup had a boom mounted to the bed. Familiar. But Dwight couldn't think where he'd seen the old truck before.

The second team, under the covering rifles of the perimeter team, filed up an arroyo, sprinted across some flats to a point where the siphon lay half buried in the ground. Each of the five men rolled over it like a circus acrobat, sprang up to a menacing crouch, and continued on toward where the pipe had been elevated over the dirt access road. The twilight was deepening, and the shadows beneath the raised section of siphon were almost black. Dwight thought he could see a cigarette coal flickering on and off there.

"Watch this," the lieutenant said, happier-looking than Dwight had seen him all day.

Assault rifles aimed forward, the two leading men of the second team charged the dark space between two siphon piers. One of them hollered, "Freeze or you're dead!" A scream immediately followed. A woman's, Dwight believed, which was confirmed when a nude figure darted out of the shadows, trying to hide her teats under her crossed arms. She collided with the team sergeant, and both of them went down. She scrambled up first, but another team member tackled her from behind.

"Oh, Jesus Christ," the lieutenant hissed.

Next, a tall, bearded man came serenely out from under the siphon. Everybody except Dwight was screaming for him to either raise his hands or interlace his fingers behind his neck or flop down on his face. He did none of these things. He just gaped around at the rifles leveled on him and placidly scratched his testicles.

"Jesus H. Christ." The lieutenant stood and bellowed, "Any ordnance or weapons under there?"

After a moment, one of men replied, "No, just a blanket and an ice chest of beer."

The lieutenant turned to Dwight. "Know him?"

"Kinda."

"Does he kinda have a name?"

"Jace Taggart."

"What about her?"

She'd finally been given the blanket to wrap around herself.

Dwight said, "Mirabelle Heckard. Lives in Seven Pines, up outta Independence."

"Work?"

"Yeah, for us. The Water and Power office in Lone Pine." Dwight felt the need to add, "Musta took the afternoon off."

"His girl?"

"I guess." Although Dwight couldn't recall having ever seen Taggart with a woman, unless one sidled up to him in the bar of the Pines Cafe. Even then, he'd seem frightfully ill at ease until she got the hint and left him alone.

"What d'you mean *you guess*?"

"Mirabelle's been everybody's girl, one time or another."

The lieutenant brushed his mustache with a knuckle, then asked, "What's the boom for on the pickup?"

"Taggart reconditions old tanks. Sells 'em."

"Tanks?"

"You know—propane, helium, acetylene. It buys his beans, I guess."

Below, the sergeant shouted, "Lieutenant, you want 'em cuffed?"

"Naw, just fill out a field interrogation card."

CHAPTER**TEN**

The sun broke over the San Gabriel Mountains as Sid Abramowitz inched up the Antelope Valley Freeway in bumper-to-bumper traffic. A line of shadow and sun crept down over Dee's sleeping face. Her eyelids twitched, then her nose, and she sneezed awake. "What's going on?" she asked, looking out the windows.

"Not much," Sid said.

"I thought morning rush hour off the desert went the other way . . . *into* L.A."

"Space shuttle. They cancelled the Florida landing due to weather. It's coming down at Edwards within the hour."

She glanced around the inside of the Blazer, the four-wheel-drive vehicle he'd drawn from the federal motor pool. "How's it drive?"

"Okay."

She yawned, then vigorously tousled her bobbed hair. He found all of it ridiculously appealing. "Coffee and grits, Sid."

"Can you wait till Mojave?"

"Mojave." Then she was looking at him, closely. "I saw your photograph on Driscoll's desk," she said.

"What?"

"You know . . . before the accident."

He wasn't sure how he felt about that. Pleased, maybe, that she had something to compare to this hideous patchwork. And then disheartened too, a feeling that had come alive when he'd heard her shower running in the adjoining motel room at three this morning. "And . . . ?" He hated asking.

"You're not that different."

"Sure."

Then she startled him by brushing his leathery cheek with her fingers. Not intimately. He could still recall what a woman's intimate touch was like. But tenderly, nonetheless, even though there were few nerve endings left in his face to register the passing of her fingertips. "You're a little less vain now," she said, withdrawing her hand.

A horn honked behind. Traffic was moving again. Stirring, he depressed the gas pedal. Something unpleasant came to him. "What's Driscoll doing with my mug shot?"

"He contacted ATF for a biographical package."

"Why?"

"I don't know—make sure the only real investigator on this thing doesn't get pulled off because of political crap."

Driscoll had phoned Sid at seven this morning. He'd been uncommonly friendly. Reported that a peaceful night had passed in the Owens Valley. No bombings. "Metro Division's apparently doing its job," Driscoll had said. His news hadn't entirely reassured Sid. Kyle Foley had spent the same night incarcerated at a youth camp in Modoc County. If, as unlikely as it seemed, the sheriff's son had figured in all the blasts, the investigation ahead would be a rocky, confrontational one with Tyrus Foley standing at every turn with his fists on his wide hips.

Sid realized that Dee was still looking at him. She was waiting. "It wasn't an accident," he said, dropping his voice a little. "You don't call stupidity an accident."

"What happened? Only if you don't mind, Sid."

No, he didn't. Part of him had been waiting for this moment. Most likely, it was the only private thing he'd ever be able to share with her. "A hot October afternoon in the Goleta oil fields . . ."

"Near Santa Barbara?"

"Yeah." He felt himself smile ironically. Barbara, the patron saint of ordnancemen. "It was dry for the coast. Santa Ana wind blowing. You could see forever. Seemed like you could just step across the channel to the islands. . . . " He braked again as all three lanes locked up. "A chemistry major from Berkeley decided to build himself a rocket and take out an oil drilling platform in the channel. Proactive ecological defense, that's what his lawyer called it in court. The kid did a decent job, too. Could've turned that platform and everybody on it into a big Roman candle. Fortunately . . ." Or unfortunately, as he'd often thought since, selfishly. "Fortunately, an oil company security guard caught him just before launch time. The kid put down his rocket nice and easy, went off to jail, and we were called in. Except I had to cover alone. My explosive tech was sick."

"How long ago was this, Sid?"

"Almost ten years." He raised his sun visor as the freeway curved sharply north. Antelope Valley lay below in light smog, North American Rockwell's huge hangars looming like gargantuan igloos over the cities of Palmdale and Lancaster. "The snag in disarming a rocket isn't the warhead. It's the motor propellant, usually nitrocellulose. Can go up in a flash, faster than you believe possible." He pressed his lips together for a moment. "I knew the grounding procedures, Dee. Knew 'em by heart."

"What d'you mean?"

"Static electricity. It was the kind of day that almost guaranteed it. *Jesus*, what an idiot . . ." He paused, amazed that after all the years, the countless mental playbacks, he could still relive that afternoon as if for the first time. Hear the dried fronds of a date palm rattling in the wind. "I remember looking up the hill at the truck, thinking of the bag of steel wool I'd left inside. I needed some to short out the contacts in the rocket motor. Just to be on the safe side so the nitrocellulose wouldn't go off. Two hundred feet. That's all I had to walk up a path through the ice plant. Two thirds of a football gridiron. But I didn't. I chanced it. . . . " Once again, he felt that sudden heat wrap around his face and hands. He'd been wearing his flame-resistant Nomex suit, another thing he'd come to regret. Had more of his body been enveloped, he wouldn't have survived. "That's it, I suppose. I rolled in the ice plant, lost consciousness."

"How long were you in the hospital?"

"Six months. Sherman Oaks Burn Center. They're sharp. They've got to be—none of their patients want to recover."

"Does the self-pity go?" she asked.

"Yeah, pretty quickly. But the anger keeps coming back. Get so damned mad at myself sometimes."

The CHP was busy keeping motorists from lining the shoulders of the freeway. The land was flat desert beyond Lancaster, and it was a good stretch to view the shuttle making its descent into the final turn before touching down on the dry lake.

"What's the worst part of it all, Sid?" Dee asked, her face almost touching the windshield as she peered skyward.

"The kids," he said instantly.

"You have children?"

"No, just kids. I'm nuts about them, you know. Overseas—'Nam, the Philippines, I had always had a bunch of 'em around me." He slowed. People standing on an overpass bridge were pointing overhead to the west. "See it?"

"Not yet."

The interruption made it slightly harder to go on. "Right after I got back to work," he said, "the Bureau flew me to a seminar in Maryland. A little girl in a restaurant . . . pretty little thing . . . popped her head up over the back of the seat, playing peekaboo. She screamed."

Dee said nothing for a while.

Sid drove on, alternately looking forward and scanning the morning sky for the shuttle.

"There it is," Dee said. "Twelve o'clock."

No more than a white speck against the pale blue sky, although it was discernibly delta-shaped. "I'll be damned."

"What's the best part of it all, Sid?"

He didn't quite believe his ears. "Huh?"

"You heard me." Her expression was blank.

He thought a moment, then grinned despite himself. "Don't have to shave anymore. Except for one graft that came off my groin."

She laughed, then he did too. But he quickly sobered for fear that he wouldn't be able to stop if it went on too long.

"Mojave, thank God," she said. "I'm going into caffeine withdrawal. There, Sid—Howard Johnson's. Good enough. I'll run inside. What d'you want? A Danish or something?"

He pulled into the lot and parked close to the front door.

"Yeah, sure. Raspberry, if they got one." He watched her go inside, her lithe body, thin hips, then lowered his forehead onto the crown of the steering wheel. Slight emotional hangover. Vague shame. But also release. Before this, he'd told the whole story only to his supervisor and a government shrink. Howard Rowe, years later, over beers. The FBI man's only comment had been, "It's an unforgivin' game, pard."

Childish voices made Sid glance up.

A young mother was leaving the restaurant with two toddlers in tow. Twin boys. Each had a helium-filled orange balloon tied to his wrist. Immediately, Sid pretended to shade the side of his face.

But then his hand fell away.

His gaze followed the balloons as they bobbed past the windshield, slid along the roof overhang.

Dee returned, carrying the coffees and a white paper sack. He sprang the door for her, and she caught the look in his eyes at once. "What's wrong?"

Dust billowed back over the Blazer. Through it, Dee had glimpses of a truck. Strapped onto its flatbed was a gleaming new section of ten-foot-diameter pipe. Sid was looking for a place to pass, but thornbush hugged the upper reaches of the dirt road into Nine-Mile Canyon. No use honking. The driver didn't have anywhere to go.

"Hunt for tiny pieces of orange nylon," Sid said, forgetting that he'd already told her this twice on the hour-long race from Mojave to the site of the second blast. "They'll be scorched. Damn . . ." He jammed the shift into a lower gear. "I found one the day after at Alabama Spillway. But I didn't see it for what it was. Thought it was from those grab straps they drape every so often into the canal."

"Where do we look?" Dee asked. "Up top here?"

"No, it'll have been thrown below the seat of the explosion."

At last, brake lamps shone through the dust. The truck pulled over and parked in a flat area that had been bladed in the scrub. It was crowded with DWP vehicles, cranes, and a trailer office for the engineer charged with the repair of the siphon. He met Dee and Sid as soon as they got out of the Blazer. "Can I help you?"

"Need to search for something on the slopes below the breach," Sid said.

Frowning, the engineer turned. A huge Caterpillar, kept from tumbling down the steep hillside by a winch cable, was reshaping the siphon bed. "I'd have to shut that down if you go up there. Rocks and dirt keep sliding down. Can you wait an hour till the operator eats lunch?"

"No," Sid said, "especially if you people are covering up where I need to look."

"Can your man take an early lunch?" Dee asked before the engineer, obviously running on frayed nerves to get the aqueduct back on-line, lost his temper. "I'm sure Mr. Driscoll would approve of that."

"Twenty minutes," the man snapped, taking a radio handset off his belt.

Dee and Sid got out. They started up the slope, fighting deep sand once again. Dust from the now-silent Caterpillar still wafted down over them. "Anywhere from here on," he said, halting momentarily to dump out a shoe. "Look for black curls too. Some of it could really be burnt."

Dee led the way.

She had a dull headache from lack of sleep, but the exertion felt good. Driscoll had not kept this promise to have her back at the motel by midnight, but she couldn't recall objecting. He really hadn't begun talking about himself, his troubled upbringing in Northern Ireland, his education, until twelve or so. He was both a hydrologist and an attorney. The advanced engineering degree had come from Delft University in the Netherlands, the law degree from Loyola Marymount in Los Angeles. She found the idea of a Belfast childhood interesting, to say the least, but Driscoll had deflected most of her questions by keeping his observations impersonal. "If there wasn't a bomb going off in Ulster every week, you'd think something was wrong."

A spot of orange caught Dee's eye. Instead of touching it, she called for Sid.

He huffed up to her side, then dropped to his knees for a closer look at the nylon shred impaled on the spines of some beavertail cactus. "Oh yeah," he said.

"Is that it?"

"That's it, lady." He took a pair of tweezers and a small plastic vial from a trouser pocket. "Which dovetails with what I just found."

"And that?"

He told her to take the plastic bag from his shirt pocket. Inside was a thick, slightly curved chip of what looked to be aluminum. "High-pressure cylinder," he explained.

"Meaning . . . ?"

"Okay, I agree, that's how our blaster did it," Jim Curlie said, eyes visibly musing over the top of a Budweiser can. "And it fits with what our lab confirmed—HBX. Military explosive." He and Sid were sprawled over their beds in the Lone Pine motel room, while Dee sat in a chair. "But what honcho do we take it to? It's still a local case, and we can't count on Foley to play it straight."

Good point, Dee realized. She and Sid were tossing their reports into a void unless someone responsible and trustworthy pulled the investigation together. "What about FBI Bakersfield?"

"Howard Rowe?" Curlie scoffed.

"What's wrong with that? I rather liked him."

"Yeah, well—ol' Howard comes across as country kin till push comes to shove," Curlie went on. "And he usually starts the shovin'."

"Jim's right," Sid said, smiling, "even though I consider Howard a close friend. Besides, it'd have to be something really major to draw him up here to Waucoba. Maybe even a directive from the U.S. Attorney's office. And then we're talking about an instant pissing contest between Howard and the sheriff. Foley hasn't forgotten that Rowe investigated him for that civil rights violation." He paused. "There's Addison, the dick from the state A.G.'s office. What d'you think, Dee?"

"He'll look into Foley's misconduct, nothing wider . . . like the bombings themselves. I heard from Driscoll that the A.G.'s investigative division is strapped for funds and taking on as little as possible at this point." Then it hit her. "Garrett Driscoll."

Sid reached for his own beer on the nightstand. "What about him?"

"We use him as our clearinghouse."

"Why him?"

"He represents the victim. City of Los Angeles. That's his clout. Foley might try to shitcan our findings if we hand them over directly. But he can't do that if DWP holds the same information. Driscoll can press for action—however reluctant—from the sheriff's office or, if need be, the U.S. Attorney."

"I don't know," Sid said, avoiding Dee's eyes. "Maybe we oughta just submit to our supervisors and let it go at that."

"Nothing'll come of it, Sid. No federal agency wants this."

"She's right," Curlie said, crushing the empty Bud can between his palms. "Everybody covers his ass, and nobody covers home plate. How many times have we seen it before?"

Sid said, "I just don't know if I trust Driscoll."

"In what way?" Dee asked.

"Not to play us against the locals to serve his own ends."

"Neither do I," Dee said, clearly surprising Sid. "Driscoll has nothing to lose by doing that. But I don't know where else to turn. He might be just what we need to get a full federal effort on the ground here."

He stared past her, through the window at the Alabama Hills. Finally, he sighed and said, "Go ahead."

Dee checked her wristwatch: 12:56. Last night, Driscoll had mentioned that he brown-bagged it most days, avocado sandwiches made by his Guatemalan housekeeper to ease his ulcer.

"Yes?" he curtly answered on his private line.

"Dee, Garrett."

Instantly, his voice turned warm. "You got my message, I take it."

"Message?"

"On your machine at home."

"I'm not home yet. I'm with Sid in Lone Pine."

"Ah." He paused, and she could visualize one of the

bouts of awkwardness that had come over him periodically
last night: faint rising of color, downward glances. She'd
been pleased to find chinks in his self-assurance. "What
time do you have?" he asked absently.

"Almost one," she said.

"Well, I just told your machine how very much I want
to see you again."

"Same here." She felt both Sid and Jim staring at her.

"I'd like to come up your way towards the weekend . . .
if you might find some free time?"

"Sounds good, but let me get back to you." She knew
at once that she'd sounded more remote than she'd wished.

"Of course."

"Garrett, I believe Sid has the bombings figured out.
How they were done." Silence. It went on so long she had
to ask, "Are you still—?"

"Yes, quite. Well, good for Sid. You said he was the
man for it."

"May I put him on?"

"Please do."

Dee handed Sid the phone. He gingerly swung his legs
over the side of the bed and sat up. "Afternoon . . ."

A wait while Garrett said something.

"Thank you," Sid said, "appreciate the compliment. But
it's just an educated guess till we collar the son of a bitch."
He motioned for Curlie to hand him his beer. "Yes, military ordnance was used. I suspect Mark Eighty-twos. Five-
hundred-pounders . . . right. Long, sleek, shaped like
torpedoes . . ." Sid paused for a sip, then dropped his own
bombshell. "Both were floated down the aqueduct. . . . "
He let this sink in a moment before continuing. The orange
shreds of nylon—Sid and Dee had found two more on a
brief stop at the Alabama Spillway site—were almost certainly from navy flotation devices. "They attach to the
bombs with harness and shackles . . . no, we didn't find any
of that gear. But I did find the suspected remains of a pressure cylinder. What? That's right, it fills the balloon with
a rush of gas . . ."

While Sid went on to Driscoll, Curlie stroked his rattail
mustache and whispered to Dee, "I betcha the blaster used
the same timer for both the balloon and the detonation. Shit,

he coulda laid those M-Eighty-twos on the floor of a canal or a reservoir days in advance. Then, in the dead of night, first the timer triggers balloon inflation . . . *pfft* . . .'' His cupped hands simulated a bomb rising ponderously to the surface and then starting to drift downstream. ''That also got the clock tickin'. The bastard had timed the rate of flow. He missed blowin' up the spillway gate. Not by much. What, couple hundred yards? But he learned his lesson for takin' out the top of that siphon. He had it down to the gnat's ass—''

The window was rattling. As the warble of the glass eased up, a rumble could be heard echoing sharply in the distance.

''Sonic boom?'' Dee asked in the stillness that followed.

Neither man answered.

She rose and went through the door, the hundred-degree heat enfolding her, leaving her a little breathless. From the parking lot she heard no aircraft. No contrails stitched the sky. A Hispanic gardener was raking leaves on the lawn outside the motel office. She asked him in Spanish from which direction the sound had come, and he pointed southward.

Turning, she immediately saw a squirt of brown-gray smoke hanging in the air above a windbreak of locust trees. ''Sid!''

He and Curlie were already coming. ''What DWP stuff's down there?'' Sid asked.

She had to think. ''I don't know. The canal runs up that way—'' She motioned toward the base of the Alabama Hills.

She felt the next blast in the middle of her chest before she heard it. Reeling, she looked eastward as a plume of smoke shot up as from a locomotive stack. Chunks of something, metal perhaps, peppered the sky. These reached their smoky zeniths, then arced down to earth again.

Dee thought that this second blast had been safely across a quarter mile of pasture—until something thudded against the motel roof behind her. And then a clang as a wad of shapeless metal bounced against the asphalt only feet from her. She was already running when Sid gave her a shove.

''Move!'' he cried.

The three of them huddled in the doorway, watching bits and pieces of steel rattle like hail on the parked cars. The rear window to a station wagon shattered, littering the covered walkway with pebbled glass. The gardener, wide-eyed, had flattened himself against a tree trunk and was staring at a section of beige-colored chain-link fence that had landed on top of his rake.

"Wells," Dee said, flinching as a third shock wave came out of the northwest and passed turbulently over them.

"What?" Sid asked.

"The city fences off its wells with chain link that color." She stepped all the way inside the room and picked up the receiver, which Sid had left dangling over the side of the bed.

Driscoll could be heard anxiously asking if anyone was there. "Sid . . . Dee . . . ?"

"Yes, Garrett," she said, feeling numb, hollow. Her hand was shaking as she wound the cord around her fingers.

"What's happening, Dee?"

"He's taking out your wells."

"How many?"

She just held the receiver toward the open door as another explosion sounded over the valley.

CHAPTER**ELEVEN**

"You were vice president of the Waucoba County Bank," Dee said, then waited.

Ephraim Bickle was peering out the window at the overcast dawn. Tropical moisture had moved in on a southwesterly during the night, and the mountains were socked in. "Glorified teller," he said at last, weakly. "But go on."

"The trouble started when the state oversight office—"

"No," Bickle interrupted. "The trouble . . . it started when L.A. set out to destroy local financial support for the farmers and ranchers of this valley. Water war's an expensive fight." He'd started wheezing. "What d'you know about bankin'?"

"Not much."

"It's a shell game . . . banker, even an honest banker, spends much of his time makin' sure there's a pea under the walnut shell when the examiner turns it over. So, the *last act* started when state superintendent saw that we—the Ritchie brothers and I, the officers—reported a credit of two hundred thousand dollars with Wells Fargo Bank in San Francisco. Wells Fargo said that was news to them. The credit was only for twenty thousand. So out of Waucoba came the examiner to turn over our shells." He shut his eyes, trying to catch his breath. "I met him at the train station and said to myself, 'Here's my funeral director.' "

After a long pause, Dee went on with what she'd learned last night from old bound copies of the *Waucoba Sentinel* at the county library. "Two million dollars couldn't be accounted for—"

"One million, nine hundred thousand and fifty-nine dollars," Bickle said, his eyelids parting.

"You and the Ritchie brothers were convicted of forty-seven counts of embezzlement and fraud."

"Numbers, numbers, numbers." The old man reached for his oxygen tube, inhaled deeply. His color improved a little.

"Yet," Dee continued, "it was never proved that you or the Ritchies spent a dime of it on yourselves. It seems reasonably clear that the money was used to keep county farms and businesses afloat while the battle against L.A. dragged on in the courts. You hoped to recoup the missing funds from the sale of bank-owned properties. But the city was the only buyer, and it had no intention of bailing you out." She lowered her voice. "The paper said the jurors wept as the foreman reported the verdicts."

Bickle nodded. "You still want to talk to this old convict?"

"Yes."

"Found out a thing or two about you too."

"Oh?"

"You're a Basquo gal. Never met a Basquo who trusted his money to a bank."

"We're a sensible people."

He gave a phlegmy chuckle. "What you want to know?"

Dee sat forward. "I need to know how far some of the people back then were willing to go, and what made them different from others in the valley."

"It's startin' up again, isn't it?"

"Yes."

"Thought I heard blastin' yesterday afternoon. I *know* I heard si-reens."

"Somebody blew up city wells. Eighteen of them. They were the first scheduled to go on-line if and when increased groundwater pumping begins. . . . " Again, Sid suspected military ordnance, three- or five-inch projectiles from naval guns outfitted with timers that had cooked off the shells between one and one-fifteen yesterday afternoon. Dropped down well casings, they had been virtually undetectable until detonation, and Sid was still out with Curlie plumbing the surviving 270 wells for more of them. The Naval Crim-

inal Investigative Service was going through the China
Lake inventories with a fine-toothed comb, although Special Agent Christy swore that no waterproof timers and
flotation devices were stored at the landlocked base.
"Ephraim, how desperate do ordinary people need to get
to do this?"

"Things aren't that desperate. Not even close to what
they were back then. I still read the paper from time to
time. I see what the pumpin' does to the water table, the
plant life. But that isn't desperation."

"What is?" she asked.

"Losing everythin' you own, findin' yourself too old to
start over again someplace else." He took some more deep
sniffs of oxygen. They seemed to revive him, strengthen
his voice. "Besides, I don't believe local folks did any of
the bombin' in those days."

Dee was flabbergasted. "Who, then?"

"We'll never know. But I did know the men and women
of this valley. The pioneers. Knew 'em well. Many of the
old families settled here after the Confederacy was
whipped. Veterans of the Rebel army. This was virgin
country. Proud, hard people. Never could picture one of
'em stealin' up to the pipeline with a bundle of dynamite.
Not their style."

"But they resisted the city, didn't they?" Dee asked.

"Hell yes, they fought back," Ephraim said, "but it was all
aboveboard. Look you straight in the eye, not sneak up on you
in the night—those were the folks I knew. You heard what
happened at the Alabama Spillway, didn't you?"

Dee shook her head.

"November sixteen, nineteen hundred and twenty-
four," he said, "the people of this valley marched shoul-
der-to-shoulder up to the spillway. Men, women, and
children led by the Stars and Stripes. They politely asked
the watchman to stand aside, then they opened the sluice
gate and let the river flow down its old bed. For days they
stayed there. Hundreds of 'em. The sheriff showed, threa-
tenin' to call in the militia. Still they wouldn't budge. He
threatened to take their names for prosecution, so they
formed lines to *give* their names. That's what kind of
sneaky bushwhackers they were."

Dee softly asked, "What finally happened?"

"What always happened. The city promised to treat 'em fairly, and then forgot those promises as soon as the people surrendered the spillway."

A rap came at the door: Tillie Aguirre warning that it was time to go. The floor nurse was on the prowl.

Dee rose. "I found one last thing in the *Sentinel*. Ten years after the trial, just back from San Quentin, you put a notice in the classifieds. You vowed to work as long as it took to pay back every dollar that'd been lost by the Waucoba County Bank."

His eyes filled. "Get out," he said.

Dwight Rainwater strode up the long sage-covered slope toward the colony. Far above the clump of trees that marked the settlement, he could see Palisade Glacier half hidden back in the Sierra. It appeared in and out of the drifting, wooly clouds, a beacon shining whitely above home for generations, glistening even in starlight. The mid-morning air was sultry, and he was sweating through the camouflage suit the SWAT lieutenant had given him. It'd rain before midnight. Hard. In a blink, the sky would grow too heavy to remain aloft. It would crack along a jagged seam of lightning and fall to earth in bluish sheets of rain.

Without stopping, he glanced back the way he'd come.

Still, no one was following him. He checked his watch. Three hours had passed since he'd stolen away from the two SWAT vans parked near Tinnemaha Reservoir and started for home.

He came to Big Pine Creek, crossed it on a fallen log, and continued along the northern bank. The wild rose thickets grabbed at his Levi's, and valley quail could be heard scampering through the dead leaves under the boughs.

A big boulder shaped like a hatbox jutted up where the little creek that wound through the colony joined the main stream. Louie Aguirre was sitting on it, drinking from a bottle. "Where you come from?" he asked, his voice raw from whiskey.

"Tinnemaha." Then Dwight added, "I deserted."

"What?"

"LAPD."

"You don't belong to LAPD."

"Well, the whole city, I guess."

Louie took a swig, then stared down at him, red-eyed. "Why?"

"I don't know," Dwight said. Which meant he didn't know how to explain in a handful of words.

"Man don't just walk off for no reason."

Dwight nodded. Louie was right.

It had started yesterday afternoon with the well bombings. He and the two SWAT teams had been resting within a few hundred yards of a well when it went up like a cannon. Nobody was hurt, but the lieutenant and his cops were furious that somebody had managed to destroy eighteen wells despite their around-the-clock sweeps. The rest of the day and long into the night, the teams roved the valley like madmen, stopping everything that moved, scaring the hell out of the locals. By early this morning, when they'd set out to patrol again, it had somehow gotten into their heads that only a Water and Power employee could have slipped the bombs down the well casings without arousing suspicion—and Dwight Rainwater knew who that person was.

The lieutenant began coyly enough, asking if there were some malcontents in the department. Dwight didn't know what to say. Attitude was a personal thing, and he had no right to express another man's attitude. His silence only gave rise to a new line of suspicion, for one of the cops then asked, "How many Indians work up here for DWP?" Three, Dwight said. "Any of them belong to the American Indian Movement?" Dwight didn't know how to admit that, returning from Vietnam, he himself had joined AIM. Most of the young men had, all in the hope of forcing change in the handling of the reservations. "Chief, you hear me?"

So, while the teams clustered around a car to harass an old man out to tend his beehives on city property, Dwight had melted into the willows and set out for home.

"They gonna fire you this time?" Louie asked.

"I guess so."

Louie offered him the bottle. Dwight hesitated. Things were bad, but not quite that bad yet. "No thanks." He leaned against the side of the boulder. Tillie, before leaving for work yesterday evening, had asked him to keep an eye on Louie, who seemed ready to stretch this bender to a full week. "Where were you all night, Lou?"

"I don't 'member."

Dwight nodded. He'd had plenty of nights like that before he'd finally gone down to the Indian Foursquare Church and gotten some help. One morning, he'd awakened to find blood all over the grill of his Pontiac sedan. His heart hadn't stopped pounding until he drove back down the road from the colony and found a squashed coyote in the middle of it. That was the same day he'd gone to the church to take the pledge.

"Any more bombs last night?"

Dwight shook his head, although the ATF agent with the burned face was running himself ragged checking all the wells.

Louie smiled slyly, drunkenly. "Who you think's doin' it?"

Dwight shrugged. Then he noticed the sleek, black pistol on the rock between Louie's legs. A Spanish job he said he'd taken off a policeman he'd killed over there. "I don't know, Lou, but those SWAT cops are pissed off enough to shoot him dead on the spot. They won't be bringin' this fella in."

Louie laughed uproariously, then took another drink. "These Amer'can cops is nothin'. But them *erdaldunak*—"

"The what?"

"Spanish." Louie spat. "They make hard-ass cops. They shoot you in a minute." He swayed woozily from the hips, but Dwight figured the pitch of the boulder top would roll him away from the water when he eventually passed out and fell. He had no intention of fighting Louie for the gun.

"Watch for lightnin'," Dwight said, moving on again. "That rock's been struck before."

"Don't matter," Louie said.

Dee had just pulled up in her Bronco when Dwight reached the colony. She'd been out all night helping the ATF men, and her boots were dragging as she headed for her bungalow. She didn't even bother to tell the kids to quit climbing all over her Fiat, which Louie had pulled inside his shed to fix before getting liquored up.

"Dee . . ."

"Hello, Dwight . . . they finally give you a day off?"

"No," he said, sliding the flats of his hands into the rear pockets of his jeans. "I walked off the job."

That stopped her.

"Really?"

"Yeah, I guess they're gonna have to fire me now."

"What happened?"

"Oh, those SWAT fellas . . ." He didn't know how to go on. He hoped, maybe, that she'd just sense what he meant. But she didn't.

"What about them?"

He grinned uneasily. "Oh, you know. They went crazy on me."

"How?"

"Kinda accused us Indians with DWP of blowin' up the aqueduct and the wells . . . best I can figure. Think we're radicals or somethin'."

"You're kidding."

"Naw."

Dee let out a breath, then said, "Don't worry about it, Dwight. I'll phone Driscoll as soon as I get some sleep."

He lowered his eyes in appreciation. She was good at patching up things. He felt better.

"Where's Louie?"

"Down at the rock on Big Pine Creek . . ." Dwight hesitated, but then decided that this was one more thing for Dee to patch up. "He's pretty messed up. Has that gun of his. Might kill himself, I guess."

Dee let out another sharp breath, then began walking down the slope through a patch of wild buckwheat.

"Want me to go with you?" Dwight called after her.

"No . . . he'll only want to fight if another set of balls is present."

Dee noisily approached Louie from behind.

She didn't figure he earnestly meant to shoot himself. But he was drunk and had a gun.

"Louie . . . ?"

He turned on his boulder perch and scowled. "I got no time for *andra gaistoak.*" Meddling, goddamned women— as best Dee could translate it.

"Who's sticking their nose in your business? I just came down to see how you're doing."

He lowered his chin onto his chest, belched.

"Tillie got held up at work," she went on. "An old woman died."

"Good, all women should die." He clumsily snapped his fingers. *"Alaxe!"* Like that. "I'd talk to a real Basque woman, but I don't wanna talk to no *Amerikanuak.*" Basque American.

Dee sighed.

"Why you do that for?" he instantly demanded.

"Nothing. I'm tired."

"You make me sick."

"Why?"

"You know."

She did. A girl from the homeland would have been content to marry a Nevada Basco with several thousand sheep and, more importantly, the permits to graze them cheaply on public lands. Winter in a travel trailer on the outskirts of some forsaken mining town and summer in mountain pasture, everything coated with the fine dust raised by the hooves of the ever-shifting flock. Louie wanted to open himself to a woman like Dee's mother had been. "You eat anything lately?"

He didn't answer.

She sat on the boulder beside him. She thought of lunging directly for the automatic pistol, but Louie had snugged it under his left thigh. He was strong and quick, even when drunk. A scuffle might end tragically. Besides, he obviously wanted to get some things off his chest before he considered dying.

"Oh, Dominica, *goddammita,*" he gasped suddenly.

Drawing closer, she threw an arm around him, hugged. "What's it this time, Louie? No work?"

"Fuck work," he said.

"Okay, it's not work."

He turned toward her, his breath sour with booze. "You really wanna know?"

"Of course."

He stared off, tears spilling down his stubbled cheeks. "Yesterday, it finally hit me, you know?" He probably meant several days prior, when he'd last been sober. "I mean hit me hard."

"What, Louie?"

"My old man, he use to say to me and my brothers— 'You know, I never see Euskalherria a nation, but you kids, yes.' And it hit me yesterday. All my brothers is gone and now *I'm* an old whitehead, and still we got no country. I'm gonna die like my old man, with Euskalherria still tore up, you know?" Snuffling, he wiped his eyes with the heels of his hands, which were roughened and covered with dried blood from stumbling around the colony these past days, part of the time on all fours. "If Ginny was alive, I could say—she see the day. But my baby's gone."

She leaned her head on his shoulder. "I still think that letter to the president could be a good idea."

He shifted away from her, and she had to sit upright again. "Sent it," he said.

"Didn't you want me to go over it?"

"I already sent it," he said adamantly. "If I wait for you, those boys over there be full of Spanish bullets."

"I'm sorry, Louie. I've been busy, but that's no excuse. I should've taken the time."

He seemed slightly mollified by this.

"You been plinking out here?" she asked.

"What?"

"Let me take a couple shots. Please, okay?"

Before he could think, he'd offered up the pistol. She knocked his hand with her own just as the transfer was made, and the automatic bounced off the rock into the pool beneath the boulder. It was at least five feet deep in midsummer.

"Dominica, *goddammita*!" he roared.

"I'm sorry, Louie."

"Damn you to hell! Now I gotta get some kids to dive for it!"

Yet, she could tell that he was a little relieved too.

She stood, stretched. She hoped that it would rain soon. The coolness would be nice as she slept. "I think we should wait on any diving till the storm's over, don't you? Water might rise suddenly.''

Louie hurled his almost-empty whiskey bottle against the far bank, shattering it. ''Shit on milk,'' he hissed in Basque.

''Walk back up with me, Louie,'' she said, heading again for her bungalow. ''It's going to thunder.''

''Fuck you.'' But, after a few minutes, he followed at a distance, staggering, swearing.

Dee took a sheaf of three-by-five cards from her uniform shirt pocket. Field interrogation cards filled out by LAPD Metro over the past days. One was from yesterday afternoon at Grant Lake, eighty miles north of Big Pine. A bar at the marina there drew Basque patrons off the summer sheep ranges in western Nevada, and Louie often frequented the place while on a toot. But Grant Lake was also the intake to an eleven-mile-long DWP stream-diversion tunnel under the Mono Craters to the headwaters of the Owens River. The subject of this particular FI had been Louis Aguirre of Big Pine. The officer had noted Louie to be ''Uncooperative and H.B.D.'' Had Been Drinking.

Reaching the colony, he now went straightway to his house, slamming the screen door behind him. From outside, Dee heard a clatter of bedsprings as he flopped, hopefully to sleep for at least a day.

She approached his Jeep pickup and quietly popped the hood. She took away the distributor cap and tossed it under her own bed as she tumbled into it with an exhausted moan.

''Dee . . . ?''

She startled, sat up. *''Who?''*

''Priscilla. Want me to turn on a light?''

''No.'' Dee felt narcotized by fatigue. Her limbs were heavy, aching, and she had a cotton mouth. She wondered with faint interest if it was dawn. ''What's the time?''

''About seven.''

Dee glanced through watery slits at the window curtain. Backdropped by pale light. ''Evening or morning?''

''Evening.'' Then Priscilla Fetterman added somewhat tentatively, ''Wednesday. It's still threatening precip. That's why it's so dark out.''

Dee lay back down. She'd slept six or seven hours, but

could have used much more. No patrol tonight, call-out only as needed. Her supervisor had warned her that the bombings had already eaten up much of his overtime budget for the month. *Phone Driscoll on Dwight's behalf.* She was beginning to wake up, to-do's sparking off inside her head. Had she dropped her dirty uniforms off at the dry cleaner's? Mended the trousers she'd ripped ducking through barbed wire the night of the first bombing?

Fetterman could be seen lifting Dee's Sam Browne belt, which included her holstered revolver, as if it were a venomous serpent off the easy chair and setting it on the floor. "Sorry to spoil your nap," she apologized. "I usually like to catch a few winks too after supper."

Dee decided not to correct her. She realized that she'd slept in her uniform. Eyes finally adjusting to the gloom, she smiled at Fetterman, the BLM archaeologist for the Waucoba Resource Area. The young woman's teeth shone whitely if only because her face was so tanned. As always in summer, she wore a terry cloth sun visor hooked around her forehead, a rumpled T-shirt over her pendulous breasts, khaki shorts, and ankle-high boots. "What brings you in from the wilds, Pris?"

"My sister's wedding. Didn't I tell you?"

Fetterman probably had, but Dee couldn't remember. "Oh, yeah." She had a pang of guilt as she realized that, thanks to the bombings, she hadn't gotten the chance to check up on the archaeologist, who was camped alone for a few months at a remote dig in the Coso Mountains. The site was being considered for a geothermal plant, although Fetterman had recently spaded and sifted down to a layer of soil yielding five-thousand-year-old Pinto culture artifacts.

"I'll be in Minneapolis for two weeks." Fetterman paused. "Sure appreciate it if you'd keep an eye on my sites for me, Dee. Word's out, I'm afraid, that I'm on to some good stuff."

"Glad to." Dee sat up, even though the heavy, moisture-laden air wanted to press her down into the mattress again. "Did you just say 'site' or 'sites'?"

"Plural." Fetterman got up. "I'll get the map from my truck."

Dee used the opportunity to wash her face, throw her light bedspread over the sheets, then open the curtain on a lead-colored twilight. The crests of both ranges flanking the valley were lost in thick cloud. The colony seemed curiously empty until Dee reminded herself that it was Wednesday evening. Everyone was down at the city park for an inter-reservation baseball game. Karl Schoenfeld, the head of the Wetlands Preservation Society and the environmental thorn in Garrett Driscoll's side, usually umpired. She thought about going to the game, but then realized that Schoenfeld would only corner her during the seventh inning stretch and bitch about some BLM practice.

Fetterman, coming back from her pickup, was squinting as if against a teasing mist.

"Raining?" Dee asked.

"Close to it." Fetterman spread her map on the bed. "I use the navy's map. It's the most detailed one of the area. I'll leave it with you."

Dee read the heading: Naval Weapons Center—North Bombing and Gunnery Range. "You want something to drink, Pris?"

"Nope, I'm gonna get toasted on the plane." No smile. Just her usual sand-blind stare. She pointed with a calloused finger. "Here's my camp, but I struck everything except the warning signs to keep out. I'm pretty much done at this lower site, so that's why I posted it. What I'm really worried about is here. . . . " Her finger shifted to the north slope of Haiwee Peak. "There's a cave up here I've just launched into. It's not posted because that's the surest way to attract the relic hunters."

"What makes you think they're on to your work?"

Fetterman said, "About two weeks ago, a truck went by in the night. No lights."

"A big truck? A semi?"

"Oh, no—a pickup, I'm sure. But it was too dark to really see. Then two nights running, last night and Sunday. Same truck by the sound of it. About the same time too, elevenish."

"Where?"

"What d'you mean?"

"Was he using a road?"

"Sure." Fetterman traced a graded BLM road that dog-legged past Coso Hot Springs before becoming an unimproved trail. It wound east, over a summit, and then down a desert canyon into an area that was marked "Restricted—possible live ordnance."

CHAPTER**TWELVE**

Dee reached Fetterman's camp site in the Coso Mountains just as the last daylight faded behind a band of lavender clouds. Switching off the dome light, she stepped out of the Bronco. The wind suddenly died, and the foliage of the spiny hopsage all around went still. Quickly, she went to the rear window, lowered it long enough to fetch her poncho. As expected, she had no sooner tossed the vinyl cloak over her head than the first big drops splatted in the dust. She pulled the drawstring to the hood tight and scanned the area. A saddle between two rolling peaks. A nearby copse of red willow marked a hidden spring.

The first wave of rain could be heard coming toward her through the brush, a muffled roar that turned into a rattle as the downpour hit the Bronco's sheet metal. The wind returned, whipped the hem of the poncho around her legs.

She walked over to Fetterman's dig.

It was an eight-foot-deep trench. At one end of the pit were chunky earthen steps leading to its bottom. The archaeologist had thrown up a stout five-strand barbed-wire fence around it, but nothing would stop the relic hunters.

Dee hadn't told Fetterman that she'd be going out to the Cosos tonight. Nor had she advised Sid. He and Curlie had enough to do lowering an electronic stethoscope down 270 wells, plus responding to anxious calls from DWP workers who now saw bombs everywhere and in everything. And there was no reason to drag the ATF men along for backup if Fetterman was right: the vehicle running without lights belonged to an artifact raider.

"But it didn't," Dee muttered to herself.

As soon as she'd traced the dotted line of unimproved road on Fetterman's map down into the navy's Coso bombing range, she'd known why the driver had sped past this camp in the dead of night, blacked out.

Methodical.

Last night, Sid had noted how keenly methodical this blaster was. Perhaps the product of a heavily regulated lifestyle. And he'd blown through Fetterman's camp at "elevenish" each time he apparently returned from the desert foothills to the east.

Going back to the Bronco, she grabbed the starlight scope off the passenger seat. While she was in Los Angeles, it had arrived by Federal Express from the Bakersfield office with a note from her supervisor: "Don't break the goddamned thing. On loan from the FBI, and Howard Rowe will have my ass."

The rain had begun to tail off into a drizzle when another squall came out of the Owens Valley. Cloud-softened lightning revealed the heart of the storm cell over the Sierra.

She set off on foot across the saddle for the highest of the two peaks. Where she walked, she idly realized, an ancient people—known only as the Pinto Culture, after the desert basin in which evidence of them had first been found—had pitched their brush huts, made tools from obsidian, buried their dead. Fetterman had been more worried about their refuse than her own safety, but bivouacking alone for weeks on end among the ghosts of a vanished people had no doubt changed her idea of what mattered and what didn't.

The nightfall was complete, but the ground seemed luminous. There was no competing blaze from any nearby cities, so the sand nearly shone under the ambient light. She started up the peak at a near trot. Off to her right, the bladed road showed like a bolt of white cloth unrolled over the mountains. This, no doubt, is what had enabled Fetterman's passing visitor to run the Coso Range without headlamps.

She reached the summit, knelt.

The rain was coming down in torrents, so she had to wait, holding the scope under her poncho. The optical device operated best under starlight, but she hoped there was enough glow from the moon, which was nearly in its last quarter, penetrating the clouds to show her shapes.

Shielding her eyes with a hand, she followed the road as it left the saddle and wound off toward Panamint Valley. Twenty or so miles to the northeast, a dim fuzz of lights shone through the rain. The mining town of Darwin. Behind it, darkly looming, was the Panamint Range, refuge of the Manson family after its killing spree in Southern California. Tyrus Foley had led the raid on an isolated ranch house to capture them. He'd personally discovered Charlie crammed in a kitchen cabinet and dragged him out by his long hair. This high desert drew them. Sociopaths who thought nothing of butchering a pregnant actress or exploding an aqueduct canal above a crowded highway.

She found herself thinking about Louie Aguirre.

She had to have a long talk with him as soon as he sobered up. Had to find out what was really gnawing at him. She'd grown up around vociferous Basque nationalism, usually mixed with alcohol, so Louie's harangues against the French and Spanish almost fell on a deaf ear. But, regardless, she'd never seen her landlord in such ragged emotional shape, although Tillie had once hinted that he'd gone off the deep end for months following the death of their teenage daughter. Still, Dee couldn't imagine him taking on the aqueduct to force the release of two condemned ETA rebels halfway around the world. He had the capability, certainly, more so than anyone else in the valley she could name. And the Basque temperament, forged by centuries of oppression and intrigue, tended toward oblique rather than direct action. But she *knew* Louie.

Yet, was familiarity blinding her to a line of investigation worth following up? *Must talk to Sid about this*, she decided.

And there lay another problem.

He was falling for her. Not even bothering to hide it, at this point. She couldn't bear the thought of hurting him, and even the mildest rejection would do that. The only solution seemed to be finding the blaster soon. Sid would go back to Bakersfield, and their friendship wouldn't be damaged.

The rainfall eased up again.

She went prone on her belly, aimed the scope eastward onto the rain-bleared hills of the bombing range.

"Merde," she whispered after a moment.

The lights of the geothermal plant, in the canyon below to the south, were washing out her view. They were invisible to the naked eye but glaring under the scope.

She lit up the dial of her wristwatch. Almost ten o'clock.

Rising, she made up her mind to drive the Bronco to a hiding place somewhere along the road. Let the driver pass by on his return. That way, she could both block his escape back into the range and herd him toward waiting highway patrolmen in the Owens Valley, whom she'd alert by radio. She had no idea if the sheriff's office would help her, so she was already mentally relying on the CHP.

She trotted down the side of the peak, keeping to a narrow sand dune heaped by the wind along a sharp ridge.

Suddenly, the nerves on the back of her neck tingled. She instantly threw herself down, cradling the scope in her arms as she rolled and came to a sliding halt. The sky lit up, and the booming crackle made her draw her head down into her shoulders. She twisted for a backwards look just as the white-hot streak faded upward—from the summit of the peak she'd just left.

She dreamed that once again she was in Papa Laguerre's old Studebaker truck, riding in the back with their sheepdogs. She had clambered up the boards of the stakeside to get as much of the cool wind in her face as she could. Ahead lay a dirt road anchored by a red setting sun, behind a rooster tail of dust that boiled hundreds of feet into the hot blue air before shredding apart. All at once, she dropped down to the bed, nudged one of the dogs aside, and peered through the rear cab window. Framing her hands around her face to block out the glare, she looked for her father. But no one was sitting behind the wheel. The truck was speeding into the sun on its own.

Dee snapped awake.

Wiping tears from the corners of her eyes, she cranked down her side window and listened through the steady rain. Nothing but the drops beating on the roof.

She never dreamed directly of her parents' deaths. Not that she didn't have a precise idea of how it'd looked, that single-vehicle rollover in a blizzard. She'd seen the grisly black-and-white photographs taken by the Nevada Highway Patrolman, the bodies ejected out into the snow. No, her sleeping mind always crept up on the loss. Most of the time, she was small, in pigtails, opening doors on a brilliant light, calling out for them.

She held her breath for a moment.

Something was approaching.

Or was it only a flight coming to or from San Francisco, one of the hundreds of jetliners that hummed over the Eastern Sierra each day?

No, it was definitely a vehicle engine.

She checked her watch: 1:34. No wonder she'd dozed off. Three hours ago, she'd backed the Bronco into a narrow, steep-walled gully off the road. It was high enough to the crest of the Coso Range not to pose much of a threat of flash flood.

The engine noise lessened, then she heard a distinct clash of gears followed by the whine of the lowest possible four-wheel-drive speed. The driver was pulling a long grade with a load.

She took her shotgun from its rack, slid a shell into the chamber, and made sure the safety was on. "Let it be him."

Smiling to herself, she recalled Garrett Driscoll's saying that, at the risk of sounding sexist, he didn't fancy her being alone on patrol "in that bloody, forsaken wilderness up there." It'd been a strange evening. Certainly not too much offered for a first date. But too much said, on her part at least. About her failed marriage, her ex-husband's obsession with environmental politics, her escape back to her Nevada hometown after the divorce. Too much. Yet, she'd been fascinated by what little he'd revealed about himself. His dreamlike coming to America, the wealthy but emotionally remote Catholic couple who'd raised him to manhood in Bel Air. Clearly, he'd been damaged by his past, yet there was something oddly appealing about that. It seemed that just when exuberant drive was close to becoming insufferable he suddenly turned shy and self-deprecating, and once again he was the ill-at-ease Irish boy arrived at Los Angeles International with a name tag fastened to an overcoat button, like a war refugee.

Dee frowned.

It sounded like the engine of a Jeep pickup. She'd heard Louie's often enough. The vehicle was now only a few hundred yards off, building speed as it topped the summit on which she waited.

She unsnapped her holster strap. "Okay, okay . . ."

Then the driver was slowing—when he should have been accelerating.

The Bronco's tire tracks. The driver had spotted them.

She'd tried to brush them out with a sage bough, but they had been too deeply impressed in the sticky alkali mud. She'd hoped, then, that the rainwater would fill them.

A spotlight winked on and filled the inside of the Bronco with a blinding dazzle. Swiftly, she aimed her own beam back at the driver but could see nothing of him or his vehicle through her rain-beaded windshield. "All right, you've made your point, moron." She was reaching for her P.A. microphone when something crunched through the safety glass. She heard the first report just as the second bullet stitched through the cabin.

"Damn!" she cried, lunging for the floorboards and trying to squeeze as much of her body as she could under the dashboard.

The spotlight went out.

She groped for the shotgun, which had landed under her, and crawled out the passenger door, rolling as she hit the soggy ground. She aimed at the road below.

Nothing.

The vehicle had sped on. She could hear mud slapping against the insides of its wheel wells.

Jumping up, she rounded the front of the Bronco. A thrill passed through her. She supposed that it was relief. Or anger. She fired up her engine, turned on the wipers, and bounced down the gully to the road. She took a moment to calm herself, then transmitted to the sheriff's office dispatcher in what she believed to be a reasonably composed voice, "Control, this is BLM-One—eleven-ninety-nine. Shots fired. I'm in pursuit, westbound from Coso Hot Springs on BLM Road Four-Sam-Sixteen. Shots fired."

"Slow down, BLM-One, and repeat your traffic."

Dee took a deep breath as she jerked the shift lever into low for a curve.

"Control," the Olancha resident deputy responded, sounding irritated, "I copied BLM fine. Shots fired near Coso Springs. I'm responding code-three from Cottonwood Canyon Power Plant."

Good, Dee thought, he—her closest help—wasn't too far out of position. He could close the Owens Valley door on this road. And nothing drivable branched off north or south into the Coso Mountains.

"BLM-One," the dispatcher inquired, "vehicle description?"

"None at this time," Dee hated to admit. "Possible pickup, that's all I have."

"But you were fired upon?"

"That's *affirmative*, Control." The wind was whistling through the two bullet holes. They were just slightly to the right of her face. She realized that she'd felt the heat of the slugs as they'd passed through the cabin. That close. She gritted her teeth together, furious. The bastard had come within inches of killing her. But still, her knees felt rubbery, and small spasms were gripping her stomach.

She flicked on her spot, fanned over the barren hillsides. The driver was far enough ahead to stop and ambush her.

The eleven-ninety-nine, the code for an officer needing emergency assistance, was starting to snowball. CHP officers from Lone Pine and Ridgecrest were responding; she could hear their hundred-mile-an-hour-plus speeds as high-pitched roars backdropping their transmissions. Even Sheriff Foley signed on, then asked to speak directly to Dee.

"Go ahead," she radioed. "I copy you."

"You all right, Laguerre?" he asked, his tone unexpectedly concerned.

"Two holes in my windshield, but I'm in one piece."

"Good, lady—you just hang on," Foley said emphatically now. "Everythin' we got is rollin' toward you. . . . " Dee's eyes involuntarily watered. The magic of eleven-ninety-nine. All feuds and accusations were temporarily forgotten. No cop within fifty miles would drag his feet. Each saw his own vulnerability in Dee's. The stomach spasms passed. "Where'd this joker come out of?" the sheriff went on.

"The bombing range," Dee said.

A pause as that sunk in, then Foley ordered his dispatcher to get the Death Valley deputies out of bed. They were to seal off both ends of Panamint Valley.

"Sheriff," Dee said, "do that, but the suspect vehicle is definitely still in front of me. I'm herding him toward you."

Foley chuckled, his own engine screaming in the background. "Sheep gal—ain't you, Laguerre?"

"Bred and dipped." She wiped her face on first one sleeve and then the other. It was splattered with mud. She licked her lips. Salty from the alkali mud. "Tyrus, advise your units to use caution. I have reason to believe he's carrying ordnance off the navy range."

One by one, units acknowledged.

A different kind of excitement came over Dee. It occurred to her that the exhausting ordeal was almost over. They had the blaster. All because Fetterman had believed that relic thieves were snooping around her digs at night. Closure. Sweet closure. Suspect in custody. Then the court battle.

The road swept close to a precipice. The cloud cover was higher than earlier, and Dee could see headlights on Highway 395. Closer, she could see emergency lights spangling up Gill Station Road, the county route that fed directly into the BLM road. The driver must have seen by now that he was boxed in. And, as if to reinforce this, the lights of the two CHP cruisers could be seen streaking out of the south and north toward the turnoff.

"BLM-One, you have suspect vehicle in sight?" the dispatcher asked.

"Negative. But I've got his fresh tire tracks." Slapdash gouges where he'd almost lost it on the tighter curves. The impressions were ruts, so heavy was his load.

"Control," the Olancha deputy said, "advise BLM I'm at the narrows at the bottom. She want me to continue up the hill or set a roadblock?"

"Roadblock," Dee insisted.

Another spate of hard rain made her boost the wiper tempo. Now and again, a cold drop flew through one of the holes and glanced off the side of her face. She picked her flashlight up off the floorboards and clamped it under her thigh. Then she drew her shotgun closer.

Firefight.

The driver had already shot at a marked law enforcement vehicle. He wouldn't go at this point with a whimper.

Flounces of rain flew into her headlights. Then something materialized out of them. "Control . . ." She paused with her thumb off the mike button, trying to make sense of it. Something large, black, glistening.

"Unit calling?"

"I've got him," Dee said, her guts clenching, growing cold. "First big curve above the narrows. He's parked in the middle of the road."

"License?"

"Negative . . ." She slowed, running her spotlight over the surrounding hillsides before sweeping it back to the pickup. "A tarp's draped over the bed and tailgate. Can't see the cab rear window to look inside."

"Wait for your backup," Foley said.

"I'm comin', BLM," the Olancha deputy said.

"Okay . . ." Dee thought a moment. "I'm leaving my vehicle and finding cover just to the north of it." She didn't want to be in a crossfire with the deputy. "I'll be on my handset." She slipped the portable radio into its belt holder and tapped in her earplug receiver. Taking her shotgun, she got out. She kept the spotlight trained on the vehicle, which was about two hundred yards down the road. She could hear its engine running, so the driver hadn't given up because of mechanical breakdown or lack of gasoline.

He wanted to come out and play.

She inched out into the scrub, watching for the wink of a gun muzzle. It was all the warning she'd have.

"Two minutes away," the Olancha deputy's voice said from her earplug.

She'd just stepped down into a shallow depression when a force—huge, swift, hammering—struck her chest like a fist. She watched her arms float outward, as if she were under water, and the shotgun tumble away. Heat followed, and the night turned a painful orange. At first, she thought she was falling, but then it felt more like being sucked into a ghostly loneliness, a place of white where the snow was piling fluffily on the undercarriage of an old Studebaker pickup.

CHAPTER**THIRTEEN**

Sid slipped into her hospital room sometime during the night. He sat in the darkness, saying nothing, his face in his hands much of the time, and when he'd gone Dee was only half convinced that he'd been there at all.

She was awakened at seven by the day nurse, had a woozy moment of horror when she glanced down toward her kicked-off covers and found her lower left leg missing. The nurse, seeing her confusion, quickly untangled the leg from the balled-up sheet and asked, "How you feelin' this mornin', honey?"

"Like hell."

"Will you try some breakfast?"

"No way." She had a ferocious hangover from the pain-killers. Queasy stomach. Fragments of the night were starting to come back to her. The ambulance ride. A flashbulb going off as she arrived at Southern Waucoba Hospital in Lone Pine, shouted questions from the media. She'd wondered if her uniform trousers had been blown off her but was powerless to lift her pounding head and check. X-rays. The emergency room doctor stitching up something on her right elbow. She now inspected that, her shoulder joint aching as she raised her arm, and saw a bandage covering the point of the elbow.

"Twelve sutures," the nurse explained.

"What else did the doctor do?" Dee asked.

"Not much. Swabbed your abrasions. No broken bones. He can't figure out how you've still got your eardrums. A few test results are due back from Reno; if they're okay you're out of here by this evening.''

"Where's my vehicle?''

"Sorry, no idea. Why don't you try a little breakfast?''

A tray was brought, but Dee left the food untouched. Half dozing, she tried to piece the night together. But a head full of medication made that impossible. She kept thinking that Sid had been with her in the Bronco as she slowed for the pickup in the middle of the road. As they stepped out, his face and hands burst into flame.

A knock startled her awake.

The tray was gone, and a check of the wall clock told her that she'd napped until ten o'clock. A hazy cast still lay over the room. "Come in," she said, then immediately wished that she hadn't.

It was Garrett Driscoll.

He was unable to entirely hide his shock at her appearance before he pasted on a smile. "Ah, thank God . . . the deputies had me convinced you were all in smithereens. The boys do love to josh the flatlanders, don't they though?'' He was clutching a rangy-looking bouquet. "Where . . . ?''

She pointed at the water pitcher, her cheeks too sore to keep up a smile for long.

"Sorry they're not store-bought. But a fine old woman in a coal-scuttle bonnet let me pick them from her garden.'' He plopped the flowers, mostly gypsophila, into the pitcher, then sat and draped one leg over the other. Slowly, his buoyant look faded with a weary sigh. "Holy Mary— you've given me a terror. I left home at three. As soon as I heard. So you must forgive me the autumn field . . .'' He stroked his stubble.

"I rather like it.''

His eyes widened innocently. "Do you now?''

"The blast . . .'' she said, feeling racked by the cross-currents of the night, the medication, Garrett's presence. She had to put everything in order.

"What of it?''

"Any human remains?''

"Ah, poor dear—nobody's filled you in, have they?''

"Someone may've tried. I wasn't exactly at the top of my game last night."

Driscoll nodded. "Well, the sheriff's men found foot tracks heading north, but the night's rain made short work of them. A manhunt, complete with a Highway Patrol helicopter, is under way this morning. No word yet." Looking at her, he shook his head as if suddenly angry. "Devilish bomb. Sid believes it to have been a thousand-pounder. Left a hole the size of a cabin in the road. Obliterated the Jeep truck . . . I believe that's what the deputies said you believe our fellow was driving." He paused. "Did you ever get a glimpse of him?"

She shook her head.

"Just as well, Dee. Thank God he didn't come back looking for you with his gun."

That made her think of her own weapon. Where was her revolver? "You hear what happened to my gear . . . the Bronco?"

"No, but I'll inquire for you." Suddenly, he rose, paced a moment, then stopped at the window, clasping his restless hands behind him.

"What kind of day is it?" she asked.

"Absolutely transcendent," he said. "Few tufts of cumulus to make the heavens seem bluer. You do have the skies in this country, don't you?"

She sat up.

"What's wrong?" he asked, brow wrinkled.

"Got to piddle."

He hurried to the bed, stooped, and came up with the bedpan.

"God no," she said, laughing for the first time. She stood, then winced as every joint and muscle in her body seemed to protest. She must have tottered slightly, for his arm flew around her waist. He helped her to the rest room and shut the door for her.

Looking into the mirror, she groaned.

Her face was peppered with tiny scabs. Bits of airborne grit, she supposed, rocketed along by the blast. Jutting from her hairline near the right temple was a grotesque bruise. She'd landed on her head, then.

She sat on the toilet.

The nurse had said nothing about a concussion, but when Dee rocked her head slightly her brain shouted for her to stop it. It even hurt to pee.

She flushed, then rose on wobbly knees.

Driscoll met her at the door, started to support her with a hand but then suddenly enfolded her in both his arms. She fell into him, let him bear up her weight. He said nothing for a few moments, then whispered breathily, "I was so damned frightened when I got the call last night. . . ." She closed her eyes as he held her tighter. "A bloody bomb got my mom and dad. Christmas shopping. They went out, and the next thing my sitter was getting a call from the constabulary. . . ." She could feel him kissing the crown of her head. "Well, nothing like a bomb to put everything else in perspective."

She looked up at him. "What do you mean?"

"Later."

"Please, Garrett."

He hesitated. "There's a move in City Hall to oust the boss and me. It's gathering steam."

"But why?"

"This is all happening on our watch. We've been called on the carpet Monday morning, although it's hoped that we'll both do the honorable thing and fall on our swords—resign—before that." He softly pressed his lips to her forehead. "I thought that was the end of the world . . . until they called me about you. Then I realized what the real end would be. . . ." His chin accidentally brushed her bruise, and she flinched. "Damn me!" He drew back, but kept a grip on her upper arms. "Bloody, damned fool! Are you all right?"

"Fine." She gave him a peck on the cheek. "I need to lie down again, Garrett."

"Surely."

When he raised the covers over her, she took one of his hands in both of hers. "Thanks for coming."

"The nurse told me you might be released this afternoon."

"Yeah."

"Need a ride home?"

"Unless somebody can come up with my Bronco."

"I'll be back at, say, five o'clock? I'm committed to speak at a banquet at seven, but I'd like to check back on you after that. If I may."

"Where's the dinner?" she asked sleepily.

"Wetlands Preservation Society up at Glacier Lodge in Big Pine Canyon. The whole county will be there." He kissed each of her hands, then said, smiling, "You're not down for the count, are you?"

She lifted her head off the pillow. "Who said that?"

He was caught off-guard and stammered slightly. "No one really . . ." But then he gave up with another sigh. "Oh, very well . . . Foley's detective. Jelks, is it? It was just an idle remark, Dee."

She frowned. So much for the comradely spirit of eleven-ninety-nine. "Need a date?" she asked angrily.

"Pardon?"

"Would you like a date for the banquet tonight?"

At that moment, Louie Aguirre barged through the door, stinking of stale booze. Tillie was right behind him, and Garrett stepped back so the couple could approach the bed.

"Dominica, *goddammita*," Louie said, then burst into tears. He started to embrace her but she fended him off with a hand.

"Where's your Jeep, Louie?"

"Jeep?" he echoed as he went on sobbing.

"We drove down in it, Dee," Tillie explained. "It's out in the lot."

"How'd he find the distributor cap?"

Tillie said, "You gave it to Dwight before leavin' last night. He came home early from the game. Don't you remember?"

She didn't, which alarmed her a little. But, exhaling, she finally opened her arms to Louie. "Come here, you crazy old Basque militant."

Over Louie's shoulder, she could see Garrett smiling quizzically.

Sid stood in the slight depression where Dee had been found unconscious by the deputies. Turning, he looked back down the road at the bomb crater. Jim Curlie was standing halfway down one of its steep banks, shoveling and sifting. He was stripped to the waist and had tied a black bandanna to keep the perspiration from pouring off his bald head into his eyes.

The technician waved good-naturedly even though Sid had yet to spell him with the shovel. He never would. Exertion in these temperatures made Sid's head feel as if it were to burst. Virtually no surviving sweat glands in his face and neck. Curlie knew this, never made mention of it, just went on shoveling and, if needed, screening mountains of bomb-churned earth.

Sid studied the small depression. Gratefully. It had saved Dee's life. The blast overpressure had vaulted the billow of rocky ground in front of her, striking her upper body but with none of the force it had had only a few yards away. All of the glass in the Bronco, including the headlights, had been reamed out. The shards were now glistening on the hillside behind where the four-wheel-drive vehicle had been parked before the sheriff's office towed it. Had she been standing on the little ridge instead of behind it, they would have found her dead, bleeding from the ears.

She'd murmured something to him in the hospital room early this morning. "It's all right, Cinch," she'd said in the predawn darkness. He had no idea who Cinch was. But the warm, dreamy affection in her voice had left him hungry for more of it. Sooner or later, he had to tell her how he felt. It'd be cowardly not to. But he knew what she'd say, and that answer would desolate him.

He strolled back down the road to Curlie.

The technician had set a small cardboard box on the lip of the crater. In it were scraps and curls of metal, all tinted with that tattletale iridescence from the heat of an explosion. None of it was recognizable. Little was even distinguishable as being either from the bomb casing or from the vehicle that had vanished in a brilliant orange flash here. Responding law enforcement had seen the fireball from forty miles away.

Curlie grinned up at him. "You know what that ignorant cracker of a sheriff asked me last night?"

"What?"

"He wanted to know if a bump in the road set this Mark-Eighty-three off." Curlie snorted.

Sid smiled. The explosives in military bombs were IM, insensitive munitions. The blaster could have taken a jackhammer to them without producing detonation. For that he had needed a triggering device. Sid guessed that he'd used a chemical delay pencil: a pliable cylinder containing a vial of acid that, once broken, activated the firing pin after so many seconds or minutes.

Curlie whipped off his bandanna, wiped his face, then retied the headband. "What's N.C.I.S. gonna do?"

Sid had talked to Special Agent Christy on the phone before setting out this morning. "They're sending an EOD team to sweep the entire range for duds."

"Jettisons, more likely," Curlie said, digging again.

Sid nodded in agreement. These bombs were dropped unarmed if the pilot experienced some in-flight difficulty. A man, walking the sprawling, sporadically patrolled range, could probably find one a day, mark the location, and come back with his vehicle under the cover of night. Not only would Explosive Ordnance Disposal now put more effort into tidying up the range, choppers and Marines in Humvees would roam over its thousands of barren acres day and night. The navy was catching its share of the political flak. Not that there wasn't enough to go around. The governor was contemplating sending in the National Guard. DWP's top brass were on the verge of being fired. Los Angeles, after reveling for nearly a century in a dreamscape filled with parklike lawns and swimming pools, had awakened to the reality that it was surrounded by a vast desert. No reliable river flowed through its borders, save the artificial one Mulholland had created. And it was now being blown methodically to pieces by some maniac.

Even with this attack on a federal officer, ATF or the FBI wouldn't be eager to take over the investigation. Let the Waucoba County Sheriff's Office take the guff for not catching the bomber. Sid knew that's how his own boss would look at it. Of course, if an arrest were imminent, both bureaus would rush in like vultures.

"Here we go," Curlie said, reaching down into his sifter as if he'd just found a gold coin. He examined the metal fragment for a few seconds, then grunted in disappointment and handed it up.

Sid saw the number at once. A seven. But not lucky this time: the rest of the vehicle identification number—on two sides of the single digit—had been sheared off. He had no clue if this was from the primary or secondary VIN. Auto manufacturers stamped both onto a vehicle's frame, the secondary one usually hidden in a location revealed only to law enforcement. Curlie and he were down to only one of the numbers, maybe. If they could ever find the hunk of steel that bore it.

Sid doffed his hat and scanned the surrounding hills, fanning himself. "How come nothing goes down in spring around here?" He could hear a car coming.

A Dodge sedan with a light bar rounded the curve below the crater and parked at a respectful distance. A deputy sergeant sauntered up carrying two paper lunch sacks and a six-pack of Heineken bottles. "Sheriff Foley's compliments," he said with a broad wink, then set the booty on the ground and retreated.

Curlie reached up for his sack. Inside was an enormous beef sandwich, dripping with barbecue sauce. He bit voraciously into it, then asked with a full mouth, "Who'd we promise a blow job?"

Dee heard Garrett Driscoll drive up.

She rushed one last time to the bathroom mirror to make sure that two coats of facial powder had faded the bruise. They had. To the mulberry color of a birthmark. The tiny scabs had washed off, but she still looked as if she'd been dug out of a bombed house during the Blitz. And her peach-colored dress looked too young for how she felt: in the last stages of osteoporosis. A vodka collins had taken the edge off her achiness, but it was still there. Dull, throbbing.

She went to the bureau, took her revolver from the topmost drawer and dropped it into her handbag. Thank God the deputies had found it on the ground near her. Then she beat Garrett to the screen door, hoping to keep him from seeing the inside of her bungalow.

"You sure you want to do this?" he asked through the rusted mesh.

Instant loss of confidence. "I look that bad?"

He drew his face close to the screen, peered through like a boy at a candy store window. Then he said quietly, seriously, "Don't make me laugh."

Beyond Garrett, she saw Dwight Rainwater slink inside his house. *"Merde."*

"Beg your pardon?"

She stepped outside. "I didn't get the chance to call you about something. My neighbor over there, Dwight Rainwater"—she lifted her chin toward Tillie's brother—"works for DWP. Twenty-some years. Somebody had the brilliant idea of having him guide a couple of the SWAT teams around the valley. Well, I don't think they understood him very well. They got heavy-handed and squeezed him for intelligence."

"Of what sort?"

"The trustworthiness of Indians working for DWP."

"Oh, Christ."

"Right," Dee said. "And Dwight walked away because that's what a good Paiute does. Confrontation's almost taboo with these people. Now he thinks he's going to be fired."

"Give me a minute. Get comfortable in the car." Garrett half jogged over to Dwight's door and knocked. After a moment, it swung open, and the former scout stood there, his expression guarded. He listened to Driscoll for a minute or so, then they solemnly shook hands, and the door slid shut.

"Done," Driscoll said, getting in behind the wheel of his anthracite-colored Infiniti and firing up the engine. "I told Mr. Rainwater he's on administrative leave, starting yesterday. He can return to his regular duties anytime he chooses over the next two weeks. The department appreciates his patience and apologizes for any overzealousness on the part of the gendarmerie."

She leaned across the seat and gave Garrett a kiss on the cheek. "Thanks."

"I could be induced to make him my administrative assistant."

"Shut up."

Leaving the colony, Garrett switched off his radio scanner and said wearily, "Whatever the disaster tonight, I don't want to hear about it."

They rode in silence. He turned west onto the paved road that followed the stream up Big Pine Canyon. The dust behind them, she rolled down her window and felt the air with her hand. It'd be deliciously cool up at the lodge. "What's going to happen?" she asked.

He raised an eyebrow.

"To you, I mean, on Monday."

"I really don't know," he said. "Certainly, a donneybrook. Some feathers will be ruffled. Others will fly. Accusations and counteraccusations. My loyalty will be tested. . . . " He left off with a perplexed shake of his head.

"Loyalty to your boss?"

"That's the rub. I must decide that before Monday. Am I more beholden to the city that hired me or to the rather timid fellow who gave me my first big chance?"

"Does it have to be one or the other?"

He tried to smile but failed. "I would've said no a few weeks ago. But these are the times that try men's souls." He lowered his visor against the last shaft of sunlight. It was shining down the center of the canyon, glancing off the ice-sculpted granite walls. "At the risk of seeming ungrateful, I think I know what I must do. . . . "

"And that?"

"I mustn't put my trust in princes, in a son of man."

She could buy that. She'd been let down by her own princes, sons of men within the federal bureaucracy. "But what *do* you put your faith in then?"

"Personal vision," he said. "One simply does what one was born to do. Whatever the obstacles. Whatever the cost." His color had risen, and he laughed. "You have the extraordinary knack of coaxing me into sounding like a pompous ass." Then he quickly changed the subject. "I found out about your Bronco. Afraid there isn't much glass left in it. And the interior's a shambles."

"Thanks. Already heard the bad news from my supervisor."

"At least you won't be needing a vehicle for a good long while. Till you recover."

"I'm going back to work tomorrow night. Our archaeologist is on vacation back east, so I'll use her truck."

Garrett looked her flush in the eye. "I wish you wouldn't do that."

"Why not?"

"I was saving this for another time—but have you ever thought about leaving the BLM?"

"No."

A tight-lipped frown, then he said, "Well, I'm in no position to offer anything at the moment, but I believe your resource management background could be put to more fitting use with Water and Power."

"I see."

"I'd certainly vouch for you . . . if you could be persuaded to consider us." He glanced over at her again. "So . . . ?"

She said nothing.

"You're right." He sighed. "My motives are quite selfish. I don't want to lose any more sleep than I have already worrying if some shaggy psychopath is putting bullets through your wind screen or blowing you off your feet."

"Garrett—"

"No answer right now." He patted her hand. "Just think on it . . . please." He pulled into the lodge's parking lot.

Karl Schoenfeld was leaning against a rough-hewn wooden porch pillar, a glass and a cigarette in his hand. He was jawing with an unlikely group of friends for an environmentalist, two county supervisors and Sheriff Foley. Years before, Schoenfeld had forged an alliance with another group interested in saving America's shrinking wetlands—waterfowl hunters. Only he could have done this. He drank Wild Turkey neat and smoked Marlboros. As usual, he'd rolled up the sleeves on his western-cut shirt to reveal the Marine Corps tattoo on his right bicep.

Garrett opened Dee's door for her. "I promise to beat a quick retreat as soon as I can."

Noticing Driscoll, Schoenfeld strolled out to collar him, just as he'd last done at the Mount Whitney Fish Hatchery. "Hey, Garrett—gotta rag on you a couple minutes."

He looked to Dee, who said, "Go ahead. I'll meet you in the bar." The first collins, although stiff, had worn off, and she felt sore all over again.

"What the hell," Schoenfeld wailed, "are you people tryin' to pull . . ."

She continued on alone toward the rambling, tin-roofed lodge. As expected, the high-altitude air was bracing, making her long for autumn. A slight breeze was shivering the leaves of the aspens along the nearby creek. She wished now that it had just been a simple date.

Foley had ducked inside as soon as he'd spotted Garrett. In obvious disgust. She now found him sitting with his detective, Ray Jelks, at a booth in the bar. The sheriff smiled warily but waved her over. "Snuggle in there, Laguerre," he ordered. He'd pushed the table over to make more room for himself. "What you drinkin'?"

"Vodka Collins."

Foley shouted it to the bartender, then took a sip from his own glass. "Quite a crowd."

"Yeah."

"But it's for a good cause. Ducks and geese. No sense in askin' folks to save a spotted owl. Can't shoot the god-damned things."

Jelks chortled, then glanced at the bandage on Dee's elbow. "You look real nice tonight."

"Not down for the count, Ray?"

He laughed it off. "You? Never."

Dee's drink arrived. She took a big quaff. "How's the manhunt going?"

"It's goin'," Foley said curtly, then remembered to smile at her again. "Oh, we'll get the son of a bitch, Laguerre. He's still here. I can smell him. Like somethin' gone bad in the back of the fridge."

"Local, you think?"

"He might be hangin' around," Jelks piped in, dabbing his bristly mustache with a cocktail napkin. "Like Manson and all the other crazies through the years. But he ain't local."

"How can you be sure, Ray?" Dee asked.

"I know my county." He laughed pointlessly again.

Foley shook an ice cube out of his glass into his mouth, crushed it between his molars. "Ray's right. Ain't local." He turned his smallish eyes on the detective. "Go mingle."

"Sure, boss. Glad to."

Jelks had no sooner left the table than the sheriff said, "An investigator from the A.G.'s office dropped by to see me this mornin'. Addison. He got the notion somewheres that fool thing Kyle threw together was loaded with powder the evenin' we found it. You tell him that, Laguerre?"

"No. I just said I suspected that it was."

"But suspectin' ain't knowin', is it?"

She rose. "Don't gloat, Tyrus," she said, walking away.

From the foyer, Garrett had flagged an arm for her to rescue him. He was still being besieged by Schoenfeld, who finally shut up at her approach. He gave her an impetuous hug that made her shoulders twinge. "Dee, so good to see you in one piece—"

Schoenfeld's head jerked as a rancher in a turquoise-studded string tie playfully snapped his ponytail. "Get a haircut, you goddamn hippie."

"I will, old man, as soon as you get a circumcision. You oughta, just for sanitation."

"Thanks for the tip." The rancher moved on into the dining hall.

Schoenfeld resumed to Dee, "What're you doin' out of the hospital?"

"It was only a thousand-pounder," Garrett said drolly. "A day in hospital per thousand. That's her maxim." He took her hand and led her to a table at the very back of the crowded hall. "I'll take solace in one thing if I'm sacked Monday . . . no more Schoenfelds."

Dee saw that Ben Whittaker and his wife were seated several tables distant. He waved at Garrett, but made no effort to join the only other DWP representative present.

Garrett smiled as he sat, but Dee could tell that he'd been stung. She'd seen the same thing at BLM, a lame-duck director suddenly treated like a pariah. She squeezed his hand under the white tablecloth.

"Something just show?" he asked.

"Yes, but only I noticed."

"Thanks," he said quietly, looking at her intently. "You are Roman Catholic, aren't you?"

"Yes, sorta . . . why?"

"Convenient."

"I'm also divorced."

"Even more convenient."

The iron triangle on the porch was rung, and the hall filled to capacity with latecomers. Schoenfeld took the podium, tapping his glass with a spoon for attention.

"I shall kill the chef if Swiss steak is on the menu," Garrett whispered.

Schoenfeld said, "I'm goin' to get things goin' early because after the late hour of the fund-raisin' portion of our last program, Sheriff Foley accused me of rollin' a bunch of drunks. . . ." This jocular arm-twisting for money made Dee a bit apprehensive. She was still saving for a swamp cooler, and some pointed public ribbing here tonight might wipe that account out. "As you know, we, the national steerin' committee of WPS, have recommended zeroin' in on the purchases of marshes in north-central Oregon. The savin' of these wetlands is key to the rehabilitation of the desert artery of the Pacific flyway, the very route that continues down through the Owens Valley. We've already made what we believe to have been advantageous land swaps and sales toward this end—less essential waterfowl habitats for absolutely critical ones. But still our war chest at present is not up to supportin' the campaign that lies ahead. . . ."

Garrett's and Dee's plates were laid before them. He grimaced. Swiss steak. She laughed as he picked up his silverware knife with a murderous gleam in his eye.

Schoenfeld said, "So, we come early and relatively sober to the purpose of tonight's event. . . ." He paused, scanning the crowd as two monitors stood by, holding slotted duck decoy banks. "Is that Mr. Driscoll of DWP I see out there?"

Garrett lofted a hand. "Guilty as charged."

"Oh, yeah? You haven't even heard the charge yet."

"Fire away."

"Do you have any idea, Mr. Driscoll, what increased ground water pumpin' will do to the little marshland remainin' in this valley?"

Dee felt embarrassed for Garrett, but most of the crowd, particularly Foley, were clearly looking forward to seeing him squirm.

Yet, he came to his feet and calmly said, "I sincerely

hope it doesn't come to that, Karl. Another severe drop in the water table would wipe out those habitats . . . forever." His words stunned the audience and caught Foley with his glass halfway to his mouth. DWP had never publicly owned up to this potential impact. All its studies indicated the contrary. Ben Whittaker exchanged a worried frown with his wife. "But this isn't something I can personally prevent," Garrett went on. "Still, I'd like to make sure that the sins of the father aren't visited upon the sons and daughters. . . ." He slipped an envelope from his inner jacket pocket and stuffed it into the waiting bank. "A check for five thousands dollars, if you please, to be recorded in Ms. Dee Laguerre's name and my own."

Silence.

Dee saw it in Garrett's unhappy smile. He knew that he was finished. He was throwing in the towel.

Then, finally, Foley started the smug clapping.

CHAPTER**FOURTEEN**

Dee got into uniform an hour early the next day. It was a calm, violet-tinted evening with the cottonwood leaves hanging limp from the afternoon's heat. Louie and Tillie had taken to the flat-topped boulder in the yard, he dozing off a hangover now in its third day and she grinding some store-bought pinyon nuts, as those she'd gathered that fall were gone. Bats jinked in the air over the colony, pounced on moths reckless enough to leave the trees. Yawning, Dee suddenly took off her Sam Browne belt and looped it around her holstered revolver. She tossed them on the front seat of Fetterman's pickup and locked the doors, then reclined on the warm granite surface beside Louie. He was snoring softly. Tillie looked up from her work at him—feeling what, Dee had no idea. Her careworn face was blank. But it was probably wrong to think that they stuck it out purely from habit. And it was naive, arrogant maybe, to wonder about the affection others felt—her own was even a mystery to her much of the time.

Tillie asked, "Want me to make you a lunch, Dee?"

"No, thanks, Till—I can grab something at Denny's in Bishop."

Garrett Driscoll had returned to Los Angeles this morning to face the music. Last night, leaving her off, he'd made no attempt to invite himself inside her bungalow. Instead, he'd waited until she was halfway to the door before saying from his car, almost defiantly, "Whatever happens down there Monday, I'm coming back for you." Then he'd driven off. Secretly, she disagreed. Only if DWP fired him was there a chance for them. Otherwise, she had little doubt she was facing the same inhuman competition with work and grand schemes that had demolished her marriage to Tyler Ravenshaw. *What attracts me to these charming obsessive-compulsive workaholics?*

Her phone was ringing.

Sighing, she eased to her feet and limped inside the bungalow. Overnight, new aches had developed, some worse than those first felt.

It was Tyrus Foley. "Abramowitz just came through for us," he said without any salutation. "We've got our man ID'ed. You want to join the fun, Laguerre?"

She rode with Foley as he accelerated up the narrow road. It climbed out of Independence toward the Sierra escarpment. He drove without lights under bright starshine, as did the four vehicles following, all sheriff's cruisers except for Sid's Blazer. LAPD SWAT hadn't been asked to join the fun. As far as Dee knew, Metro hadn't even been told about Jace Earle Taggart. That was his name. He finally had a face too, and she was holding it, a high-resolution fax off his driver's license. His haunted brown eyes glared out from a darkly bearded face. Six-three in height and 240 pounds, fully capable of winching and muscling navy bombs into the bed of his 1964 Jeep pickup, to which Sid and Jim Curlie had finally located a piece of chassis with the secondary VIN stamped into it.

She could recall having seen Taggart once before. It'd been the evening of the Nine-Mile Canyon blast. The surly beer drinker, sitting on the porch rail outside the south county bar, who'd told Kyle Foley that he wouldn't buy booze for him—there'd already been too much death on the highways. Remorse over the drowning deaths of the two actors?

The raiding party was not headed directly for Taggart's residence. That was across the valley, up Mazourka Canyon, an area of played-out mines and widely scattered shacks. LAPD SWAT had passed along an FI card placing Taggart near the aqueduct with a Mirabelle Heckard of Seven Pines, a small subdivision on the open alluvial plain a few miles to the west of Independence.

Her place was the first target.

Meanwhile, a deputy had the mouth of Mazourka Canyon under surveillance, should Taggart come or go.

Dee had a dozen questions about the man who'd nearly blown her apart, but Foley's mind was rightfully on the raid. Holding the microphone with the same hand, he punched up the scrambler and ordered Sid to drive to the spot behind him. Abramowitz would go in even ahead of the entry team, clearing the way of any possible booby traps.

"All right," Sid said. He sounded exhausted. The heat, Dee figured, plus the tedious, fruitless search for more bombs in the wells.

She could see the lights of Seven Pines across the rising sagelands. Open country. That was why no one was using headlamps. A string of lights racing up from town would alert Taggart in an instant.

She cracked her window for air. Bit nauseous. She was beginning to feel the excitement of two nights ago, that this was all close to ending. But it was tempered by having seen what Taggart could do when cornered. The deputies seemed uneasy at the prospect of facing him. Sid had suited up as if for war, Nomex suit and helmet with face shield.

"I'd just as soon kill that crazy son of a bitch," Foley mused out loud. "He'd be a demon to hold in detention for any time." Then he transmitted, "This is it, folks." He turned into the subdivision and immediately parked on the shoulder, letting Sid and the cruisers go past. "That itty cabin dead ahead. Yellow porchlight on."

"Her car's there," another voice noted over the airwaves. Ray Jelks's.

Foley and Dee stepped out, stood behind their open doors.

The smell of the sage seemed intense, as did the rasping of the crickets. The cruisers surrounded the place, drivers bailing out without closing their doors. A silhouette darted past the porchlight. Another, shotgun visible at port arms.

Dee struggled not to brace for another explosion. Only now did she recall the awful heat, the irresistible force of the one the other night. She thought even Foley and she were too close to the cabin, everybody was too close for what she remembered.

A voice—Sid's, she believed—whispered, "Clear!" Then wood could be heard splintering. The entry team rushed through the front door. Muffled shouts. A woman's scream, earsplitting. Commands to freeze, show hands.

Dee prayed that no gunshots would follow. Her teeth began to hurt. She made herself stop gritting them.

Foley had his .45 automatic out as he waited. What had he really meant when he said that he wanted Taggart dead? Did he want the man silent forever—to save himself?

"He's not here!" somebody finally cried.

"You cut the phone line?" Foley hollered back.

"Affirm."

"Let's go have a look, Laguerre." Holstering, the sheriff hurried ponderously for the shack, his pocket change jingling. "I just knew it wouldn't be that simple."

Two deputies, on previous instruction, jumped back into their sedan and sped off to reinforce the man bottling up Mazourka Canyon. Sid, holding his helmet under his arm, was already getting back into the Blazer. The entire operation started to shift across the valley to the assembly point below Mazourka Canyon as Dee followed Foley through the front door of the cabin.

The inside smelled of hot wax and wine.

A candle seemed to be burning on every flat surface inside. The glow was jarring, grotesque. Jelks was sitting on a corner of the bed in the combination living room and kitchenette, muttering to the young woman. Mirabelle, apparently. She'd drawn the sheet around her large breasts and was sobbing. "Why d'you keep doin' this to me?" she whined.

"Oh, Mir," the detective said, reaching over and massaging her neck, "come on now."

Ignoring her, Foley was grinning at a balding man sitting rigidly in an armchair across the room. "Why, Counselor," he said in a mocking tone to the Waucoba County deputy district attorney, "I applaud your energy in beatin' us here . . . but don't you think the prosecutorial thrust should follow the arrest?"

The man rose, pivoted slightly away from Dee to tuck

in his shirttail and zip up his trousers. "Is this some sort
of joke, Tyrus?"

"Yes," Foley said, shuffling around the room, blowing
out candles. "After thirty years . . ." *Poof.* ". . . it all seems
like some sort of joke. . . . " *Poof.* "Only thing a man can
do is make sure it ain't on him."

"Meaning?"

"Unless Miss Heckard discussed the love of her life,
Jace Taggart, with you—you're free to go, Counselor."

"Who's Jace Taggart?"

Foley made a sweeping gesture with his hat toward the
door. "Need a ride? I don't recall spottin' your car any-
wheres close."

"It's close enough."

"Oh, I see."

The deputy D.A. went out, and Foley winked at Jelks.
"You doin' any good?"

But the detective looked no less chagrined than the attorney had. He got up from the bed, approached the sheriff,
and said low, "Sir, remember when the wife and I kinda
separated . . . ?"

"No."

Jelks grinned pathetically. "Come on, Tyrus, don't kid
like that. I told you all 'bout it."

" 'Bout what?"

"Mirabelle and me. We kinda had a thing . . ."

"What's this got to do with you askin' 'bout Taggart?"

"Well . . ."

Dee sat beside the woman on the bed, took a tissue from
the box of them on the nightstand and handed it to her.
"Mascara."

"Thanks." Mirabelle wiped her eyes, then blew her nose
and explained defensively, "I haven't seen Jace since that
day."

"What day?"

"Monday. The last time you cops scared the holy shit
outta me like this."

"Do you see him often?" Dee asked.

Mirabelle seemed confused by the question.

"Is he a friend?"

"I don't know what he is. . . . " The woman paused, her

lips trembling slightly. "Weird. That's what he is. Just weird."

"How?"

"He talked me into takin' the afternoon off work. For a picnic, I thought. A date. He was all hyper about it. He bought beer and took me down along the aqueduct . . . under the pipeline . . ." She averted Dee's gaze for a moment. "I like it outside. He said he does too. But then nothin' happened. I mean, we got all ready for somethin' to happen, but I stayed ready all afternoon. All he did was lay on the blanket and brood. He wouldn't say about what. And he seemed kinda relieved when those L.A. cops found us."

"Relieved?"

"Yeah. I think he said 'Finally' when they pointed their guns at us."

Dee shook a Kent out of the pack on the nightstand and lit it for her. "Have you seen Jace since Friday?"

"Huh?"

Smiling, Dee handed her the cigarette. "I'm getting the feeling he isn't exactly your steady."

"Oh, for sure. It was just that one time. Never before and not since. I thought it'd be different, you know. But it turned out to be a big zero."

"Where do you work?"

"DWP, Lone Pine."

Dee realized that Foley and Jelks were stepping outside to give her and Mirabelle some privacy. But the detective turned at the door. "Hey, Mir . . ." He pointed at a small metal object on the mantel of the river rock fireplace. "What good's it gonna do inside here?"

"I keep forgettin' to put it on the car," she complained. "I will."

Jelks went out, and Dee asked, "What is it?"

"Bumper beeper," Mirabelle said. "It's like a trackin' device in case your car gets stolen. Ray sells 'em on the side. Five-ninety-five installed. You interested?"

Dee shook her head. "Did Jace ever ask you about your job, the department?"

"Never. I don't think he said a hun'erd words all afternoon."

"What did he talk about?"

"Oh, I don't know. . . . " She shrugged, sucking her cigarette coal bright. But then her eyes widened. "I don't remember the words so much. Just the feelin' he gave me."

"Yes?"

"Jace Taggart don't want to live much. He's lookin' for a way out."

"How d'you know that?"

"I just know. My daddy kilt himself when I was little. So I just know about these things."

"Okay." Dee smiled. "Thanks. Try not to think too much about any of this. You're not in trouble."

"Yeah," Mirabelle said, snuffling into another tissue, "but it's sure hard on your concentration, you know?"

"I bet."

Dee joined Foley on the small porch.

"Well . . . ?" he asked.

"She barely knows him. Hasn't seen him since Monday, when LAPD found them under the siphon."

"Mazourka." With that, the sheriff started back for his sedan. They were the last to depart for the assembly area.

"It was staged," Dee said, getting in.

Foley gunned the engine, turned around with tires screaking. Again, no headlights. "What was?"

"The love feast SWAT broke up. Taggart never touched her."

Foley chuckled skeptically. "She tell you that?"

"I believe her. Don't you see? Look at us tonight—running around with no lights, just because nothing can move across this valley without being spotted."

"So?"

"Taggart couldn't help being seen delivering his floating bombs to the intakes. But he could do something about *how* he was seen."

After a moment, Foley grunted. "You mean he wanted L.A. SWAT to laugh him off as the nature boy who likes to slap belly buttons under the siphon?"

"Right. He wanted them to wave him through next time they saw his Jeep."

The sheriff grunted once more, then turned his headlamps on for as long as it took to pass through Independence.

"You know something about him, Tyrus," Dee quietly said. "Something that would give sense to this."

Foley extinguished the lights as he turned eastward onto the road for Mazourka Canyon. "I know a thing or two," he finally admitted. "God only knows if they make sense."

"Tell me."

The last-quarter moon had risen almost directly behind Waucoba Mountain.

Foley looked at her sideways, then frowned and said, "Taggarts lived up in Round Valley north of Bishop. Pioneer stock, lost their homestead in the thirties to Los Angeles . . ." So much for the suspect not being a local, as the sheriff and Jelks had both insisted last night. "After losin' their own place, they rented another old farmhouse along Pine Creek owned by DWP. Well, along came the early seventies, and the city decided to get out of the landlordin' business. There was more to it than just that. By turnin' out their tenants they saved water on those sites, plus put more pressure on the housin' market. As few people as possible in the valley. That's always been their aim. . . ." He slowed for something in the road. A coyote, which scampered for the low brush.

"What'd Jace's father do?"

"Drank. Worked now and again up at the Pine Creek Tungsten Mine in the dry shack. Miner's change room. Rest room attendant."

Jelks's voice came over the radio, "That you comin', boss?"

" 'Bout three minutes away. Go ahead and start Abramowitz and the entry team up the canyon." Foley hung up the microphone. "Anyways, the city started evictin' folks and then razin' these places. Ol' man Taggart ignored the notices. Somethin' clicked, I suppose. He was done with movin' on. Well, DWP had an answer to a number of hardheads like the Taggarts—they watched and waited till one of these families went to town, then rushed in the bulldozers and flattened the house. Contents and all." He fell quiet for a few seconds. "Jace had a younger sister, forget her name. Doesn't matter. Eight or nine. She wasn't right in the head. I don't know what you call it, but she didn't speak and was always crawlin' off someplace dark to hide. DWP

boys would go through a place before startin' the demolition, but they missed her. She'd gone up into the attic,
jumped inside a big steamer trunk.''

"Oh, Jesus." Dee rolled her window all the way down.

"Ol' man Taggart and his wife had left Jace to watch
her. He was no more than thirteen at the time. Kids are
kids, and he went off with an Indian buddy to catch
snakes." The pavement ended at the mouth of the canyon,
and Foley fell in behind Jelks's car. Despite the rain of two
nights ago, dust enveloped both sedans. "The city settled
with the Taggarts out of court. The ol' man drank it up.
Jace went off to the navy, came back and joined the workin' poor."

Dee studied Foley's jowly profile in the wan moonlight.
"Why didn't you suspect him right away?"

"Lady," he said, with rising anger, "I know a hun'red
diff'rent stories just like this one. Owens Valley's an old
battleground, and a hun'red people got just as much cause
as Jace Taggart to try to blow Water and Power off the
face of the earth." He gestured hotly at Jelks, whose brake
lamps blinked on and off. "Ray there, his daddy was crip-
pled by the water dicks and their goddamn bats. Left him
in a wheelchair for life. Ray had to quit school and go to
work when he was sixteen. Don't you think he might want
to do exactly what Jace did?"

"Does he?" Dee calmly asked.

Foley ignored the question. After a moment, he said,
"What I've gotta find out is—what set Jace off *now*, after
all these years?"

Sid saw the monofilament trip wire as soon as he approached the open door to the small machine shop. It glistened like a fresh strand of spiderweb. He thumbed off his
flashlight and turned to the deputies, who stood in single
file some yards behind him. "I've got one. Back off,
okay?"

Quickly, they withdrew well out into Taggart's storage
yard and sat on some of the rusted tanks protruding from
the sagebrush. Propane, oxygen, helium, acetylene. According to Dee, Taggart had had a boom on his Jeep, which
explained how he'd picked up and transported something

as heavy as a one-ton bomb. No vehicles now anywhere on the property, a patented mining claim in a gully with a spring.

And no Taggart.

Assisted by a canine unit, the deputies and Sid had already swept the grounds and the filthy hovel the recluse called home. Amazing that he'd never contracted Hanta virus, an often-deadly bug found in rodent droppings, for the shack floor was blanketed with them. He'd eaten a hasty meal of Vienna sausages and canned beans, leaving the remainders to spoil on the table. This had probably been immediately upon his return from the blast that had nearly gotten Dee. The deputies figured that he'd hoofed it out of the Coso Range to the Death Valley highway, then hitchhiked the rest of the way to Independence.

Sid lit up the underside of the machine shop steps.

Nothing. No pressure-sensitive trigger.

"Sid . . . ?"

He scooted around on his knees toward the voice. Dee was standing out in the brush. Too near for the kind of ordnance Taggart preferred to use. "What?" he asked irritably. The inside of his head felt thick, stuffy. He'd left his helmet in the Blazer. Just too hot to wear it. He'd almost passed out during the sweep up at Seven Pines.

"Curlie advises he's en route with the truck."

"Good. That all?"

"No . . ." She shifted her weight to the other foot. "Why don't I stand by? You know, in case you need me to go for something?"

Like steel wool, he realized. "I'll be fine. It's a rule in this business—no more personnel than necessary. I wouldn't even let Curlie stick around. Go back up to the road. In fact, I'd feel more comfortable if the deputies went with you."

She began walking toward the tanks, where the cigarette coals of the deputies were winking on and off.

Sid crept up the steps. Time for the first gamble. He didn't figure Taggart had the capability to rig a light-sensitive trigger, so he flicked on his beam. The device was nailed to the inner wall, its guts clearly visible: several bricks of plastique taped together plus two obvious triggering mechanisms. A pull wire, to which the monofilament was attached, and a self-destructing, watertight timer—U.S. Navy issue, no doubt. It was ticking.

Thorough.

Taggart was thorough. He wanted a detonation no matter what.

Sid glanced toward the yard. He'd heard Dee murmuring to the deputies, but she'd moved on alone and the men were still lounging on the tanks.

Quickly now, he dug the electrical blasting cap out of the plastique. Taking a pair of wire-cutters from the tool bag he wore around his waist, he snipped the two wires leading from the pull wire and timer. Done. But then he noticed something about the bricks. Wrong color for plastique. Too gray. He scraped one of them with a fingernail and sniffed.

"Shit."

Duct seal, not plastique. He rested his forehead on the back of his hand for a moment, thinking. Taggart had set up an elaborate tease. Had he been willing to let it go at that?

No, Sid decided. This blaster had always delivered an explosion. He had no sense of humor.

On a sudden suspicion, Sid began shredding apart the duct seal with his fingers. Then he froze. The blood rushed to his already full head. He'd found a trembler switch. By all rights, he should've been injured by this time. At least a couple of fingers blown off. The switch, closed by the slightest jarring, should have been connected to another blasting cap.

But it wasn't.

The two fine red wires that issued from it wound down through a hole Taggart had drilled in the floor.

Sid backed out of the doorway, scuttled down the steps, and tore away the wooden skirting around the foundation with a big screwdriver. The wires continued down a post into the ground.

He could hear a muffled ticking.

Using a wooden probe, he felt something hard buried just beneath the surface. He uncovered it. A second timer, encased in epoxy resin to keep Sid from stopping it. Two white wires, covered with an inch of dirt, trailed off toward the tanks.

Spinning around, Sid shouted at the deputies, "Run!"

But they did no more than stand, gaping at him.

"Get away from the tanks!" He began duckwalking toward them, following the wires, gently running them through his hands. He couldn't just sever them. He was now afraid of a collapsing circuit: as soon as he cut one filament, a secondary power supply circuit would come into play, igniting the device. Taggart had known precisely where the deputies would pass the time while Sid dealt with the dummy IED. Thorough, again. Diabolically.

"Move!"

They were moving, but it was all nightmarishly slow, a few of the younger men loping toward the road, but the others almost shuffling through the knee-high brush as if they were afraid of tripping.

Sid continued to follow the wires.

Any disarming would have to be done on the explosive device itself. The realization staggered him, but he told himself that he still had some time. Taggart could've set an instantaneous blast with the trembler switch had he wanted.

Then, as he approached the tanks, it came to Sid what Jace Taggart had wanted. The disarmer. Not the deputies.

He dropped the wires and came to his feet.

Taggart had suckered him by using the only means that would work. Delayed Sid's own escape by making him think he had to go ahead with a complicated takedown to save others.

He started running. He could see the deputies ahead of him, almost to the road now. A spotlight from one of the cruisers was casting a blinding path for them to follow through the scrub. Other cars were backing down the hill toward the main canyon, dust swirling around them. He looked for Dee, but couldn't make her out in the confusion. He prayed she hadn't come back for him. Then his vision went orange, and he was breathing fire. He felt himself being picked up, sucked into the sky. A pink mist enveloped him. He stopped struggling and started floating.

CHAPTER**FIFTEEN**

Dee was allowed to go along with Sid on the medical flight to Northern Waucoba Hospital, in Bishop, the best equipped hospital in the county. The EMT needed help to hold the pressure dressings in place, and Dee was already awash with the agent's blood from having applied tourniquets on the ride in Foley's sedan down out of Mazourka Canyon. Sid's right leg was gone from the knee, the left from the midpoint of the shin. A flying chunk of propane tank, the sheriff figured. Sid's scarred face had been scorched black by the fireball, and his ears were now completely burned off. He seemed to come close to consciousness as the helicopter swooped down to the hospital parking lot. He rocked his head from side to side, but Dee was left wondering if she'd only imagined the brief, frothy smile behind the translucent oxygen mask.

Sid was wheeled into ER immediately upon arrival, then swiftly on to the operating room.

A nurse offered Dee a shower and a patient gown. She shed her bloody uniform and stepped into the hot needles of water. A nauseating moment came and went: a pink tea was twining down her legs into the drain.

Then, too numb to cry, she took a chair in the waiting room. The chair seemed too big. The room too. Or maybe it was because she felt so small. Hollow. She didn't try to rest her burning eyes. Each time she'd closed them before she'd seen Sid lying as rigidly still as a mannequin in the fireball that seemed to light up the entire canyon.

She got up and phoned Sid's supervisor. Her own. Then

she sat again. She couldn't even recall what she'd just said to the two men.

She tried to nap. But couldn't.

Five hours later, Jim Curlie arrived, his ATF jumpsuit covered with char and ash. "Finished with the prelim stuff at the scene," he said with a vacuous grin. And he was talking too loudly. "I figure the prick set off a two-hundred-and-fifty-pounder right under some propane and oxygen tanks." Then his grin faded, and his eyes held hers in silence. "How's . . . ?"

It took her a moment to shake off the numbness. "Alive, last I heard. That was a half hour ago." She rubbed her face with her hands. It was stiff with dried sweat. Had she forgotten to wash it in the shower? "It's his lungs that have them worried. They were already messed up from the first accident." She shook her head. "No," she said fiercely.

"No what?"

"He didn't want it called an accident." Anger came and went like lightning. She wasn't sure what the provocation had been. Maybe it just wanted out. "What happened, Jim? What'd he do wrong?"

"Nothin'. I know that old EOD line about there bein' no such thing as an accident. It's bullshit. I've seen disposal guys go through the door and right into a blast. Never even had a chance to unpack their tools. Luck and time were against 'em, and if that ain't an accident I don't know what is. . . ." Curlie started to reach for his cigarettes, but then noticed the No Smoking sign. "Got a return from N.C.I.S. on Taggart. He was navy all right, torpedoman aboard a nuclear sub. Secondary specialty as a diver. That explains how he knows his way 'round ordnance like he does—"

"Later, Jim," Dee said.

Curlie's sooty fingers trembled as he stroked his mustache. "You want somethin' to drink?"

"No, but there's a soda machine down—"

"I mean somethin' to *drink*." He took a chrome flask from the top of his boot.

"God yes," she said, grabbing it. Bourbon. Excellent bourbon.

At seven, with sunlight streaming in through the waiting room windows, Curlie gave Dee a hug and left to pick up a federal investigative team at Bishop Airport and take the various special agents down to the Mazourka Canyon crime scene. Sid had been out of surgery for nearly two hours. Dee had learned this from the weary-looking surgeon, who suggested that she go home. All that could be done had been done. But, under prodding, the doctor admitted that Sid probably wouldn't last the morning. He was fighting for his life, but often that wasn't enough. Not with inhalation burns and massive shock. "I'll stay," Dee said. "Somebody needs to be here for him."

She wondered if Sid had any family left. He'd never said.

At ten after ten o'clock, a cool touch on her arm startled her awake. The head nurse from the intensive care unit. Dee asked, "Is he—?"

"Not yet," the woman said with an odd look in her eye, "but he needs your help."

"Did he ask for me?"

The nurse knelt, took Dee's hands in her own—and lapsed into a poignant silence that said everything.

Dee, getting light-headed, asked, "How can you be—?"

"I can give you a dozen reasons why, each one enough on its own to make this terminal. But he goes on suffering. Are you his partner?"

Dee nodded, fighting tears.

"Tell him it's all right to go," the nurse said. "He'll trust your voice. Can you do this?"

The interior of the ICU felt like night, low lights. Dee could hear Sid breathing painfully, thunderously as the mechanical ventilator forced air into his lungs. A blue corrugated tube entered an incision in his lower throat. The nurse let Dee go on alone to him. Up close, she could hear the secretions in his lungs bubbling. The scars on his face were charred tatters. His eyes were dull, but she thought that they had tracked her approach. "Sid, it's Dee. . . ." Trying not to cry only made it worse, so she just held one of his bandaged hands for a while. When she had her voice back, she said, "I know why you're fighting this. You beat it once before. But you can't do it this time. No one could. . . ." The bubbling in his lungs became a low rattle. "Oh, Sid . . ." She leaned over and kissed a less burned spot on his forehead, then whispered the awful words, "It's okay to die . . . it's okay, sweetheart . . ."

Jace Taggart peered anxiously out from the hinge crack in the boathouse door. The waters of Grant Lake, slate-colored under the late afternoon shadow of the Sierra, were being whipped by the breeze into echelons of small waves. These marched toward the east, broke whitely against the rock dam.

At one o'clock this afternoon, a DWP crew had showed up, half of it by two-ton truck and half by boat. A crane in the bed of the truck lowered a grate over the intake, and a pair of wet-suited divers flopped backward out of the boat to weld it onto the pipe that was the opening of an eleven-mile-long tunnel. It passed under a series of gray volcanic cones and dumped the waters of the Mono Lake Basin into the upper Owens River.

Taggart turned away from the door and sprawled on the dock, which was bobbing slightly. It was dark in the abandoned boathouse, almost as dark as the interior of a steamer trunk, but he could see the bright orange flotation device, the five-hundred-pound bomb to which it was harnessed, gliding up and down on the swells. The hull of the fourteen-foot aluminum boat was knocking against the edge of the dock. The sound was driving him nuts. It was like a small, bony fist rapping for release.

He reached for the brandy bottle, took a swig. Another. He was sorry now that he'd taken more speed this morning. Sleep would be impossible tonight, and he'd have nothing to do except drink. Ride the runaway elevator.

The job was temporarily off, thanks to the new grate on the intake. The easy times were over. This, the using of the last of DWP's three main intakes, almost felt jinxed. The trouble had started with the delay coming in off the bombing range. A lousy flash flood. Then he'd been boxed in on the Coso Hot Springs Road between the BLM ranger to the east and half the law enforcement in Waucoba County to the west. He'd lost the thousand-pounder he'd hoped to use on the tunnel tonight. The fiver he'd already had on hand would do considerable damage, but nothing like what he could've caused with the bigger bomb. He'd also lost his

Jeep pickup, although it'd quickly been replaced for him with a long-bed Chevy van. He kept it at a trailhead parking lot nearby.

Puttering was coming his way.

Taggart shot up to look through the door crack again, then shifted for a view westward. A bass boat was coming from the direction of the marina, although the wind had driven all the other craft off the lake. Spray was breaking over the bow. A solitary figure was aboard, sitting in the chair near the tiller.

Taggart reached over and took hold of his carbine with a jittery hand.

The man in the boat cut the motor and glided into the tiny bay on which the boathouse sat. A splash followed as he threw over an anchor, and then silence except for the chop slapping against the hull.

Taggart aimed at the man's back.

The man stretched and yawned.

Taggart's forefinger applied faint pressure to the trigger, just enough to make the hammer rear up.

The boat, skimmed along by the wind, came to the end of its anchor tether near the boathouse door. ''Get that god-damn thing off me,'' the man said, his long, reddish-blond ponytail whipping over his shoulder as he twisted around to glare through the crack at Taggart.

Reluctantly, Taggart lowered the carbine, then leaned it against the wall.

''You rang . . . ?'' Karl Schoenfeld picked up a rod, cast a hooked worm into the shallows. Taggart had flown an old sock from the boathouse flagpole as a signal.

''It's off for tonight.''

''Why?''

''They welded a grate over the intake.''

Schoenfeld exhaled. ''Shit.'' The tip of the rod jiggled as he got a nibble, but he didn't set the hook, and the line went slack again. ''What d'you need?''

''Underwater cutting rig.''

''Where am I gonna find that around here?''

''You're not. I know a place in San Pedro.''

''Too close. Southland media's got the word out to any-body and everybody who sells pressure cylinders.''

"There's another outfit in Bremerton."

"You mean *Washington*?"

"Yeah."

Schoenfeld lit up a Marlboro, and the delicious smoke wafted through the crack. Taggart had run out this morning. "I don't want either of us to show our faces in the Northwest yet."

Face. Northwest. Inwardly, Taggart saw a flash of the old man's bloody face, the crushed nose, the broken eyeglasses on the linoleum. "Toss me that pack," he said. "I'm clean out."

Schoenfeld took a one-ounce lead weight from his tackle box, dropped it into the hard pack before chucking it onto the outer dock of the boathouse. Taggart reached through the wide crack, scooped it up. "What's the news outside?" He felt cut off, isolated from the world, just as he had on board his submarine for months on end.

"Abramowitz died this mornin'." Curiously, Schoenfeld said this with an utter lack of satisfaction—after he'd told Taggart in a panic that the game was up unless the ATF man, the best on the coast, was taken out of the picture.

Taggart took a thoughtful pull on his cigarette.

This death, like those of the two actors, meant nothing to him. Unlike the first one. His first. The old man up in Wasco County, Oregon. Schoenfeld had parked down the road from the farmhouse. *Punch him around a little*, he'd said, the rain tinkling on the roof of the Oldsmobile, *let him hear the limb creak under him. That way, when I come back in the mornin', he'll put two and two together, be in the mood to sell when I bring it up. Don't say nothin'. You don't have to.* But Schoenfeld must have known that things would get out of hand. And they had. From all the brandy and speed, maybe. The old man spat on Taggart, who kept hurling his fists until he finally realized that they were covered with blood. He'd driven the bridge of the old man's nose right up into his brain. Schoenfeld and he dumped the body in the Columbia River, and months later the Wetlands Preservation Society bought the land from the old man's relatives. At a bargain rate. Nobody wanted to live in a house where a murder had gone down.

Taggart washed away the taste of this memory with a

swallow of brandy. "DWP still all fucked up over this?"

"Royally," Schoenfeld said. "You've got them on the run. Heads will roll this time. Whole city is scared shitless they'll be recyclin' piss for drinkin' water."

"Good," Taggart said.

"What about San Francisco?"

"What about it?"

"Can I get what you need there?"

"I guess. I just don't know of a place off the top of my head."

"Why don't you blow the grate?" Schoenfeld asked, frowning as the tip of his rod began jerking again.

"I'd have to go with multiple charges. Still might not open enough bars to squeeze the Mark Eighty-two through. We're fucked if that happens. I won't have time for a second shoot."

Schoenfeld landed a small rainbow trout. "How you fixed for money?"

"Fine," Taggart said. He hadn't spent much of the fifty thousand Schoenfeld had already given him. Not that it mattered. Things like that no longer mattered. He couldn't see beyond this time, which had scared him at first. But not now. He had enough methamphetamine to keep him from getting too low, enough brandy to keep him from getting too high. He figured he could manage to ride the elevator up and down just a bit longer, until the cable inside his feverish brain snapped and he was left at peace. Like his sister. He'd dreamed of her the other night. She'd been able to talk, and she'd thanked him, told him that he'd like the other side better. Everything felt the same all the time. No ups and downs. Bliss.

"Aw, what a shame," Schoenfeld said, reaching into his tackle box for a pair of pliers. "Hooked him too deep to let him go . . ." Then he turned and smiled coldly up at Taggart. "So deep I'll have to tear his guts out to get my hook back."

"Schoenfeld," Taggart said sharply, but then he made himself shut up.

"Yes?"

Taggart lit a second cigarette off the first. "Nothin'."

"You sure? We never talk, Jace. After all these months, I still don't know you."

"Just as well."

"Really?"

Then it slipped out of Taggart. "It ain't you who's got me on the line, Karl," he said bitterly. "And it ain't what you probably got stashed away in a safety-deposit box on me."

"Well, what then?"

Taggart spun away from the door crack and braced his hands against the wall. Blood. But he couldn't quite bring himself to admit the forever unspoken to Schoenfeld, that he'd been hooked and his guts torn ever since he'd seen blood dripping from that crushed steamer trunk among the wreckage of his father's house.

"Like I say, Jace," Schoenfeld's voice drifted inside, "we gotta talk sometime." After a few minutes, he started up the motor and left.

Garrett Driscoll pounded on Dee's door one last time, then turned in frustration to the middle-aged Indian woman who was grinding something on the big rock in the yard. "The truck's here . . . is she?"

"Only if she wants."

Garrett frowned, then wondered if she was giving him tacit approval to try the knob. "To hell with it." The door was unlocked, which made him feel foolish for having knocked in the first place. It took a few moments for his eyes to adjust to the gloom. Dee was lying on her bed in a terry cloth robe. He parted the curtains, admitting just enough twilight to see that she was asleep, Walkman headphones on. He waved through the window to the DWP driver who'd brought him from the airport, and the man nodded, crept away, scattering some Indian kids playing some kind of stick-and-ball game.

He looked at Dee again. The nasty bruise near her temple was just starting to turn yellow. Next to her on the night-stand were two bottles and one glass. He read the labels: anisette and cognac. He winced at the thought of mixing them.

He could hear a tinny sound, music coming through the headphones. Gently, he removed them, listened a moment. Edith Piaf.

"Dee . . . ?"

Her eyes slid open with an intoxicated slowness. The whites were red. "What . . . ?" She had to lick her lips.

"I flew up as soon as I heard." Instantly, he regretted having said that, for it visibly all came back to her.

Her eyes closed again. "What time's it?"

"Almost eight." He sat beside her on the bed. "Do you want to sleep some more?"

She shook her head.

He noticed her uniform bundled up in a clear plastic bag at his feet. It was blood-soaked. "Is there anything I can do while you rest? For him? Any arrangements?"

"He's already on the way home."

"Where?"

"Hawaii. Turns out he had a sister in Honolulu. Autopsied and en route Reno Airport by four." She reached blindly for her glass.

"It's empty, love."

She rose on an elbow, but then winced, remembering the stitches there too late. She poured in two fingers of transparent anisette, then two more of honey-colored cognac. She must have noticed his look, for she explained, *"Sol y sombra."*

"Pardon?"

"It's called sun and shade. Basque after-dinner drink, but it's pretty good after most anything. Try . . ."

He had a sip. Not as bad as he thought it'd be.

"Well?" she asked.

"I don't know how I feel about it."

"Exactly. It's for when you don't know how you feel."

He set the glass back on the stand, glanced at her again, but her expression was lost in shadow. The light was going swiftly behind the Sierra. "What can I say, Dee?" he whispered.

"Don't say anything." Her arms reached up and drew him down to her.

A long while passed in silence. The light went almost entirely while they held each other. Then he felt her fingertips exploring the contours of his face, his nose and lips and chin. She was crying without making a sound.

"Dee . . ."

"Quiet," she gasped, snuffling.

He thought it best to get up, but his attempt to rise made her cling harder to him. Sobs were turning her breath shuddery, but she started kissing him, deeply, fervently.

His own arousal was so sudden he felt a little ashamed. "Only if you want, Dee," he said, realizing the instant after that it was what the Indian woman had said to him a few minutes earlier. "It can't be the drink. Not the first time for us."

"I can't get drunk, Garrett," she said, her voice soft and forlorn in his ear. "I've tried all afternoon."

CHAPTER **SIXTEEN**

Dee turned off Mazourka Canyon Road onto the narrow trace that ended on Taggart's property. She was still driving Priscilla Fetterman's truck and would be until the replacement windshield and windows for her Bronco arrived from Reno. The front seat was crammed with her own gear, peppered with little sparkles of glass from the blast on the Coso Hot Springs Road, plus the archaeologist's dusty assortment of artifacts, trowels, and topographical maps.

Garrett had already gone from her bed by the time she'd gotten up at six this morning. The car the Bishop DWP office had no doubt sent to pick him up had failed to awaken her. He'd left a note, explaining that he had to be back in Los Angeles should the ax fall sooner than expected. He promised to phone her tonight. Then she noticed the light blinking on her answering machine. The message was from yesterday afternoon at four o'clock. Howard Rowe, the special agent in charge of the FBI's Bakersfield office. He explained that he was now head of the team looking into Sid's death. The U.S. Attorney's office had made the call that the FBI, not ATF, would be the leading investigative agency. Best not for the ATF to look into the loss of one of its own. Too close. Rowe had asked Dee to meet him at Taggart's place in Mazourka Canyon at eight this morning.

She'd expected the day to begin with a dreamlike languor dogging everything she attempted. Not to mention a hangover. Instead, she felt a restlessness that made sitting still impossible. She had to keep moving.

She slowed for the gate to Taggart's property.

Jim Curlie's bomb truck was parked among six nondescript government sedans. In addition to the multiagency investigative group under Rowe, ATF had committed its National Response Team. Dee could see some of these agents and technicians down in the big circle of scorched brush left by the explosion. Others were going over the shacks. Rowe was standing off a ways from the activity with his counterpart from ATF's Bakersfield office, Sid's boss. They were conferring, heads down. The FBI man was wearing an Indiana Jones felt hat. Rather self-consciously, she thought.

Dee shut off the engine and tucked the keys in a pouch that ran along the front of the seat. In case somebody else had to move it, quickly. Suddenly, her breath caught in her throat. Something had cut her thumb. "Damn." Sucking on it, she gingerly reached down with her other hand and brought out a ten-inch-long ceremonial obsidian blade. One of Fetterman's relics. Flaked volcanic glass took on such a fine edge it was being experimented with for surgical instruments.

She got out, slamming the door in frustration.

Curlie glanced up from a sifter and waved. He seemed alone, withdrawn, in the swirls and eddies of busy men. After a moment, Rowe broke away from Sid's boss and shambled up the slope to her. "Ms. Laguerre . . . ?"

She nodded. He seemed to take forever to come all the way up to her. A hot, ringing stillness hung over the canyon.

"Nice meetin' you last week at DWP." He offered his hand. Sweaty. Then he realized that she was looking at the hat. He smiled. "Doesn't become me, does it? But the dang thing's a gift from my granddaughter, and she'd be heartbroken if the news photographers caught me not wearin' it."

She attempted a smile. "Call me Dee."

"Howard. Mind if we walk, Dee? Not a whisper of breeze since midnight."

She fell into step with him. "Out here all night?"

"Yep. Grabbed a few winks in Curlie's truck." Then

Rowe paused. "Sidney thought a great deal of you. Told me so every time he phoned."

She wished that he hadn't said that. Her eyes started up again.

He looked closely at her. "Your first?"

She had to think about that a moment. Yes, she finally decided. She'd lost some fellow BLM employees over in Nevada, but they hadn't been partners, exactly. Not the way Sid had felt to her. "I guess so."

"Well, I pray it's my last, Dee. I retire in October. I'd hoped it would be smooth sailin' till then." They left the road and went over to rocky outcropping, halted. Across the valley she could see the Alabama Hills, the spillway at their northern end where it had started, seemingly eons ago.

"Don't mean to alarm you, Dee," Rowe said, "but your hand's bleedin'."

"Oh." She took out her handkerchief, wrapped her thumb in it. "Should be more careful when you borrow an archaeologist's truck. Indian weapons tucked all over the place."

Rowe appeared not to have heard her. His gold-rimmed glasses had slipped, and he nudged them back up to the bridge of his nose. "Did Sidney say anythin' before the end?"

"No. He never came around."

Rowe nodded, disappointed.

"You expected something?" Dee asked.

"Maybe. Was Sidney ever threatened? Him specifically?"

"Not that I ever heard. But we Feds aren't exactly beloved out here."

"Understood."

"I don't," she said angrily.

"Sorry?"

"I don't understand. Not this morning." She couldn't believe how wrathful she felt all of a sudden.

Rowe clasped his big hand to the back of her neck and gently squeezed. "Boil it all off. Won't go no further. I promise."

But she couldn't open up. Not without breaking down.

He seemed to see this too. "What do threats have to do with anything?" she asked.

Rowe dropped his hand and started back along the road. She caught up. "Sidney was set up. The antitamperin' mechanisms, the total configuration—all designed to take him out. Just him."

"But aren't triggers like that common on IEDs? Sid said something about always looking out for them."

"Sure. To protect the device long enough for it to go off. Not to kill the disarmer."

"Is that what happened, Howard?"

"Well, what else was the point of the blast up here? No DWP facilities. As far as we can tell, no evidence layin' around the place was destroyed, other than the bomb itself. This Taggart fella coulda just as easily carted it off when he pulled up stakes and skedaddled."

She grabbed Rowe by the sleeve as they reached Fetterman's truck. "I want a part in this, Howard. I don't want to be left out. I *can't* be," she added, her voice cracking.

He patted her hand until she let go of him. "I'll be in touch." Then he strolled on down to rejoin the others.

Speeding out of the canyon, she noticed a sheen of dust rising languidly to the north. Sheep. Just down in the past several days off the sparse summer pastures high in the desert mountains. She was drawn to them, something familiar on a day in which everything felt raw and strange. They were milling around a water tank in a wire grass meadow. From here they'd be trucked farther north to fresh pastures. The long-distance drives of the past, a solitary shepherd nudging the flock along a few miles a day for six months or more, were gone forever.

She braked and approached the shepherd, the flock flowing around Fetterman's truck. Even in her own childhood, the man might have been Basque. But not now. Chilean. Aristocratic bronze face like an Incan prince. Through her open side window, she asked him if he'd seen any unusual cars coming to and from the canyon over the past week. Apparently, he didn't understand her Spanish, and she certainly didn't his Andean dialect. She thought it was hopeless until he shaded his eyes for a look back toward the road leading into Independence. Rolling along it were three rigs pulling sheep trailers. They raised huge clouds of dust as they turned off and approached the herd.

The outfit was Basque-owned, a big one based in the Central Valley, but the foreman ramrodding the transfer was El Salvadoran. He made this clear as he climbed down out of the cab of the lead truck. His English was good, and he repeated Dee's question to the Chilean.

"Yes," the translation quickly came back, "he's seen many cars. All police. Many."

"Any other kind?" Dee asked.

"No, not coming to and from, as you say. But there was a Chevy van parked over there Friday morning." The shepherd and then the foreman pointed at some ruins of an old train station along an abandoned narrow-gauge line that ran the length of the valley.

"What happened to it?" She tried not to appear impatient as she waited for the translation. These people were so naturally obliging.

"A man walked down out of the canyon, took the keys off the front wheel, and then drove back up in the van. He came down two hours later, and the herder did not see him or the Chevy since. It was the color of rust, this van."

"Please ask him to describe the man."

Instantly, she caught the words *grande* and *barba negra*. Big, darkly bearded.

"Thank you," Dee said.

Pulling away, scattering the ewes before her, she reached for her microphone. She asked the sheriff's office dispatcher for a meeting with Foley but was advised that he was out of the county until late this evening. Modoc, perhaps, visiting Kyle.

"Jail sergeant's available," the dispatcher offered.

Dee thought about it, but finally said, "Negative at this time." Only if the information came through Foley would it be trusted and acted upon. Besides, she didn't want Taggart to be alerted by the grapevine. That might only force him to scuttle the van.

Instead, she pressed the gas pedal to the firewall.

Over the next four hours, she hit every tiny settlement in the lower county, looked over every vehicle on Highway

395 in case Taggart had switched to another. She walked through every bar—ignoring the rowdy jibes—swung through every campground, checked every shady place where Taggart might linger while waiting for nightfall. She went as far east as Darwin, the northern edge of the navy bombing range, and then south through Panamint Valley and Ridgecrest to Nine-Mile Canyon. There, she followed the dirt road under the aqueduct until it petered out in pinyon flats. At the end of that time, she had nothing except two hundred more miles on the odometer and a near-empty gas tank.

She parked above Haiwee Reservoir, the southernmost intake into the system. Where Taggart had submerged the bomb that had suddenly bobbed to the surface on its balloon and glided into the aqueduct the evening she and Sid had been eating hamburgers near Ridgecrest.

Getting out, she sat on a rock in the shade of the cab and glassed the calm, green waters. A small boat was stitching back and forth near the dam, towing something on a cable. She brought the two-man crew into focus. Sailors in swim trunks. And on shore was their gray van marked "United States Navy—Explosive Ordnance Disposal Unit."

Rising, she reached through her open window for the microphone. "Control, BLM-One . . ."

"Go ahead."

"Can you advise what the navy's doing at Haiwee?"

After a moment, the sergeant himself came on. "Go to scramble, BLM." When she'd done so, he continued, "They're towin' a side-scan sonar, searchin' for possible devices on the bottom. They'll be doin' all the reservoirs this week."

"Thanks."

And the first California National Guard units were due sometime tomorrow. Garrett had told her that last night— as if the news meant his entire life was finished. LAPD Metro was being pulled out, and the army was on the way. The people of the valley betrayed nothing outwardly, although Dee suspected that Paris had awaited the Wehrmacht with only slightly more smoldering resentment.

She leaned against the truck, gazed all around. The view

exhausted her: mile after mile of hot scrubland, convoluted ridges and canyons. Vast. Yet, Jace Taggart was out there somewhere. She trusted, just as Tyrus Foley had said, that the blaster hadn't beaten his retreat yet. The sky and the dry bed of Owens Lake commingled in a mirrorlike ripple. Her eyes quickly sought the comfort of the genuine water in Haiwee Reservoir. Somewhere under the surface was the site of an old way station. Near the only spring for miles around, submerged now as well. In 1864, while the husband was away, the station was attacked, possibly by the Paiute, possibly the Shoshone, maybe even the Mojave. The wife and son had been murdered. In retaliation, the local whites massacred forty Paiute men, women, and children. All over water, most likely. A spring.

She closed her eyes.

The past was never a comfort. Not the real past. It was as violent and seemingly pointless as the present.

Then her eyes snapped open. "Ephraim."

Tillie made Dee wait in the corridor until some unpleasantness was dispensed with. Only then, as the woman shuffled out carrying an opaque plastic bag, was Dee allowed to enter the room. Ephraim Bickle's eyes were almost lifeless today, but she thought a flicker of recognition came into them as she took the chair.

"Afternoon, Ephraim."

She was afraid that he might recall their last meeting, when he'd ordered her out. She decided to steer clear of his personal past, although she'd learned more about it from Tyrus Foley. Of the Ritchie brothers, the owners of Waucoba County Bank, for whom Bickle had worked; one had died in San Quentin and the other had committed suicide, hanged himself, two days after being paroled. Ephraim alone had come home to face the music, running that quixotic ad in the newspaper promising to repay all that had been lost in the bank. Unfortunately, his good intentions brought on a flurry of lawsuits that tied up what little he made as a gas station attendant in Big Pine, and his health gave out before he could ever come close to honoring the promise. He had been in this room for nearly thirty years, doubly cursed with longevity and ailments that refused to kill him.

"Missed lunch," he finally said.

"Pity."

He chuckled raspily at the irony in her voice. "What you want this time?"

"I came to tell *you* something."

"Oh?"

"You were wrong."

"How gracious."

"It is a local. Jace Taggart." Then she said, trying not to sound too bitter, "He killed a friend of mine."

Bickle's head eased back into his pillow. "Knew some Taggarts years ago. Round Valley people."

"Same family."

"So you're here to crow?"

"No, Ephraim. I've come to tell you as much as I know. Then I'm asking you to tell me what you think. Will you do that?"

Eventually, he gave a weak nod and shut his eyes.

And so she began. Ten minutes into it, she was sure that he'd fallen asleep when suddenly he said, "First bomb middle of the system, second the lower part, then back to the middle, hittin' the wells . . . I got that much right?"

She couldn't help but smile. "Yes . . ." She went on until there was nothing left to tell, then sat back and waited.

His eyes opened, clicked toward her. "Demands."

"What?"

"All this bombin', and no demands? What kind of moron would do that?"

"Somebody who believes the city murdered his sister," Dee replied.

Bickle mulled that over. "Naw," he finally said, "the thinkin's too pretty for that."

"Pretty?"

"Symmetrical. If it was Taggart on his lonesome, and he's the mad dog you say he is—why, he'd tear through DWP's system from one end to the other. He'd go out like a meteor. No, if he's in it at all, somebody's got a leash on him."

"How can you be so sure?"

"Pattern. There's always an accidental pattern to deceit. Don't ask me why. Just is. Somethin' unconscious in even the most crooked mind to work it all out square. Hell, the Ritchies and I proved that. The bank examiner chalked out our little scheme on a blackboard for the trial—I couldn't believe how damn symmetrical our machinations were. What the Ritchies and I hoped was a financial thicket turned out to be a formal garden."

"Show me the pattern, Ephraim. I don't see it."

"Middle, lower, middle . . . next, it'll be upper."

"The upper system?"

"Goddamn right. Happened just that way in the twenties. A dynamitin' on the Alabama Hills canal. Then the siphon down south in Nine-Mile Canyon. Next the well field. And finally the penstock to a powerhouse way up in the Owens Gorge." Bickle looked doubtfully at her. "How old you figure this Taggart kid is? Old enough to throw the same exact curveball in two games seventy years apart?"

Taggart sat in his wet suit in the dimness of the boathouse, shaking. The brandy and the speed were tussling with each other inside his bloodstream, but he couldn't let the booze's mellow warmth win. Not now. Beside him on the dock was the portable underwater oxygen-acetylene cutting rig that Schoenfeld had left about an hour ago in the aspens across the road. It was now almost six o'clock, and the wide crack around the door was a square of gray evening light. Taggart popped two capsules, washed them down with the last of his brandy, then lowered the mask over his face and clamped the mouthpiece between his teeth. Turning, he inflated the bladder to the cutting rig, then slid with it under the surface.

He swam beneath the door, out of the blackness into the jadelike waters of the little bay. Stroking with one hand, clutching the rig with the other, he flutter-kicked past a school of German browns. The fading light was still strong enough to sparkle off the gold in their scales.

To his ears came the rhythmic hiss of compressed air.

He kept an eye out for hulls overhead. One of them might be a DWP boat, guarding the intake, although Taggart had seen no one from the department since the crew had installed the grate yesterday morning. Hopefully, the city was satisfied that a few iron bars would do the trick.

Taggart checked his waterproof watch. Six-ten. By now, Schoenfeld would be parked up on Parker Ridge in his Volkswagen van, overlooking the lake, keeping watch. They'd agreed that this would be the final blast for a while. No longer the simple task it'd been at the outset, lowering the bombs into an unguarded canal or reservoir and letting the flow sweep them toward their targets. If a grate had been installed here, Taggart could count on finding them everywhere.

Boulders began to appear along the mossy bottom. First sign of the rock-and-earth dam.

Then there it was on the bottom: the five-hundred-pounder, sleek and menacing-looking.

Last night, after the quarter moon set, Taggart had towed the bomb behind the aluminum boat to within twenty yards of the intake, then hit the pressure release on the balloon. The Mark Eighty-two sank to the bottom forty feet below. It had lain there ever since. More than enough helium remained in the tank to reinflate the flotation device, giving the bomb just enough buoyancy to rise within five feet of the surface and slip, unseen, into the tunnel through the butchered grate.

Taggart came to the lattice of bars, stood with his flippers on the lowermost horizontal one. He could feel the weight of the current on his back as it gushed toward the intake, the dark tunnel beyond. He latched the cutting rig to a bar, then opened the valve on the oxygen tank. A big bubble wobbled slowly up. Inside this he quickly lit the acetylene torch with a flint.

Then he started slicing through bars.

Dee approached Grant Lake from its upper end, having checked the campgrounds and trailhead parking lots along a fifteen-mile-long loop. She'd been tempted to grab a bite in the village of June Lake, but at that moment the sun had dipped behind Carson Peak and made up her mind to use the last of the daylight before looking to any creature comforts. She'd now put over four hundred miles on Fetterman's truck since morning.

Grant Lake spread glassily between the rocky moraines that enclosed it, a few boats here and there, fishermen spread along the shorelines.

She fought a yawn and lost. She felt frazzled, but couldn't make herself turn for home.

A driveway wound down to the marina. Its bar catered to anglers but was frequented by Basques who, like Louie Aguirre, came from miles around. It wasn't owned or run by Bascos, but had become a watering hole for them in the days before the federal government had cut back on the grazing allotments in the high meadows above the lake. Somehow, there always seemed to be a couple of old white-heads sitting inside or out on the patio, and Dee was tempted to drop by for an ox tongue sandwich, the house specialty.

But she didn't.

There was one more trailhead lot to drive through before going down to the intake, the northernmost one of the entire system. The one Taggart had yet to use. A blast in the middle of the long tunnel that started there would prevent the diversion of Mono Basin streams for years. Sid had said that the tunnels would be hardest to repair.

She wasn't sure that there was anything to Ephraim Bickle's notion of symmetry, but it appealed to her in her present muddle. If nothing happened after a few hours of stakeout, she'd go on twenty miles to the BLM fire station atop Conway Summit and grab a bunk for a few hours' sleep. Her vision was starting to blear double on her.

She crept through the lot, checking license plates. Hikers from all over the country left their vehicles here before trekking off into the Sierra. Hard to concentrate. A Ford Econoline slipped past, baby-shit yellow. Her ears were ringing from fatigue. Must reach that bunk soon. She was halfway past the Chevrolet van before she suddenly sat erect. Rust-colored from a coat of primer. It was all she could do to keep from braking. She forced herself to drive on at precisely the same speed. Thankfully, two hikers flagged her down at the outlet to the lot and asked for trail information. She had none but made up something about erosion on the switchbacks while she glanced back at the van. No sign of anyone through its windshield.

The hikers waved good-bye, and she wrote the Chevy's license plate number on her pad.

Turning back onto the loop highway, she continued eastward. *Steady*, she reminded herself, *you're being watched*. She had no doubt of that. Taggart would keep a careful watch before and during whatever he had in mind here.

She passed the barricaded road that descended to the dam and the intake midway across it. No one was fishing from the railed crest.

Only when she was well below the dam did she reach for her microphone. "Control, this is BLM-One . . ."

Her transmission was answered by a squelch noise. She tried again. A voice came faintly through the waterfall-like roar: "Unit tryin' to raise Control, try from another location. You're completely unreadable."

She bit her underlip, thinking. There were several radio blind spots throughout the Sierra, but this canyon wasn't one of them. She'd never had a problem here before. Nor did she believe that bad atmospherics where to blame. Calm day, no sunspot activity she knew of. She switched to DWP's channel. The same blocking sounds followed. Even channel 9 on CB was being jammed.

"Christ," she said, accelerating.

It was going down right now. Taggart was moving on the intake. And the nearest phone was miles away, other than the outdoors one at the marina, which she felt sure was under surveillance.

She glanced all around. No vehicles in sight, other than those whose headlights were coming on a few miles below along Highway 395. The first dirt road to the right appeared through the bitterbrush. She took it. She kept her speed down so too much dust wouldn't roil up out of the deep-green growth. A small herd of mule deer bounded ahead of the truck through the twilight. She dipped across a dry gulch, the old bed of the creek which now flowed down the tunnel.

Something bright in the rearview mirror caught her eye.

A sheriff's cruiser was speeding up the road she'd just left—toward Grant Lake. The deputy was running his emergency lights but no siren. She boosted the volume on her radio and was treated to the same cacophony. She tried anyway. "Sheriff's unit going code toward Grant . . . ?"

Nothing.

She thought about turning around and going after him, but then saw that she was well south of the dam. She could approach the intake from the opposite direction of the deputy. If Taggart was still in the area, they had him caught between them.

She braked, threw the shift lever into park, and grabbed her radio handset and shotgun. Trotting through the brush, she fumbled to clip the mike onto her uniform shirt lapel and jam the plug into her ear. A welter of confusion came over her. What was bringing the deputy here? She hoped that it wasn't something as silly as a disturbance at the marina bar. Taggart would slip away, down the road nobody was blocking. Damn him for screwing up the airwaves.

But then, out of the blue, came the deputy's voice through her earplug. As clear as it could be. "Control, I'm at the dam. ETA on a backup?"

"Unknown, CHP's closest. Rollin' from Sherwin Grade—"

"Control," Dee said breathlessly, jogging up the moraine that formed the south bank of the reservoir, "BLM-One . . . at Grant . . . I can back . . . I'll back . . ."

The deputy asked, "Where are you, BLM?" His voice was shaking as he transmitted on the run over his own handset, "Don't see you."

"South of the dam . . . what's your activity and where?"

The dispatcher answered for him. "All units respondin' to Grant Lake, we had an anonymous report five minutes ago of suspicious activity at the intake. We have two units out at the scene, June Lake resident and BLM."

Dee turned her ankle on the rock-cluttered slope, dropped to a knee. It made no sense. She'd just seen the intake. Nothing had looked out of the ordinary to her. Why had someone called in? Anonymously, she reminded herself. She got up again and topped the moraine at a hobble. The pain quickly wore off.

Two hundred yards across the lake, she could see the deputy crouching on the catwalk over the intake. He was clasping his automatic pistol and flashlight together, aiming them down into the water. He shouted something, but Dee couldn't make out the words.

She kept running.

CHAPTER**SEVENTEEN**

Taggart thought he heard something on the catwalk above. Then the vibrations were so clearly telegraphed to him he shut off the cutting torch and listened. Heavy footfalls. Suddenly, a flashlight beam slanted down through the water, probing. It passed over him, moved on a few yards, then swept back and held steady. He could catch glints of gold on the silhouette above: star-shaped badge, cap piece, nameplate.

Deputy sheriff.

Taggart grabbed the partially cut bar he'd been working on and bent it outward. He fully expected bullets to sizzle down toward him, but he ignored the threat and swam with the cutting rig for the bottom. Long strokes with his free hand and a furious kick quickly left the reach of the beam behind.

He rested the rig on the silt and opened the oxygen and acetylene valves. A frenzy of bubbles snaked toward the surface.

How had this happened? The small glow of the cutting torch wouldn't be visible until well after dark. He'd checked every five minutes and seen no one along the crest of the dam. No boats, not even trollers, had come this way.

Taggart then took his diving knife from its sheath and cut the tether to the bladder that neutralized the weight of the rig. Instead of slicing all the way through, he left a strand, no more than a nylon thread. The buoyancy began straining against it. This done, he slid the knife under his wet suit along his inner forearm. It felt cold against his skin.

Muffled shouting. The deputy was shouting something at him now.

Slowly, Taggart came to the surface and breached about ten feet out from the man. "Hands up!" he was bawling, obviously terrified even though he was looking at Taggart over the sights of an automatic pistol. "Put your goddamn hands up!"

"Can't keep afloat that way," Taggart lied, his flippers churning leisurely beneath him.

The deputy was eyeing the dome of bubbles off to Taggart's left. "What's that?"

"There's two of us."

"Is he comin' up?"

Taggart pretended difficulty hearing, swam closer.

"Is he gonna surface!"

"I signaled . . . but it's up to him." Taggart treaded water even nearer. "He's got a speargun." The deputy's boots were about eighteen inches above him, and the muzzle of the pistol was almost touching his face.

"A *what*?"

At that instant, the cutting rig bladder shot two feet into the air, scattering droplets for ten feet all around. As the deputy swiveled his weapon and flashlight toward it, Taggart kicked powerfully and reared up out of the water. He'd already drawn the knife from his wet suit and now, reaching the zenith of his lunge, used his left forearm to turn the muzzle of the handgun even farther away from him. A shot went off, echoing in the intake pipe. As he began sinking back down, Taggart buried the knife to the hilt in the deputy's groin, below the body armor vest that was visible beneath his uniform shirt. The man screamed. Letting go of the knife, Taggart seized him by the shoulder straps and pulled him down between the catwalk railings. They plunged below the surface together.

Struggling, the deputy found the mouthpiece, yanked it out.

Taggart let him have it for the moment. Instead, he found the knife where he'd left it. Freeing it, he began delivering overhand blows to the face and neck. A black mist envel-

oped them, and the deputy's arms went slack. He began
floating upward, spread-eagled, trailing a dark stream that
was unraveling like smoke.

Taggart reinserted the mouthpiece and got his breath
back. He felt strong, furiously alive. He took hold of the
deputy by his heavy belt and dragged him down toward the
opening in the intake. The current into the tunnel felt like
a hard, running tide.

He let go of the deputy, and the man tumbled away into
the blackness like an astronaut in weightlessness.

Rushing now, before the light was gone, Taggart swam
along the bottom to the bomb. He started the timer. Twenty
minutes. That gave him five minutes to maneuver it through
the intake and another fifteen for it to float to the place
under the volcanic craters where tons of loose ash would
crash down, closing the eleven-mile-long tunnel, perhaps
forever. Schoenfeld was sure that even the five-hundred-
pounder would end the hijacking of water from the Mono
Lake Basin, its shoreline wetlands, for years.

Taggart felt the old elation returning. It always followed
the low times, restored him, filled him with energy, told
him he could do anything. He felt like crying with happi-
ness.

He turned the valve on the flotation device inflater and
the orange balloon began to fill again. He wanted just
enough buoyancy to float the bomb through the grate opening without anything showing near the surface.

But then, once again, a flashlight beam came dimly down
through the water from the catwalk.

"Repeat your traffic, BLM?" the dispatcher requested.

Dee was so sickened she couldn't speak for the moment, yet she continued inching along the blood-spattered
catwalk toward the pistol and the black metal flashlight,
which was still on. She kept her shotgun trained on the
water as she tried once more. "Control," she transmitted
over her handset, her voice low, "eleven-ninety-nine . . .
deputy down . . ."

"Condition?"

"Unknown. Stabbed . . . he's in the lake." Dee still
couldn't believe how swiftly it had happened, the sharklike

lunge by the figure in the wet suit. The deputy, a large man, being effortlessly snatched into the water. She'd been able to take no more than a few strides toward the intake before it was over.

She now picked up the light and shone it below.

Nothing. A green murk now that the twilight was spent. No sign of the deputy. A stream of bubbles was breaking the surface, but it wasn't coming in pulses, like a diver breathing.

She was frighted, her knees felt weak, and she was fighting for air, but something—remembering Sid, maybe— made her shout, "You're mine, Taggart!"

Far off, sirens were coming. That made her feel a little better. Help was only minutes away.

But what was this?

Something bulbous was slowly working its way up from the depths. It was orange-colored. She brought the stock of the shotgun up to her cheek, blinked in confusion—until she recalled the orange scraps of nylon. The flotation device and bomb, coming up off the bottom. Just as the others had before slipping into the intakes at Charley's Butte and Haiwee.

The trigger slid back under the pressure of her right forefinger.

But then she eased off.

She had no idea if the double-aught buckshot could set off the bomb. Lowering the shotgun, she aimed the flashlight, which she'd been clasping to the forestock, around the sides of the approaching bomb. She could see nothing of Taggart.

"Hurry those backs, Control," she said, activating her lapel microphone with her chin, "I've got an explosive device."

"Copy . . . will advise ATF."

Then, putting down the flashlight, Dee climbed over the railing and balanced herself on the outer lip of the catwalk. The bomb was almost to the intake. She could plainly see the ballon about two feet beneath the surface. Once it's past you, she told herself, it's gone for good. But for how long was the timer set? She reassured herself by remembering that the two previous floaters had been set to blow after hours had elapsed.

She put her shotgun on safety.

Grasping the top rail with her left hand, she leaned over and dipped the gun, butt first, into the water. The balloon plowed into it, the fabric denting as if it were underinflated. The heavy bomb pushed against her, but she'd stopped it for the moment.

Red and blue lights appeared in the corner of her eye.

The first backup had arrived, a CHP cruiser.

She shifted the shotgun as the current tried to push the device to one side. Then something pale darted up around the bomb and seized the stock, jerked it. She let go of the gun as soon as she could react, but it was too late.

She was falling.

The water was deep and cold. As her plunge bottomed out she felt two things at once—the current moving her and a hand wrapping like a vise around her ankle. She kicked, losing her boot, and the hand shifted, gathering a fistful of her trouser leg. She tried to reach for her revolver, but Taggart pinioned her arms. She kneed him, striking him in the head, for she heard his faceplate crack. They came up a few yards apart, she spluttering and he growling as if he'd been cut. The balloon rubbed against her back.

She was astonished to see that they and the bomb were fifty feet inside the intake, being swallowed by the frigid darkness. They had about two feet of headspace. Her ears popped, and she realized that something just downstream was thundering. Taggart must have heard it too, for like her, he began swimming the crawl upstream, frantically, toward the dim half-moon of light at the opening. Without flippers, she soon fell behind. Yet, she saw that he too was losing the struggle. The light was getting smaller.

Taggart gave up with a howling laugh.

Calmly now, for she knew that she must ready herself, she unholstered her revolver and jammed it as best she could down a front trouser pocket. Next, she shed her last boot, then unbuckled her Sam Browne belt, let it sink. Finally, sculling around with her cupped hands, she faced the cascade.

The darkness was now total.

It felt like a road dip. Oddly, she recalled one from her girlhood. Cinch Holland, her first love, would speed up his old pickup for the sharp rise and then the belly-tingling plummet. Floating and falling. The same sensations, except now she was hammered by frothing water against a wall. The pipeline had just angled and then dropped several feet into the tunnel.

She felt for her revolver. Gone.

The current smoothed out but was no less driving. Reaching all around, she made sure Taggart wasn't close by, then tested first one side of the tunnel and then the other. Slick cement. No handholds of any sort.

She was shivering violently. Her legs were cramping.

Steeling herself, she let all the air out of her lungs and went under until her toes touched bottom. The water was running about eight feet deep. She surfaced, gasped for breath, then made sure once again that Taggart was nowhere near.

Scissor-kicking, she reared up and brushed the ceiling with her fingertips. Again. Something tubular was up here. A small-diameter pipe of some sort. She realized that her splash was still echoing in the underground calm.

"Give it up, bitch," Taggart said with a sick glee that made her stomach turn. "May as well enjoy it. When my baby blows, this whole tunnel's gonna be like a rifle barrel." He sounded to be maybe fifty feet upstream of her. "And if that ain't bad enough—explosion carries harder in water than it does in air. We can't run and we can't hide!"

She treaded water as quietly as she could, gnashed her teeth together against the cold. The scalding feeling was subsiding, but she was becoming sluggish. She shook her head, trying to stay alert.

His words finally sank in.

She had to get to the bomb. Disarm it, somehow, and then swim ahead of Taggart. She'd seen the outlet to this tunnel. What now—nine, ten miles to the south? Nearby was a dude ranch. She imagined the lights, told herself how cheering it would be to finally see them. There'd be help there. No doubt a firearm or two. But what had Sid said about an amateur like her trying to disarm a device? *Don't, Dee. Just don't. But if you absolutely must, pull out the electrical blasting cap. If it blows, you lose some fingers, maybe your sight. If the explosive goes, you lose everything. . . .*

She began swimming forward, a quiet breaststroke.

"Didn't mean to call you a bitch," Taggart said, sounding genuinely sorry all of a sudden. "Hell, I'd have nothin' against you if you hadn't thrown in with the city. All you. That ATF guy and the poor son of a bitch deputy back there . . ." He paused as if he were waiting for her to say something. He too was swimming: she could hear his labored outbreaths. "It was you stakin' me out down there in the Cosos . . . right?"

Dee rolled over onto her back. Still kicking under the surface, she unzipped her trousers, wriggled out of them. Too heavy. Her shirt was too, but she wanted the slight warmth she believed it trapped. Something slithered out her right sleeve: her sutures bandage.

"You okay?" Taggart asked. "You still with me?"

Suddenly, a string of small globes blinked like fireflies along the ceiling the entire length of the tunnel before going out again. Two seconds later, the lights came fully on, a bulb in a wire cage every fifty feet for as far as Dee could see in both directions. It'd been an electrical conduit she'd felt with her fingers. The bomb was floating about a hundred feet ahead.

And Taggart was swimming forty feet behind, his wet beard glistening, his eyes blazing. "Wait!" he ordered.

Dee swam overhand for the bomb as fast as she could. She could hear him bellowing something, but she didn't stop and turn until her hands were clinging to the balloon. He'd delayed long enough to draw his knife. She could see it flashing in his fist as he porpoised toward her, using his fins and free hand. He'd shucked off his tanks.

She hurried around to the front of the balloon—and, looking downward, cried out in shock before thrashing several feel ahead of the device.

The deputy's corpse was being pushed along, wedged between the underside of the flotation device and the top of the bomb. His blank eyes were open, distended, and she could see grisly knife wounds to his neck and throat.

From upstream, Taggart was closing on her.

She forced herself to pat the deputy's pants pockets. She was hoping to find a hideaway, a small automatic many cops carried hidden as a backup. Nothing but keys. She ripped open a round leather case on the deputy's belt, took out the handcuffs, and hurled them at Taggart.

He stopped long enough to figure out what she'd thrown at him before shaking his head. The cut from where she'd broken his faceplate was bleeding. "Don't do that," he said contemptuously.

And then she sprayed him with Mace. She'd slipped the canister from the deputy's belt while Taggart flinched at the splash of the handcuffs. The stream of tear gas dribbled in an arc into his eyes, but he quickly dunked them underwater and came up again grinning.

Then Dee found the deputy's Buck knife. She slid it from the case, unfolded the blade. Deliberately, so Taggart saw every motion.

"You wouldn't even if you knew how," he said, inching closer alongside the balloon.

"I grew up around sheep," she said, her voice seething with fear and anger. "Must've nutted a thousand lambs. Don't see how you'd be much different, Taggart."

He snorted but then sobered and advanced no farther.

Dee dislodged the corpse and gave it a shove so she could ride the nose of the bomb. Her legs were now so tight and heavy she could barely keep kicking. The body, limbs outstretched, drifted back. As it began to pass him by, Taggart glanced at it dispassionately, then sank his knife into its back. He wrenched the blade in a grinding circle, tearing muscle and gristle. The sound echoed horribly off the ceiling. He roared with laughter at the look on Dee's face. "That's right, lover," he bawled, jerking the knife out, dousing it clean. "I'm in it now!"

The corpse fell behind.

She lowered her forehead against the balloon for an instant. Taggart's reach was at least a foot longer than hers. She could never hope to win a knife fight with him.

The timer.

As if reading her thoughts, Taggart, with a theatrical flick of his wrist, read his watch. " 'Bout seven minutes." His look softened to a scowl. "You're beat, ain't you? You're acceptin' it. Well, so'm I. Truth is, I've had enough.''

"Of what?" she stalled, thinking.

"The city. DWP. You can't beat 'em. You can't beat millions and millions of people. . . . ''

Dee nudged the balloon up slightly, furtively peered under it. She could see two wires, one black and one red, strung from Taggart's end of the bomb to the nose, where they entered a quarter-inch-wide hole.

"Truth is, I'm a goddamn fool." His tone, mercurial, had turned desolate.

"How?"

"Oh, I reckoned everybody in the valley would rise up and join me. But they din't. They din't give a shit. They want L.A. out as long as somebody else does it." Dee had just grabbed the wires when he growled, "Don't even think of it."

She held his gaze, tried to guess which way his mood would swing next.

"I got where you can't tamper with this one," Taggart went on, smiling proudly now. "One little jar, and you've blown the timetable by six minutes. You in such a god-awful hurry to die?"

She let go of the wires. She saw no reason for him to have added antihandling mechanisms to this device. It'd been designed to go directly underground with little chance of anybody discovering it prior to going off.

Yet, he'd murdered Sid with such a trigger.

He started toward her once again, but instead of brandishing the Buck knife she said, "Was this all for your sister?"

He halted, eyes turning thoughtful, pained. Hanging on to one of the bomb fins, he eased down into the water until the surface poured over his bottom teeth. Then, rising up again, he spat and said, "For everybody. Big places can't just keep rippin' off little places. And that is the thing what's so hard to get across. . . . ''

"What d'you mean?"

Taggart was gazing up at the lights as they slipped past. "I . . ." He paused, then finally looked at her again. "I really din't want to kill that G-man. But he was breathin' down my neck. So was that poor deputy. See, they din't try to understand what I was out to do. They din't care, for chrissake.''

''What are you out do?''

''Save my country,'' he said emphatically.

''America?''

''No, no, no—the Owens Valley's my *country*, not the U.S. of A. I served that other country. Six years. And know what it done to repay me? Stuck me in the brig. And if that rat hole wasn't shitty enough, they finished it off by plunkin' me in the looney bin.''

''They say what for?''

''Bipolar disorder,'' he said derisively.

Manic-depressive was the old term, Dee realized. No doubt, his mood was cresting right now, the top of the cycle in which he believed himself capable of anything. The more impossible the better. Still, she felt she had to try something before she turned her attention back to the bomb. ''Surrender, Taggart. Help me defuse it and let's both live through this.''

She thought he was wavering when he said with an infuriatingly reasonable tone, ''Can't do that. Thanks for askin', but I just can't. There's law at both ends of this tunnel by now. They've switched on the lights and have probably shut off the flow by now. They want me bad. I killed one of their own, and I know how that feels. God, don't I?'' He was staring inquisitively at her. ''What are you? Italian or somethin'?''

She stole a glance at her wristwatch. Three minutes, twenty seconds. Approximately. ''Basque.''

Chuckling, Taggart rolled his eyes. ''Shit, I'm in for it now. I crossed a goddamn Basquo.''

Dee peered down the tunnel. It seemed to go endlessly, the lights merging at a distance into a single yellow line. The view gave her a moment of vertigo, as if the tunnel were a bottomless well she was falling down. Ordnance. Her arms and legs were in gooseflesh. She knew nothing about it. Did the wires lead to or from the timer?

''What brought you all to the dam?'' Taggart asked.

That made her stop counting the seconds. The Chevy van had been left for him below Mazourka Canyon. The call this evening to the sheriff's office had come anonymously. "Tip-off."

"What?"

"Somebody called in. Didn't leave his name. Said you were at the intake with a bomb."

"Me . . . by *name*?"

"You're Jace Taggart, aren't you?"

He looked bewildered. "You sure of that?" But then he caught her trying to look up the wires toward where she thought the timer to be. "Oh, for chrissake," he fumed, elbowing the balloon aside, "you wanna see the fuckin' thing?" It was taped to a kind of bracket on top of the five-hundred-pounder. He leaned across the bomb casing to read the dial, using the tip of his knife as a pointer. "Fifty-four seconds, all right? What'd this bastard sound like?"

"Don't know . . ." Inwardly, she was counting. *Forty-nine, forty-eight* . . . "I didn't take the call. Dispatch center did."

Then Taggart slapped the water with a hand and said, "Oh, fuck it. Fuck it all. I don't give a damn. Be my friend," he implored. "Don't give a damn too. Let's go out together not givin' a goddamn for nothin'."

Finally, she could stand waiting no more. She tugged on the wires, squinting, bracing. A blasting cap popped out of the hole and dangled loose.

"Don't do that!" Taggart shouted, lunging at her.

She pushed off from the nose of the bomb with both legs, still clutching the wires with one hand and fending him off with the knife in the other. *Nineteen . . . eighteen* . . . The timer broke free of its tape binding, and Taggart grabbed it, yanked with all his might, drawing the six-foot length of wires tight. Dee let go of her end, and there was a glint in the air between them as the aluminum detonator snapped back at him. Like a bola, the wires flew around his neck. He groped for the cap, but then tried to do something to the timer.

A sound like a firecracker stopped him.

Dee had shielded her eyes with her forearms. She now lowered them and waited for Taggart to come at her again.

He was clasping the flat of his hand to the left side of his neck, pressing. Yet, bright red arterial blood oozed through his fingers and down his wrist. His eyes were dimming. In seconds, he'd lost his color. *"Damn you . . ."* Her heart stopped as he thrust his knife toward her in a useless gesture of vengeance. But he seemed to realize that he couldn't swim toward her with his knife and still keep pressure on his blown carotid artery.

"Just as well," he murmured, "just as well." Then he gave a sickly, hopeless grin as his head began lowering into the water. "Fuck me."

Dee was still treading water well ahead of him. "Who left the van off for you, Jace?"

His face was half submerged. A single eye glared back at her. Then it closed. His face went under, and his hand floated away from his throat. Blood continued to flow for a few seconds, curling darkly in the water, then stopped. Like the deputy's, his body lost speed and fell behind the bomb.

She thought to jab her knife into the balloon and sink it, just in case Taggart had rigged another way for it to go off. But she was too weak to swim ahead on her own.

She went back to the nose and hung on, crying soundlessly. Nothing in her felt like crying, but out it came as she shuddered and clung to the bomb. She had no feeling left in her fingers. Her legs refused to kick any longer, and she hung limply on to the cold steel.

Fifteen minutes later, maybe longer, she could see the outlet of the tunnel. A strong light was being aimed up it.

"Coming out!" she shouted.

"Ranger Laguerre . . . ?" a voice boomed over a P.A.

"Yeah, code four!" No assistance needed. "Coming out!"

"You all right?"

CHAPTER**EIGHTEEN**

Dee asked Howard Rowe for the window seat. Drowsy-eyed, he gladly surrendered it. Below, the Oregon Cascades were inching past, a series of white-capped volcanic cones jutting northward from the sage-covered Columbia Plateau. She could pick out Klamath Lake, then cobalt-blue Crater Lake, but after two vodka collinses she was more in the mood to cloud watch. The flight from Reno to Seattle-Tacoma International Airport was skimming through tufts of cumuli, a foglike grayness pressing against the window one moment, brilliant high-altitude sunshine the next.

Rowe eventually dropped off, and his head sank onto Dee's shoulder.

He'd said nothing when Dee demanded late last night to go along with him to Washington State. She argued that she was the sole federal officer who'd been on the case since the first bombing. Her own supervisor backed her going, if only because the national director had finally realized that, whether he liked it or not, his agency was in the middle of a case making headlines every few days. And then came some unexpected support: Foley told Rowe that he trusted Dee to uphold Waucoba County's interests in Bremerton. Without costing the county a dime, she realized. But, in fairness, one of his people had been murdered—and the sheriff wanted anybody even remotely involved.

Puget Sound Naval Base.

Shipping labels on two crates found in the Chevy van had been addressed to the facility near Bremerton, Washington. One crate contained flotation devices, the other timers. N.C.I.S. was already working on the theft, but Rowe wanted to hurry them along. The purpose wasn't so much to retrace Taggart's tracks as it was to locate his accomplice. Dee's information that the van had been left for him below Mazourka Canyon had been enough to convince Rowe that Taggart hadn't acted alone. In fact, he'd already decided that the logistics of the bombings precluded a solo effort, and there was the possibility that the accomplice had stolen the balloons and timers, or had at least gone with Taggart to the Northwest.

The male flight attendant—blond, crisply handsome, but with a slight lisp—whispered so as not to awaken Rowe, "Another?"

Dee nodded. "Thanks." Then her gaze drifted out the window again. She'd killed somebody in the line of duty once more. Second time within twelve months. Not a bureau record, but it certainly put her in contention. She felt nothing but a pulpy hollowness at hour fifteen since emerging from the tunnel. She nurtured the feeling, protected it with regular doses of vodka. She'd feel too much in time, judging from the last experience. But that would have to wait until Taggart's partner was in custody.

She owed Sid that much.

Rowe stirred, yawned, then realized with an embarrassed smile that he was camped on Dee's shoulder.

"It's all right," she said. "But I told the attendant to cut you off."

He sat up, glanced past her. "See the Columbia yet?"

She shook her head, took another sip of vodka.

He studied her a moment, tried to pass off the examination with another smile, but then asked, "You gonna talk to somebody professional 'bout last night?"

"I will."

"Sooner the better, Dee."

"You think I need a confessor?"

He laid his hand over hers. "I think you did it bang-up."

That's what everybody seemed to believe, except Dee herself. But she knew now that this sort of thing never felt clean. So she turned a partially deaf ear on both the praise and her own inward voice of doubt that she'd had to kill Taggart.

DWP and the city, of course, were ecstatic. Not only had the blaster been stopped, there'd be no trial to publicize the vulnerability of the aqueduct system. Garrett, although beset by his own alligators, had positively gushed with relief and pride over the phone early this morning to her: "How'd you do it, love? How could anyone have done it?" The locals, according to Louie Aguirre, were in tacit agreement with what she'd done, if only because Taggart had killed a deputy.

"That anonymous call . . ." Rowe said, musing out loud.

"Yes?" Dee sat up. This was what she needed. Her mind back working, not playing emotional bumper pool.

"You'd think somebody in the county woulda recognized it."

"I know," Dee said. Recorded by the dispatch center, it had been replayed at the briefings of every agency in the area. No one was familiar with the middle-aged male voice, although the caller had apparently made no attempt to disguise it.

Rowe asked, "Could anybody on or around the lake have spotted Taggart underwater?"

"I don't see how. I wasn't aware till he . . ." Again, the brutal swiftness came back to her. ". . . he took down the deputy."

"What about the light from his cutting torch?"

"I drove by the dam when he had to be using it to open the grate. Didn't see a thing." She could almost read Rowe's mind. Doubtlessly, he was suspecting what she herself had from the beginning: Taggart's sidekick—or one of them, if several were involved—had turned on him. But why steal a vehicle for him and then, a few days later, drop the dime on him? The van had been stolen, and rather cleverly too. It belonged to an army private in Korea for another six months. His home was in Trona, a small mining town near Ridgecrest, and the van had been stored in an old mill on a remote claim. Had Taggart not been found, the theft would still be unreported. "What d'you think, Howard?"

He just smiled. An ingrained FBI trait: cards close to the vest, always. "I think we gotta find that caller."

"What about evidence from the van?" she asked. An FBI technical support team had torn it apart, dusted every surface for latent fingerprints, blotted the upholstery and carpets with adhesive tape for hairs and fibers. "Any prints?"

"The owner's and Taggart's, of course. One interestin' fresh partial . . ." Meaning not enough friction ridge pattern to readily identify the person, if he or she had prints on file. "But no match from the computer yet." Rowe leaned out into the aisle for a check on the progress of the lunch cart.

Dee still wasn't hungry.

Rowe suddenly asked, "What was the hair color on that gal Taggart was seen with down along the aqueduct?"

"Dark brown. Why?"

"The boys found a long reddish-blond hair in the van. Must belong to a friend of our army private's."

The attendant knelt beside Dee, smiled gorgeously. "Ms. Dominica Laguerre . . . ?"

"Yes."

"Pretty name. Call for you on the Sky Phone."

"Ring right back on my cellular, if you want," Rowe said as she got up.

"And break it like I did your starscope?" She went forward, grabbing the back of a seat at one point to keep her balance. *Slow down on the Smirnoff's.* She picked up the receiver. "Hello?"

"You won't believe this," a giddy voice said.

She failed to recognize it for a split second. "Garrett?"

"You honestly will not believe this."

Then she remembered. It was Monday. His showdown with the city council. "What happened?"

"The impossible. The fantastic. Damn, but I love you—"

"Slow down." Curiously, she didn't feel like hearing that.

"I went in a whipping boy and came out the heir apparent. I'm acting director, Dee. They handed me the whole ball of wax. Temporarily, at least. Finally, they're listening to new ideas. They realize they must. My dear God, I'm scared to death. But happy. Out-of-my-mind happy. And I

do love you, dammit. I've got my shot at the brass ring,
Dee. A long shot, but it's mine.''

"Congratulations.'' She realized the instant after she said
it that her voice was flat.

"Is that all?'' He sounded stung.

Turning, she saw that all the passengers in the front row
of the cabin were eavesdropping. "No, Garrett, I'm as
pleased as you are. I want to hear all about it as soon as
we get together again. . . . '' At the very least, she was baf-
fled over how he'd managed to turn what had sounded like
a certain bloodbath into a coup d'état. She bit her lip a
second, then tested him, despite herself. "When will that
be?''

"Shortly, love. I promise. Things will be rather hectic at
the outset. But I'll see my way clear to drive up in a week
or two. We've got to talk. About you. Your future. You
can't stay where you are. I know it's exciting stuff, but you
just can't. I absolutely need your help from now on. But
we can talk this over when I see you. No more than a
fortnight, promise.''

"All right.''

"I love you, Dee.''

"Good-bye, Garrett.''

The Bremerton car ferry pulled back into its Seattle slip
at eight o'clock that evening. Dee slumped wearily in the
backseat, listening to the murmur of the boat's diesels and
a light rain falling on the government sedan's roof. Rowe
was dozing openmouthed in the passenger bucket seat. Behind the wheel sat a special agent from the local FBI office.
When Rowe had mentioned on the plane that their contact
would be Indian, she'd visualized a Yakima or a Nez Perce.
But Randas Shetty was originally from Bangalore, India,
and found Columbus's mistaken identification of Native
Americans a tiresome nuisance. "I refuse to call myself an
Asian Indian American,'' he'd explained, driving away
from the airport. "I'm quite simply an Indian American.
That's the truth of it. But as soon as I put it that way, I'm
asked to show my war bonnet and arrows.'' Other than that
sensitivity, Randas was a genial man in his early forties

with warm eyes and a suit that grew more rumpled the longer the day went on.

Turning now, he smiled back at Dee and said quietly, "I'm sorry you came all this way for so little."

Dee shrugged. "Not your fault, Randas."

"No, but still a shame."

N.C.I.S. had made little progress on its investigation into the theft of the flotation devices and balloons. Rowe and Dee were given a thick sheaf of transcripts of interviews with more than fifty warehousemen at Puget Sound. None claimed to have known Jace Taggart. The submarine base there had been his home port in the mid-1980s, and while that would explain his familiarity with the various storage facilities the N.C.I.S. agent didn't believe that Taggart had breached base security and burglarized a warehouse. They suspected inside collusion and were still working that angle.

Either way, Dee sniffed futility. They were looking for Taggart's accomplice, not evidence to prosecute a dead man.

"Here we go," Shetty now said, driving through the open bow of the moored ferry into Seattle's waterfront district. The wet streets glistened blackly under a now-steady, drenching rain.

"Oh, my." Rowe awoke, stretched, big-eyed. "Long day."

"Indeed," Shetty said. "Let me just drop by the office and see if any of those returns have come in. Then it's straight to the motel with both of you."

Five minutes later, he parked outside the federal building, unfurled his umbrella, and ran inside.

"Any ideas?" Rowe asked.

Her mind was a muddle. "Maybe in the morning."

"You bet."

"Howard . . . ?"

"Uh-huh?"

"Did Sid have any friends in Bakersfield?"

"Me. He had me, my wife. We had him over at least once a month. And all the high holidays. Like Super Bowl Sunday."

She smiled. "Thanks."

Shetty came down the steps much faster than he'd ascended them. He'd forgotten his umbrella inside. He got in and switched on the dome light. "Perhaps all is not lost, my friends." A rain-speckled sheet of fax paper was passed to Rowe, who held it up to the light. "This just came in from our Portland office."

Rowe slowly smiled. "Taggart got himself a traffic ticket that went to warrant in Hood River County, Oregon."

An Oregon state trooper had written the citation eighteen months before. He was on duty the next morning, so Dee and Rowe, after catching a four o'clock flight to Portland and picking up a rental car, met him at a coffee shop overlooking Bonneville Dam. Three dams, really, anchored around two islands midstream. Any of the channels made the flow of the Owens River a pittance in comparison, she realized. The trooper's name was Norwood. He had a crew cut and bore himself like a West Point cadet. He began by apologizing why he didn't recall much about the traffic stop. He'd scratched out over a thousand cites since that night in February a year and a half ago, and Interstate 84—his portion of it that ran fifty miles along the south shore of the Columbia—was "a sewer for every piece of shit trying to flush himself out of the Northwest."

Dee lowered a fork full of runny egg that had almost reached her mouth.

Rowe tried to put Norwood at ease. "That's all right, son. You'd be a mental case if you could recall everythin' that precisely. . . . " He then went over a copy of the citation with the trooper. Taggart had been doing excessive speed in a 1988 Oldsmobile, maroon in color. No license plates, but a sticker in the windshield from California DMV, a temporary transfer slip, with a lengthy number the trooper had copied down. Apparently wrongly. Rowe had telephoned the night shift in Sacramento, which informed him that it was an incomplete number. He asked them if they might "fiddle with the digits a tad," but the supervisor said that they'd just started a twenty-four-hour-long downloading of data and didn't care to fiddle with anything. It'd be difficult enough to deal with ordinary information requests, let alone fishing expeditions. Disgusted, Rowe hung up, vowing to call the Sacramento office of the FBI in the

morning to send an agent over to shake things up at DMV.
"Now, son," he went on to Trooper Norwood, "you note
here that there was one passenger."

"If I marked it, it's true."

"Male or female?"

Pause. "Uh, male . . . no, disregard that. I'm seeing long
hair. Jesus, I don't know."

Dee wondered if her own disappointment was as evident
as Rowe's. The voice calling Foley's dispatch center the
other night had been male.

"That's fine," Rowe said. "Did you have a feelin' the
Olds was stolen?"

"No."

"But you didn't copy down the vehicle registration information, right? Or match it to Taggart, confirmin' him
the owner?"

"Those California forms are like Greek to me. I let it go
with the number on what I took to be a transfer slip of
some kind."

"Is there a possibility the passenger was the owner?"

Norwood shrugged, took a slug of coffee. But then his
eyes widened. "You know, I remember the driver saying
something like, 'First time I get behind the wheel the whole
fucking trip, and look what happens.' "

Rowe took a three-by-five color photograph from his inner jacket pocket. Taggart on the cooling table at the mor-
tuary in Bishop. The sheet had been pulled up to conceal
the blasting cap wound on the side of his neck.

Norwood smirked. "I take it his pedal-to-the-metal days
are over."

"Is that your driver?"

The trooper frowned. "I remember the beard, but other
than that . . . just another raggedy-ass mope ripping down
the interstate. I see two guys a week who could be his twin
brother." Rowe had reached across the table to retrieve the
photo, but Norwood continued to clasp it, scrutinizing.
"But you know, there's something about this face . . ."

"Oh?"

"Yeah, I'm not sure what."

Dee pressed, "You mean something other than your traffic stop?"

"Right." Norwood gave back the photo, then reached for his campaign hat. "You shown this to Hood River S.O.?"

Rowe said, "No."

"Might be worth a shot. Sorry, but I got to ride."

"Ride," Rowe said, "and thanks."

Alone, Dee and Rowe ate in silence for a few minutes, then Rowe slipped his cellular from his jacket pocket and grumbled, "Let me phone Sacramento and see if they can hustle an agent over to that goddamn DMV."

The homicide detective at sheriff's headquarters in the county seat of Hood River leaned back in his swivel chair and tapped the photograph against his lower lip. Through the window, Dee could see the rain-flattened waters of Lake Bonneville being split into a V by the wake of an ocean-going freighter that had come up the lock.

Rowe wore a tired, impatient look as he waited for the detective to say something. Anything. Finally, he could no longer keep quiet. "Ding any bells on anythin' you're workin'?"

"No," the man said, but then he stood and turned for an oak filing cabinet behind his desk. He took out a thick folder and, sitting again, opened it atop his blotter and began leafing through what Dee realized to be law enforcement bulletins, many of them yellow with age.

He licked his right forefinger with infuriating thoroughness between each page.

Rowe and she had hoped to be back in Portland by late afternoon, then possibly catch an evening flight to Sacramento. They now agreed that their best chance of identifying Taggart's accomplice lay with California DMV. Rowe had phoned FBI Sacramento twice now, and was promised both times that an agent would be sent to hurry the search as soon as possible, but he'd been given the impression that his request had a low priority.

"Here," the detective finally said, scooting a copy of a composite sketch across the desk. "Wanted for questioning. One of two suspects. No details on the other. Homicide, February before last. What d'you think?"

Dee and Rowe inclined their heads over it for several moments, then exchanged a quick, satisfied glance. "Whose case?" Rowe asked the detective.

"Wasco County, just to the east of us."

Dee and Rowe had dinner that night with a few severe
friends, then coffee and a nightcap. Several drinks
Rowe said. "Rowe said. Dee said." Rowe

CHAPTER**NINETEEN**

The rain had stopped, but the eastern slope of the Cascades
was shrouded in low overcast. The late afternoon light was
being strangely deflected by the cloud cover, so that it almost seemed like morning. Or no recognizable time of day.
Stepping out of the rented car with Rowe, Dee decided that
the moment felt timeless. The investigator from Wasco
County, who'd led them down into the Tygh Valley at seventy miles an hour, got out of his unmarked Ford and tried
the gate. It barred entry to a farmhouse visible across several hundred yards of weedy pasture.

"Locked—dammit," he said, turning to Dee and Rowe.
His name was Cole Leach. He was a string bean of a young
man, no more than twenty-five, with lank red hair and a
staid manner. His briefing at his office in The Dalles about
the one-and-a-half-year-old homicide had been thorough,
although questions of clarification turned him defensive
now and again.

"That's all right, son," Rowe said as he and Dee ambled
over to the gate. "We can use the exercise."

The three of them climbed over the pipe gate. As Leach
landed, a strand of hair fell across his eyes, making him
look even younger than he was.

Rowe asked, "How long did the pathologist figure the
victim's body was in Lake Bonneville?"

"Several months by the time it showed up in the lock."

They started walking up the drive, which was already
returning to meadow. Dee noted that, in the rain shadow
of Mount Hood, she was back in sagebrush country.

Washed by the two-day summer storm, it cloaked the surrounding hills with a silvery green that seemed too vivid to be real. Much of the property was marshland. Black dots, coots, could be seen gliding among the reeds choking a long string of ponds.

"Afraid I couldn't get the key to the house from the new owners," Leach went on. "But you can peek in the windows."

Dee asked, "Who are the new owners?"

"Audubon Society, I think."

"*The* Audubon Society?"

Leach's eyes turned evasive. She wanted to tell him to relax: despite his callow age, he was one of the more competent and obliging rural detectives she'd encountered. But she didn't know how to do this without pricking his already sensitive dignity. "I'm really not sure," he finally admitted. "Some nature outfit like that. They bought it on account of the ponds and all. Not the house. I hear they're just gonna tear the old place down. It's a big property. Stretches in a one-mile strip all the way from the White River to Wapinita Creek."

"How far's that?" Dee asked.

"Oh . . . ten miles, maybe."

"You mind confirming the ownership for us?"

"No, ma'am," Leach said. "I'll get back to you by Friday on it."

She'd already given him her card. He'd come through, she believed. He hadn't balked when Rowe asked to interview the postal carrier who, on a rainy morning two Februarys ago, had seen a darkly bearded man in a maroon sedan parked against the traffic along the road near the farmhouse. Yes, there had been another person in the car, the driver on this morning, but the postman's view of him had been blocked by Taggart, who he swore was the passenger as soon as he saw the photograph. One detail provided by the witness had no doubt sidetracked Wasco County's investigation: the postman recalled the vehicle as being a Buick, not an Oldsmobile. He hadn't noticed the plates or the absence of them.

"Home sweet home," Leach tried to quip as they went up the front steps.

Suddenly, Dee wanted to go back to the car.

Everything about this—the surreal light, the heavy atmosphere and dripping willow trees—was coming too closely on the heels of the other night.

Yet, she joined Leach and Rowe at the kitchen windows and shielded the sides of her face with her hands to block out the sulfurous glare. The sun was starting to break through the clouds. A somber kitchen. Appliances from the fifties. Old linoleum. Almost beyond a reasonable doubt, Jace Taggart had beaten an elderly man to death here. But why? What purpose had been served by that? Nothing had been taken, according to Leach. Nothing of real value had been here, except the land—and how could Taggart have hoped to gain that by killing the owner?

Dee and Rowe had already surmised that Taggart had been on his way home to the Owens Valley from Bremerton when he stopped off here. But there was a problem with that too. U.S. Highway 197, which wound down through the Tygh Valley from The Dalles, was not the most direct route to the eastern slope of the Cascades and then the Sierra Nevada, virtually the same mountain range.

Taggart had come out of his way to this farmhouse. And then had driven back north to the Columbia to dump the body.

Rowe stood back from the window. "You save the victim's clothing?"

"Yes, sir," Leach said. "Sweater, pants, and underwear. No shoes and socks on him after all those months. And I cut off a lock of his hair. It's all in our evidence locker."

"Good boy."

Dee could tell that Leach didn't know how to take Rowe's patronizing compliment. Hard being an authority figure so young. "Do you have a line on the car?" the investigator asked. "The Hood River dick said something over the phone about this Taggart guy being scratched for speed by OHP the day prior to our homicide."

For a few moments, Dee thought Rowe was going to play the same old FBI game. Suck local law enforcement dry. Share nothing. But then he said, "Our office in Sacramento is workin' on it. I'll let you know if we locate the Oldsmobile."

"Not a Buick?"

"No. Our identification folks will go over it for blood, hair, and fibers. Particularly the trunk. So hang on to your evidence with both hands, son."

Squinting through the smoke of his companion's cigarette, Tyrus Foley smiled across the table at Mirabelle Heckard. She looked pretty, her long-lashed eyes especially. She'd batted neither of them earlier at five o'clock when Foley, having spotted her coming out of the Lone Pine DWP office, invited her to dinner in Mammoth Lakes. Mirabelle had been asked out by so many married men it no longer evoked even a moment of hesitation. She hopped into the sheriff's Dodge, and they were off to Mammoth. Foley quickly realized from her sidelong looks that her expectations for the evening were different from his own, but he did nothing to set her straight. It was fun to flirt after so many years, and he'd felt quite spry as he escorted her on his arm to a window booth at Whiskey Creek Restaurant.

"I hope all that hoopla the other evenin' at your place," Foley now said, "didn't rattle you too much."

Her pretty eyes narrowed. He'd put much the same question to her on the drive up, but she'd failed to take the bit in her mouth. This time, after two gin fizzes, she said somewhat dolefully, "I just got to stop havin' so many boyfriends." Then, God only knew why, she must have thought she'd offended Foley, for she reached out and softly grazed his jowls with the back of her hand. "But it's so nice for you to get me out of the heat." As if suddenly reminded of the temperature down the hill in the valley, she pinched her low-cut blouse between her thumbs and forefingers and lifted it off her sticky bosom, fanning herself.

It was all Foley could do to remind himself that this dinner was being paid for out of the special appropriations fund. "It's a shame Jace went the way he did," he went on. Privately, he thought that Taggart had died just fine, having killed one of his deputies.

She nodded, then gazed sadly out the window at the forest, dark with evening shadow. "I love pine trees," she whispered.

"You know, I always took a special interest in him."

Her eyes shifted back toward Foley. "Really?"

"Don't say anythin'—but I doctored his juvenile record so he could get in the navy. Wrote a letter makin' him sound like a goddamn Boy Scout."

"Oh, that was sweet."

"He was a hellion, Jace Taggart. But his heart was in the right place. His head never was, but that's a different matter. The Taggarts was always a crazy bunch, but when my family was bein' pushed into a corner by the city . . . they were always there, lendin' support, takin' up our fight as their own. I figure I owed Jace a helpin' hand if only because he was the last of the Taggarts . . . know what I mean?"

"He scared me," Mirabelle said.

Foley paused.

Taggart and Mirabelle had spent all of an afternoon together, most of it buck naked. People talked too much when they were paired off nude. Maybe they figured their souls were visible too. "He scared lots of folks. But he was dangerous only when cornered . . . like any other wild creature." He snapped his fingers for the attention of the boy waiter, the usual ski resort airhead with an Arabian tan and a cocaine grin. "Two more, hoss." Then the sheriff turned back to Mirabelle. "Honey, can I ask your honest opinion about somethin'?"

She spread her hand against her breast, flattered. "Sure."

"You figure Jace did what he done alone?"

She had to think about that. "Uh . . . no, I kinda doubt it." But she had nothing to add.

"He ever mention any friends of his?"

"Not that I recollect."

"Did he ever talk about *anybody*?"

"Like who, Tyrus?"

She gave Foley a vapid smile which somehow gave him the confidence to ask, "Like Ray Jelks . . . just on an off chance?"

"I don't remember anythin'." She frowned.

"Somethin' wrong?"

"No."

" 'Bout Ray, I mean."

Mirabelle pursed her lips a moment, probably just so she wouldn't seem too quick to criticize. "My brother says he ripped me off."

"Your brother?"

"Well, my half brother, really. He's over in Korea now. The army. But before he left, he said I coulda got that bumper beeper Ray sold me for half the price at Circuit City."

Foley stared meditatively at her a few seconds, then said, "That's right, you're originally from Trona, aren't you?"

Garrett Driscoll was on Sunset Boulevard, waiting for a red light at La Cienega, when his cellular phone rang. It was Dee's supervisor in Bakersfield, finally returning his call. The BLM man apologized for the delay in getting back. Dee was staying at the Quality Inn at the Portland Airport. He then gave the number, which Driscoll wrote on his palm. "Thanks ever so much," he said, signing off, accelerating westward again.

He took a minute before dialing. This could prove the most important call of his life. He tried to put the day's distractions behind him. What seemed a thousand telephone calls.

Punks were lining up for the trendier heavy metal clubs, Mercedes and BMWs for valet parking at a strip joint. A teenage prostitute waved at him from a bus bench. Not exactly the Tinsel Town he'd imagined from a Belfast slum.

At last, Garrett punched up the number. Two minutes later, he had her on the line. Her voice moved him. She sounded sad, exhausted.

"I'm on my knees, Dominica Laguerre."

"Why?"

"For saying the wrong thing yesterday. The stupidest possible thing. I'm not going to wait a bloody fortnight to see you. I'm going to see you as soon as you get home, and if that's not in the cards presently I'm getting on a plane for Seattle or Portland or Nome, if necessary."

"No need."

His breath caught in his throat with that. He could feel

her slipping away, and he knew that his fear would make him sound confrontational unless he was very careful. "You're on the way home then?"

"Yes, morning flight to Reno. Eleven o'clock."

He relaxed slightly. "I can meet you for dinner tomorrow night. Where does one dine in Big Pine?"

"Don't, Garrett. I'm beat. Wait for the weekend."

He paused to keep his disappointment out of his voice. The last tacky glitter of Sunset Boulevard went out like a sparkler, and the dark, sylvan neighborhoods of Beverly Hills enfolded him. He failed. "I'm dreadfully out of step, aren't I?"

"No. Let's just not rush anything."

"Of course. You couldn't be more right."

"How's the new job going?"

"Beastly, but I love it. How are things for you and Special Agent—who is it now . . . ?

"Howard Rowe. Fine. He's flying from here to Sacramento in the morning. . . . " She seemed to hesitate, but then went on, "We've got a lead on Taggart's accomplice, an Oldsmobile the two of them drove up in this part of the country eighteen months ago. No plate number, but we have some DMV documentation on it."

"Terrific. Then you're zeroed in."

"Not quite. Chipping away at it. That's why Howard's off to Sacramento in the morning. To cut through the red tape."

"Dee . . . ?"

After a moment, she asked, "Yes?"

"You're not going public with speculation about an accomplice, are you?"

"Why d'you say that, Garrett?"

"Well, we just got a lid on this. You did it, really. By doing what you did the other night. And you wouldn't believe the sense of relief that's settled over the city. Angelenos are finally reassured that there won't be any more water rationing than what they're facing now. Oh, don't get me wrong—they've woken up. They know now what they must do to survive as a metropolitan area. But they see the light at the end of the tunnel, and I hate now to tell them, on the basis of a few assumptions, that the nightmare could go on.''

"Somebody helped Taggart," she said evenly, "and I'm going to find him, Garrett."

"Are you positively sure of that?"

"Yes. And I know he's just as dangerous as Taggart was. Either he or Taggart, or both of them, beat an old man to death up in Oregon. He's mine before the week is out. I know it."

"Be careful, love," he said lightly. But then he blurted, "Let this Rowe chap take the point. You've done your bit for God and country, and I'd go out of my mind if something happened to you. Do you understand what the hell I'm saying?"

Silence.

"You're right." He sighed, then chuckled helplessly. "Mr. Driscoll is entirely out of order. It's just that he's mad in love with you and overly prone to these unreasonable outbursts. Are we still on for this weekend?"

"Yes."

"Until then, Ms. Laguerre."

"Good-bye, Garrett.

He realized that he'd missed his turnoff through the gate into Bel Air. He made the next right and wound up into the Santa Monica Mountains, toward the home he'd inherited and almost feared to show her. She'd grown up in a travel trailer. She'd freely admitted that on their Palm Springs date. Some day, he'd take her to Belfast, show her the dingy row house in which he'd spent his boyhood. Then, she might understand.

After retiring from LAPD, Royce Gilmer had bought property on Topaz Lake, a trout-rich reservoir straddling the California-Nevada border seventy miles south of Reno. He'd built a shingled cottage and a boat dock, gained forty pounds, and developed the bad habit of telephoning old buddies in the wee hours when drunk. His more acceptable habits included going fishing each morning at daybreak during the season.

His bathroom light was now shining through the four-thirty darkness.

Karl Schoenfeld waited on Gilmer's dock, dying for a smoke. To the east, the sky behind the Sweetwater Mountains was just starting to brighten. Faint swells were knocking Gilmer's boat against the pilings, lapping over the granite boulder that barely broke the surface in the shallows near the dock.

Schoenfeld was remembering the old days with Gilmer—but not with a great deal of sentimentality. They'd worked together for seven years, until the Special Intelligence Unit had been disbanded. It'd been great fun, those years, filling dossiers on entertainers, politicians, athletes. But then came the outside investigation, the media circus, and finally the Parker Center brass covering their own asses by portraying the unit as a cabal of rogue cops.

It ruined a lot of careers, that investigation.

But only Schoenfeld had had the balls to burglarize its offices. There he discovered the informant within the unit, the man of conscience who claimed he didn't "hold truck with invading people's privacy." Sergeant Royce Gilmer, who'd been allowed to take a medical retirement while everybody else was sacked. The same Sergeant Gilmer who, on the sly, had sold the juiciest portions of those dossiers to *National Enquirer* for thousands of dollars. Schoenfeld hadn't confronted Gilmer right away. It was money in the bank. He'd let a few years slide past before knocking on Gilmer's front door here at Topaz. The man had pretended to be pleased, although Schoenfeld could smell the fear on him. "Bill Schuyler," Gilmer said, using Schoenfeld's real name, "what the fuck are you doing here?" After a couple of beers, Schoenfeld told him. Gilmer paled. He stammered that he'd been forced into it. Did the other guys know? They were a rough crew, and Gilmer had good reason to be terrified of them. But Schoenfeld told him to relax. He had a new life now and there was no reason they couldn't be friends. "That's great, Bill. That's how I want it. What you doin' . . . and what's with the long hair?"

Schoenfeld told him that he was in the environment business. "I'm gonna save the goddamn planet."

"Get outta here."

"I'm serious."

"Really?"

"Yeah," Schoenfeld said with an icy glare, "and the name's not Bill Schuyler anymore. Think you can memorize a new one, or do I have to dust you?"

Suddenly, as Schoenfeld watched, the bathroom light went out.

He slipped quietly into the waist-deep water and ducked under the planking. Gilmer came out his front door with tackle box and rod in hand, then circled his eighteen-month-old Mazda Navajo. Paranoia dies hard. Satisfied that his car was all right, he tramped toward the dock, a fat little man in a Dodgers warm-up jacket. It was just light enough to read the team letters.

Glancing up and down the muddy beach one last time, Schoenfeld satisfied himself that it was deserted.

He could see the bulge under the jacket on Gilmer's hip. The snub-nosed .38 special he wore everywhere. The man would talk. He'd talked once before. Loyalty meant nothing to him. Fear worked with him, but Schoenfeld would soon lose that grip on Gilmer if pressure developed from another quarter. He would willingly tell everything he'd ever done to help the WPS. Most recently, calling the sheriff's office on his cellular phone—so the call couldn't be automatically traced—to report suspicious activity at the Grant Lake intake.

Tennis shoes drummed overhead.

Crouching in the cold water, Schoenfeld smiled.

There had been no agonizing over this decision. He'd known it would one day come to this the instant he'd opened the investigation's informant file.

As Gilmer leaned over to put his rod and box inside the boat, Schoenfeld seized him by the wrist and yanked. The man tumbled into the water. Before he could take a breath, Schoenfeld dunked him, held him under so his only thought for a few crucial seconds was to reach the air—and not for his revolver. Then Schoenfeld obliged Gilmer, lifting the smaller man by the back of his gray hair and the seat of his trousers. He gasped, then began to shriek as Schoenfeld dashed him headfirst against the boulder. Just once. Gilmer lay limp on the surface, but Schoenfeld submerged him until the stream of tiny bubbles died out. Then he let go.

Quickly now, he passed beneath the dock and waded

along the beach, his wet ponytail whipping against his back.
He kept to the water for at least a hundred yards before
running up a rocky stretch to the cover of the pinyons.
Daylight was coming on fast, so he avoided the scattered
cottages and mobile homes as he walked, not ran, toward
his car, which he'd left on a highway overlook above the
lake.

He smiled again as he climbed the last bit of slope. Nothing was going to change his world.

CHAPTER**TWENTY**

Dee stared up at the departure board in the Reno-Tahoe Airport terminal, then nearly ran to the Trans-Sierra Airlines desk. "Why's the one o'clock flight to Bishop been cancelled?"

"Something mechanical," the agent said. "But the plane oughta be ready for the four-thirty run. Want a seat aboard it?"

Dee mulled it over. No other airline ran into the Owens Valley, and the Joad family had made it from Oklahoma to California faster than the Greyhound ran from Reno to Big Pine.

"Yeah." She sighed, taking her ticket folder from her purse. She wasn't pleased to hear about mechanical problems for a reason other than the four-hour delay. Trans-Sierra's sole surviving aircraft was a World War II–vintage DC-3. Years ago, its sister ship had plowed into a peak near Bishop, scattering a movie crew over a quarter mile of mountainside. It'd been something mechanical then too.

Turning back for the lounge, she resisted dropping a few quarters into the terminal's slot machines, saving them instead for the newsstand. There were papers from all over the world, but her eyes were drawn to the *Los Angeles Times*. The headline for the feature story in the left-hand column read:

OWENS AQUEDUCT BOMBINGS
The Men and Women Behind the Badges

She was the first cop featured. *"Merde,"* she said, tossing a dollar-fifty onto the counter.

Louie Aguirre and her supervisor were the named
sources on her. No apology from the staff writer for not
having contacted Dee other than mentioning that she was
on temporary assignment somewhere in the Pacific Northwest. Praise from the national director: "Ranger Laguerre
has been the kingpin, the constant, in this violent and
chaotic investigation. I don't see how it can be brought to
a successful conclusion without her continued contributions
on the scene." Dee shrugged—that wouldn't hurt, especially after the political fallout of her Nevada tour. There
was some boilerplate about the Basque character, stamina,
and independence, all that. Then some common misinfor-
mation that Bascos had brought their sheepherding skills
from the Old World to the New. *Bullshita. They hadn't
known sheep from Shinola when they got off the boats.*
They'd been farmers, fishermen, and city dwellers in the
homeland, not graziers.

Then Dee read something that made her groan. "Damn
you, Louie."

He'd suggested that all Owens Valley Basques, including Dominica Laguerre, were in an uproar about the im-
pending execution of the two ETA men by the Spanish
government. This text appeared right under Dee's official
photograph.

Then she heard her name being paged.

She found the nearest courtesy telephone. "Laguerre."

"Dee, it's Howard..." Another cellular phone. Nobody
was safely out of touch anymore. The background noise
told her that Rowe was in a speeding car. "Listen, don't
have much time. I'm almost to Placerville..." Fifty miles
east of Sacramento, she calculated. A sleepy gold country
town. "Does the name Rogelio Escamilla mean anythin' to
you?"

She took a moment. "No."

"All right," Rowe said. "Foley drew a blank too. Our
boys in Sacramento didn't get 'round to buggin' DMV till
this mornin'. Not their fault. Had a bank hostage situation
in Folsom. Anyways, Escamilla popped up as the current

registered owner on our Oldsmobile. Lives in Placerville, so we're jumpin' on it ASAP.''

She kept running the name through her memory. But Escamilla evoked nothing. Certainly not one of several large Mexican-American clans in the Owens Valley. And Taggart had reportedly associated with virtually no one, excepting Mirabelle Heckard for one afternoon to make his travels up and down the aqueduct system seem comical to LAPD. ''Are you trying a registration history as well, Howard?'' she asked on a sudden thought. ''The car could've been sold.''

''Yes. But it's involvin' a hand-search, and I still don't have word yet from our agent who's over at DMV.'' Rowe murmured some instructions to the driver, apparently, then came back on the line. ''I just wanted to keep you up on things, Dee. You be home this evening?''

''Yes.''

''I'll give you a jingle.''

''Thanks, Howard.''

''This is it,'' Rowe said, dropping the cellular phone into the flap pocket of his jacket. ''North on Highway Forty-nine, toward Coloma.'' The driver, an obscenely young special agent, turned up the winding two-lane highway and punched the accelerator. In the last few minutes, he'd loosened his tie and collar button. Unheard of in Hoover's day. And his shirt had a pink tint. An ungodly pink tint. White—that's all a G-man wore back when ''Thompson'' meant a submachine gun instead of a water seal paint. ''Slow down now. We don't wanna go by the damn place at ninety.''

The young agent frowned. Rowe had already forgotten his name. Curry or Kerby. Something inane like that.

The sedan passed in and out of the shade thrown by blue oaks and scraggly digger pines. It was a hot, parched country—the western foothills of the Sierra—this time of year, with all the grass bleached gold by the sun. Rowe reminded himself to keep an eye out for poison oak. It was the only brush that stayed March-green over the long, rainless summer. A vile, oily green. He'd gotten a bad case of it on a wild-goose chase along the American River during the Frank Sinatra, Jr., kidnapping in the sixties.

"Silver Lord," a voice crackled over the radio. The ID technician, who was following in his van some miles behind.

"Go ahead."

"I'm at the intersection. What d'you want me to do?"

"Pull into Placerville and find some shade. Will advise when it's clear."

Rowe then said to Curry or Kerby, "Keep it steady at fifty." They went past the house. Rowe stole a quick glance, memorized the scene with it, then faced indifferently forward again. A small ranch-style dwelling with a big tin outbuilding, set at least three hundred yards back off the road in thick chaparral. He had seen the Oldsmobile. It'd been repainted a gaudy turquoise color. A valance of dingle balls in the rear window.

"Slow down, son." They'd have to drive over a dry creek ditch on a wooden bridge to approach the house by vehicle. But Rowe had already dismissed that idea. "Park behind here," he said, pointing at an abandoned service station. "We're gonna take a hike."

"There snakes around here?" Curry or Kerby asked as they got out of the car.

"Hell yes, there's snakes. Worst snake country in the world, the Mother Lode. Rattlers as thick around as your forearm ..." Rowe hiked a trouser cuff to show his shin-high Acme boots. "That's why I wear these."

They set off through the chaparral, Curry or Kerby on his tiptoes as if he expected a huge rattlesnake to lunge at him out of the dead leaves any second. Suddenly, Rowe halted and gestured for the young agent to do the same.

"What?" Curry or Kerby whispered.

"Don't you smell it?"

"That funny mediciny smell?"

"Ether," Rowe specified, then continued on, slower now, more cautiously. They came to the dry creek bed, which had angled away from the highway. Resting in the wilted ivy covering its banks were several five-gallon water bottles. He jogged down to the closest one, stiff-kneed. A brown residue coated the inside. He took a swipe with his finger, sniffed the stuff, then drew his revolver.

Wide-eyed, Curry or Kerby did the same.

Rowe motioned for him to peel off to the right. Curry or Kerby gravely nodded, and together they crested the far bank. A blast reverberated through the manzanita as soon as they'd stepped on flat ground, and Rowe had a fleeting glimpse of a Mexican male adult with a Fu Manchu mustache ducking back through the front door of the house with his shotgun.

"Goddammit," Rowe growled, sidling behind the stout trunk of a digger pine. Curry or Kerby was blasting away at the house with his handgun. "Hold your fire, *men*!" Rowe shouted.

But the young agent stopped pulling the trigger only after the second snick of his firing pin striking a spent primer. He found cover behind a rock and shrugged sheepishly at Rowe as he reloaded. "I hit anything?"

"Yeah," Rowe said low, "you blew the holy shit outta the roof." Then he shouted toward the house, "Rogelio Escamilla—this is the FBI. We've got the place surrounded. Come out with your hands up right now and you can make last call on tortillas and beans at county jail!"

No response, as expected.

Leaning his back against the tree, Rowe holstered his handgun and then reached for his cellular phone. He dialed 911 for the El Dorado County Sheriff's Office, advised them of the situation. Units were on the way. "Thanks," he wearily signed off, scratching his back against the nicely furrowed bark.

"What do we do?" Curry or Kerby whispered.

"Son, you do what you will. I'm about done with this goddamn business. It's gettin' where you can't run down a simple goddamn homicide lead without stumblin' on a goddamn methamphetamine lab."

Curry or Kerby looked sorry that he'd asked.

Dee's ears popped, and she awoke.

The Trans-Sierra DC-3 was descending over the brush-dotted volcanic tableland just north of Bishop. The sun was halfway behind the Sierra, but still blazing fiercely. Below lay Lake Crowley, at the head of the now-dry Owens Gorge, a mini–Grand Canyon.

She'd been dreaming of the farmhouse up in Oregon's

Tygh Valley, except that in the jumbled terrain of sleep
she'd confused the surrounding sagelands with those of the
Owens Valley, for an aqueduct pipeline ran behind the old
place. A ribbon of steel through the unworldly green scrub.
Detective Leach still led Rowe and her up to the kitchen
windows. She still cupped her hands around her face and
peered inside, but instead of seeing nothing but old appliances and worn linoleum she saw Sid lying on the table.

At that instant, she'd awakened.

Obeying the captain's instructions, she brought her seat
upright and checked her belt. She felt so bleak it was a
struggle not to cry. But not yet. Sid would understand.
There was still so much to do. Must rest tonight and get
on with finding Taggart's accomplice in the morning.

The jouncing fuselage seemed like a cage, a coffin. She
wanted out, badly. Her eyes took her to the ground below
again. A glinting penstock ran along the lip of the Owens
Gorge down to a DWP power station. This pipeline reminded her of the one in her dream, the steel ribbon behind
the farmhouse.

Garrett.

She suddenly realized how much she wanted to see him.
She didn't want to be alone this weekend. She wanted to
be outside somewhere with him, in strong sunlight, taking
in the lilting music of his accent.

Rowe had expected Rogelio Escamilla to bolt through
the oaks and manzanita, which would have been fine with
him. His interest was the Oldsmobile, not an illegal drug
lab. But Escamilla kept holed up inside his little house until
El Dorado SWAT showed up, and then three hours beyond
that while a hostage negotiator back at the Placerville headquarters tried to establish rapport with him. Finally, Escamilla came out the front door, hands lofted, barechested in
order to flaunt his prison tattoos, and the SWAT boys ran
up, dropped him face-first into the dust, and cuffed him.

Rowe stooped over his head. "How do, Rogelio."

"Aytch," Escamilla said while the SWAT sergeant emp-
tied the contents of his pockets.

"Pardon?" Rowe asked.

"You're fuckin' up my name. The gee is like an aytch. It's Rohelio."

"Oh, sorry, son," Rowe blithely said.

"How'd you find me, man?"

"The car."

"Car?"

"You bought your Olds from a fella named Royce Hilmer, right?"

The folds around Escamilla's eyes scrunched up. "Who?"

"Gilmer," Rowe said, chuckling to himself, "outta Lake Topaz, just over the Sierra here." During the wait for Escamilla to make up his mind to surrender, the agent at DMV in Sacramento had finally come through with the registration history.

"Yeah, big dude with a ponytail."

"You sure, son?"

"What's it matter, man? You fuckin' got me. This big *gavacho* come over the hill to a car show. Had a For Sale sign on the Olds. So what?"

Rowe mused for a few moments, then rose and stepped away from the prisoner. The ID technician had just pulled up in the van, and Rowe told him to start going through the Oldsmobile. Then he phoned the Douglas County Sheriff's Office in Nevada for the second time in the last hour. On the first call, he'd learned that Royce Gilmer, a retired LAPD dick sergeant, was dead as of dawn this morning, drowned after falling off his boat dock and bashing his head on a rock. "Yeah, Toby," he said to the same detective, "it's Rowe again. Quick question for you, son—what's the physical on Gilmer? Big man with a ponytail, by chance?"

"No way. Five-nine, two hundred, gray hair blocked at the nape."

"Appreciate it." Rowe disconnected and strolled over to the technician, who was going through the trunk first, as he'd been told. He was carefully collecting possible fibers and hairs by dabbing sticky tape over the oil-stained carpet.

Rowe checked his wriswatch. Almost six. He decided to try to catch Dee Laguerre at home. But after the fourth ring, her answering machine came on. "Dee, Howard. Forget Escamilla. He bought the car from a retired cop in Topaz

Lake. . . ." Briefly, he told her about Gilmer's death. "But I got an inklin' we're after an associate of his, big Caucasian fella with a ponytail. That mean anythin' to you? Phone only if you got somethin', otherwise I'll be in touch. Bye."

"Whoa," the technician said, grinning. Hands gloved, he'd just swabbed a portion of what Rowe had thought to be an almost invisible oil stain in the trunk carpet with orthotolidine, a chemical that turned a bluish green in contact with even minute traces of blood. Rowe could see the tattletale color change from six feet away.

"Good," he said, "we didn't waste a goddamn trip, for once."

The colony was deserted.

Wednesday evening, Dee remembered. Everyone was down at the town park for an inter-reservation baseball game. Pulling up alongside her bungalow, she sat a few moments longer behind the wheel of Fetterman's truck, engine idling. She was tempted to drive to the game, lie in the cool grass, and enjoy Tillie's quiet company. But, tired and grimy after the day's travels, she finally turned off the engine and trooped through her door.

The interior was hot and stuffy after being shut up for three days. She'd take a long bath and then lug her mattress out onto the grinding rock. Hear the wind in the big cotton-wood tree all night, let it carry off all the ugliness trapped inside her head.

On the way to the small walk-in closet, she glanced at her answering machine light.

Unblinking. No messages.

Opening the closet door, she reached up into the darkness for the pull string, groped blindly a moment before finding it. The light came on with a click. She laid her suitcase on the floor, unzipped it, began shaking out and hanging up her badly wrinkled clothing. She thought about buying something new at Penney's in Bishop for the weekend. A cotton dress, maybe.

She carried the suitcase to her bed, culled her unused underwear from the used and put them in the top dresser along with her revolver. Always a hassle to get the damned thing aboard a plane.

"Hot," she groused, then went to the window. She threw back the curtains and tried to raise the sash window. But it was stuck. Last week's rain. She cracked the front door a few inches for some draft, then went into the bathroom and began running the taps on the old claw-footed tub that Louie swore had come out of a whorehouse in Mina, Nevada. It made her smile to think of the girls lounging in it.

She examined her face in the mirror. Her bruise was quickly fading. Thank God. Behind her, she could see the front door creep back, opening wider. A moment later, a soft breeze came to her, wrapped around her sweaty skin like drifting snow. Dropping her clothes to the floor, she stepped into the tub and slid down. Too warm. She flipped off the hot tap with her big toe, then let the quiet thunder of cold water lull her toward drowsiness, the coolness inching up her legs, past her thighs.

Garrett.

Be careful, she reminded herself, soaping her neck and shoulders. She didn't quite trust her wanting to see him again—after she'd resolved to let things die between them. Yet, he'd phoned last night to admit that he'd been wrong about his focus, something Tyler, her ex, had never done until it was too late.

She heard the door latch.

Rising up on her arms, twisting around slightly, she saw that the door had been blown shut. The breeze had been nice, but she was too comfortable to get out and reopen the door. She eased down again, thought about supper. Her appetite was returning. But there was nothing in her tiny refrigerator except some collins mix and a head of celery that, at last inspection, looked like it'd come out of Tutankhamen's tomb.

She sat up with a jerk.

She smelled propane. The gas was heavier than air, so she reached with a soapy hand down along the floor and wafted a puff up into her face. Definitely propane. "Damn." She was grasping the sides of the tub to get up when something whipped around her neck. Her hands flew to the thick bristly thing just as it tightened and jolted her out of the water and halfway to her feet. It felt like a horse's mane.

"There," a male voice snarled. *"There!"*

Her vision began to gray as the flow of blood to her brain slowed to a trickle. She cocked her arm and jabbed backward with the point of her elbow, slamming into ribs. But the pressure continued.

The man was breathing with a heavy, surflike rhythm.

She was slowly passing out. Everything looked washed out, transparent. She quit trying to pry the bristly thing off her neck. Instead, she clawed at his eyes with her fingernails.

He cried out, a bellowing gasp, and the thing fell away from her throat.

She dived for the far wall, spinning around onto her back just before she slammed into it—and doubled her legs to push him away. He came for her, his face dark with rage and exertion, his ponytail jouncing against the wet front of his shirt.

She kicked, but Karl Schoenfeld was so large and heavy she only turned him to his side.

His scratched eyes watering, he reached out for her, took hold of a wrist and wrenched. She ignored the pain and smashed her heel into his nose. His head flopped against the floor, and he let go of her arm with an infuriated grunt. A swift dribble of blood formed a pool on the linoleum under his nostrils.

She crawled over him, shaking off a brief grip around her ankle, rose, and ran for her dresser. In the corner of her eye, he streaked for the door—her only door—and rammed his back against it, pinning it closed. Let him. She wanted only her revolver. She flung her top drawer onto the bed and rummaged through her underwear.

Then Schoenfeld gave a sultry, knowing chuckle.

Dee glanced up. He was brandishing two handguns. One was an automatic, probably a nine-millimeter, and the other was her own revolver. He wiped his bloody nose on a rolled-up shirtsleeve. His usual white shirt.

The propane connection to her heater was hissing. He'd no doubt loosened it.

She hurled the drawer at him, but he just ducked to the side and came up grinning as he tucked her wheelgun into his waistband and leveled the pistol on her.

"Do it, you son of a bitch," she said, oddly fearless. The moment had come too quickly for fear.

But Schoenfeld hesitated, his eyes darting around the room.

Then she realized. He wanted to make it look like a propane accident. He'd tried to throttle her, hoping that fire damage to her body, her neck, would destroy any marks of strangulation.

She said, "It's not going to work now."

"What?" He wiped his nose again.

"A bullet wound won't be erased by the fire."

He nodded, pensively, then reached down and retightened the propane connection with his left hand. The hissing stopped. He looked at her. For an ugly split second, as she stood naked before him, she thought that his desires had shifted. But no. He stood tall again and studied her with worried eyes. There was only one thing he wanted to do before fleeing. And now he wasn't sure how to do it.

"I'm going to put something on," she said matter-of-factly.

He raised his pistol to eye level but didn't stop her as she went to the closet door and took a fresh uniform down off the rack. It was still wrapped from the dry cleaners. She slowly ripped off the plastic, then put the shirt and trousers directly on. A move back toward the bed for her strewn underwear might make him think that, out of sheer desperation, she was getting ready to rush him. The uniform clung to her wet skin.

She had to slow this all down. She had to create time in which to find a weapon. Delay him long enough for somebody—Louie, anybody—to return from the park. The light was fading. Soon, someone would come home.

She realized that Schoenfeld was standing like a cop as he trained his automatic on her. Knees wide-set and flexed, both hands clasping the weapon.

"Step away from the closet," he ordered. His eyes were still shifting as he tried to think of some way out of this. He was doing everything with his future in mind, she realized, otherwise she'd already be dead. If possible, he intended to stay right were he was. The Owens Valley.

"You're an ex-cop," she said, complying, taking two slow paces toward the center of the room.

He admitted so much with a faint smile.

"And you and Taggart killed that old man up in Oregon."

Schoenfeld's face hardened. She knew that if he denied involvement, he was no longer sure about killing her. If not, she had even less time than she thought. "That was never meant to happen," he finally said. "Accidents just happen when you deal with explosive personalities."

"Yours or Taggart's?"

"I never set foot inside that farmhouse."

Dee took a deep breath, trying to settle down her pulse. Weapons. Her service shotgun was lying across the floorboards in Fetterman's truck, parked just outside the door. And then there was Louie's Spanish pistol. But where was it? Inside his house or still at the bottom of the creek? *"Why?"*

Schoenfeld shrugged. "Supreme test. Any eco-moron is willin' to die in the defense of Mother Earth. But what matters is that you're willin' to kill for her."

"That's not it, Karl. It never wore well on you."

"Oh?"

"You blew the whistle on Taggart. It was you who arranged that call to the S.O. I just know it. Right before Taggart could have really hurt the aqueduct. You stopped him . . . why?"

"He'd become a liability."

"Just when he was on the verge of causing maybe irreparable damage to the system?"

Schoenfeld nodded thoughtfully. "Your director back in Washington was right. Without you on the ground here, the Feds don't have a fuckin' clue."

So much for the value of publicity. Schoenfeld had obviously read the *Times* article. She started to say that the federal effort on the case was now a team effort enlisting the FBI, N.C.I.S. and ATF—but he barked for her to shut up. Then, in the silence that followed, he ran a worried hand over his hair and down the back of his head, stopping at the knot in his ponytail, which he gripped in frustration. She could tell that he was at a loss what to do. That was more dangerous than his having a plan. It left him more prone to spontaneity.

"You mind if we leave?" she tested. "I don't want to involve these people. Is your car just outside someplace?"

Schoenfeld stared back at her. "No, too far for me to drag you to it."

"We can take my truck if you like."

At last, he said, "All right." But as she started to go for her boots, in the corner, he said, "No way. Leave 'em."

She knew why. She'd never be able to run across any rocky alluvial fans on this side of the valley in her bare feet.

"The keys," he said.

She scooped them off the top of the dresser as he opened the door two inches and peered out, his nine-millimeter still on her.

"Let's go," he said. "You drive."

Outside, the evening air hit her sweaty skin like ice. She hadn't realized how profusely she'd been sweating. Schoenfeld too. His shirt was soaked.

"Get in the passenger door," he snapped, taking the keys from her. He opened the lock and gestured with the pistol for her to slide across to the steering wheel. She was careful not to glance down at the shotgun, which was wedged almost out of sight beneath the seat. She had to scoot over the archaeologist's accumulation of junk and her own, on top of which was her Kevlar bullet-resistant vest, which she seldom wore because of the desert heat.

She'd no sooner settled in than Schoenfeld grabbed the shotgun and laid it in the bed of the truck.

Her heart sank.

"Gotta take care of government property," he quipped, tossing her the keys. "We need good relations with the BLM. Let's go."

Backing up, she furtively glanced around the cab, looking for something to go at him with. Nothing really. A clipboard. Pens. Then she noticed the obsidian flakes on the floormats.

"Get a move on it, Laguerre." He yanked out the radio microphone and hurled it through his side window. Then, he scanned the various frequencies with a smirk. Sheriff's, DWP, CB emergency—they were all being jammed.

"You did that the other night at Grant Lake too," Dee said.

"Amazin' what a security blanket the radio is to the police mentality," he said, switching off the squelch noise. "Take it away from the average cop and he's afraid to act on his own. He can no longer summon his precious fuckin' backup."

"Is that why you did it the other night?"

"No. I didn't want one of you to find Taggart at the intake too soon."

"You wanted him to have no way out, then. You wanted him dead."

Schoenfeld didn't reply.

"Did you plan for the deputy to die?"

"No," Schoenfeld said somberly, gazing through the windshield. "Another accident." Then he stiffened, and as Dee glanced away from him, forward, he jiggled the muzzle of his pistol against her ribs.

A DWP truck had just turned off onto the colony road and was coming toward them. Dwight Rainwater, she realized, coming home from the baseball game. Her one chance, she told herself. This was it. If she squandered it, she was Schoenfeld's. Was Dwight alone? Yes, thankfully . . . no kids with him.

"Here's how it goes down," Schoenfeld said deliberately. "Say somethin' in passin'. Somethin' cheerful and brief. If you get a wild hair up your ass—you both die here and now."

"Your nose," Dee said.

"What?"

"Blood on the tip of it."

As he leaned over into the mirror on his side, moistened his fingertips and rubbed, Dee slid her left hand into the seat pouch and closed it around the ten-inch obsidian blade Fetterman had left there. Schoenfeld slid his pistol under her vest, barrel facing her.

Dwight slowed to talk to her. "Hey, Dee . . ."

She braked for just as long as it took her to say, "Sorry, Dwight—I've got a call. Tell Ginny I'll be late." The name of the Aguirres' dead daughter. Dwight looked quizzically at her. By that time, she was already swinging around the obsidian knife with her left hand and rising off the seat by pushing against the vest with her right. Everything then happened in the same instant. Schoenfeld screamed as the blade plunged into his waist just below the floating ribs. There was a deafening blast, and the cab filled with white smoke. She knew that the bullet had passed beneath her but wasn't sure if it might have gone through the door and somehow hit Dwight. She sprang the latch and leaped for the bed of the DWP truck, hollering as she landed, ''Punch it, Dwight!''

For a sickening moment, nothing happened. She saw that the blood-covered blade was still in her grasp. She flung it away in revulsion. Then she was thrown against the bed liner by the sudden acceleration.

''Don't stop, Dwight!'' She sat up, looked over the top of the tailgate. Through the boiling dust, she saw Schoenfeld stagger out of the still-crawling BLM truck, holding his side with one bloody hand and the pistol with the other. He cranked off a round, and Dee went flat again. ''Faster, Dwight!''

When she rose two hundred yards later for another look, Schoenfeld was on his knees, vomiting. The truck had veered off the road and been pulled to a stop by the thick sagebrush.

Dee scrabbled forward and cried to Dwight through the rear window, which he'd opened. ''Your hunting rifle . . . get it as soon as we stop!''

He dipped his head, his eyes frantic. ''What—?''

''Later, Dwight. Just get the rifle and plenty of ammunition to hold him off. He'll come back at us.''

They reached the house, and Dwight stalled the engine by letting up on the clutch while still in gear. He ran inside, and Dee jumped down. The dust obscured her view along the road. Through the kitchen window, Dwight could be heard tapping telephone keys. ''Line's dead, Dee!''

''I know,'' she said, watching the dust thin, ''and don't bother with your truck radio either. The rifle, Dwight!''

Then it materialized out of the lifting murk: the grill of Fetterman's truck. Schoenfeld had turned around and was coming cautiously back toward the colony. The barrel of her shotgun was jutting out of the driver's side window.

"Dwight!" She prayed nobody else would return from the game right now. Schoenfeld would use them. He'd take them as hostages.

At last, the screen door banged shut and Dwight appeared with his aught-six and a box of cartridges. Dee took the rifle from him, then five rounds, which she fed into the magazine with twitching fingers. Blood was running down from her right elbow. Her stitches had broken. And grasping the stone blade had opened her palm.

Schoenfeld slowed, then backed up into a dip in the road.

"No," she said, realizing that she'd have to go after him now. Before somebody blundered into him coming back from the park. She slipped the box from Dwight's hands and said, "Stay here, all right?" She walked a short distance down the road, but then went out into the chest-high sage and bitterbrush for concealment.

Rocks bit into her feet.

She halted, listened. She could no longer hear the engine of the BLM truck. The scoped rifle was a clumsy weapon for a close-up fight. She'd be at a disadvantage against the shotgun and handguns.

A jackrabbit broke from hiding, loping downslope through the brush and away from the road. Was Schoenfeld on the move?

She startled as something whisked against a branch behind her.

Reeling, she swiftly lowered the rifle. It was Dwight. He'd brought her boots and Louie's pistol. "Wonderful," she whispered. She traded him the rifle for the pistol, and together they advanced toward the truck. They hadn't gone far when a wisp of black smoke curled up from the ravine into which Schoenfeld had backed the vehicle. It was followed by a deep rumble and an orange fireball that mushroomed up into the twilight.

They stopped, and Dwight squinted through his scope at the ravine. "That's that, I guess. He set fire to your truck."

Dee jogged over to a boulder, stood atop it, and peered all around, especially at the slope below the road. But it was no good. The light was going, and the sageland was dotted with glacier-strewn granite rocks. They shone like a thousand white shirts.

CHAPTER **TWENTY-ONE**

Most of the colony's residents had gathered around the grinding rock. The men and boys toted their hunting rifles and shotguns, and Louie Aguirre had gone down on picket to his wailing boulder along Big Pine Creek. Dwight Rainwater asked to build a bonfire for the light it would cast out into the sage, but Dee said no. It was better not to illuminate everybody.

She was leaning against the side of Foley's sedan, massaging her throat. The lingering effects of Schoenfeld's ponytail felt like the onset of strep.

The sheriff was seated behind the wheel, with one boot planted outside on the ground and the microphone in his fist. "I wish to hell," he groused to Dee, "these folks'd put away their arsenal."

"Not a chance, Tyrus." Their encampment had been attacked. They were frightened, angry. It was in their starlit faces, memories passed down from the old days, the small massacres that had gone unrecorded by white history but were still recounted on the reservations. These people were big supporters of the NRA.

"Last thing Karl's gonna do is come back here," the sheriff went on.

Dee wasn't sure about that. Schoenfeld had focused on her. Somehow, he'd become convinced that if he eliminated her he could go on with the life he'd made for himself in the valley. However irrational, killing her and anyone standing in the way might be the only plan he had left, even if his purpose had shifted unconsciously to revenge.

A murmur of radio traffic made Foley sit up, draw his boot inside. "Go on ahead," he said.

Dee stood and drew closer to hear the dispatcher, but by the time she neared the car door the transmission had ended. "Two of my boys," Foley explained to her, "got Karl's V-dub bottled up at the trailhead lot, head of the canyon." He lumbered out of the Dodge and hollered for an idle deputy to back the others nine miles up Big Pine Creek. Yet, he didn't go himself, and from that Dee realized that he privately figured what she did: Schoenfeld was no longer up there. It was nearly two hours now since he'd set fire to Fetterman's BLM truck and faded into the brush. With the flaming wreck blocking the only road into the colony, she and Dwight had been unable to contact the sheriff's office until Louie and Tillie had driven up twenty minutes later.

The cruiser sped past the telephone repair truck, emergency lights going.

Foley sat again. On his dashboard in a manila envelope was the obsidian knife she'd plunged into Schoenfeld's side. Even looking at the package, knowing what was inside, brought back the sensation of tearing skin and muscle.

Foley was smiling at her under the glow of his dome light. The shadow of his large head fell around her boots. "You sure have lousy luck with gov'mint vehicles, Laguerre."

"That I do." As far as she knew, her Bronco was still in a Bishop shop, awaiting new glass from the factory. Then something hit her. He hadn't seemed particularly mystified that one of the most popular citizens of the Eastern Sierra had tried to strangle her to death. She asked, "Rowe kept you up on the developments from our trip, didn't he?"

"He did," Foley said. "Had a chat with him this afternoon on the phone. Now we finally know who went up north there with Taggart, don't we though?"

Dee nodded.

He must have caught drift of her suspicion, for he suddenly dropped his voice and said, "I was two steps behind you all, Laguerre. . . ." He punched in the cigarette lighter. "I knew ol' Mirabelle Heckard was holdin' out, and that

poor gal can't hold out for long with anybody. . . . '' The
flicker of a smile before he lit up a Havatampa. Dee found
it vaguely guilty. "Funny how you can begin to suspect
the folks 'round you when an investigation turns stubborn
on you.''

"Like who?''

"I won't say, exactly, just that I was lookin' sideways
at one of my own boys. Little things he'd said and done
lately. So I took Miss Heckard out for a steak and a couple
highballs . . .'' Another guilty smile before he reached up
and extinguished the overhead light. "Girl like Mirabelle
always knows more'n she admits or even realizes. That
Chevy van Taggart got his hands on . . . ?'' He exhaled
cigar smoke around Dee.

"Yes?''

"Belongs to her half brother from Trona. Diff'rent last
name put us off the scent.''

"Did Mirabelle help leave it off at the mouth of Mazourka Canyon?'' Dee asked. It would have taken two drivers to do that, unless Schoenfeld had hiked back into
Independence.

"Good possibility Mirabelle did just that,'' Foley said.
"But she wouldn't own up to it.'' He paused. "Fascinatin'
evenin'. Eventually, we got goin' through her love list.
Somewhere in the middle was Karl Schoenfeld. News to
me. I'd heard he got all his servicin' up at Janie's . . .'' A
small brothel just over the Nevada border. "She said he
was forever askin' questions 'bout DWP. That didn't surprise me. Karl was always finaglin' to get a leg up on city
operations here in the valley, and who better to do that
with'n Mirabelle?''

Her sleeves were rolled up, and Dee touched the clean
bandage on her elbow. The doctor from the Indian health
clinic had dropped by and put in fresh sutures, plus
swabbed the cuts on her palm. "What about Schoenfeld
and Taggart?''

"Just where I led her next. Karl had heard about the
death of Jace's kid sister. Asked Mirabelle if Taggart was
still stewin' over that. She said she didn't know him well,
but she'd heard he was all a mess upstairs because of what

L.A. done to his family. So that's who got him riled up again 'bout his sis—Karl.''

"When was this conversation?" Dee asked.

"Two years ago, she said."

"You try to question Schoenfeld?"

"This mornin'. I went by just to have a chat with him. Not there."

The dispatcher advised that the backup had arrived and the deputies were approaching Schoenfeld's VW van. A fairly new Westphalia with tinted windows and a generator, Dee recalled.

"Fancy vehicle for a fella who has to fund-raise to make a livin'," Foley mused out loud. "Ain't it strange how suspicion always gets its edge after the fact?"

A long-term plan. Intricate and far-flung operations. Not a spontaneous revolt. And Ephraim Bickle was right: it had been most likely instigated by an outsider. Schoenfeld. Yet, there was still something out of tune about his involvement. Deep at heart, Karl was a reactionary, not a revolutionary. She'd met enough eco-radicals during her marriage in San Francisco to see now that he'd been impersonating one, almost contemptuously.

A deputy at the trailhead lot reported that the VW was clear, although there was a jumble of "electronics-lookin' stuff and an antenna" inside.

"His jamming equipment," Dee said. "He's been blocking our traffic."

"Leave it be," Foley ordered into the microphone, "and keep away from the vehicle. I'll be rollin' ATF. Copy, Control?"

"Affirmative. I'll phone their motel."

Dee saw Sid for a split second—scarf, sunglasses, and hat.

The deputy came on again. They'd found broken glass in an empty parking lot.

"Shit," Foley said. "He took a goddamn hiker's car."

Dee realized the problem at once. No way to identify the vehicle except by contacting the two Forest Service district rangers serving the central Sierra, who'd have to be roused out of bed to go through the wilderness permits for license plate numbers.

"Shit," Foley repeated. "He'll be clear outta the country before we get a vehicle description."

Louie was walking in from below, his flashlight beam bobbing along the ground. "Tyrus," he boomed as soon as he noticed the sheriff's sedan, "what you doin' 'bout this *bullshita*? That bastard damn near kill Dominica, *goddammita*. You gonna let mad dog killers stroll right in our place anytime they want?"

"Don't start on me, Lou."

"So nothin', you mean. Just like American gov'mint 'bout them kids the Spanish gonna murder. Nothin'!"

"Look." Foley sighed. "I'm gonna say it for the last time, Lou. Your two Basquos killed cops. Granted, dago cops, but they was still cops. If your boys had blown up some soldiers, it'd be a diff'rent thing, and I'd be glad to write a letter on official stationery for you. . . . "

Dee noticed the telephone repairman slowly driving her way. She stepped over to meet him. "All done," he said through his side window. "Checked the line into your house too."

"Thanks," she said, immediately turning for her bungalow.

The interior was cooler than before. She'd found and removed the shims Schoenfeld had wedged into the double-hung window to keep her from using it for escape. A breeze off the Sierra was flowing through the screen.

She dialed Information for the number of the Wasco County Sheriff's Office. Dispatch answered on the eighth ring. Finally transferred to the sleepy-sounding watch commander, she begged him to have Detective Leach call her back as soon as possible.

Then she hung up and went into the bathroom. At the sink she doused her face with cold water, washed the stickiness off the back of her neck. There was a ring of bruise around her throat the color of a fresh hickey. *"Merde."*

Her bathwater was still standing in the tub. Bending over to pull out the stopper, she once again saw the water being churned by her feet, her vision fading to gray while Schoenfeld's breath exploded in her ear. For the first time, she felt the vulnerability, the nakedness of those moments. Then another feeling, anger, welled through this, and she hurled the plug against the wall.

Her phone was ringing.

"Laguerre."

"Dee—Howard Rowe. You get my message?"

"No. You mean my answering machine?"

"Yep."

"Nothing was on it when I got home."

"Well, listen. The ball's back in your court. You know any big white losers over there with a long reddish-blond ponytail?"

A giggle came. She tried to suppress it, but that only increased the urge. The release was intoxicating. And, of course, Rowe sounded confused.

"What's wrong?"

She sobered herself by staring at the door, imagining Karl Schoenfeld braced against it, herself nude and virtually helpless under the muzzles of two handguns. She took a breath, then said, "He tried to kill me this evening, Howard. He was waiting for me when I got home."

"You're kiddin'."

"No. His name's Karl Schoenfeld. Head of the Wetlands Preservation Society. Tried to strangle me with his ponytail, then blow up my place with propane."

"My God, you all right?"

"Well enough. He's still at large, Howard, but has an obsidian knife wound to the side."

"You *stabbed* him?"

"Yeah," she said as if realizing it for the first time.

"What d'you mean *obsidian* . . . the stone?"

"An Indian artifact. Only thing I had within reach."

"Jesus Christ . . . poor kid."

"I hope you mean me."

"Hell yes, I mean you," Rowe said gruffly.

"I'm okay, Howard. Really. Pissed off but okay."

"Well, this Schoenfeld went on quite a spree today. I'm almost sure he killed a retired LAPD sergeant at Lake Topaz this mornin'. A Royce Gilmer. Know of him?"

"No."

"That's what my message was about. He was the registered owner of the Oldsmobile at the time Taggart—and now Schoenfeld, I suppose—swung by the Tygh Valley and beat to death our Oregon farmer.''

''Schoenfeld's an ex-cop, Howard. . . . '' Glancing at the underwear littered over her bedspread, Dee realized that she still had none on. She kicked off her boots and dropped her trousers to the floor. ''He as much as admitted so to me, so the link to the Topaz retiree dovetails . . .'' Stepping into her panties, she froze a second. ''The partial print. From inside the Chevy van Taggart used. Shouldn't we send it to LAPD, their fingerprint database?''

''Already on the way.''

''And that long blondish hair. God knows there must be a couple of them around my place now. I'll start looking.''

''In the mornin', Dee. You take a stiff belt of good whiskey and turn in, you hear?''

''Yes, sounds good,'' she fibbed. Sleep would be impossible tonight.

''I'll fly to Bishop first thing tomorrow. We'll put our heads together over an early lunch. I just got the preliminary return from the pathologist. Why doesn't anythin' come in when you need it? Taggart's blood was chock full of meth. After today, I got a good notion what lab it came from. But all that can wait. You take care.''

''Thanks, Howard.''

She finished dressing, donning even her Sam Browne belt to ward off the aftertaste of that earlier nakedness. Revolver. Schoenfeld had hers. She was thinking of asking Louie for the loan of his pistol when the phone rang again.

''Ranger Laguerre?''

''Cole?''

''Yes, ma'am,'' Leach said. ''Did you get the message I left this mornin'?''

''No,'' she said drolly, ''a number of them seem to have been erased.''

''Well, I left one. Honest.''

''I'm sure you did. Listen, I need to ask if you have anything yet on the new owners of the Tygh Valley property.''

''That's what I called about,'' Leach said. She could hear papers rustling. ''There's been two owners since the victim's family sold out. First was . . .'' An embarrassed pause. "I was wrong about the Audubon Society. I got the 'society' part right, but it was the Wetlands Preservation folks."

Dee wasn't surprised. "Do you know if a Karl Schoenfeld handled the transaction up there in Wasco?"

"Uh ..." More rustling of papers. "That name doesn't ring a bell. Some lady out of Santa Cruz. Her card's here someplace. She's like executive vice president."

It figured. Not likely that Schoenfeld would have shown his face up in Wasco again. "That's okay for now, Cole. Who's the present owner?"

"C and C Transportation Company."

"You ever heard of them before?"

"No, ma'am. Says here it's incorporated under the laws of Nevada."

"Who signed the documents for them?"

"Some guy named Smith."

"Transportation," Dee said after a moment, rubbing her sore neck and throat. "Any talk of a new rail line being laid through your country?"

"Nope."

"Warehouse complex, anything like that?"

"Nothin' I've heard of."

"Does private land surround the farm?"

"No way. We're mostly government property on this side of the Cascades. It's BLM land north and south of the Tygh Valley. Jeez, it's probably federal holdin's of one sort or another all the way south to the borders with California and Nevada."

A female voice broke onto the line. "This is the operator, I have an emergency call for Dominica Laguerre."

Her heart started racing. "Let me call you back in the morning, Cole."

"Surely." Leach hung up.

"Go ahead, operator."

"Dee ... ?" Garrett Driscoll said. "Dee, are you there?"

"I'm here."

"Thank you, operator." He waited a few moments for her to get off the line, then said, "I've been going out of my bloody mind. Ben Whittaker phoned to tell me Karl

Schoenfeld tried to kill you. Can that be *right*?"

"Yes."

"What possessed the man?"

"I have no idea." She added nothing more.

"Well, that settles it, woman."

"What?"

"You're coming down here until this all blows over. You're staying at my place in Bel Air. The housekeeper will be here to let you in. Copy down this address . . ."

"I'm not copying down anything, Garrett. I have work to do."

"The hell you say!" he exploded. "You are to pack right this instant and drive down—"

She slammed down the receiver, then went to the assortment of bottles atop her dresser. She chose the cognac for a straight gulp. She was more agitated than she thought she'd be. Still holding the bottle, she crossed the room to the drawer she'd thrown at Schoenfeld. The back had been broken out of it, but she nevertheless began dumping her underwear inside. She was sliding it back into the dresser when a knock came at the door.

It was Foley, who took something from his jacket pocket. "Thought you might be able to use this." A six-inch revolver. "The spare I always keep in the trunk. My first service piece."

"Thanks . . . come on in."

She slipped the wheelgun into her holster. He sank heavily into her armchair, eyed the bottles.

"Care for a drink, Tyrus?"

"Never say no."

Not in the mood to entertain, she poured him what she was having, cognac. He hoisted his glass at her. "Here's to closin' this all out."

"Amen," she said, sitting on her bed.

After downing his drink, he smiled reflectively at her. She could tell by the look in his eyes that he wanted to broach something. But he palavered for the moment. "Must be interestin' livin' up here with these folks. Diff'rent perspective on things, the Paiute outlook." She gave a remote nod. Her mind was still on Garrett. "I'm told their prophet, Wovoka, said that us whites would vanish because of our

own excesses . . ." Her attention came back to Foley. He
was talking about the Nevada Paiute who, a hundred years
ago, had had visions that gave rise to the Ghost Dance
Religion. "Funny what losin' your way of life does to
you."

"You mean your life, Tyrus? What L.A. did up here?"

"Yes," he said softly. "But eventually, you figure out
the real casualties are your kids. They're hurt—oh, not directly. But through you. It echos through you, all your feelin's, all the things you ever said. It falls on them. . . ."
She realized, astonished, that his eyes had moistened, even
though they now evaded hers. "I never meant to suggest
you were a liar over that pipe bomb thing, Laguerre. But
it can make you crazy, as crazy as poor ol' Wovoka, to
realize that your son will have no future in his own mother
country . . . even if the damn kid was in the wrong." He
rose and took a huge breath to clear his eyes. "Well, you
try'n sleep. The boys'll be around periodic all night."

Dee said nothing as he went out.

Thirty minutes later, Garrett phoned back. She let the
answering machine deal with his long plea for her to talk
to him. "We can't let this get out of hand," he said, almost
choking on his words. "*Please*, Dee, don't make me press
this issue. . . . I'm only thinking of you, your safety . . ."

The digital display on her alarm clock read 12:10.

On the volcanic tableland ten miles north of Bishop was
Mustang Mesa, a settlement of widely spaced houses. Many
of them were owned by Southern Californians who came
up only two or three times a year. Karl Schoenfeld knew
of one such retreat: the owner, a Hollywood cameraman,
had contributed to the WPS. Headlamps out, he crept the
hot-wired Toyota Corolla behind the weathered house and
then nose-first into the empty horse shed. He killed the
engine. He slumped a moment, forehead against the top of
the steering wheel, clasping his blood-soaked windbreaker
against the wound. Stupidly, he'd taken the jacket from his
VW before abandoning it in the trailhead lot up Big Pine
Canyon—and forgotten his cellular telephone.

At least he still had his forty-five, snugged in his waistband.

He sat up, nauseous and weak.

"Just a bit more," he promised himself, disheartened by how eerily thin his voice sounded. He tossed the windbreaker between his shoes and opened the glove box, fumbled around. Locating a penlight, he shone it on the wound. It'd stopped bleeding. He parted the sharply incised lips and peered down a narrowing tunnel, inside himself, past a layer of yellowish fat, dark red muscle, and then—he didn't know what. A kidney?

"I'll kill her," he gasped. "I'll fuckin' kill her!"

Staggering out, he uncovered a nearby stack of hay bales and began dragging them behind the rear bumper of the Toyota, building them into a screen. The exertion made him almost pass out, and he was afraid that the bleeding would start again. But it didn't, a quick check with the penlight revealed.

Five minutes later, he was shuffling north past the lights of the last house and out into the low scrub.

For the first time, he wished that he had some of the speed Escamilla had brought over from his Sonora lab to Taggart. Anything to keep him on his feet until he could arrange for help. Escamilla. The man called Howard had mentioned him on Laguerre's answering machine. Was Rogelio in custody? If so, he had to be bailed out—and silenced. Just as Gilmer had been. Something might yet be salvaged if both men couldn't testify.

Schoenfeld had to stop. Catch his breath.

A sliver of moon was throwing its light against Wheeler Crest behind him, a sheer wall of granite. To the east reared the White Mountains, their west slope in shadow. A prison. This valley was a prison, and its single artery, Highway 395, a gauntlet—by this time—of deputies, highway patrolmen, and Feds. There was no way he could get out on his own, not in this condition. He'd heard of a robber in the fifties who'd hit a Bishop bank and then hiked over the Sierra to Fresno. But that fugitive hadn't had a deep gash in his side.

Schoenfeld came to the edge of the mesa and, halting, looked down into the Owens Gorge onto fjordlike Pleasant Valley Reservoir. The winding waters were glimmering in the faint moonlight. At their head stood a cluster of starkly lit buildings, the DWP hydroelectric plant and its employee residences.

He started down the steep, bouldery slope into the gorge. Each footfall was a jolt to his side, an invitation to vomit.

"Not far now," he coaxed himself. Soon he could rest.

He reached the bottom, collapsed to his knees on some soft mud along the otherwise rocky beach. The powerhouse office would be deserted at this hour, the controls to the great humming machinery on autopilot, alarms set to awaken the on-call operator in his nearby house. Schoenfeld got up, reeled slightly before working his way along the water to the footbridge over the channel of the once-free Owens River. There was some genuine shame to that, penning up a river inside a steel tube.

As expected, the powerhouse door was locked.

Schoenfeld groped along the top of the sill for the key, then let himself in. Not much in the way of security, but public access was barred by a gate across the only road into the plant. The whine of the turbines made his already light head ache. He caught his reflection on the glass partition that shut the office off from noise. Deathly pale. He burst through the door and, without flicking on the neon ceiling fixture, went straightway to the first aid kit mounted on the wall, opened it atop the desk. He popped four aspirin into his mouth, ground them up, and swallowed. Then, lying down on his uninjured side against the cool cement floor— in case he fainted—he crushed an ampoule over the wound, letting a trickle of Merthiolate wash down into it. The pain was immediate, chilling. He didn't totally lose consciousness, but for a few seconds he was on the grass at the police academy a thousand years ago, panting for breath after one of the qualification runs through Elysian Park.

At last, he had no choice. He had to throw up. He scuttled over to the trash can, relieved himself.

Finally, he sat in the chair. The wall clock read ten minutes after midnight. He dialed.

The line was busy.

CHAPTER **TWENTY-TWO**

Dee lay atop the grinding rock on her mattress. Tillie slept below her on an army cot, Louie nearby in the bed of his Jeep pickup. His snoring resonated tinnily in the sheet metal of the truck. Across the streamlet, Dwight dozed in a beach chair, his rifle resting across his thighs. Nearly all of the Paiute had come out-of-doors to sleep, as if they didn't want to be caught unawares by anything. They sprawled on blankets, some in the moon shadow of the trees, some out of it. A child whimpered.

Dee listened. The breeze was stirring the cottonwood leaves overhead.

Every hour, almost to the minute, a deputy cruised through, waking everybody with his spotlight. Dee wanted to tell him that Schoenfeld no doubt had a watch, but instead she lay still while the light passed over, glanced around at the human shapes on the blankets.

Before turning in, Dee had phoned her supervisor. Without meaning to, she'd alarmed him. He was sending two additional rangers to the Owens Valley: "Expect them by early afternoon. And Dee—I want you to think of your own safety now. Above all else. This is just turning too ugly. Think about taking some vacation, if you like."

Safety.

There was none in life. Feeling safe was just an illusion. These past two weeks for her—this was how it was for most of the world all the time.

The people of the colony knew that instinctively.

Tillie suddenly sat up.

She quickly scanned the surrounding sagelands, a hazy gray under the moon. Next, her head turned toward the south end of the valley, the route by which the Mojave would have come raiding so long ago. And then toward Big Pine Canyon, looking far up to the pass down which the Yokut would have come stealing. Finally, the woman eased back down. Only temporarily reassured. Sometimes it slipped out of these people in unguarded moments: the conviction that sooner or later the whites would exterminate them entirely. How this would happen they never said, although during the Second World War they'd watched Japanese Americans brought to this valley and put behind barbed wire.

Louie's paranoia was more spelled out. He'd spent his youth in sheep camps that were occasionally attacked by cowmen.

Dee tried to clear her mind and sleep.

She thought of snow, vast and unbroken expanses of snow covering the high range of the Nevada on which she'd been born and raised. But, obstinately, a new thought protruded through it.

Bel Air.

So that's where Garrett lived. He'd never said, and he had dropped her directly off at the motel the night they'd gone to Palm Springs. Bel Air was a long way from Belfast, but this evening she'd seen a glimmer of the chromium hardness that had come from his youth. She'd been as much frightened as angry at the sheer personal fascism of it— and his blindness, every bit as galling as her ex-husband's—to the fact that she had a job to do, obligations of her own to keep.

Drowsiness came at last. The promise of a swift blackness comforted her, but instead of that she drifted in and out of a shallow half sleep. Fragments of dreams. Sid Abramowitz said something to her, but the words were too far away to catch.

She opened her eyes. Waucoba Mountain was being backlit by the first hint of dawn.

A jackrabbit came bounding into the colony, through the sleeping people. Strange, she thought. The big hares seldom left the brush.

She'd tucked her Sam Browne belt under a corner of the mattress at her head. She reached under, felt for Foley's revolver in her holster. Still there. Nothing showed out in the sage, not even the coyote Dee half expected to see, the one that might have flushed the jackrabbit.

"What time's it?" Tillie asked from the cot. She had morning shift today at the sanitorium.

Dee checked her watch, then whispered, "Five-fifteen."

Tillie shut her eyes again.

Dee sat up to watch the sunrise. These past days had been so full she wondered what would happen before it set this evening. Don't dwell on that, she told herself. Two more BLM rangers were on the way. One was being flown in all the way from Lassen County, almost on the Oregon border.

Her face grew still.

Leach from Wasco County had said something about BLM lands stretching southward from that farm in Tygh Valley all the way to the Oregon border. Northward too, if she recalled correctly. The farm was a critical private link in a long chain of federal holdings. And last evening, on that awful ride from the colony to the spot at which Dee had reached for Fetterman's artifact in the seat pouch, Schoenfeld had said something about the bureau too. What was it? She strained for an echo of his voice. *We need good relations with the BLM.* And then she saw it in her mind's eye, saw it as clearly as if she were holding the Environmental Impact Statement in her hands. *Draft Report: Tygh Valley Water Diversion Project*, one of the EISes on Garrett Driscoll's desk at DWP headquarters.

Tillie had stood.

"What is it?" Dee asked.

The woman didn't answer. Her gaze on the brush.

Dee grabbed her Sam Browne belt, then slid down off the rock and into her waiting boots. She strapped on the belt. Dwight had risen from his beach chair and was listening intently, gripping his rifle with both hands. All had come to their feet.

A covey of quail exploded from the scrub to the south, the fat little birds whirring through the air. Dee watched to see if they'd pass through the colony and on out into the brush again, but they sailed into a wild rose thicket behind Louie's house and remained there. Whatever was approaching—it was coming from all sides.

"Dwight," Dee said, "get on your radio and contact the sheriff's office." As Rainwater jogged for his truck, she told Louie, who was standing in the bed of his pickup, "Climb down—and get behind something."

She realized that her telephone was ringing.

But she'd just had a glimpse of a dull black helmet in the ravine into which the streamlet flowed. "God no," she said, suddenly not knowing what to do. She ran her eyes over all the women and children, the young boys with .22 rifles, the men like Dwight who were trying to remember what they'd done in Vietnam.

It was LAPD SWAT moving against them. She was almost sure of it.

Her phone was still ringing.

"Answer that, Tillie," Dee ordered. "Whoever it is, tell them to get hold of Sheriff Foley. We need help right now."

Time. She needed time.

Unholstering, she fired a single round skyward. That would make them all flop down, trying to figure out where it'd come from. "Hang tight, everybody," she said. "And don't fire at anything or anybody unless I say."

"We got the right to protect ourselves, Dee," an old man said.

"I know. But we're outgunned. So let's keep calm."

Tillie appeared at the door of Dee's bungalow with the phone in her grasp, trailing the cord behind her. "It's them, Dee," she said.

"Who?"

"The fellas out there in the sage."

"Who are they?"

"They wanna know what that shot was about."

"Tell them I'm a federal officer and I'm armed," Dee said. "That's what the hell it was about." As Tillie relayed the message, Dee felt a vulnerable ache between her shoulder blades, as if she could feel a sniper taking a bead on her there. Had Schoenfeld enlisted some retired cops to come at her? The more she thought of it, she just couldn't believe that active LAPD could be persuaded to do this. Unless they'd been convinced that they were moving on saboteurs. But Metro was gone several days from the valley. "Till, ask them who they are—right *now*."

She finally did so, they said, "Secret Service."

"What!" Dee exclaimed.

"This fella says he and the others are Secret Service, Department of the Treasury. His name's Special Agent Young." Tillie cupped her hand over the mouthpiece. "Colored boy."

Dee clasped her forehead, rubbed. *Think.* The phone call might be a diversion while the assault was launched. Whoever they were, she couldn't think of a better way for them to hamstring her than to call themselves Secret Service. She made up her mind not to take the phone herself. She had to be aware of everything all around the colony. "Dwight!" she shouted. "What about the sheriff?"

He stood at the open driver's door to his DWP truck. "Rollin'. Foley and most everybody else too. Resident deputy should be here in a couple minutes."

Good. Even though, if it were indeed Schoenfeld out there, the arrival of the sheriff's office would only spark what might end up a bloodbath.

"Dee," Tillie said, "this fella Young wants to talk at you."

"Tell him I'm busy passing out ammunition to my federal deputies. And ask him why they're here."

Dee made a sweep through the colony, making sure the women and children were inside the houses, behind kitchen appliances if possible. Again, she told the men and boys not to fire unless she said so first. Returning to the grinding rock, she could hear Tillie asking in dismay, "But what you want my Louie for?"

That gave Dee pause. She turned on him, and he offered a slight shrug. "Louie, goddammit—do you know what this is about?"

"Maybe," he said, quiet-faced, pocketing his pistol.

"Merde." Then she went over to the bungalow and grabbed the receiver from Tillie. "Ranger Laguerre, BLM."

"Yes," a black accent said icily, "we'd like to talk to you too."

"Fine. If you are who you say you are, you won't mind doing this. A deputy sheriff's on the way. He'll reach your perimeter within minutes. More local law are right behind him, so I don't suggest screwing with him. If you open up against him, my people are going to start picking off the black helmets we see out in the sage. Half of my people are 'Nam vets. They've been in more firefights than you ever will. Understood?"

After a beat, the voice said, "Go on."

"Have the deputy walk in to me with the credentials of your people on the scene."

"All my people?"

"Yes." One forgery was probable, five or six of them that much less so. "Every last one."

"That'll take time."

"I'll take time over blood any day of the week. How about you, Special Agent Young?"

"So," Young said, sitting on a corner of the table in the interrogation room at the Independence jail, "you have absolutely no interest in the establishment of a Basque homeland." He was indeed a special agent from the Los Angeles office of the Secret Service, a svelte young black in a tasteful charcoal suit. "Did you hear me, Ranger Laguerre?"

"Yes. The statement's absurd. And please sit down on my level."

He stared at her a moment, then descended into the chair across the table from her. "Where were we?"

"You were trying to establish my feelings about Basque separatism. First, you accused me of being a fellow traveler with the Euzkadi Ta Askatasuna. When I tried to deny that without betraying my heritage, of which I'm justifiably proud, you then accused me of not giving a damn about my people. That's where we were."

Young arched an eyebrow. "Do you resent this interview?"

"Yes."

At least that made him smile. "How long have you known Mr. Aguirre?"

"About a year."

"Are you related to him?"

"Possibly."

"I beg your pardon?"

"There aren't that many Bascos in this country. Louie and I have last names that may be derivations of the same clan name from the border region of the homeland."

"Would you say that he's a loyal American?"

"Oh, Jesus."

"That his primary loyalty is to the United States?"

"Gee, I don't know. But I'll wager some Chinese Communists thought so. In Korea, they punched holes in his legs with mortar shrapnel while he dragged his wounded captain back to an aid station."

This time Young didn't smile. "This is serious, Ranger Laguerre."

She knew that. That's why she'd told Louie, before the agents put on the cuffs, to demand an attorney at once—and listen to that attorney. "Okay," she said, folding her arms over her chest, "I'm willing to be convinced. Convince me, Young."

He took the photocopy of a letter from the inner pocket of his jacket.

Dee immediately glanced at the signature. Louie's. A hand-scrawled letter to the "Presidente of the U.S.A." She read it once, twice, then looked at Young. "This is zip. At best, borderline. He never threatens the president—"

"Never directly. But he does promise 'evill things to come' if the two ETA terrorists are executed." The agent paused. "I have information that you helped Mr. Aguirre with this letter."

"Oh, hell yes, Young. A master's degree, and I'd let him tack an *e* on 'president' and an extra *l* on 'evil.' " Then it hit her. "Who's your informant? You wouldn't come up here with your special operations boys on a letter this weak. Who's juicing it up?"

He finally broke off a long stare. "I'm not at liberty to say. But I assure you he's reliable. And you're wrong about us not checking out this in any event—the president comes to Reno in a week to address the national convention of

Veterans of Foreign Wars. Aguirre is registered to go . . . or were you aware of that?''

She hadn't been, but kept silent. "Anything else on him?''

"Yes, a field interrogation card placing him at Grant Lake, where I understand you recently encountered some difficulties with a bomber. Any chance Aguirre was tied up with Taggart?''

"None.''

"I wouldn't be so sure of that. Aguirre's a commercial blaster, correct?''

She hurled back at him, "And how long have you been working this case, Young?''

He looked angry enough to finally demand her revolver and Mirandize her, but at that moment she could hear Howard Rowe's drawl out in the corridor. "Howard?'' she called.

"You all right, sugar?''

"No, there's smoke in here—bad.''

The door burst open, and Rowe entered. He was standing very erect. "Hope I'm not interruptin' anythin'.''

"You are,'' Young said coldly. "I'm interviewing Ranger Laguerre.''

"Well, Sheriff Foley's filled me in, and I know enough to say you're barkin' up the wrong goddamn tree. Louie Aguirre's just a hot-tempered ol' sheep-knocker, but if he wanted to kill the president—why, the womanizin', liberal son of a bitch would already be pushin' up flowers.'' He broke off scowling long enough to smile at Dee. "Had lunch yet?''

"Nope.''

"Let's go.''

"Hold it.'' Young rose, hooked his thumbs in his waistband. "If you don't mind, I am conducting an interrogation—''

"Minute ago it was an interview. I'd take her gun if you mean to get rough. She's already killed one man and maybe another this month, and these things tend to happen in threes. Meanwhile, she and I got some work to do.''

Young reached out and laid his hand on Dee's shoulder to keep her from rising.

She couldn't believe the change in Rowe's face. "Son," he hissed, his jaw muscles tight under the skin, "I been lookin' for a place to shit all mornin', and I think I just found it. You unhand her right now."

Young stood pat. "Understand you're ready to retire, Rowe. You prepared to fuck that up?"

"Yep."

At last, uncertainty crept into Young's eyes. He took two steps back and looked away.

Out in the hall, Rowe was completely himself again as Dee and he strolled for the entrance. "William Schuyler," he said as if it meant something.

"Who?" Dee asked, still trying to get her bearings. Was Louie all right?

"Karl Schoenfeld's real name was William Schuyler. We got a return on the partial print from LAPD. He was a dick assigned to a special intelligence unit. Got disbanded some years ago for playin' Gestapo with the public. Schuyler was sacked, then sued by a good number of the folks he'd spied on. Contempt of court slapped on him for failure to pay judgments. So he vanished."

Dee stopped briefly at the front window. "Louie's lawyer show up yet?"

"Yeah," the desk sergeant said, "in with him now."

"Thanks." That made Dee feel better. She turned back to Rowe. "It goes beyond Schoenfeld, Howard."

He looked surprised. "How do you know?"

"I don't positively. But I will as soon as I see somebody in Bishop."

"Well, let's get up there."

"Not both of us, Howard. He won't talk with you there. I'm not even sure he'll open up to me."

Rowe finally nodded. "You contact me, lady, before you leap. Is that understood?"

"Yes, promise." She gave him a quick kiss. "And don't fuck up your retirement on my account."

"Hell, for slappin' that priss on his skinny ass? They'd just dock my unused sick leave. Do I look sick?"

Foley was walking in from the parking lot as she came

down the front steps. "Where you runnin' off to?"

"No rest for the wicked, Tyrus."

"Christ, Laguerre—do I gotta put a bloodhound on you?"

"Don't let them push Louie around...okay?" she said, getting inside her Fiat and immediately rolling down the windows.

He gripped her upper arm. "I won't. He's local. One of mine."

Ben Whittaker was in the backyard of his West Bishop home, sitting on the grassy bank of the tiny creek that ran through the neighborhood, soaking his bare feet in the clear flow. It was a private yard, screened by liquid ambers and silver maples. A gas-powered mower had stopped mid-swath in the thick saint augustine grass. Dee shuffled her feet through the rough lawn so as not to startle the man in charge of DWP's valley operations.

He turned but didn't smile. "Why, Dee."

"Your wife was kind enough to tell me just to come back." He started to get up, but she said, "Sit down, Ben—and no, I don't need anything to drink."

"What brings you here? Not another bombing, I hope."

"No, I think the bombings are over." She sat on the bank, dipped her hand into the water, ran it over her face. "Home on a Thursday afternoon?"

"Mental health day."

She smiled. Whittaker had snubbed Garrett Driscoll the night of the WPS dinner at Glacier Lodge. She'd tacked it up to the decline of Garrett's fortunes, but now she wasn't convinced of that. "I need your help, Ben."

"Sure."

"Don't promise so quickly. It has to do with DWP."

"In what way?"

"Long-term projects. Does one of them involve the Tygh Valley in northern Oregon?"

He leveled his eyes on hers, but said nothing.

"Somebody died up there, Ben. Murdered for his land, which was the only private holding along what I think is a proposed aqueduct route. I'm going to find the person responsible for that and everything that's happened here in the Owens. I don't care who it is—he's going to jail.''

"Are you sure of that?" he asked skeptically.

"Yes."

Whittaker glanced away, then did a soft flutter kick in the water. "The Columbia and Colorado Diversion," he said, almost whispering.

She closed her eyes for an instant. C and C Transportation.

"I was just a rookie engineer when it was first proposed. Everybody thought it was the solution to all our problems. And I mean all of us in the broadest possible sense—everybody living in the Southwest. Take high-quality Columbia River water from below Bonneville Dam and convey it south, across eastern Oregon, down the length of Nevada and finally into Hoover Dam as the terminal reservoir. It's still a damned good concept. And the engineering's quite feasible. But it was felt that the legal and political factors made the project impossible. So the C and C plan was shelved. Almost forbidden to discuss.''

"But Garrett Driscoll's resurrected it."

"I don't know that for gospel."

"Help me, Ben," she begged.

"You *emotionally* ready to go to war with him? Didn't look that way to me the other night up at the lodge.''

"He's already fired the first shot. I've got no choice now."

Ben let out a long breath. "I can feel it in the works. Engineers and water resource people from Oregon, Nevada, and Arizona milling around every time I drop by headquarters. I got a hunch—and I'll deny it, dammit, if anybody asks—that the groundwork's been laid for a big water bond issue. The most expensive water project in history. People down south are scared, really scared that their taps will run dry." He paused. "Driscoll saw his opening. The day we all flew down to headquarters, I spent most of that afternoon with the boss.''

"I know."

"Well, you don't know this—he told me he was afraid Driscoll was getting set to cut the legs out from under him. And that's just what happened. Driscoll sank his own mentor, the man who'd pulled him up out of the engineering department.''

Dee recalled what Ephraim Bickle had said about the pattern of blasts in the valley. "Repair work," she said.

"What about it?"

"First the canal near the Alabama Spillway was hit, then the siphon. Wells that weren't even pumping. Then an aborted strike at the Mono Craters Tunnel. That honestly wasn't a surefire plan to bring the system to its knees, was it?"

"No," Whittaker admitted. "Canal was fixed within days. Siphon will be back on-line sooner than expected. Even had the tunnel been completely shut down, the city's been expecting a court order any day now to cease and desist transporting water out of the Mono Lake Basin—that's on the qt from our legal department."

"So the damage was more dramatic than significant."

"I suppose." Whittaker shook his head. "All I ever wanted to do was bring people water. Makes everything possible. Water. Life itself. I saw it as opportunity. Jobs. Hope. Coming out to California from the Mississippi I grew up in was like arriving in the Promised Land. Opportunity. Dreams realized. Is that so bad to give people, Dee?" After a few moments' silence, Whittaker said, "He's coming up today. Already en route."

Garrett, she realized. "Where will he go?"

"Here sometime this afternoon. He wanted one of my set of keys."

"To what, Ben? Keys to what?"

Just when she thought that he wouldn't reply, Whittaker got up and said, "To all the locks along the Owens Gorge."

CHAPTER **TWENTY-THREE**

Dee concealed her Fiat under an old willow tree. A hot southwesterly was waving the stringy boughs back and forth across her windshield.

Leaving Ben Whittaker's house, she'd made straightway for this spot just off the northbound lanes of Highway 395. It lay between the settlement of Mustang Mesa and Owens Gorge Road. At first, she'd had every intention of telephoning Howard Rowe from the mom-and-pop market on the mesa. But then she'd realized that Driscoll might see her getting in or out of the car. She didn't believe he'd seen the Fiat on his visits to the colony. Louie had pushed it into his shed for repair.

She watched the traffic speed past, her eyes programmed to pick out Driscoll's anthracite-colored Infiniti.

It'd come to her with a jolt while Young was grilling her at the county jail. The afternoon the wells had started exploding near Lone Pine. She'd been on the phone to Driscoll when he asked her for the time. He had a wall clock in his office and habitually wore a wristwatch, but he asked her as if some expected moment was coming, or had already passed without result, and he was getting edgy. He'd known that the wells were ready to go up at any second.

Then, she'd shrugged it off as *just Garrett*, ever the absentminded engineer, asking for the time with timepieces within sight.

But now his razor-sharp focus stunned her.

He'd fomented a water crisis. First to supplant his boss and then to terrify Southern Californians into financing a project that boggled the imagination with its scope and cost. The Monday morning massacre at Los Angeles City Hall had been an exquisitely planned power grab, leaving Driscoll as the only apparent solution to an almost impossible dilemma.

It was all falling into place with a sharp, metallic click. *How is it that every recalcitrant in America has Earl for a middle name?* he'd quipped during the meeting at DWP headquarters. Jace Earle Taggart. She shut her eyes, felt the wind pass over her damp skin like a ghost.

Then, suddenly, she was fumbling for the door latch.

She staggered outside, saliva welling in her mouth. She braced her hands on her knees and bent over, the willow branches wrapping around her like tentacles.

After a few minutes, the nausea faded. But her revulsion didn't.

She'd heard herself telling Driscoll how good Abramowitz was. *Sid will get this blaster. Sooner than later, I believe.* Sooner would have been a problem for Driscoll and Schoenfeld, the ex-intelligence cop working for him. They'd no doubt planned to dispense with Jace Taggart as soon as his sabotage had convinced Angelenos that long lines at water trucks were coming. The two men had been careful to pick a time and a place at which Taggart, strung out on methamphetamine, felt so trapped he'd fight to the death.

She stood straight, staring through the foliage at the traffic. Then she froze. Driscoll's face. She'd just seen it flash by. Not in his Infiniti, but in a white Ford sedan.

She got in, started her engine, but counted to thirty before pulling out onto the highway.

Driscoll glanced at his rearview mirror before turning off onto Gorge Road. Nothing unusual in the way of vehicles, not even a Highway Patrol black-and-white. He drove at moderate speed across the sun-baked tableland. It looked like a continuous plain far to the east, but it wasn't—a precipitous canyon lay in between, the old course of the Owens River before DWP had funneled it down from the Lake Crowley Dam to the hydroelectric plant in Pleasant Valley below. He now drove under the penstock, the huge pipeline that, along with two tunnels, carried the flow fourteen miles down to the turbines.

On the seat beside him was a canvas satchel. A day pack, as it was called in this country.

That other country.

Ever since dawn had brightened the overcast Bel Air sky, his mind had been going back to the old days. Somehow, calling it a childhood didn't quite feel right. But it'd been intense, that other life. One's attention keenly concentrated. Alert but careful to exhibit just the right degree of nonchalance. He'd only been twelve, but his baby face had helped recommend him for the chore of delivering bombs for the IRA. He'd carry them in a shopping bag, the plastique bumping against the side of his leg as he walked up some narrow Protestant street under a leaden Antrim sky. Hard men, those Provos who'd recruited him for the work. But they'd taught him one indispensable thing: the world turns on the deeds of single-minded individuals. Eventually, his parents took delivery of a bomb of their own. Part of a Protestant reprisal campaign. No secrets in Northern Ireland—the Ulster Defense Association had been on to the doings of young Driscoll. But after the burials, he'd gone on with the job, knowing full well that his actions had cost his parents their lives. Single-mindedness. Get the bloody thing done. The task is all, the alpha and the omega.

He stopped at the first gate.

Getting out, he carefully stretched and yawned, then strolled over to the padlock.

From this point, the road plunged down into the gorge. He swung back the gate and stood a moment on the brink, surveying the pinkish cliffs of volcanic tuff, cut perpendicular by the Owens over aeons. "So here's the final road to damnation," he said quietly, without bitterness. He had killed before. By toting plastique to human targets, he had indeed killed. So this would be nothing new.

He drove through, then got out once more and locked the gate behind him.

Last night, Schoenfeld had phoned from the hydroelectric plant, the place they'd agreed he should go if things went awry. Driscoll put aside his anger and calmly told him to crawl into the bed of the damkeeper's truck before first

light, throw a tarp over himself. Reaching the dam, Schoenfeld was to wait for the keeper to go inside the outlet control house before hiking down the face of the rock dam and
hiding in the sluice gate pipe. There was no reason for any
DWP worker to go inside there, and it would be cool.
Schoenfeld, sounding half delirious, told him to bring a
doctor. He was going fast. "I'll see what I can do, lad,"
Garrett had promised, even though it was impossible. No
doctor was going to be brought into it at this late date.

He reached the bottom of the chasm. The road was in
shadow, but the air was still hot. He'd turned off the air-
conditioning and rolled down his window—to listen as best
he could over the engine noise for other cars. He glanced
up. The cliffs were whittling down the sunlight to a few
streaks furling like yellow banners across the towering
stone faces.

He hoped to find Schoenfeld dead. But it was a small
hope. Karl was a rugged man. Driscoll had realized that the
first time he'd seen him. It'd been on the television news,
and with all the other detectives of that ill-fated intelligence
unit ducking for cover, William Schuyler alone sailed
through the proceedings with a coldly defiant grin. He
didn't admit a thing. Nor did he accuse anyone else. No
surrender. Schuyler was Provo material, without a doubt,
and he also proved to have a fine greed, which made him
manageable.

Driscoll had come to the last gate.

Stepping out, he glanced up at the dam. Crowley Reservoir had been an alternate target all along, so this was no
departure from the plan. He opened the lock and pushed
back the gate, leaving it open so he wouldn't be delayed
when coming out in fifteen minutes. Then he drove ahead
another hundred yards, nosed the Ford inside a rusted section of huge penstock pipe, and parked. The pipe had been
damaged by a slide and set aside for removal. The sedan,
then, couldn't be seen from either the crest of the dam or
the lip of the gorge.

"No surrender," he said, as he had so often long ago.
Then he reached inside the satchel and started the navy-
issue timer. One of two he'd buried in his Bel Air backyard
as spares, should Schoenfeld need them for Taggart. The

dynamite and blasting caps were from DWP's demolition stores.

Thirty minutes.

More than enough time to deal with Schoenfeld, then get back to Highway 395. There'd be no sign of the explosion until the Owens, after more than fifty years, gushed down its parched channel into Pleasant Valley Dam. Karl would ride that torrent. In pieces. Blown to bits while apparently carrying the torch for his late partner in crime, Jace Taggart.

Driscoll left the car and jogged down into the riverbed. Sand spilled inside his oxfords. He slowed as he entered the sluice gate pipe. Taking a flashlight from the day pack, he shone it forward. "Karl . . . ?"

Schoenfeld was sitting with his back against the steel plate that separated him from millions of tons of water. His head was slumping.

"Karl, lad . . . ? Driscoll grinned: the man was already gone. He himself would be done and back to the highway in no time. Home by evening.

But then the head raised, and the fever-swollen eyes parted into puffy slits. Schoenfeld grunted, a breathless grunt, then asked groggily, "Gare . . . ?"

"Don't sound so surprised. Did you think I'd forsake you?"

Schoenfeld didn't reply. He just dully watched Driscoll's approach.

"Let's have a look at you."

"So it goes," Schoenfeld croaked.

"What goes?"

"You wind up the king of California, and I wind up pissin' blood."

"Truly?"

Schoenfeld nodded. "Bitch clipped a kidney."

Driscoll didn't like her spoken of in that way, but he held his tongue. Retribution was just minutes away. He took a small first aid kit from the pack, then snugly tucked the satchel itself into a corner of the sluice gate.

"Where's the sawbones?" Schoenfeld asked.

"In Bishop. Wouldn't come with me. House calls are passé, even if you wave ten grand under a doctor's nose—"

"Oh, Christ, man."

"Listen—I've got to take you to him. That's all. So let's start with a nip of codeine . . ." Driscoll slipped a tablet between the man's lips. "Sorry, no water." Schoenfeld swallowed it dry. A placebo. Sugar-coated sodium chloride was all. The remains would be autopsied, and as simple as it would be to poison the man, Driscoll wanted nothing to indicate that drugging or any form of trauma had preceded the effects of the blast on the body.

"What're you thinkin', Gare?" Schoenfeld's glassy eyes were hard on him.

He considered. "I'm thinking I could use a mule to get you to the car."

"No, you're not."

"Oh?"

"You're thinkin' what I was right up to this mornin'—eliminate this and that fucker and you can go on with the game. Court's a fair bet if the prosecution is short of witnesses." Schoenfeld swept a pistol up from between his legs and pressed the muzzle between Driscoll's eyes. "Right, *lad*?"

"Nothing of the sort, Karl." But then he slowly smiled. "Not that it didn't occur to me, though."

"Here we go," Schoenfeld said with a sickly chuckle.

"But I have far too much faith in modern forensic science to try to dispose of your carcass, Karl. All my purposes are served if you live to squander your Swiss bank account on Brazilian whores and Bacardi's rum."

"Horseshit."

Pretending to ignore the pistol, Driscoll felt Schoenfeld's forehead. "You're burning up."

"I'm dyin' by the hour. But you're an impatient son of a bitch. You're gonna grease the skids."

"Then shoot, lad." Driscoll smiled again. "Blow the light out of my head. Part of me would thank you, I'm sure."

Schoenfeld's gaze seemed to drift out of focus, and then he winced. Driscoll could almost imagine the line of pain running up the nerves from the wound to the man's uplifted arm. It was agony even to grip a pistol at this point. But there was something more than suffering in Schoenfeld's eyes. A dim spark of hope. Rum and whores.

"Ah, dear Karl, so you're not ready to give it up."

At last, Schoenfeld lowered the weapon. "Get me outta this godforsaken valley, Driscoll," he rasped.

"I'm bloody well trying—"

But then Schoenfeld's head lolled to the side. He'd fainted.

Driscoll slipped the pistol, a nine-millimeter Beretta, from Schoenfeld's loose grasp and laid it behind him on the floor of the pipe. He looked over the wound. Infected already. Nasty way to spend one's final days, but he'd told Schoenfeld to get out of the country as soon as he'd learned from Dee that she and the FBI had followed the evidence trail up to Tygh Valley. None of this would have happened had Schoenfeld obeyed.

Well, he'd never disobey again.

Driscoll took a damp washcloth from the first aid kit, then covered Schoenfeld's mouth and nose with it. The man roused slightly, tried to gulp in some air, then grabbed for the cloth and began struggling. Feebly. Driscoll kept the pressure on.

Dee drove the BLM road that paralleled the western rim of the gorge. She stopped every quarter mile and hiked out to the precipice for a look over. The tumbling depths made her dizzy: she felt as if the bottom of the chasm were falling away from her. That and last night's sleeplessness left her queasy.

She hadn't seen Driscoll's Ford since he'd left Highway 395. But she trusted that he was somewhere below, otherwise his car would have churned up dust on the same road she was now using. The Fiat was covered with it.

Schoenfeld.

She could think of no other reason for Driscoll to have come to the valley today. He meant to deal with his co-conspirator. Perhaps help him. Perhaps murder him. There was a precedent for killing the hired help. Taggart. She remembered his look of dismay in the tunnel when she told him that someone—Schoenfeld, it turned out—had betrayed him to the sheriff's office. She was sure that he'd gone to his death never knowing that he'd been in the employ of the second most powerful man in DWP. Schoenfeld had known perfectly well who he was serving: *We need good relations with BLM.*

Dee parked for the last time. The top of the Crowley Lake Dam was within sight. Driscoll could have gone no farther on the asphalted lane that meandered along the bottom of the gorge.

She jogged out to the lip and went prone.

No Ford.

But after a minute, she noticed two faint lines arcing through sand into a dented section of ten-foot pipe. A small concrete building stood on one end of the dam's crest, but it made no sense for Driscoll to have approached it from the chasm bottom and then have to clamber up several hundred feet of ankle-turning rock fill.

He was down there somewhere. With Schoenfeld.

The only route below was a steep talus slope. She started down it, slowly, trying to keep the rock debris from clattering in little avalanches. Dust streaked up from her feet and swirled out of the shadow and into the sunlight. She decided that it was no use halting to let it dissipate. She was committed now, and it was best to get down as soon as possible.

Off to her left, a rattlesnake warned her with a low buzz to keep clear. "Don't worry," she whispered.

She reached the old river channel and flopped down among some black willows. From here, the Ford was visible. She was about to check it out when she saw foot-sized divots angling down the sandy bank. They continued up the riverbed and into the sluice gate outlet at the base of the dam.

Backtracking a short way, she traversed the talus and approached the outlet from the side.

Voices were echoing out of it. "Get me outta this godforsaken valley, Driscoll," Schoenfeld was saying deliriously.

She shuddered, recalling the sensations of plunging the obsidian knife into his flesh.

But she drew Foley's revolver and descended to within a few yards of the big cement pipe. There, feeling exposed, she gave thought to heeding Rowe and backing off until help could be somehow summoned. Her radio handset was at the bottom of the Mono Craters water tunnel.

Yet, she had Driscoll and Schoenfeld trapped, undeniably together. There might not be another opportunity to take them down as cleanly linked as she could here—even though a man like Karl would come out firing. He'd take his chances with a rush and a running firefight to the Ford. She had no idea what Driscoll would do—try to talk his way out of it, maybe. Somehow, she felt that he could be persuaded to give up. Maybe, deep down, that's why she'd come alone. But she wouldn't delude herself. Driscoll had arranged for Sid's murder.

She found herself wishing that Rowe were there.

The ground on which she stood was sandy. It would absorb and not deflect bullets into her face, so she lay down again, gripping the revolver in both hands. Think ahead, she told herself. Was there a telephone inside the cement house atop the dam? If not, she could still march the two men up the rock face and try to hail a fisherman in a boat. Usually by late afternoon, a few boats were anchored there.

A strange sound reverberated outside to her. She didn't know what it was. Water gurgling?

She couldn't see directly down the pipe. Purposely, so the two men couldn't see her either. But the continuing sound made her crawl to the right. Inside, a flashlight seated on its butt was shining palely against the overhead. A silhouette passed back and forth in front of it, a confusion of activity.

The sound ceased.

After several moments, the silhouette picked up something and then dropped it against a rusted metal partition. A slack-armed body, she realized with horror. All doubt evaporated, and she raced up to the opening. "Garrett!" she cried. "Don't move!"

But Driscoll dropped down out of sight, into the shadows below the cone of light. "I'm armed," he answered, his voice sharp with anger and surprise. And then, a heartbeat later, he asked almost gently, "Dee . . . ?"

"Put it down, Garrett," she insisted, "and come out now!"

"Dee?" He sounded dumbfounded. "How'd you—?"

"Never mind. Just come out." She'd sidestepped so that

most of her body was beyond the opening. Only her gun hand and half her face showed.

"Are you alone?"

She thought to lie, but then something—the notion that she alone could convince him to surrender—made her say "Yes."

In the silence that followed she could feel him frantically thinking, turning over every possible option, including shooting her, no doubt. She had to remind herself how remorseless he was. Sid. And then Taggart. "Do you want me to bring poor Schoenfeld along?"

"How is he?"

"Dead."

She ground her teeth together, then said, "Oh?"

"Yes, he was dead when I arrived. Looks like he was passing blood all night."

The flashlight went out, and Dee realized that even her partial exposure was too risky against the circle of daylight Driscoll now faced. She ducked around the corner, squatted on her heels. "Then there is life after death."

"Love?"

"Damn you," she said, her voice more shaken than she wanted, "don't lie to me . . . not me!"

"Lie?"

"When's it stop? When your aqueduct stretches from the Columbia to the Colorado? Or will it then be some new bigger project worth that much more killing and deceit?"

After a moment, a soft, jaded laugh echoed from the darkness. "Perhaps. Not that prevaricating comes naturally, love. I'm a rather straight-forward fellow, you know. But God saw fit to plunk me down in a crooked world and then give me the burning desire to better it. . . ." She could hear him crawling. When he spoke again, his voice seemed closer. "But I do lie with the best of them when the need arises. Karl wanted you and not that deputy lured to Grant Lake, but I said no. I lied and told him, 'She doesn't have a clue'—when I knew damned well better."

Sweat had beaded on the tip of her nose. She wiped it on her sleeve. The possibility of surrender. Was he broaching it? "Then why was I spared, Garrett?"

"I'd fallen for you. Like a bloody fool. And I went on

falling even when I felt you tightening the noose around my neck. You have some qualities I could do without, Dee Laguerre. But still I was willing to lie to the Secret Service last night.''

"That Louie and I meant to kill the president, for god-sake?''

"Yes.''

"Why say such a thing, Garrett . . . revenge?''

"Not at all. I'd hoped it'd keep you on ice today and out of harm's way, at least until the flimsiness of the accusation showed through." He sighed. "I should've known better.''

All at once, she felt terribly weary. She'd just realized how long this might drag on. With Driscoll testing her every inch of the way. He could be heard crawling forward again. He wanted out of the trap. He was preparing to strike. "May I ask a personal question, Dee?''

"I suppose.''

"Do you have any feelings for me?''

She buried her face in the crook of her arm for a moment. "Dee . . . ?''

She looked forward again, but bit her tongue to keep from answering. Sid. She thought of Sid.

He laughed again, but pathetically now. "I was afraid of that. Well, it was a fond dream. Still, I'm glad for that night, and I thank you, Dee.''

"Don't,'' she said, not knowing why. She just didn't want gratitude for something like that. She wiped her sweat-bleared eyes with her left hand, trying to clear them.

"Now to business,'' he said.

She braced for a rush.

"There's an explosive device in here, Dee. I can't check my watch right now, but let me just say—each second's getting a trifle more exhilarating than the last.''

"Disarm it, Garrett—and come out.''

He said nothing for at least thirty seconds, then: "I just don't think I can do that, love.''

She thumb-cocked her revolver, making for a faster trigger pull, a more accurate shot. He was going ahead with the plan that had started with the blast below the Alabama Spillway. He'd taken Schoenfeld out of the picture to restart that plan toward its conclusion, and now it was her turn to die. She imagined the cramped, sweltering interior of the Ford's trunk. She'd wind up there unless she calmed down. The advantage was hers. He had to break from shadow into sun.

"See, love," he went on, "long before I met you, I fell in love with an anecdote. It concerns the great William Mulholland, paddy extraordinaire..." Thinking of the blast, the deluge that would follow, she scrambled back to the bank. Revolver still trained on the opening, she jumped on top of the sandy shelf and went prone again. She was now about sixty feet from the outlet. "November... nineteen hundred and thirteen, it was. I do so love the autumn in Southern California. Thirty thousand Angelenos gathered at the terminus of the aqueduct. The last gate was opened, and down a concrete channel they flowed, the beautiful bright waters..." Dee saw that at least fifty yards of flat, open ground lay between her back and the nearest boulders. Driscoll went on, his words almost covering the sounds of his forward progress. "As chief engineer of the grandest water project in the history of mankind, Mulholland was asked to make an oration. Know what he said, Dee? He simply said, 'There it is.'"

"If you come out with a weapon in your hand—I'll kill you, Garrett!"

"That's all I ever wanted, love. The opportunity to do something so monumental only understatement could put the capstone on it...."

"Garrett—!"

Then he burst from the opening.

A sharp breath seized in Dee's throat as she tried to make sense of what she was seeing. Driscoll was carrying Schoenfeld, shielding himself with the corpse. An echoing crack and then the whine of a bullet near her head drew her attention to the automatic pistol he'd propped on the dead man's shoulder.

She fired twice. She heard two sickening thuds, but both hollow-point rounds had burrowed into Schoenfeld without passing through. Driscoll, meanwhile, kept up a steady fire that landed short but sprayed sand into Dee's face.

Blindly, she pulled the trigger once more, then rolled to

the side, waiting with a pounding heart for her eyes to stop watering. She believed that Driscoll had dropped the corpse to the ground and was shooting from behind it.

At last, she saw well enough to pick out Driscoll's head. She fired two more shots. Both missed. That left her one cartridge loaded.

Driscoll must have been counting too, for he vaulted over the body and charged her, his blazer spreading in the breeze as he ran toward her, pumping more bullets. She waited as long as she could before loosing her final round. It came close enough to his face to make him drop. As she rolled on her back to reload, she heard a whisper fly past her ear. His automatic had at least a dozen cartridges in its magazine. She tried to jam a sand-covered cartridge into the cylinder. Another whisper, even closer. All her spare rounds were gritty.

The echoes off the chasm walls made it sound as if a hundred guns were going off.

Fingers trembling, she tilted her head back for an upside-down glance toward Driscoll. He was coming on again, grimacing, tears streaking his face as he fired. Then something above him caught her eye. A bulky figure on the crest of the dam. Driscoll was being surrounded by little spurts of sand. Bullets. Suddenly, one of them slapped into his back. The air wheezed out of him as he went down on his chest.

Dee turned over.

Still grasping the automatic, Driscoll reached behind with his free hand to explore the gunshot wound, offering her a twisted smile as he began stemming the flow of blood. He tried to speak. '' 'There it —' '' But at that moment Tyrus Foley fired again from above. Driscoll's head slammed forward against the riverbed.

The last report faded away. The dust Driscoll had raised wafted skyward, vanished.

"You hit?" Foley shouted down.

She could only shake her head. Her fingers went on loading cartridges as if of their own will.

"Driscoll dead?"

Nodding, she managed at last to holster the revolver. She was rising numbly to her knees when the explosion came.

Not as loud as she'd expected. But almost instantly a wave surged out of the pipe, covering Driscoll and Schoenfeld. First white with foam, it then turned deep green as tons of water continued to pour from the ruptured sluice gate. The muffled roar of the blast lived on and on in the confines of the gorge until it rumbled like distant thunder.

She was sure that the bodies would be swept along by the crest all the way down to Pleasant Valley Reservoir. But, after a minute, they reappeared in a wide eddy just downstream of her, circling head to toe as if they'd been lashed together.

CHAPTER**TWENTY-FOUR**

Dee drove her Bronco up the road toward Grant Lake. A week of cool, cloudy weather had closed out August, tricking some of the aspen trees into turning their leaves early. These formed streaks of gold and scarlet in the otherwise lime-green groves.

It was now Labor Day, and the weather had become summery again.

Two days ago, the Spanish government had executed the two ETA rebels. They'd gone to their deaths unrepentant, shouting, "Long live *Euzkadi!*" Louie had taken the news better than Dee would have expected. From that moment, he went about his usual business in the colony with a quiet pride. It finally came to her why. The Secret Service had unknowingly given him the means to endure this outrage. He'd been arrested, though only briefly, for the sake of the homeland. His name had been counted.

She rounded the last curve and ignored the intake off to the left. Instead, she focused on the marina. More trucks than usual for a gathering. The executions had reminded many that they were Basque, that even the Palestinians were well on their way to having a homeland of their own.

Turning down the steep driveway to the bar, she reached over to steady the cardboard box on the passenger bucket seat. From it came the mingled smells of moth crystals, wool, and old leather.

The state attorney general had decided to take no action against Tyrus Foley. It'd come down to the fact that Dee could never have gauged the weight of Kyle's pipe bomb with her eyes, helping substantiate whether or not it'd been filled with powder the night the sheriff came to the Charley's Butte intake to retrieve it. She'd retracted nothing under further questioning by Addison, the A.G.'s investigator, but neither was she upset when Tyrus skated on this one. He'd settled a desperate fight in her favor, after all—even though his motivation in following her to the Owens Gorge had been distrust. "You're just like the goddamn FBI, Laguerre," he explained. "Share nothin' and leave a mess in your wake. . . ." So he'd attached one of Ray Jelks's bumper beepers to her Fiat while she was inside his jail, being interrogated by Special Agent Young.

She found one last space among the pickups in the marina lot, smiling at a bumper sticker: "Pass With Care—a Basque Never Forgets." Killing the engine, she heard the music. Guitars, mandolins, flute and drum, and an accordion.

Howard Rowe had retired early by running out his unused sick leave. He and his wife were touring the West in a Winnebago "as big as a goddamn elephant." A week ago, Dee had received a postcard from him. The Dalles in Oregon. Howard had circled a stretch of Columbia shoreline in the photograph and inked in a balloon: "Where those lowlifes probably dumped that farmer's body."

She shed her Sam Browne belt, hid it and her holstered revolver under the front seat, then carried the box into the rest room shack behind the bar. She took off her uniform. A silver disk dangled on a chain between her breasts. A Saint Barbara's medal. Sid's sister had sent it from Hawaii. It'd come with his effects, and she'd remembered his telling her on the phone that he wanted to give it to his partner at the conclusion of the investigation.

In truth, she'd felt little these past three weeks.

An offer of some leave from her supervisor—she hadn't wanted to waste vacation in this mood—had been declined, so he'd sent her for ten days on a temporary detail to support another ranger in Klamath River country, where the Hoopa Indians were contesting state and federal salmon-fishing regulations. A quiet assignment. The Hoopas were winning in court. She mostly patrolled the hot, steep, grassy country, thinking of nothing, just driving, letting a searing wind blow over her through the side window. Air-conditioning still felt morguelike.

Ephraim Bickle had stopped talking. Before leaving for Northern California, Dee had dropped by the sanitorium, told him everything, thanked him. According to Tillie, he quit speaking after this. She saw nothing unusual and unhappy in his silence: the old man was simply getting ready for the other side.

Dee reached inside the box, brought out a long-sleeved linen blouse and put it on. Then a black skirt and a pair of knee-high woolen socks that had been left their virgin color. Finally, she slipped on the *albarkas* and wound the long laces over the socks. These flat leather shoes had been her mother's. And her grandmother's before that. They'd survived a winter Atlantic crossing and a range war in Nevada during which the Laguerres' cabin was burned to the ground by cattlemen.

She studied her own eyes in the mirror. She was struck by the sadness in them. A sadness she wasn't sure she felt through the dogged numbness of the past weeks. Howard had been right. She probably should've talked to somebody professional. This was depression. Yet, she hadn't felt like talking, and depression was nothing new in the world. Hers didn't feel terribly unique. The Laguerres before her had buried their murdered dead, mourned them in silence, then gone on, perhaps with eyes changed like hers now.

But they'd done something to regain life. To go on. She'd recalled what just this morning, upon learning of the gathering at Grant Lake.

She tossed her uniform inside the Bronco, locked it, then went around to the patio from which the music was coming.

Louie was squirting wine into his open mouth from a *bota* when he noticed her. The red liquid dribbled down over his chin as he lowered the wineskin. "Dominica . . ." he said, his eyes growing wide as they ran over her costume. No *Dominica goddammita* for once. He turned to Tillie. "Look, Mama—she's back!"

Tillie smiled from her table, head warmly inclined.

A young man in a white shirt and brand-new Levi's stepped up to Dee. Fresh off the boat from the homeland. He invited her in halting English to join him in the *jota*, a

Basque fandango. She wasn't sure her feet were still up to
the quick and intricate steps, but he pulled her with gentle
insistence to the center of the patio. Somehow, her body
remembered. She began dancing it all out of herself.
Slowly, over the timeless hours, it spiraled out of her like
black smoke, sheered off into the mountain sky. How foolish it now seemed for each generation to try to reinvent
life, for the pressures and the sorrows were the same from
age to age, and how much better she would've felt had she
recalled sooner what her grandmother had said in the glow
of a sheep camp fire. *We would die if we could not dance.*